Waves of Mercy

Books by Lynn Austin

All She Ever Wanted
All Things New
Eve's Daughters
Hidden Places
Pilgrimage
A Proper Pursuit
Though Waters Roar

Until We Reach Home
While We're Far Apart
Waves of Mercy
Wings of Refuge
A Woman's Place
Wonderland Creek

REFINER'S FIRE

Candle in the Darkness
Fire by Night

A Light to My Path

CHRONICLES OF THE KINGS

Gods & Kings
Song of Redemption
The Strength of His Hand

Faith of My Fathers
Among the Gods

THE RESTORATION CHRONICLES

Return to Me
Keepers of the Covenant

On This Foundation

Waves of Mercy

LYNN AUSTIN

BETHANYHOUSE
a division of Baker Publishing Group
Minneapolis, Minnesota

Published by Bethany House Publishers
11400 Hampshire Avenue South
Bloomington, Minnesota 55438
www.bethanyhouse.com

Bethany House Publishers is a division of
Baker Publishing Group, Grand Rapids, Michigan

Printed in the United States of America

Library of Congress Cataloging-in-Publication Data

Names: Austin, Lynn N., author.
Title: Waves of mercy / Lynn Austin.
Description: Minneapolis, Minnesota : Bethany House, a division of Baker Publish-
ing Group, [2016]
Identifiers: LCCN 2016017386| ISBN 9780764218781 (hardcover : acid-free paper) |
ISBN 9780764217616 (softcover)
Subjects: LCSH: Self-realization in women—Fiction. | Life change events—Fiction. |
GSAFD: Christian fiction. | Love stories.
Classification: LCC PS3551.U839 W39 2016 | DDC 813/.54—dc23
LC record available at https://lccn.loc.gov/2016017386

Cover design by Dan Thornberg, Design Source Creative Services

17 18 19 20 21 22 23   10 9 8 7 6 5 4

For Lyla Rose
with love

"Grandchildren are the crown of the aged."

PROVERBS 17:6 RSV

For I am convinced that neither death nor life,
neither angels nor demons,
neither the present nor the future,
nor any powers,
neither height nor depth,
nor anything else in all creation,
will be able to separate us from the love of God
that is in Christ Jesus our Lord.

———————

Romans 8:38–39 niv

CHAPTER 1

Anna

LAKE MICHIGAN
1897

I am living my nightmare. A violent storm has overtaken our steamship, and as we mount high on the crest of a wave one moment, then plunge sickeningly into a watery trough the next, I am certain we are about to sink. Everything is happening just as it does in my nightmare—the one that has haunted my sleep for as long as I can remember.

Mother and I huddle inside the passenger deck as the wind hurls rain and waves against the windows. Thunder rumbles and booms like barrels full of cannonballs rolling downhill. I close my eyes as daggers of lightning slash the dark horizon. Above the roaring wind I can barely hear my own whimpers or Mother's voice as she tries to soothe me.

"Shh . . . Don't cry, Anna."

I'm a grown woman of twenty-three, but she tries to calm my fears the same way she did when I was a child and would awaken at night, screaming in terror from the nightmare, shivering as if the icy water had swallowed me alive.

But I am not dreaming. We are aboard a ship called the *City of Holland*, fighting to cross Lake Michigan in a terrible storm. The boilers pound and throb beneath my feet like an urgent heartbeat, mimicking my own heart. I'm dizzy from the wild pitching and swaying as the ship rolls on the lake like a toy. I never should have agreed to travel by steamship, but in my haste to leave Chicago I chose what seemed to be the quickest and most direct mode of travel. A tragic mistake. How could I have forgotten the nightmare that tormented my childhood? I'm going to die and I don't want to.

"Shh . . . Don't cry, Anna," Mother soothes. "I'm right here."

But my father is back home in Chicago, and that's how this real nightmare differs from the dream I've had all these years. That's how I know that Mother and I will both die. In my dream, Mama and I abandon our sinking ship with the other passengers and climb into a crowded lifeboat. Suddenly a towering wave slams into us, capsizing the lifeboat and plunging us into the frigid water. The shock of it sucks the breath from my lungs. My skin tingles and burns as if on fire. We sink beneath the water, clinging to each other, pulled down by Mama's heavy skirts and petticoats. I can't see, can't breathe. She kicks and struggles to reach the surface again, and when we finally do, people are screaming and shouting for help all around us. The vastness of the lake muffles the sound. I see Father frantically treading water a few feet away from us, dressed in his dark suit and waistcoat. Mama thrusts me toward him, begging, *"Please! Save my daughter! Save her, please!"* I don't want to let go of Mama, but Father pulls me into his strong arms and keeps my head above the lashing waves. When I look back, Mama has disappeared. The only thing visible above the swirling water is her hand as if she is waving good-bye. Father lunges to grasp it, but he's too late. Mama is gone, devoured by the churning black sea.

I always cry out as I awaken from the dream, but I can't awaken from this nightmare. I clutch my mother so tightly she gasps. "Anna, let go a little. I can't breathe!"

8

"Father isn't here to save us this time. We're going to sink, and I don't want to die!"

"We aren't going to sink, darling."

I'm not convinced. I recall the very last service I attended at the Chicago Avenue church, and the sermon topic now seems prophetic. The minister described a sudden storm like this one on the Sea of Galilee, making the scene as vivid as my nightmare. Jesus was asleep in a boat and His friends awakened Him, fearing they were about to sink. Jesus shouted, "Peace, be still!" and immediately the wind and waves died down. They were saved. *"Jesus can calm the storms in your life, too,"* the minister had said. Then he'd asked, *"Have you made Jesus your Savior? Is He beside you when you sail life's stormy seas? If you died tomorrow, would you go to heaven?"* I wanted to rise from my pew at his invitation and walk down the aisle with the others, but I was afraid. Now, because of that sermon, I'm aboard this ship in a violent storm. William had forbidden me to go back to that church, and when he found out I had defied him, he ended our engagement. I left Chicago to give my broken heart a chance to heal, sailing with my mother to a lakeside resort on the other side of Lake Michigan. It seems we will never reach it.

Another clap of thunder booms, and it sounds more distant now. "Everything is going to be all right, Anna," Mother says. I wonder if she's speaking of the voyage or my shattered heart. Perhaps both. "Open your eyes and see." She untangles our arms, and I lift my head from where I've buried it against her pin-tucked shirtwaist. "See, darling? The storm is blowing past us. The sky is lighter over there. It shouldn't be much longer now, and we'll be there." But the shoreline still isn't visible, and the storm-tossed lake continues to seethe, promising a rough ride to the Hotel Ottawa on the Michigan shore.

"This is so much like my nightmare, Mother. Remember? Remember how I used to wake up at night, screaming? I haven't dreamt that I was drowning for a long, long time, but this storm is bringing it all back. That dream used to feel so real!"

"You're going through a difficult time right now. It's only natural to be upset."

I loved William and I thought he loved me, but he broke my heart when he ended our engagement. I press my fist against my heart and feel it beating like a wounded bird's. "It still hurts," I say. "I know, darling . . . I know."

But my mother doesn't know the real reason why William no longer wants to marry me. It has to do with religion in general—and the church on the corner of Chicago Avenue and LaSalle Street in particular. "*I told you I didn't want to hear any more about that place, Anna,*" he had shouted. I had never heard William raise his voice before. "*I told you to stop going there. It's making you crazy. I forbade you to go back there, but you defied me!*"

William believes, as my parents do, that churches are places to be married and buried, places that Chicago's fine families attend at Christmas and Easter and other special occasions. William says that flagrant displays of emotion such as those seen at Mr. Moody's evangelistic rallies and in his Chicago Avenue church are for the ignorant, immigrant masses, not refined people like us. Yet something drew me back there, even after William forbade me to go. The church seemed wonderfully familiar to me, and the minister's words touched a deep, empty part of my soul, the part that feels like the photographs I've seen of Chicago after the Great Fire with nothing but blackened sections of tottering walls and lifeless, rubble-strewn streets that stretch for miles and miles. When I tried to tell William how I felt and why I had gone back, he ended our engagement. "*I can't have my wife, the mother of my children, falling for such nonsense.*" I wonder if he will mourn for me when he learns that this ship has sunk and I've drowned.

The steamship continues to rock and pitch. The view out the windows is blurred by rain and fogged by our breath on the inside. I can still feel us climbing to the tops of the waves, then sliding down the other side again. If Jesus was aboard with me, could He truly shout, "Peace, be still!" and calm the seas? William doesn't believe in miracles.

When Father learned that my engagement had ended, he was shocked. He had arranged my courtship with William in the first place, and he feared I would be ruined by gossip when the other members of our social circle heard the news. "I'll talk to William," he'd promised. "I'll see what I can do to smooth the waters." Do I want William to take me back? I think I do. I think I still love him.

Hours seem to pass until I hear one of the other passengers say, "I see harbor lights!" Mother pulls her lace-trimmed handkerchief from her sleeve and wipes the foggy window, but I don't see anything. And even if we are near the harbor, our ship could still run aground on a sandbar. That's what happens in my nightmare. That's why Mama and I have to abandon the ship in my dream and board the lifeboat.

"We could still run aground on a sandbar."

I don't realize I've spoken aloud until Mother places her gloved fingers over my lips and says, "Hush, Anna."

"That's the harbor," the same passenger says. "I recognize the Holland lighthouse." A few people stand up to look, and they nearly fall over on the unsteady deck. It seems to take years to reach the shore as the ship battles against the surf. When I finally see the channel entrance leading from Lake Michigan into the smaller lake, the opening seems impossibly narrow. How can the captain avoid the stone piers on either side with the waves crashing over them? Somehow he does. We navigate the channel and enter Black Lake, which is no less calm than Lake Michigan. I see the lights of the resort glowing in the darkness, the dark shape of the sand dune looming behind it, illuminated by distant flashes of lightning. More lights twinkle from a row of cottages and from the other hotels on the opposite shore of the narrow inland lake.

At last I hear men shouting outside on the slippery deck as they maneuver the ship into place beside the Hotel Ottawa's dock. Porters bearing umbrellas run to assist passengers as we disembark. I stand up, eager to get off this ship, yet not at all certain that my trembling legs will carry me. The deckhands have to grip my waist to get me off safely as the ship bobs up and down in the choppy water. I'm horrified to have a stranger manhandle me so intimately.

"There you go, miss," the man says as my feet touch the ground. My knees buckle, and he grabs me again as I nearly fall. "Whoa! You all right, miss?"

"I'm fine." I push away his hands. Mother and I squeeze beneath a single umbrella. The ground moves beneath my feet as I wobble up the wooden walkway to the main door. I sink into the first chair I find inside the hotel lobby and wait while Mother attends to our room keys. It will be very strange to be without our lady's maid during our stay. Mother wanted to bring Sophia along, but I insisted that I wanted to be completely alone. We will be wearing casual clothing while we're here, freed from our corsets and obligations, so there's no need to have our dresses laid out or our hair elaborately pinned. I have no idea what I'll do with myself all day or how long it will take for my heart to mend.

"The porter will show us to our rooms," Mother says when she returns with him and our room keys. "Dinner will still be served for another hour."

"I feel too ill to eat," I tell her. "I simply want to change out of my traveling clothes and lie down."

Our adjoining rooms are in the original hotel building, not the expanded annex. They're small but lovely, and mine has a view of Black Lake and the *City of Holland* still moored outside at the dock. It didn't sink in the storm; Mother and I didn't drown in Lake Michigan. But as I watch the bobbing ship and the dancing whitecaps in the distance, I silently vow to travel by train back to Chicago when it's time to leave. I'll never board another ship as long as I live.

CHAPTER 2

Geesje

"Would you like a ride home, Geesje?" one of the other old-timers asks me after the meeting ends. People refer to us as the "old-timers" because we are the few remaining Dutch settlers who first came to Michigan from the Netherlands fifty years ago. But I certainly don't feel old.

"No, thank you, Mrs. Kok," I tell her. "It's such a lovely summer day, I believe I'll walk. Besides, I need to stop by Van Putten's Dry Goods on my way home."

Mrs. Kok rests her wrinkled hand on my arm. She seems frail to me; but then, she must be in her mid-seventies now, nearly ten years older than me. "Are you going to take part in all these parades and things that they're planning for the celebration, Geesje?" she asks. "It seems like they're making too much of our town's fiftieth anniversary, doesn't it? How did those fifty years pass so quickly?"

"I don't know," I reply, laughing. "It doesn't seem that long ago to me, either." And yet it has been a lifetime. My lifetime. "I need time to think about all their fancy plans before I give the committee my reply," I say. "If you'd like, I can stop by your house later this week, and we can mull it over together."

"That would be very kind of you, dear. Good day to you."

"And to you, too, Mrs. Kok." I make my way out of the bank building where the meeting was held and onto the bustling street, glancing up at the new clock tower to see the time. I can't decide if it's a good thing to be continually reminded of the hour or a bad thing. We had little need for watches and timepieces in the early days. The town clock is a sign of progress, I suppose, like the rows of wooden poles and the tangle of wires that web the sky above the street. And like the new electric arc streetlamps that have replaced the old kerosene ones, putting the village lamplighter out of work. At least someone had the good taste to use Waverly Stone for the new bank building and clock tower instead of slapping together another wooden and brick structure. The locally quarried stone gives the tower a sense of permanence—although Holland is still a far cry from the beautiful cities I left behind in the Netherlands, with their centuries-old buildings and cobblestone streets.

I wait for a horse-drawn wagon to pass, then cross River Avenue and walk up Eighth Street. For all the progress our town has made, I don't understand why the streets remain unpaved. Even the ancient Romans had sense enough to pave their roads. The Semi-Centennial Committee had better pray it doesn't rain during the anniversary celebration or their parade floats and marching bands will be mired in mud.

After making my purchase at the dry goods store and chatting with Mrs. Van Putten about the town's upcoming festivities, I pause for a moment to watch construction on the enormous wooden and canvas archway they're building, spanning Eighth Street from one side to the other. The committee showed us a drawing of what it will look like when it's finished, including a portrait of *Dominie* Van Raalte on top, high above the center of the arch. How he would have hated that!

14

I'm sitting in my favorite chair knitting later that afternoon when my son Jakob stops by for a visit, bringing fresh eggs from one of his parishioners. "How did your meeting with the Semi-Centennial Committee go, *Moeder*?" he asks. We speak to each other in Dutch at home, as our family always has.

I stop knitting, letting my hands and the half-finished sock rest on my lap. "Goodness, what a lot of fuss they're planning—parades and speeches and marching bands and such. And that ridiculous arch on Eighth Street that they're wasting money on. Although I do think it's nice that the local Indian tribe is coming back to be part of the celebration after being squeezed out of town years ago. The chief will be giving a speech."

"What do they want you and the others to do?" He unfastens his clerical collar as he speaks. He looks so much like his father in that moment that it surprises me.

"No speeches, thank goodness. They want us to ride on one of the parade floats. Silliness, if you ask me. And they want me to write down my story for a book they're making about the history of our city. Everything I can remember about leaving the Netherlands fifty years ago and settling here."

"That sounds like a splendid idea. You're going to do it, I hope."

"I don't know. . . . I wouldn't know where or how to begin."

"Why not start with why you decided to leave the Netherlands?"

"I didn't decide. My parents did. I was seventeen years old."

"You know what I mean. You should tell some of their story, too. Why they left their home and the Netherlands church. It's important for your grandchildren and the generations after them to know what took place and why we're here."

I look away, lifting my knitting bag and checking to see how much yarn is left on the ball, stalling for time. When I glance up at Jakob again, his impatience has made a deep crease between his eyebrows. "Are the other settlers who were here from the beginning going to write their stories, too?" he asks.

"The committee wants them to. But you know I can't write

very well in English, Jakob. It would embarrass me if people saw how poorly I spell."

"I'll help you. Joanna and I will make certain it's perfect before you hand it in."

"I don't know . . ." I pick up my knitting and wind the yarn around my fingers so I can finish the row. The needles whisper softly as they slide against each other, as if telling secrets. "I'm not sure if they only want to know what happened during those years and all the hardships we faced, or if I should tell them the whole truth."

Jakob blinks and sits down on the chair across from me. "What do you mean, Moeder?"

I don't reply. What I'm asking is: Should I tell the truth about all the times I despaired of God's love? The times when I doubted and my faith was shaken and I turned away from Him in anger? *Nay*, sometimes it was more than anger—it was rage. Those feelings are part of my story, too, the part I've kept hidden all these years. Do they belong in this book they are making about our past?

"Of course, tell the truth, Moeder. It's for the historical record, isn't it?" The crease deepens, and he runs his finger between his collar and his neck again. "Please give it serious thought—if only for our family's sake. I hope you'll tell them you'll do it."

"*Ya*," I say with a sigh. "*Ya*, I suppose I will tell my story."

"Good." Jakob stands again. He never stays long. "If you'd like, I'll bring you a notebook to write in the next time I come. And some ink and a good pen."

"I would rather use a pencil." That way I can erase what I decide not to share.

"Some pencils, then. Do you need anything else before I leave?" I shake my head, and he bends to kiss my cheek. His thick hand rests on my shoulder for a moment. His wooly beard tickles my face as I inhale the clean scent of his Castile soap. "I'll see you on Sunday, Mama, for dinner." He turns, and I watch him stoop his head as he ducks through my sitting room doorway. When did the flaxen-haired, barefooted boy I once held on my lap turn into this tall middle-aged man?

I begin knitting again. I don't want to think about the past just now or stir up buried memories. I need to concentrate as I turn the heel of the sock and start knitting the foot. I should have measured Jakob's foot while he was here. The socks are for him. I hear my kitchen door open and close in the distance. "Did you forget something, Jakob?" I call out.

"It's me, *Tante* Geesje." I look up, surprised to see the boy who lives next door standing in my sitting room doorway. But Derk is no longer a child, either. He's a man now, as tall as my son.

"Well, Derk! For goodness' sake!" I stuff the unfinished sock into the bag with the ball of yarn and struggle out of my chair so we can hug each other. "How wonderful to see you! It's been much too long—since Easter Sunday, I believe."

"I know! And I'm so sorry that it's been that long. These past few months have flown by so fast with all of my studies at the seminary and final exams—and then I started my summer job the day after school was out. How are you, Tante Geesje?" He calls me *tante*—his aunt—but we aren't related.

"As good as can be expected after all these years. Come, let me fetch you something to eat. I think there are some cookies left in the tin." I speak as if he is still the motherless child who used to run errands for me, carrying coal up from my cellar on cold winter days and emptying my ash bucket, not the grown man he has become. Derk and I took care of each other for many years. He would show up in my kitchen at just the right time, when I was feeling lonely and needed someone to talk to, as if God Himself would whisper in Derk's ear and send him to my door. "Tea or coffee?" I ask. "Or maybe a glass of milk?"

"Don't fuss, Tante Geesje. I just stopped by for a minute to see how you're doing."

"But you'll need something to drink with my almond cookies. They're your favorites."

He grins. "In that case, milk, please." He sits in his usual place

17

at my kitchen table, his long legs sprawling, his smile lighting up the low-ceilinged room. He has grown to be as solid and good-looking as his grandfather was at that age. Should I write about his grandfather when I tell my story? Wouldn't my son be shocked! But I don't think Derk would be.

He opens the cookie tin and chooses one while I poke at the fire and add some wood and move the kettle over where it can boil. "Tell me everything you've been doing since I saw you last spring," I say.

"Well, let's see. My classes at the seminary have ended for the term—it was a very challenging year, but only one more year to go now. Did I tell you I'm working at the Hotel Ottawa for the summer?"

"Doing what, dear?"

"A little bit of everything—carrying guests' bags to their rooms, taking care of the rowboats and canoes, maybe giving sailing lessons or excursions around Black Lake if anyone signs up for them. You know how I love to sail." Derk gulps the milk I've poured for him.

We talk like the good friends we have always been as I sip my tea and Derk empties my cookie tin. "May I ask your opinion about something, dear?" I say after a while. "I could use your advice."

"You can ask me anything, Tante Geesje, you know that. Although I'm not sure my opinion is worth much."

"It is to me. . . . I met with some people from the Semi-Centennial Committee today, and they want me to write the story of how I left the Netherlands to settle here fifty years ago. They want to put all the old-timers' stories into a book for Holland's fiftieth anniversary celebration in August. What do you think?"

"You should do it. I would love to read your story. I was always sorry I didn't pay more attention to my grandparents' stories when they were alive. They didn't talk about the past very often."

"I don't blame them. I don't like to recall those hard times, either. . . . My son Jakob thinks I should do it, but I don't know how much of the truth I should tell."

Derk sets down his glass. "What do you mean?"

I blink away my sudden tears. "I can describe how the fever struck, and what it was like to hear the church bell tolling as I buried loved ones in the graveyard. But should I tell how hard I had prayed, day and night, begging God to spare them? Or how I raged at Him for letting them die?" I trace the pattern on the tablecloth with my finger as I speak, not looking up. Derk rests his broad, unwrinkled hand on top of mine, stilling it. My tears break free at the warmth of his touch. "If I'm going to relive my story, I think I should tell all of it, the whole truth, ya? But what will people think when they read it? Young people like you imagine that their grandparents and even men like Dominie Van Raalte were filled with faith, never wavering in what they believed. What will happen if I reveal all the cracks in that perfect picture?"

"I think you should tell the truth, doubts and all." Derk's deep voice has turned soft. "If only for your own sake. Write down everything that's on your heart, Tante Geesje. I'll read it, if you'll allow me to, and help you decide what should go into the book and what should stay between you and God."

I nod and pull my hand free to dry my tears. I pour more tea into my cup. Derk will be a minister someday, so perhaps he needs to know how far away God feels to a mother when she loses her child. He needs to know how hollow his words of comfort will sound to her. I hope he won't think less of me or my imperfect faith after all is said and done.

"Ya, Derk. That is what I will do, then," I say. "Thank you." I sip my tea while I wait a moment for the sadness to lift. "So is there a special girl in your life these days? A handsome, young dominie like you should be married or else the young ladies in your church will be too distracted to pay heed to your sermons." I expect him to laugh but he doesn't.

"There was someone," he says, looking down at his empty glass. "Caroline is beautiful and funny and full of life. I met her at a gathering of young people from three area churches and fell madly in love with her. I asked her to marry me . . . but she said she didn't want to be married to a minister, and that's what God has called me to be. Her father is a minister, and she said they never have time for their wives and families. I suppose she's right. She broke up with me about a month ago. There's been no one else since her."

"I'm so sorry, Derk. Forgive me for prying."

"No, that's all right. I'm pretty much over it," he says with a slow, sad smile. "But if you've ever had your heart broken when you were my age, promise me you'll tell me all about it in your book."

I feel my face grow warm. "We will have to see about that," I say. "I won't make any promises."

After Derk leaves I feel too restless to sit and knit socks again. I'm eager to begin my story and wish I had the new notebook Jakob promised. I rummage through my desk, searching for paper, and find a few sheets of stationery. I also find my daughter Christina's letter, the last one she ever wrote to me. I don't need to read it. I know it by heart. She was coming home like the prodigal in Jesus' parable. But unlike him, she never arrived.

I tap the sheets of stationery into a neat stack and search for a pencil. Then I sit down at my desk and begin to write.

CHAPTER 3

Geesje's Story

**THE CITY OF LEIDEN, THE NETHERLANDS
52 YEARS EARLIER**

On the night of my fifteenth birthday, a huge brick shattered the window of Papa's printing shop and ended my childhood. The crash awakened me, and when I heard Papa thundering down the steep, narrow stairs to investigate, I jumped from my bed and followed him. The brick lay in crumbled chunks near the printing press. Shards of glass were scattered across the floor like pieces of ice. Nothing remained of the huge window with Papa's name painted on it except a jagged hole that invited the brisk night air inside. Bricks don't fall from the sky by themselves. Someone had deliberately thrown it through our window.

"Don't come in here," Papa said, shining a lamp all around the shop. "You will cut your feet on the glass."

"I want to help you sweep up." I hated the way the broken glass and ugly pieces of brown brick marred Papa's pristine shop floor. I wanted to put everything right.

"In the morning, Geesje," he said gently. "Go back to bed. There's nothing we can do tonight." I did as he said, but it took me a long time to fall asleep again. I never did hear Papa return to bed. I found out later that he had stood guard downstairs all night.

In the morning, not only was there a mess inside the print shop, but we discovered our attackers had also splashed red paint across our storefront and emblazoned the word *heretic* on our door. Paint dripped from each letter like blood. "Who did this?" I asked Papa. "Who would do such a thing? And why?"

"It's because of the *Afscheiding*," Papa said. "People don't like it that our family has seceded from the government church to start a new one."

"But why would someone do this?" It made no sense to me. Weren't we all followers of Christ in both congregations, even though our church had to meet in private homes instead of in a building?

"They think they can intimidate us into returning to the state-sponsored religion."

As soon as Papa's apprentice, Maarten, arrived, Papa sent him to purchase boards to nail over the shattered window. The broken slivers of glass tinkled like silver coins as I swept them from the print shop floor. I thought of the Scripture verses I had memorized in catechism class: *"A new commandment I give unto you, that ye love one another . . . By this shall all men know that ye are my disciples, if ye have love one to another."* This was not an act of love.

Our lives changed that night, although it took several months for our family to realize it. I felt violated, my sense of safety and security destroyed along with the window. I had rarely known fear until the night of this cowardly act, my childhood in Leiden as lovely and whimsical as the bubbles of light that used to dance on my bedroom wall on sunny days. The narrow brick house where I grew up overlooked *de Nieuwe Rijn*, and Mama said the bubbles were reflections of sunlight off the river's surface. If the day was cloudy and there were no dancing bubbles, I knew the river would look as dark and dense as molten steel.

Papa's print shop occupied the first floor of our home on Nieuwe Rijn Street, a ten-minute walk from Leiden University. Leiden is a beautiful city with centuries-old buildings, brick-paved streets, and canals that weave through the avenues like vines. I loved to watch from my bedroom window as flatboats and houseboats floated past, to hear the hinged wooden drawbridge creak open to let the masts of sailing ships slip through. Sometimes I would stand by the edge of the water with my older sisters, Anneke and Geerde, and feed stale bread to the swans. On market days, we would walk with Mama along the Nieuwe Rijn all the way to the *Stadthuis* and shop along the way at the colorful booths piled high with cheese and vegetables and flowers—always flowers.

"I have been thinking, Geesje," Papa told me at lunch after I'd helped him clean up. "I don't think you should walk to your sisters' apartments by yourself anymore."

"But they need my help with their little ones. It isn't very far." Both sisters had married a little more than a year ago, Anneke first and then Geerde. Now they'd each given birth to a baby boy.

"I'm sorry. But until we find out who did this and the vandals are punished, it may not be safe to go out alone. People know that a family of Separatists lives here. They seem to be watching our house. You could be in danger."

I had never felt in danger before. I loved walking through Leiden's beautiful streets by myself, following the winding river to where Anneke and Geerde lived. "What if Mama and I went together?" I asked.

Papa wiped his mouth and stood to return to the print shop. "Even if there are two of you, I'm not so sure."

"Well, I'm not afraid," Mama said. She was a tiny woman who was sometimes mistaken for a child when she covered her graying blond hair with a bonnet. She was as fearless as a biblical matriarch. "Our heavenly Father will watch over us."

"That's very true, my dear. But I still don't want Geesje to go out alone."

"I-I'll go with her, sir." Papa's apprentice spoke so rarely that we all turned to him in surprise. Maarten was two years older than me and had worked for Papa since he was twelve. We had all watched him grow from a spindly boy who knew nothing about the printing business into a sturdy adult who was now Papa's right-hand man. He also was a Separatist, like us. "I'll be happy to walk with Geesje—if you can spare me for a few minutes, that is."

Papa wagged his head from side to side, a sign that he was thinking. "That might work. Just don't go out alone, Geesje."

I never defied my parents or argued with them because one of God's Ten Commandments was to honor my father and mother. To disobey them would have been a sin. For as far back as I could recall my family lived a life of devout faith in God, doing our best to follow the Bible's teachings. My parents had seceded from the official state-sanctioned church before I was born, believing that the stiff, ritual formality of the national church made God seem cold and distant. They wanted a more vibrant faith, worshiping a God of love, a faith that adhered more closely to the Bible's teachings rather than manmade traditions. I grew up eager to serve God in any way that He asked me to. I imagined that would mean marrying a devout Christian man and raising a houseful of children, feeding the poor, helping the sick, and spreading the love of Christ. I thought my faith was very strong. I didn't realize, back then, that faith that is never tested isn't true faith at all.

The first time that Maarten walked with me to Geerde's house, we both felt awkward. For one thing, I had never been alone with a young man before, even though Maarten was almost like a brother to me. And for another thing, we made a mismatched pair—Maarten tall and solid and thick-shouldered, while I was so short and small-boned that the top of my head barely reached his chin. He was as dark-haired as one of the Spaniards who had invaded the Netherlands generations ago, while I was blond and fair-skinned. Neither of us spoke a word to each other that first day.

The intimidation at Papa's shop gradually grew worse. The painted slogans reappeared on our storefront almost as quickly as Papa and Maarten removed them. Many of Papa's regular customers stopped bringing him their business. Some of the vendors in the marketplace refused to sell to Mama and me or to other members of our Separatist congregation. I didn't understand why all of this was happening, but I became very grateful for Maarten's silent, protective presence with me whenever I ventured out.

By the time a year had passed and I turned sixteen, Papa's declining business and the growing animosity of our neighbors forced him to make a decision. He invited Anneke and Geerde and their husbands to our home one Sunday after church to tell all of us the news. "I have decided to leave Leiden altogether and move my print shop to the town of Arnhem."

"No . . ." I breathed. This was our home. We couldn't leave Leiden. I covered my mouth, careful to keep my thoughts to myself. My sisters also seemed shocked by the news.

"Dominie Albertus Van Raalte, who was one of the founders of the seceding church here in Leiden, has recently moved to Arnhem," Papa told us. "He used to preach to our congregation until he was driven away a few years ago. The Separatist church in Arnhem is larger than the one here, so we won't have to endure religious persecution alone."

Mama reached for Papa's hand as if to show everyone that she supported him. "This has been a very difficult decision for us to make," she told my sisters. "It will be hard to say good-bye and leave you and your families behind in Leiden." My sisters and I were already tearful, but Mama remained strong. She would shed her tears in private.

"But perhaps you will decide to come to Arnhem, too," Papa said, addressing his sons-in-law. "If you'd like, I will see if there is work for you there."

They showed little enthusiasm for the idea and their promises were vague, even though they also were Separatists. The only one who seemed eager to move to Arnhem with us was Maarten, who had finished his apprenticeship at age eighteen and was now Papa's assistant. "I would like to move there with you," he said, "if you will allow me to. My parents are remaining here."

25

"Of course, of course!" Papa said, slapping his shoulder. "We will run our new printing business together."

Everything moved quickly once the decision had been made, and we began the arduous task of packing up our household in hopes that Papa's business would prosper in a new city. I said a sorrowful farewell to my sisters and two little nephews and to the lovely city of Leiden.

Papa found a building to rent in Arnhem near the train station, only a short walk from the *Nederrijn* River. Papa's shop and our kitchen were on the ground floor, the apartment where we would live was on the second floor. Maarten seemed content to sleep in a room in the attic beneath the dormers, although how he kept from hitting his head on the rafters was a mystery to me. I worried he would become a hunchback from crouching up there every night. On our second day in Arnhem, Dominie Van Raalte paid us a visit. Papa left Maarten in charge of the shop and invited him back into our kitchen for coffee. Mama and I were still unpacking but the cookstove was hot and so was the coffeepot. Dominie Van Raalte wasn't much taller than me, but his warmth and charisma made him seem like a much bigger man.

"The church is welcome to meet here in my print shop," Papa told him as they sat down at our table.

"Thank you. I'm very grateful," the dominie said. "I will gladly accept your offer." He blew on his drink to cool it and took a sip. "But keep in mind, only nineteen people will be allowed to meet inside the shop at a time."

"But why? We can fit many more than nineteen people out there," Papa said. "If we move my desk aside and clear away a few other things it should be no problem at all to squeeze in fifty people."

"It isn't a matter of space. The king has declared the Separatists to be 'secret agitators.' It requires government consent if twenty or more people wish to meet for religious services that aren't part of the State Church. And official consent is nearly impossible to obtain."

I could tell by the angry look on Papa's face that he was prepared to defy this ridiculous law. Mama quickly spoke up before he had a chance to object. "What will happen if there are twenty or maybe twenty-one persons inside?"

"The authorities will come in and break up the meeting. The owners of the house or business will be punished with heavy fines for disobeying. Several of our ministers have already been fined for holding illegal meetings and even put into prison." Papa learned later that Dominie Van Raalte himself had spent time in prison for disobeying. "We are not wealthy people," he continued. "The fines are a very heavy burden to bear. Yet some of us believe that being able to worship freely is worth any price."

"There is no way around this law, then?" Papa asked.

Dominie smiled his calm, patient smile. "We have discovered a few ways. For instance, we could have nineteen people meeting inside your shop, while others stand outside, listening through the open doors and windows."

"That is what I will do," Papa decided.

"And when the weather is pleasant," Dominie continued, "we sometimes hold outdoor services near the border of two towns. If the authorities from one town come to break up the service, some of us can quickly disperse to the other town so we are not all meeting in one place."

The church met in Papa's print shop on our first Sunday in Arnhem. Mama and I and a few other women listened from our kitchen behind the shop, while exactly nineteen people gathered around the huge printing press out front. Dozens more jammed the narrow alleyway on the side of the shop and crowded along the sidewalk in front of the open door to hear Dominie Van Raalte preach. Everyone agreed it was worth the discomfort to be able to worship together and to hear Dominie's stirring sermon assuring us of God's abundant love.

The joy we all felt was short-lived. A few nights later a gang of ruffians threw an avalanche of rocks and bricks through the window of Papa's new shop. The sound of shattering glass startled me from sleep. This time the attack didn't end with one window. Our tormentors continued throwing stones and bricks until nearly every window in our apartment had been smashed. Then they lobbed more rocks through the shattered openings, trying to destroy the furnishings inside.

"Geesje! Get into the closet!" I heard Papa shout. My wardrobe was on the other side of my bedroom and I could see silvery shards of broken glass littering the floor. I crawled beneath my bed instead, as Papa and Maarten ran downstairs to the shop. I closed my eyes and prayed for their safety as shouts and cries and the sound of thudding stones came from the shop below me.

At last everything grew quiet. Too quiet. What had happened to Papa and Maarten? *Please, God . . . please, God . . .* I prayed. Then I heard the unmistakable sound of footsteps coming up the stairs. I was still hiding beneath my bed, so I squeezed as far back against the wall as I could, my heart pounding like the thudding rocks. The bedroom door creaked open. Someone stood in the doorway. I could see his wooden clogs from the crack beneath my bed. I clamped my hand over my mouth to keep from screaming.

"Geesje . . . ? Are you all right?" a voice whispered.

Maarten.

"I-I'm under here. I-is it safe to come out?"

"Yes. The thugs are gone. . . . But be careful. There is glass all over your floor."

I felt so shaky I could barely crawl out. Maarten shoved some of the glass away with his foot, and as soon as I emerged, he caught me in his arms and lifted me onto the bed. "I was so scared!" I exclaimed as he hugged me tightly for a moment.

"I know. Me too." He pulled away, and I saw a dark shadow on the side of his face. When I tried to brush it away, it felt wet. Blood.

"Maarten, your head is bleeding! You're hurt." He reached up to feel his forehead, and I saw him wince.

"They pelted us with rocks."

"That cut should be washed and bandaged." He helped me find my shoes, then we climbed down the narrow, winding stairs to the kitchen. Mother had lit a lamp and was tending to several cuts on my father's face and arms. She nursed Maarten when she was finished.

"What were you two thinking?" she scolded as she worked. "You never should have gone out there. They might have killed you!"

"I will do whatever it takes to defend my home and my family," Papa said.

"Why is this happening to us?" I asked. "Why doesn't God protect us?"

"He is protecting us, Geesje," Papa soothed. "They threw all those rocks, yet none of us was badly injured."

"And remember what Jesus said?" Mama added. "'The servant is not greater than his lord. If they have persecuted me, they will also persecute you.'"

The next day, Dominie Van Raalte and some other men from our church came to help us clean up. "Where were the authorities last night?" Papa asked as he shoveled up stones and broken pieces of bricks and tossed them into a bucket. "Why aren't they searching for the men who did this?"

"I'm sorry to say this isn't the first such incident," Van Raalte replied. "These ruffians have grown bolder and bolder because they know that the city officials will look the other way."

"So we can expect this to happen again?" I asked. I wondered if I would ever feel safe at night.

"Our church will help you make shutters for your windows that you can close at night," the dominie replied.

"And I will sleep downstairs in the shop from now on," Maarten added. "I'll make sure no one harms you, Geesje." The purple bruise on his forehead had swollen to the size of an egg. He would always have a crescent-shaped scar there as a reminder of that terrible night. His dark eyes looked soft when he gazed at me, and it gave me a funny, watery feeling inside.

That was the first time I became aware that Maarten thought of me as more than a friend or a little sister. In the days that followed, I noticed that he became so flustered whenever I walked into the print shop that he would forget what he was doing and his round face would grow very red. His reaction amused me, and so sometimes I went into the shop for no reason at all except to test my power over him. Then I would laugh to myself after I returned to the kitchen. Maarten was pleasant-looking in a gangly sort of way—like an oversized puppy that might eventually grow out of its awkwardness. I had always thought of him as an older brother, but after we moved to Arnhem, I began viewing him through the eyes of the other young women from our congregation. They giggled and blushed whenever he was around, and the braver girls made excuses to talk with him. These girls quickly befriended me as a way to get closer to him. "Does he have a girlfriend?" they would ask. "Please, tell us what he's like!" A few even asked to be introduced to him. I was happy to play matchmaker but timid Maarten declined all their offers.

"Geesje, come for a walk with me down to the Nederrijn River," Papa said one evening after dinner. I could tell by the somber expression on his face that he had something important to discuss. I never would have guessed that it would be about Maarten. "Listen, Geesje," he said as we walked arm in arm. "Maarten approached me the other day and asked for permission to court you."

I stopped walking, dragging Papa to a halt as I looked up at him. For some reason the request filled me with dread when I knew I should have felt excitement. "What did you tell him?"

"I told him that of course he had my blessing. I believe you're old enough and mature enough to think about marriage in another year or so, but I said that the decision to court him would be up to you. I won't force you against your will." I felt relieved and started walking again. It was a warm spring evening and the streets were crowded with people who were taking advantage of the fine weather. "The only thing I will demand of any of your suitors, Geesje, is that he must be a believer."

"And a Separatist, like us?"

Papa wagged his head from side to side. "I would need assurances that his faith and his commitment to Christ are genuine."

We paused when we reached the river. I gazed out at the wide expanse of water, and the birds wheeling and calling overhead. The Nederrijn was nothing at all like the river in Leiden, and I felt a pang of homesickness. "Maarten has all of the qualities I could wish for in your future husband, Geesje. He is already like a son to me. If the two of you were to marry, my printing business could remain in our family."

"I will think about it, Papa," I promised.

"Do more than think about it, *lieveling*. Pray about it."

I was a compliant, obedient daughter. I usually did whatever my parents thought was best for me. Maarten was a man of very strong faith and would make a fine husband—but I wasn't sure I wanted to be his wife. To be honest, shy, soft-spoken Maarten seemed boring to me. Even so, I might have allowed myself to fall in love with him, especially after the tender way he'd treated me on the night we were attacked. But then the king's soldiers arrived in Arnhem, and everything changed. . . .

HOLLAND, MICHIGAN, 1897

I have run out of stationery. The rest of my story will have to wait until Jakob brings me a new notebook.

CHAPTER 4

Anna

HOTEL OTTAWA
1897

I didn't sleep well in the plain, unfamiliar hotel bed. My childhood nightmare returned after that terrible storm, and once again I dreamt that Mama and I were abandoning the sinking ship for the lifeboat. I heard the pitiful screams of drowning passengers and watched Mama sink beneath the waves. I'm awake now, and yet I still can't stop shivering. Bright sunlight slants past the curtains, but I have no idea what time it is, nor do I care. I came to the Hotel Ottawa so I'd have time to think and to lick my wounds like an injured animal. I climb from the bed and rummage in my trunk for something to wear—I was too tired last evening to hang up my clothes properly, and they are strewn across the chair and floor. I change into a shirtwaist, a simple, loose-fitting skirt, and my traveling jacket, then brush my hair, leaving it unpinned. Why fuss when I no longer have a fiancé to impress or a calendar of social obligations to keep? I feel surprisingly liberated as I head outside.

I can tell it's early because the grass still sparkles with last night's rain, and the summer sun hasn't had time to warm the storm-swept air. A few hearty guests are already walking toward the sandy beach on Lake Michigan, but I stay well away from that terrifying expanse of horizonless water. I find a place to sit on a bench facing the much smaller Black Lake and watch the water splash against the pilings. *The City of Holland* is no longer moored at the dock, and a family of ducks swims near the shore. They bob up and down on the waves like toys in a carnival game, dipping their heads into the water until their tails point straight up to the sky, then righting themselves again. I know nothing about wildlife and wonder if this is how ducks feed.

It's so quiet I can hear my own breathing. There are no traffic sounds as in Chicago, no streetcars or trains or rumbling carriage wheels or horses clomping down cobblestone streets. The only sounds that disturb the stillness are crows calling and birds chirping and water slapping against the dock—until some fool shatters it by calling, "Elizabeth! . . . Elizabeth!" His voice is loud and insistent. I don't turn my head, ignoring him as his footsteps hurry along the path, coming in my direction. He stops beside me, panting, and thumps my arm playfully. "You're such a tease, Elizabeth. Why are you ignoring me?" I finally look up, and he steps back in surprise. "You aren't Elizabeth!"

"No, I am not. Which is precisely why I didn't answer you." I comb my blowing hair out of my eyes with my fingers.

"I'm sorry," he says. But instead of excusing himself and moving away, he remains where he is, towering over me and scratching his head as if bewildered. I turn to him again, scowling at his rudeness. He is about the same age as me with eyes the same gray-blue color as the lake. His hair is so fair it's nearly white. His eyebrows, which are still raised in surprise, are pale as well. "It's astounding," he says. "You look exactly like Elizabeth. You could be her sister!"

"I have no sisters, I assure you. Or brothers either, for that matter." The polite thing for him to do would be to excuse himself and leave. Instead, he sits down on the bench beside me and extends his hand. "I'm Derk Vander Veen. I work here at the hotel . . . well, for the summer, that is."

I ignore his outstretched hand, then realize I'm being just as rude as he is. Besides, I came here for a reprieve from all the stiff social rules and mores. "Anna Nicholson. How do you do?" I extend my fingers, palm down, and he holds them awkwardly, as if unfamiliar with the proper way to greet a lady. The first time William and I were introduced, his touch caused a rush of heat to travel up my arm to my cheeks even though I was wearing silk gloves. I have no such reaction this time even with bare fingers. "I arrived on the steamship last evening from Chicago. In the storm," I tell him.

"That was some storm, wasn't it? It's going to take all morning to clean up the downed branches."

"I was quite certain we would sink to the bottom of Lake Michigan. I'm not at all sure why we didn't."

"It wouldn't have been the first time a ship was wrecked in a storm like that one. I could tell you quite a few stories about the ones that didn't make it. It's kind of a hobby of mine."

"No, thank you." My voice sounds prim. "I don't care to hear about sinking ships. I've already decided to take the train back to Chicago when my holiday ends."

He laughs, although I hadn't meant it as a joke. I find it strange that I can't recall William's laugh. Maybe he laughed in the beginning when we were first courting, but certainly not in the last few months when everything began to fall apart like a house made of bricks without mortar. "Do you have family here in Holland?" Derk asks. "You must."

"Why must I? What makes you say that?"

"Look in the mirror!" he says, laughing again. "You look just like the rest of us Hollanders. This town was settled by Dutch immigrants, so a good many of us have fair skin and blond hair and blue eyes. Like mine. Like yours."

I have always known that my parents adopted me as a newborn, so I suppose there is a chance that he's right and that my ancestry is Dutch. I rarely think about being adopted and haven't had any

34

interest in finding my birth parents. Even so, I find it intriguing that he thinks I resemble this girl named Elizabeth. Might she be a relative?

"You could pass for a Hollander if you wanted to," Derk tells me. "You could claim to be Elizabeth's cousin or some other long-lost relative, and people would believe you."

"Is Elizabeth your girlfriend?"

"No," he says quickly, shaking his head. "No. She's my neighbor's granddaughter. I can't afford a wife until I graduate. I'm studying at Western Seminary here in Holland to become an ordained minister."

Something stirs inside me. I want to ask if he will be a minister like the one in my parents' church or like Reverend Torrey in the church that William forbade me to attend. I have no idea how to frame such a question, so instead I ask, "Have you always wanted to be a minister?"

Derk grins. "No, when I was a boy I wanted to be the captain of a sailing ship and travel around the world. That's why I know so much about all the shipwrecks on Lake Michigan." He smiles so easily. Once again I think of William, who gives away smiles as if they are rare coins that must be doled out carefully. "I gave up the idea of sailing the world when God called me to the ministry a few years ago," Derk finishes. What an odd thing to say—that God *called* him. I want to ask him what he means, but he stands up. "I need to get back to work. It was very nice meeting you, Miss Nicholson. I hope we can talk again sometime."

"Good day," I say with a polite nod, but I doubt we'll speak again. I can't imagine that the Hotel Ottawa would encourage conversations between staff members and guests. I watch Derk lope across the grass, wondering how he'd dared to approach a woman of my social standing in the first place without a proper introduction. Then I realize how casually I'm dressed. He can't tell that I'm from a wealthy Chicago family. Besides, he had mistaken me for Elizabeth—unless that was just a ruse. Mother warned me about the ways of unscrupulous men. But why didn't she warn me that a respectable man like William, a man who was above reproach, could hold my heart in his well-manicured hands and crush it in an instant?

The bench feels cold and hard beneath me. I stand and walk back to the hotel. Derk is picking up downed tree limbs and stacking them in a pile. He gives a little wave when he sees me. *"God called me to the ministry,"* he'd said. But how had he known that was his purpose? I think about what Reverend Torrey said in one of his sermons: *"God has a plan and a purpose for your life."* Those words had intrigued me—and they had made William furious. He said that my purpose was to be his wife, the mother of our children, to assist him with his social duties as the son of one of Chicago's foremost families. He said that wanting more than that was ridiculous and selfish and insulting to both of our families. I think William feared that I was turning into a suffragette, when all I really wanted was to fill the emptiness inside. Something important seemed to be missing in my life, and I had an overwhelming urge to find what I had lost.

I rarely think about being adopted, yet after my conversation with Derk, I wonder if perhaps I was born for a different purpose. What if God's true plan for me has been thwarted by my adoption? Could that be why I feel so empty and restless? Or perhaps it *was* God's purpose that I be adopted, and I am *called* to become William's wife.

I don't know. I'm so confused!

I reach my hotel room and knock on Mother's adjoining door to see if she is ready for breakfast. "I was wondering where you were," she says when she sees me. I can tell by her cursory glance that she disapproves of my windblown hair. Even in casual clothing my mother is dressed fashionably.

"Shall I go down and choose a table?" I ask.

"Yes. I'll be there in a moment. But please comb your hair first."

I wait until Mother and I are both seated and our breakfast arrives before saying casually, "An odd thing happened on my walk this morning. One of the hotel workers mistook me for a woman named Elizabeth. He said she was Dutch, and that I looked Dutch, too. Do you know what nationality I really am?"

For the space of a heartbeat, Mother's expression can only be described as frightened. She is rarely flustered—no matter how awkward the social situation—and is always ready with an appropriate reply. But for a few interminable seconds, she is speechless. When she recovers she looks away and says, "I have no idea. . . . Do you see our waiter, Anna? I would love some more tea. How about you?"

"No, thank you. But I wondered—"

"What shall we do today? They say the beach is lovely. Is that where you went for your walk?" Her attempts to change the subject annoy me and pique my curiosity even more.

"So, is it possible I might be Dutch?" I ask.

Mother is too well-mannered to sigh, but I can tell she wants to. "The adoption was handled privately, through our lawyer. We have no way of knowing the details."

"Is there a way to find out?"

"I don't think so. . . . Is that our waiter?" She waves him over and asks for more tea. When he's gone she says, "What difference would it make to know, Anna? You're my daughter, and I couldn't love you more if I had given birth to you."

"I know, I know." But I silently plan to ask my father the same question the next time I see him. "Do you think Father will join us here?" I ask.

Mother knows me too well. "Your father doesn't know anything about your background either, Anna, so please don't ask him. You'll hurt his feelings."

"Have I hurt yours? I didn't mean to." The waiter arrives before she can reply, and I watch him fill her teacup. He is wearing a white vest and black bow tie, as if he's serving in a fine Chicago restaurant—not in a resort in the wilds of Michigan. I shake my head when he offers me some. "None for me, thank you."

"Of course you haven't offended me," she says when the waiter is gone. "I suppose it's only natural to be a little curious at times.

But most girls would envy the life that your father has given you. Questioning him might make you seem ungrateful."

She's right. And maybe that's why William became so angry with me. He was giving me everything a woman could dream of—a handsome husband, wealth and prestige, a beautiful new home, a wedding trip to Europe—yet I had told William I felt empty inside. Because I do.

"Very well, I won't ask Father," I say.

"Good girl. Now, how shall we spend our first day here?"

CHAPTER 5

Geesje

HOLLAND, MICHIGAN
1897

I'm walking home after visiting Mrs. Kok as I promised I would do, and I decide to take a shortcut through Market Square, where the trees will offer shade on this sunny summer afternoon. I still call the square by its original name, Market Square, even though they renamed it Centennial Park twenty-one years ago to honor the hundredth anniversary of the Declaration of Independence. When Dominie Van Raalte donated this patch of land to the town, he thought it would be used the way market squares back home in the Netherlands were. Instead, our townspeople prefer to shop the American way, from storefronts lined up in rows along the main street. Market Square is just a village park now.

As I emerge from the park and onto the street again, a carriage slows to a halt beside me. "*Hallo*, Moeder," the driver calls.

"Jakob! What brings you into town on such a fine summer day?"

"I'm on my way to see you," he says as he steps down. He rests his hand on my shoulder and bends to kiss my cheek. "I brought you the notebook I promised. Are you heading home? I'll give you a ride." He helps me climb onto the carriage seat and hands me the new notebook. I feel a shiver of excitement as I rifle through all the blank pages waiting to be filled.

"Thank you, dear. This is just what I need. I've been visiting with Mrs. Kok—remember her? One of the other old-timers? The committee wants her to tell her story for the anniversary book, too, but she's going to write hers in Dutch. Someone else will have to translate it."

"You've decided to do it, then? I'm glad."

"Well, yes . . . and I've been stirring up a lot of old memories in the process." We halt in front of my house a few minutes later. "Do you have time to come in for some coffee?" I ask. "It's cooler inside, I think." Jakob always looks so hot in his stiff clerical collar and dark suit. His round, bearded face is flushed and damp with perspiration.

"Not today, Moeder, I'm sorry. I have two more parishioners to visit this afternoon, and they'll fill me to bursting with coffee before I'm through. Next time, I promise."

It's on the tip of my tongue to ask if I need to be sick or dying before Jakob would have time in his busy life to sit and talk with me—but then I remember Derk's story about the girlfriend he'd loved, and I bite my tongue. Jakob's work for the Lord must come first, of course. "Well, thank you for the notebook, dear."

"Here are some pencils, too," he says, digging in his coat pocket. "You did say that you preferred to use a pencil, didn't you?"

"Ya. These will be perfect." Jakob helps me down, then climbs onto the seat again. He waves good-bye as he drives away.

I've done enough visiting around town for today. After splashing some water on my sweaty face, I'm ready to sit down and return to the past. The clean, lined notebook pages look inviting. I sharpen one of the new pencils and begin.

40

Geesje's Story

THE NETHERLANDS
50 YEARS EARLIER

The year before we moved from Leiden to Arnhem, the potato blight struck crops throughout the Netherlands. All over Europe, too, for that matter. The leaves and vines withered and died in a mushy black mess before any potatoes had a chance to form underground. The farmers and poor people—and there were plenty of both in our congregation—went hungry that winter. In the spring, shortly after we arrived in Arnhem, farmers planted their potato crops again. We were all filled with hope and faith in God's goodness that year: the farmers trusting that their crops would prosper, and our family trusting that Papa's new print shop would succeed.

We had replaced all the window glass in our new shop after that terrible night. A carpenter from our congregation fashioned wooden shutters that Papa and Maarten could close at night, including a huge pair to protect the shop's front window. The shutters may have kept us safe from bricks and stones, but they made the inside of our apartment as dark as a cave.

"At least our tormentors will leave us alone now," Papa said at breakfast one morning. He spoke too soon. Mother and I were about to leave for the market square when we heard voices and heavy footsteps inside the shop. I peered through the door from the kitchen, then quickly slammed it shut again.

"Mama! Soldiers! The shop is filled with soldiers! Are they going to arrest Papa?"

My mother was a tiny woman, yet her faith in God made her fearless. "Stay here," she ordered before marching through the kitchen door in her apron to see for herself. Too frightened to remain alone, I followed at a safe distance. "What is going on?" she demanded to know of the men. "This is a print shop. Are you here on printing business?"

Father hurried to her side and draped his arm around her shoulder. I wasn't sure if he was protecting her or the soldiers.

"The captain has just informed me that four of his men will be quartered in our apartment from now on," Papa told her. "We will be required to provide their room and board."

"But we can't afford such an expense. Our new business isn't established yet." Mama broke free and took a step toward the captain. "And we have an unmarried daughter in our household. It wouldn't be proper for her to share space with strangers—soldiers, no less!"

The captain was unmoved. In fact, the corner of his mouth twitched in amusement. "If you have room enough to hold religious meetings, then you have room enough to house my men. My decision is final."

Later we learned that we weren't the only members of our congregation who were forced to billet soldiers. Dominie Van Raalte himself wasn't spared, and his wife had five small children to care for. We were outraged. And helpless. The four soldiers, all young men in their twenties, moved in with us that very afternoon, forcing Mother and me to cook for them and clean up after them. They decided that the attic where Maarten slept wasn't good enough for them, so they confiscated my bedroom, leaving me no choice but to sleep on a pallet in my parents' room.

I can't begin to describe the bitterness I felt. I longed to spit in the soldiers' food before serving it to them. We only wanted to worship God with all our hearts, free from the stale, lifeless routines of the established church. We wanted to live as servants of Christ, not servants of a state-controlled church system that kept God at a cold, remote distance and watered down all His commandments. I didn't understand why we were being forced to suffer for that freedom.

On Sunday, the dominie reminded us in his sermon of how Christ had suffered at the hands of Roman soldiers. Yet as they had cruelly nailed Him to the cross, Jesus had said, "Father, forgive them; for they know not what they do." If Jesus could forgive His tormentors, then we must also forgive ours. Dominie finished his sermon by reminding us of these words from the book of Hebrews: "'Let brotherly love continue. Be not forgetful to entertain strangers; for thereby some have entertained angels unawares.'"

I doubted that the coarse young men living with us were angels. Yet the sermon had touched my parents' hearts, and they made up their minds to serve these intruders the way Jesus would have—humbly and joyfully. Mama shared our meager meals with them without complaint, giving them the best portions even if we went hungry ourselves. She sang psalms and hymns as she cooked and washed dishes, especially if the men were in the house with us. She not only swept up after them, she even cleaned the mud from their filthy boots every night. Papa invited them to join us in our tiny sitting room in the evenings, although the men preferred to go out on the town, instead. "These soldiers don't deserve such kind treatment," I argued after they had eaten all our bread one morning, then left our breakfast table without a word of thanks.

"That may be true, Geesje," Mama replied. "But neither do we deserve the kind treatment God gives us. He offers us grace, and we must do the same for others, even those who we think are undeserving."

I had a lot of time to think that morning as I hung the soldiers' bedding from the windows to let their blankets air in the morning breeze. I decided I would follow Mama's example and work cheerfully from now on, responding to the men's ignorant grunts and demands with a smile and a polite reply. But I would have to pray for the Holy Spirit's help in doing so. I couldn't walk the extra mile or turn the other cheek as Christ commanded me to do without His help.

Slowly, almost imperceptibly, I began to notice a change in the men as the days passed, especially in the fair-haired soldier, the tallest of the four, with the lean build and muscled arms of a farmworker. He was the most talkative of the four, the most outgoing, and he also had the heartiest appetite. "Thank you, miss," he said one morning after I'd given him the last of our butter for his bread.

I hid my shock and said, "You're welcome." Then I added, "I'm sorry, but I don't even know your name."

"It's Hendrik, miss. And this is Gerrit, Pieter, and Kees." He gestured to the three others. They didn't speak. Since they had been billeted with us to punish us, I suppose they thought it their duty to treat us rudely.

"My name is Geesje." I smiled at Hendrik, and when he smiled in return my face suddenly felt as warm as if I had opened the oven door. His deep-set gray eyes resembled liquid metal, the color of De Rijn River on a cloudy day in Leiden.

"I know, miss," he replied. "I have heard your family calling you that."

Mama and I made a point of addressing the soldiers by name after that. And following Hendrik's example, the others began removing their boots at the door instead of tromping dirt inside. They made sure there was enough food to pass around before heaping their own plates. They even bowed their heads when Papa prayed before meals, although Hendrik was the only one who remained at the table afterward to listen as Papa read aloud from the Bible.

The change in Hendrik so intrigued me that I started observing him from a distance. Of course the only time I could stare openly at him was when everyone bowed their heads to pray for our meals. One evening when I peeked from behind my folded hands, Hendrik was staring back at me. I could feel my heart trying to escape from my rib cage. Neither of us looked away until Papa said, "Amen." Mama asked me to pass the bread, and my thoughts were so scrambled I passed the butter instead. I had never reacted this way before but I recognized the symptoms—this was the addle-headed way Maarten always behaved around me.

The following evening Mama had an errand to run after supper, bringing a pot of soup to a new mother in our congregation.

I was washing the dishes by myself in the kitchen when I glanced over my shoulder and saw Hendrik standing in the doorway. The room seemed to grow very warm. His nearness made me suddenly aware of my soiled apron and my messy hair, falling loose from my braids after a long day of housework.

"May I ask you something?" he said. I nodded, my throat so tight I wasn't sure I could make a sound. "Why have you been so kind to us," he asked, "when we are such an inconvenience to you?"

I swallowed to loosen the lump in my throat. "Because . . . because we're Christians . . . and it's what Jesus would do."

When Hendrik didn't reply I grew nervous. His face didn't reveal what he was thinking. I had never spoken to a stranger about my faith before, and I worried that he might laugh at me or mock my family. I knew I shouldn't care what he thought of me, this soldier who had been forced upon us. And yet I did. I held my breath as I waited for his reaction.

"I have never met people like you and your family before," he finally said. "People who live the way the Bible tells us to live." He gazed directly at me, his expression open and frank. It unnerved me. Maarten was always too shy to look directly at me, staring at his feet or the table or the wall beyond my head, instead.

I leaned against the work counter, the dishes forgotten. "Are you a Christian, too? Do you know the Bible?"

He ran his fingers through his fair hair, which was darker at the roots, making it stick up in places like a small boy's. "My parents baptized me in the village church. We attended services there when I was growing up. We learned about the birth of Jesus and how He died on a cross, but knowing those things didn't seem to make a difference in anyone's life."

"That's why we left the State Church and started a separate one," I said. "We think Christians should do more than just agree with what the Bible says. We should obey it and do things like loving our enemies."

Hendrik still stood in the doorway, and I was afraid he would leave now that I had answered his question. I didn't want him to.

"May I ask you a question?" I said. I waited for him to nod. "Why did you become a soldier?"

He leaned against the doorframe, shoving his hands into his trouser pockets. "My parents died in the cholera epidemic nine years ago." His gaze never left my face. "I was eleven. I lived with my aunt and uncle for a while, but they had too many children of their own and couldn't afford to keep feeding me. I couldn't find regular farmwork after the potato blight, so joining the army seemed like my only choice."

"Do you regret your decision?"

"No. . . ." He hesitated before saying, "It brought me here."

I felt a growing excitement that I couldn't explain. I wanted Hendrik to stay here in the kitchen and keep talking with me, so I asked him another question. "Where did you grow up?"

"In a little farming village in the province of Groningen. You've probably never heard of it. May I?" he asked, gesturing to a kitchen chair. "I don't want to keep you from your work. . . ."

"Ya, please. Sit down."

"My family was very poor," he continued. "I loved them very much, but I don't recall us ever being as happy as your family seems to be."

I realized how lonely Hendrik must be, living far from home, his parents gone, and I was glad I had been kind to him. "We are happy," I said. "And the church is like a family to us. We don't have much, but we help each other out."

"I've noticed that. You Separatists aren't at all what I expected."

"What did you expect?" I smiled, and when Hendrik smiled back, I felt like I was floating above the floor.

"We were told that the Separatists were crude, ignorant people. And that you had radical beliefs. I imagined I would see all kinds of strange rites and rituals."

I laughed out loud and sat down at the table across from him. We lost all track of time as we talked about our lives and our families, our hopes and our dreams. I told him about growing up on De Rijn in Leiden and how much I had enjoyed the excitement of city life. He told me how he used to play in the fields and along the dikes with his three brothers as a boy. They had died in the cholera epidemic, too, along with his parents and grandparents. "I have only one sister left," he said. "She still lives in our village in Groningen."

"Are you able to travel there to visit her?"

"No. I haven't seen her since she married three years ago."

"Will you stay in the army all your life?"

Hendrik shook his head. "I don't want to. I would love to have a patch of land of my own to farm someday. I want to work with my hands and have a family—like yours." He paused, then asked, "What about your future, Geesje? What do you wish for?"

I realized that I didn't have an answer. "I don't know . . . I haven't thought much about it. I imagine I'll have a husband and children one day. But for now, God hasn't told me what His future plans for me are."

"Does God always speak to you in such a . . . a direct way?"

"Not with a voice I can hear," I said, laughing. "But I believe that if we pray and ask for guidance, He'll help us decide what to do."

We were still sitting at the table talking, the dishes unfinished, when Mama returned from her errand. I had learned a lot about Hendrik, and he fascinated me. After that first night, he often lingered in the kitchen after supper to talk with Mama and me instead of going out on the town with his three friends. I looked forward to those evenings more and more, and I often caught Hendrik watching me while I worked. Was I imagining it, or did he seem to want to be near me as much as I wanted to be near him? I stole glances at him whenever I could and decided he was the handsomest man I'd ever met. Everything about him was attractive, from his tall, lean frame, his tousled blond hair and warm gray eyes, to his easy smile and friendly personality. Each time we talked, he never failed to make me laugh.

I didn't know what I was feeling, at first—this breathless giddiness whenever I was near him and the hollow emptiness whenever he was gone. I didn't know why I felt a surge of happiness whenever

I heard him and the others returning home, their feet tromping up the wooden steps, their deep voices laughing in the distance. Then one day as Papa sat at the kitchen table, weary after a long day in the print shop, Mama came up behind him and began kneading the tension from his shoulders. He sighed and reached back to cover her hand. I had witnessed these simple gestures dozens of times, but that day they spoke to me of how much my parents loved each other. I longed to massage the ache from Hendrik's shoulders at the end of the day and feel his tender touch in return. Was I falling in love with him?

Throughout the next few months I tried to deny my growing feelings for him. I didn't understand them. And I knew for certain that my family would never allow me to marry a man who didn't share our faith. Maarten also took a liking to Hendrik and they became good friends. Hendrik would often sit and talk with Maarten while he tidied the print shop at the end of the workday. One evening, Maarten stopped me on my way upstairs, his voice hushed with excitement.

"Geesje, do you have a minute? There's something I want to tell you."

"Ya . . . what is it?" Maarten had made no move to court me even though Papa had given him permission, yet I feared he was about to declare his love or offer a marriage proposal. The last thing I ever wanted to do was to hurt Maarten, but how could I accept his advances? As it turned out, that wasn't at all what he wanted to discuss.

"I have such wonderful news, Geesje. You know how I've been talking with Hendrik, the tall soldier with the sandy hair? He has been asking many, many questions these past weeks, and tonight he said he wants to become a believer!"

Hope and joy bubbled up inside me. "Really? That's wonderful news!" My excitement wasn't for the same reason as Maarten's. I wouldn't have to deny my feelings for Hendrik if he became one of us. It seemed like a miracle to me.

"Ya, it's really true," Maarten continued. "Just think! The king put Hendrik here in our home to punish us, but God brought good from it. Will you pray for him, Geesje? And pray that I'll know the right words to say to him?"

"Ya, of course I'll pray." Poor Maarten couldn't know that his kindness to Hendrik might mean sacrificing his hopes of marrying me.

I lay on my pallet that night, wide awake with excitement, listening to the low rumble of the soldiers' voices through the thin wall, punctuated by occasional laughter. I couldn't hear what they were saying, but Hendrik's voice, the deepest of the four, sent shivers through me. *Love your enemies*, Jesus taught. And I had obeyed. Now His command had transformed into something I never imagined or intended. For the first time in my life, I was in love.

CHAPTER 6

Anna

HOTEL OTTAWA
1897

I rise early, before breakfast, so I can take a walk outside before the sun grows too hot. I love this time of day when the air is fresh and clean and the dew still twinkles on the grass. Today the sky is dotted with high, gauzy clouds and the waters of Black Lake are a lovely silvery blue. I sit on my favorite bench, near the water where Derk mistook me for his friend Elizabeth the first day, and watch the family of ducks swimming near shore. I have seen Derk only from a distance since then, when he is taking care of the rowboats or toting trunks and suitcases for hotel guests. Today I watch him load a picnic basket onto the hotel's small sailboat as he prepares to take passengers on an excursion. Advertisements and flyers in the hotel's lobby advise guests that we can sign up to go sailing at the concierge's desk. I watch until Derk's passengers—a young couple who can't seem to take their eyes off each other—are seated in the boat and Derk sets sail out onto the lake. Their laughter carries across the clear water. I can think of nothing I would hate more than stepping onto another boat.

Mother has news for me later as we sit across from each other at breakfast. "A letter from your father arrived in this morning's post," she says. She pulls it from the envelope and reads part of it aloud to me. "'Tell my dear Anna that I saw William at the club the other night, and we spoke briefly about their broken engagement. He told me he would be open to further conversation regarding a reconciliation but perhaps at a later time.'"

I could easily imagine William sitting in an overstuffed club chair in his starched white shirt, holding a fragrant cigar between his fingers and frowning at the very mention of my name. But Father is an important client of the bank that William's grandfather founded, so William wouldn't dare shout at him the way he shouted at me, especially in the hushed tranquility of their private men's club, where the servants whisper and walk on tiptoe.

"What do you think, Anna? That's good news, isn't it?" Mother asks.

"I don't know . . . can we talk about something else? I still need more time to think."

Mother honors my wishes, although I can tell she is biting her tongue. When we finish eating, she runs into a guest from Chicago she has befriended named Honoria Stevens. They decide to sit on the hotel's wide veranda and leaf through the latest copies of *Vogue* fashion magazine, planning the gowns their seamstresses will create for the fall social season. I'm sure they'll also spend a good deal of time complaining about their servants back home and the hotel's untutored staff. "You're welcome to join us, Anna," Mother says.

Nothing would bore me more. "Maybe later," I tell her. "I want to walk to the beachfront on Lake Michigan this morning."

"In that case, why not invite one of the nice young ladies we met at the piano recital last night to go with you?"

I give a vague nod in reply, but I have no intention of asking

51

anyone to join me, least of all those giddy girls. I already know that their conversation will be superficial and boring, like the idle conversations I'm forced to endure when paying social calls and receiving visitors back home. Such visits rarely ease my loneliness or fill the longing I have for a close friend. I haven't had a real friend to laugh with and confide in since my school days. The girls I knew at school are all married now, and I'm practically an old maid at my advanced age of twenty-three. But it took me longer than the other girls to overcome my shyness and to grow up enough to begin courting and become engaged. Father sheltered me as his little girl, and no suitor was ever good enough in his eyes until William came along.

"Well, be sure to wear a hat when you're on the beach," Mother cautions. "And long sleeves so the sun doesn't darken your skin."

I do as I'm told and return to my room for my sun hat. I still haven't worn the new bathing costume I purchased before leaving home, nor do I want to wear it now. I have no desire to dip so much as a toe into either lake. As I'm leaving my room again, I decide to bring my diary along—not to write in but to read. Perhaps I can discover where things went wrong between William and me. And maybe I can decide if I still love him.

The short walk to the beach takes me along the channel that connects Black Lake to Lake Michigan. Several small boats are sailing through it this morning, taking advantage of the calm water to venture out onto the big lake. A handful of fishermen try their luck along the edge of the channel, casting their lines into the glittering water. I stand and watch the activity for a while before pulling off my shoes to walk barefoot in the warm, sugarlike sand. A group of children play in the water nearby, squealing with delight as the waves wash over them and destroy the sand castles they're building at the water's edge. Another young family has brought along a picnic lunch, and as they spread it out on a blanket, a trio of bold seagulls inches closer.

At last I sink down in the sand and open my diary to the first entry:

January 1, 1897

I attended a New Year's Eve party with William last night in the ballroom of his family's mansion. Everything was dazzling—the decorations, the food, the ladies' gowns, the orchestral music. William stole my breath away in his tailored black evening suit and tailcoat. We danced until my feet ached and the champagne I sipped made the room begin to whirl. William was by far the handsomest man in the room with his wavy dark hair and neatly trimmed beard and mustache. His eyes are the same rich mahogany color as the woodwork that decorates his mansion. I saw the jealous looks in the other girls' eyes, knowing that I was the lucky one who had won William's heart. After midnight we snuck down to the servants' hallway, and I let William kiss me when no one was looking. His kisses made me even dizzier than the champagne. Oh, how I long for the day when we are married and we can be together all the time, holding each other much closer than we are allowed to now.

Tears fill my eyes at the memory of that evening and the stolen kisses we shared. We had gazed at each other the same way the young couple had when I watched them this morning, climbing into Derk's sailboat.

I skim a few more diary entries, remembering the wedding preparations Mother and I had begun to discuss—the guest list, the wedding dinner, the gowns and other clothes for my wedding trip to Europe. William and I hadn't chosen a date yet, but he did decide to hold the reception in his family's ballroom since his home is larger and more opulent than ours. We would live with his parents at first, until our own home could be built. William knew exactly what he wanted our mansion to look like and how every room would be furnished. The thought of planning and furnishing an enormous home on my own seemed overwhelming to me at the time, so I was quite happy to leave everything in his capable hands. William is very decisive, while I'm terrible at making up my mind. Little did I know that he would take over all of the other important decisions in my life as well, including which church I should attend.

My stomach rolls like the nearby waves as I turn back to my diary.

January 7

It finally stopped snowing this morning, and by the afternoon I longed to get out of the house. I summoned our driver and asked him to take me for a carriage ride, wishing I had a friend to join me—someone who would enjoy a brisk winter ride as much as I do. The city looked like a fairyland with a new coating of snow sparkling on all the trees. The frigid air blowing off Lake Michigan made my nose hurt when I breathed it in, but I felt so alive!

On my way home the driver came upon a carriage accident that blocked the way, so he turned down a side street, then another and another until we ended up outside a church on the corner of Chicago Avenue and LaSalle Street. I have been to that church before, I am sure of it, but I can't remember when or why. The entrance, which faces the corner, is through a round, brick tower that resembles a castle turret. Parked in front of the door was the Gospel Wagon that I'd often seen around Chicago during the World's Columbian Exposition three years ago. The music and singing were so festive that I asked my driver to stop for a moment. When we did, a woman ran right up to my carriage and handed me an advertisement inviting me to come inside and hear a world-famous evangelist. I instructed my driver to wait, and I stepped out of the carriage.

The moment I walked through the doors, I knew I had been inside before. Everything was so familiar! I lingered in the rear of the church and listened for a moment. The min-

ister talked about Jesus as if He was his best friend. Then he described the loneliness and emptiness we all feel, and said that Jesus could fill that empty place. "God loves you," the minister said. "He has a plan and a purpose for your life."

The sermon wasn't finished, but I knew my driver was waiting for me, so I slipped outside again. But the minister's words remained with me all the way home, warming my heart like a tiny candle in the snow.

I asked Mother if we'd ever gone to the church at that address when I returned home. "Certainly not!" she replied. I questioned if I might have gone there with Father, but Mother simply stated that our family has attended the same church our entire life.

It's late now, and I need to turn out the gaslight and go to sleep. But I still can't shake the eerie feeling that I've been to the castle church before. Nor can I forget the minister's words. Does God really have a plan and a purpose for my life?

January 9

I dreamed about the castle church last night. Mama and I were there together, listening to a sermon. Then I awoke to a dreary, gray day with nothing to do. Mother is in bed with a cold, so I bundled up in my warmest coat and boots, intending to walk down our street and back again. But on a whim, I hailed a passing cab and asked the driver to take me to the castle church. I had no idea if there would be a service there in the middle of the afternoon, but it turned out that there was. The same preacher from a few days ago was speaking, and this time I stayed for the entire sermon.

I look up again, gazing out at the thin line on the horizon where water and sky meet, remembering what happened the following evening. William and I had been on our way to the theater together, and I was excited to tell him about the sermon I'd heard. I had barely begun speaking when he interrupted me. "What were you doing in a place like that, Anna?" His voice was as cold as the January night.

"What do you mean? It's a church, William. A Christian church."

"Places like that attract the very lowest sort of people. The ministers are often charlatans who like to bilk innocent people out of their money."

"No one asked me for money—"

"Even so, stay away from there." It was an order. He spoke to me the way he might speak to a servant or one of his employees at the bank. I tried to explain how something seemed to be missing from my life, and he grew angrier still, saying I was insulting him and my parents when I spoke that way. Then he smiled and said, "Let's talk about something else." He was very sweet to me for the rest of the evening, holding my hand and stealing kisses and telling me how beautiful I am. "Your hair is the color of spun gold," he said. "I can't wait to see it hanging loose around your beautiful face."

I close the diary, unable to read any more. The sun is growing very warm, so I rise to my feet to walk back to the hotel. My mother and Mrs. Stevens are sitting on one of the side porches, their heads bent close together like conspirators. They don't see me, so I wait at the bottom of the steps, peeking through the bushes rather than interrupting them. I know it's impolite to eavesdrop, but Mrs. Stevens speaks so loudly that I can't help overhearing her.

"I found out that my husband has been seeing another woman on the side," she tells Mother.

"Oh, you poor dear!"

"I gave him an ultimatum, then told him I was coming here by myself to give him time to think." She dabs her eyes with her lace handkerchief as Mother murmurs in sympathy. I know I should leave, but I can't tear myself away.

"This must be so painful for you, Honoria. But if it's any consolation, I'm told that these little affairs are quite meaningless."

"That's what Albert said—but it isn't meaningless to me!"

"I understand. . . . But the hard truth is, your husband isn't the first gentleman to have a little fling, nor will he be the last. It's much more common than one might imagine. The husband of an acquaintance of mine had an affair with their Swedish parlor maid."

My mouth drops open in surprise. I try to figure out which of Mother's friends she might be referring to, but many families in our social circle have Swedish servants—including my own family. Our lady's maid, Sophia, is from Sweden.

"What if—heaven forbid—the woman has Albert's child?" Mrs. Stevens asks.

Mother holds her hand, patting it gently. "I've heard of that happening, too, Honoria. Usually the girl can be paid off and convinced to give up the child for adoption. The stigma for a single mother and a bastard baby from any social class is too great to bear."

"I still don't know if I'm ready to forgive Albert."

"And yet you must. A divorce is ruinous for women of our standing."

I finally slip away, already wishing I hadn't eavesdropped. I know I'm very naïve when it comes to worldly matters because my parents have sheltered me all my life. So it has never occurred to me that my father—or William—might have a dalliance with another woman, or that Mother—and I—would be expected to forgive him and look the other way. I hurry around the building and run up the steps into the lobby, wishing I could simply disappear, and I nearly collide with Derk, who is coming toward me with a suitcase in each hand.

He does a double take, then grins and says, "I almost called you Elizabeth again!" I push past him and hurry up the stairs to my room.

As I fumble to fit my key into the lock, tears of shame burn my eyes. I was adopted. My real mother gave me away. I have always known this was true, but after overhearing Mother and Mrs. Stevens, I wonder if I might be the product of an illicit liaison. Is this why Mother doesn't want me to question Father about it?

I finally get the door open and rush inside, closing it behind me as if I'm being pursued. I sit down on the edge of my bed, feeling sick. Our young Swedish lady's maid is as blond and fair-skinned as I am. So are both of William's Swedish maids. My chest hurts so badly I can barely breathe.

CHAPTER 7

Geesje's Story

THE NETHERLANDS
50 YEARS EARLIER

Against all reason and common sense, I fell in love with Hendrik. He had been sent to our home to punish us, yet I thought about him nearly every minute of the day and dreamt about him at night. I made excuses to talk to him whenever I could, even though we were never really alone. And the more I got to know him, the more I longed to be with him all the time. He was a wonderful storyteller, and my family often gathered in our sitting room in the evenings and listened as Hendrik told us about all the places he'd been stationed and all the adventures he'd had. He could describe a scene so vividly that it was as if we'd traveled there with him. One of his ancestors had sailed to the East Indies on a spice ship, and he kept us enthralled for hours as he retold tales that his family had passed down, tales of exotic islands, pirate ships, terrifying storms at sea, and of long days waiting in the doldrums for the wind to rise. I listened to Hendrik spellbound, studying his handsome face. I loved the endearing way he raked his fingers through his fair hair until it stood on end. I wondered what it would be like to feel his arms around me. Or taste his kiss.

I had no idea if Hendrik felt the same way about me until one afternoon when I was hanging clothes on the line in our tiny backyard. I heard the back door squeal open, but I didn't turn around, thinking it was Mama. When she didn't speak, I finally turned and saw that it was Hendrik. The moment our eyes met, a wave of heat seared through me. My heart started beating faster than it ever had. I couldn't draw my gaze away from him. Hendrik didn't look away, either.

"Geesje . . ." he said. I couldn't move, couldn't speak. He took a step closer, and I wanted him to kiss me. "Geesje, I don't know what it is that I feel for you, but I know that I've never felt this way before. You are such a beautiful person and . . . and I want to be near you all the time."

I opened my mouth to reply, but nothing came out. Hendrik usually wore a confident grin on his face but not that day. The expression on his lean, handsome face was somber, his pale brows arched above his gray eyes as if asking me a question. I had never seen him so tongue-tied before.

"I-I know that your father could never allow me to marry you," he continued, "because I don't belong to your church. But the months that I've lived here have been the happiest ones of my life." He swallowed and took another step closer. "I wake up in the morning to the sound of your singing. Your smile is more beautiful to me than the sunshine. I just learned that I may be transferred out of Arnhem soon, and I'm terrified because I don't think I can live without you." His face blurred as tears filled my eyes. "Geesje . . . please say something."

"I love you," I said.

"You . . . you do?"

I nodded. Hendrik quickly glanced all around, then pulled me to himself, clutching me tightly as we hid behind the line of flapping towels and aprons. The top of my head barely reached his chin, and he rested his cheek on my hair for a long moment. The warmth and strength of his embrace was everything I had imagined it would be. And more. "Geesje, tell me what I need to do so that I can hold you this way for the rest of my life."

I didn't know what to say. I only knew that I wanted the same thing that Hendrik did. And that I would dream of his wonderful embrace for many nights to come. Much too soon, he released me. I felt shaken, as if I stood out in an open field during a powerful storm. I bent to finish pinning the laundry on the line, worried that my mother would peer out of the window to see what was taking me so long. "The man I marry must be a Christian," I finally said.

Hendrik lifted the basket for me so I wouldn't have to bend. "Ya, I understand how important your faith is to your family. I have been listening from my bedroom on Sunday mornings whenever I'm not on duty. The dominie's words are very moving, and I want to live like you and your family do. I have been bringing my questions to Maarten, and he has very kindly explained everything to me. I want to become a true Christian, if God will have me. Even before I knew that I loved you, I wanted this."

Against everything I had been taught, I threw my arms around Hendrik again, the basket crushed awkwardly between us. "That's wonderful, Hendrik! I'm so glad! We can be together for the rest of our lives if you make a profession of your faith as a Christian!" Everything was falling into place. When I pulled away again, I said, "I'm sure Dominie Van Raalte will be happy to talk with you and welcome you into our congregation. After that, nothing will stand in our way."

He smiled his dazzling smile, then grew serious again. "My faith will have to remain a secret for now. The captain and the other soldiers can't find out that I've become a Separatist until after my term of duty is over."

"When will that be?"

"Not for another year and a half. Pieter and Kees are already suspicious of my interest in your meetings—and in you—but I don't think they will give me away."

Once again I returned to the mundane task of hanging laundry as if my world hadn't just changed completely. My mind spun in a dozen directions, and I could barely make my fingers work. I had never felt so happy.

"There is just one thing," Hendrik said, and the solemnity of his voice made me afraid. I stopped pinning laundry. "Maarten has been a very good friend to me. I have known from almost the first day I moved here that he is in love with you. He says there is an understanding between him and your father and that if you agree, the two of you will be married one day."

I looked away, knowing as Hendrik did, how deeply hurt Maarten would be. Gentle, patient Maarten. "Ya, he has been part of our family ever since he became Papa's apprentice years ago," I said. "I know he cares for me. And I've always been fond of him. But I'm not in love with him. . . . I'm in love with you."

"How will we ever explain to him that the soldier he has befriended and the woman he loves . . . ?"

"Neither of us meant to fall in love, Hendrik. But I feel certain that God meant for us to be together. I believe that's why He brought you here to live with us."

"Really? . . . How do you know?"

"Because my heart tells me it's true. Maarten will be hurt but he'll understand. Besides, he deserves to have a wife who loves him fully and truly. I'm not that woman."

"So what should we do next? Will you wait another year and a half until I'm discharged?"

"Ya, of course I will! Go talk with the dominie, Hendrik. Tell him everything we talked about. He'll tell us what to do next."

Hendrik promised that he would as soon as he found a way to do it without his fellow soldiers finding out. He would face very stern discipline if it was ever discovered that he'd joined the enemy.

After that magical afternoon in our backyard, Hendrik and I looked for ways to be alone for a few minutes nearly every day, sometimes in the open, sometimes in dark hallways and back stairwells. We held each other close whenever we could, and a few of those times he kissed me. It was the most wonderful sensation I had ever experienced. One afternoon we arranged to meet in the backyard again, hiding behind a clothesline full of bedsheets so we could kiss. Then a gust of wind blew, uncovering our hiding place, and when I looked up Maarten stood in the back doorway, watching. Hendrik called to him, but he disappeared inside.

"Oh, no," Hendrik groaned. "I don't want you to get into trouble, Geesje. Do you think he'll tell on us?" At that moment, I didn't care if my parents were angry or even if they punished me. Hendrik's kisses made any punishment worthwhile. I had never felt so happy in my life.

"I don't know. Maybe I should go talk to him," I said.

"No, I'll do it." Hendrik gave me a quick hug, and I watched him cross the yard to the house in a few quick strides.

In the end, Maarten never told Papa what he had witnessed. But before Hendrik had a chance to talk to the dominie about becoming a Christian, before either of us had a chance to take another step toward spending the rest of our lives together, two terrible blows struck our community. The first blow came when the potato blight destroyed all the crops yet again. The blight affected everyone. Thousands of farmhands were out of work with no way to support their families. Wealthy landowners lost an important source of income. The poorest people in our nation faced starvation. Papa's printing business barely had been able to pay the rent, much less feed us and four hungry soldiers. Now the blight would cause the price of everything to go up, including the taxes Papa was forced to pay. The men in our congregation began holding worried meetings as they prayed for guidance in this worsening crisis.

The second blow came within days of the first. Hendrik and the other three soldiers left our house as usual right after breakfast, then returned barely an hour later. I was sweeping the walkway in front of the print shop when I saw them coming back. Hendrik looked worried, and he touched my arm briefly as he walked past me. I followed them into the shop and heard Pieter tell Papa, "We were told to pack our gear and prepare to move to Utrecht."

"Utrecht?" Papa asked. "I'm sorry to hear that."

I stood frozen in the doorway of the print shop as their footsteps thundered up the stairs to my old bedroom. I was stunned by the news and too upset to finish sweeping. I heard the floorboards creaking above my head as they moved around, hastily packing their things. My world was coming to an end. I grabbed a piece of paper and a pen from Papa's desk and scribbled our address on it. Within minutes, the footsteps thundered down the stairs again and the men trooped back through the print shop.

"Wait a moment, please," Papa said as he paused from his work. "Before we say good-bye, I would like to pray for you, if you would allow me to." All four men bowed their heads while Papa prayed for their health and safety, and for God's blessings on their lives. The steady *thunk* and *swoosh* of the printing press rumbled in the background. I saw Hendrik wipe his eyes when Papa finished.

Mama hurried in from the kitchen with a package wrapped in brown paper and tied with a string. "Here's some bread and cheese and a few apples for you to share on your journey. We will miss you."

Maarten shook Hendrik's hand. "I wish you Godspeed," he said.

I followed the men out the door and into the street with my broom, not caring who saw Hendrik and me together. We barely had time to say good-bye as we stood outside on the busy street, longing to hold each other one last time. "I love you, Geesje," he said. "I want to marry you if you'll wait for me."

"I'll wait forever if I have to. I love you, too."

Hendrik glanced at his three friends who had started walking without him as if unwilling to risk being late for duty. "I promise to come back for you the moment I'm discharged. I'll save every cent of my pay until then so we can be married right away."

"We can write to each other until then. Here's my address."

He took the paper from me and tucked it into his pocket. "I'll write as soon as I get to Utrecht and let you know my address."

"It's going to seem like an eternity until we see each other again." Hendrik's friends had reached the corner and were crossing the street. I wiped the tears from my eyes so I could take one last, lingering look at the man I loved. "You'd better run," I said.

Hendrik nodded. Tears filled his eyes, too. "I love you, Geesje." Then he turned and sprinted down the street without looking back. A feeling of dread crept over me as the space lengthened between us. I wondered if I would ever see him again.

CHAPTER 8

Anna

Today is Sunday, and it seems odd not to attend church. Last night I dreamt once again that Mama and I were sitting together in a church service. I must have been very young in the dream because my feet stuck straight out from the pew instead of touching the floor. When I looked over at Mama, she was crying and wiping her eyes with her handkerchief. I thought it odd that it wasn't one of the Belgian linen and lace ones she always carries, but a plain square of white cotton, hand-embroidered with blue flowers. Her tears frightened me. My mama shouldn't be sad. I patted her arm to soothe her, and she smiled at me through her tears and pulled me close. "It's all right, darling," she said. "These are happy tears." Then she took a white peppermint from her bag—my favorite candy—and placed it in my palm, folding my fingers around it. "Here, darling." I put the candy on my tongue and let it dissolve slowly in my mouth so it would last longer. When I woke up, the dream had left behind a lingering sadness.

I get dressed and eat breakfast, then walk down to the pier and sit on the bench, watching the Sunday fishermen lined up along the dock with their poles jutting out over the water. I have my diary with me, and I'm still reading through it, slowly reliving the events of the past five months. I see a pattern emerging. I have been unhappy for quite some time, even before William ended our engagement. Shouldn't the months before my wedding be the happiest days of my life? Shouldn't the glorious excitement of being loved by someone and loving him in return fill my days with laughter and joy? Instead, I've felt a deepening loneliness, even when surrounded by people—and especially when I've attended Chicago's genteel social events. I have written again and again in my diary that I feel as if I don't belong there, that I am somehow different from the other young women in my crowd.

Ever since that first January day when my driver took a wrong turn and ended up on the corner of Chicago Avenue and LaSalle Street, I have been inexplicably drawn to the castle church—as if hooked by a fisherman reeling in his catch. Was that the church in my dream last night, or am I only imagining that it was now that I'm awake?

I am still sitting by the water's edge when a steamship arrives from the town of Holland, which is only a few miles away at the eastern end of Black Lake. The quiet morning is suddenly filled with excitement as picnickers and bathers disembark to spend the sunny summer day here at the beach or along the shores of Black Lake. Many travelers are dressed in their Sunday best, and my attention is drawn to a woman who steps off the ship with her little boy. He is wearing a white sailor suit and blue cap, and he lets go of his mother's hand the moment he reaches the end of the gangplank, eager to run. His mother grabs him and pulls him back. "Wait, lieveling! Don't run near the water," she says. "Hold my hand, lieveling."

A shock tingles through me at the foreign-sounding word. I

know that word. Mama spoke it in my dream last night after I'd noticed her tears: *"It's all right, darling."* But she hadn't said *darling*, she'd said *lieveling*. Somehow I know that it means the same thing. I watch the little boy, and I can almost feel the peppermint in my palm as Mama curls my fingers around it. *"Here, lieveling."*

For a long moment I feel paralyzed. Am I losing my mind? William said that the castle church was making me crazy. Is it true? My diary slides from my lap and falls to the ground as I leap to my feet. I want to chase the woman and ask her what nationality she is, what language she is speaking. But how can I ask a stranger such a question? Besides, she and her son have disappeared into the crowd.

The mother had thick, golden blond hair like mine. I was the envy of all the girls at school because my skin was so fair and my hair was so thick and curly. I can't recall ever seeing another woman with hair like mine. Our Swedish maid's blond hair is as fine as silk.

I sit down on the bench again, too shaken to walk much less run after them. I bend to retrieve my diary. When I sit up again, the sun blinds me as it reflects off the lake. I squeeze my eyes shut, trying to remember Mother speaking to me in another language when I was a child. But why would she? And what language would it be? Mother's ancestors were English. So were Father's.

I pull my straw hat down to shield my eyes and open my diary to the place where I stopped reading.

March 9

I don't know what to think. Last evening in his sermon, Reverend Torrey asked us the same question that Jesus asked: "For what is a man profited, if he shall gain the whole world, and lose his own soul?" The question haunts me. The answer eludes me. William will be giving me "the whole world" when we marry, yet my soul feels lost and empty. I had told Mother I was going to visit a friend yesterday, but I went to

*the castle church instead. I know it's wrong to tell lies, yet
I find myself doing that very thing. When I arrived home, I
went into Father's library and searched for the huge family
Bible that he keeps on one of his shelves. The servants are
the only ones who ever touch it, and that's only when they
dust the bookshelves each week. I carried the heavy Bible up
here to my bedroom so I could read Jesus' words for myself.
The sermon gave me so much to think about. I already know
I'll go back to the church again, in spite of William's order
to stay away.*

March 12

*I've been reading the Gospel of Luke from Father's big family
Bible. I was deeply moved by the parable Jesus told about
a rich man who had no pity on a poor beggar named Lazarus. The story reminded me of the question that still haunts
me: "For what is a man profited, if he shall gain the whole
world, and lose his own soul?" I wish I had someone to talk
to about everything I'm reading. I have so many questions.*

March 13

*It's after midnight. I've just arrived home from a dinner party
with William, and I'm so upset that I know I won't sleep. The
dinner was at the Mitchells' magnificent new mansion, and
there were endless courses of food. I watched people nibble
at each course or take a sip or two of their soup, and then
the servants would clear away our plates and bring the next
course. Naturally, there was entirely too much food to eat.
And I realize that this is the way these elegant dinner parties
have always been. But as I dined beneath the gilded ceiling
and dazzling chandelier, I couldn't stop thinking about the
rich man in Jesus' parable and the poor beggar, Lazarus, who
would have gladly eaten the crumbs from his table but was*

*never given any. The uneaten food tonight would have fed
a family of immigrants for a week. And on the carriage ride
home afterward, that's exactly what I told William.*

*But he stared at me as if I were crazy and said, "Which
immigrant family?" Then he asked where I was getting such
wild ideas.*

*I told him they were from a story in the Bible, that Jesus
told a parable about a rich man who never helped a poor
beggar. But he cut me off and stated that his family gave very
generously to charity. "And so does your father."*

"But in Reverend Torrey's sermon he said—"

*"Who? What sermon? There's no one by that name preach-
ing at our church." I realized my mistake too late. William
had been holding my hand as we rode home, but he suddenly
let go, practically tossing my hand back into my own lap.
"You went to that ridiculous church again, didn't you? After
I told you not to."*

I couldn't reply, my throat was so tight with tears.

*"Your silence condemns you, Anna." Then William turned
away, gazing out of the carriage window not at me, his chin
lifted in contempt.*

*"William, please listen . . . I don't understand why you're
so against that church." But he shook his head, refusing to
say another word to me for the rest of the ride home.*

I can't read any more diary entries, or I'll begin to weep. William had forced me to choose between him and the church, and
by continuing to sneak back there to attend services, I had chosen
the church. Had I been foolish to do so? I remember feeling so
lost and alone at social events, even with William by my side and
dozens of people surrounding me, and yet that emptiness always
lifted when I sat by myself in the pew, listening to the minister talk
about God's unfailing love.

I stand and slowly walk back to the hotel's wide front porch. The
walkways are crowded with people and I look all around, hoping

to see the woman and her little boy again. I still can't imagine how I understood the foreign words she said to him.

My mind bounces from that mystery back to William again. If he decides to give me another chance, should I take it? He would give me everything I could ever want—except the freedom to attend the castle church. I could never go back there again. *"What is a man profited,"* I wonder, *"if he shall gain the whole world, and lose his own soul?"*

CHAPTER 9

Geesje

HOLLAND, MICHIGAN
1897

I stand just outside the door of Pillar Church, gazing in dismay at the rain that has begun to fall, spotting the steps with dark circles. "It looks like we should have ended our gathering a few minutes ago," I tell the other ladies. "I hope you all brought umbrellas."

"I don't mind a little rain," the dominie's wife says. "We accomplished a lot of work for the Lord this morning." We all murmur in agreement, and after saying good-bye to my friends, I unfurl my umbrella and prepare to plunge into the rain. Dominie's wife stops me. "I just wanted to thank you for leading us in prayer today, Geesje," she says. "You always seem to know exactly what to say and do and how to pray. We would be at loose ends, sometimes, without your wisdom to guide us."

I feel my cheeks grow warm at the unexpected praise. I thank her and set off for home. By the time I arrive, my leather shoes and the hem of my skirt are soaked, and I find myself wishing we still wore wooden shoes like in the old days.

The warm, incessant rain makes my house feel like the inside of a dog's mouth. It's too steamy to leave the windows closed, too damp to leave them open; too muggy to knit, too wet to work in my yard. I wonder what Derk does out at that great big hotel on rainy days like this. I'll have to ask him the next time I see him. He and his father ate Sunday dinner with me here yesterday after the service, and I gave Derk the first few pages of my story to read.

"This is fascinating, Tante Geesje," he told me when he came to the place where I'd stopped writing. "I wish you had more for me to read. I don't think I've ever heard the story about the soldier you fell in love with, have I? What happened next? Is he the man you married?"

I didn't think I could tell Hendrik's story out loud and still keep my composure. It's difficult enough to find the words to write about him after fifty years. "Hendrik's story is very long and complicated, Derk," I told him. "I promise I'll let you read it when it's finished, but I need to tell it in my own time and in my own way."

"I understand," he'd said. "I'll try to be patient and wait."

Now I putter around my kitchen for a few minutes, looking for something to do. The rain is still coming down hard. How in the world do all the guests out at those big hotels keep busy when they can't go to the beach or sail on the lake or even go fishing? I can't imagine having days and days of uninterrupted leisure like those wealthy guests do—although I suppose, with their mansions full of servants back home, they're accustomed to a more leisurely life than I am. We Dutch are a hardworking people, and we give ourselves only one day of appointed rest each week, the Sabbath day. When I recall how hard we all worked when we first arrived here in America—to near exhaustion, at times—I cannot imagine what men like Dominie Van Raalte, God rest his soul, would think of the grand hotels that now line the shores of Black Lake. Or the rows and rows of cottages that are inhabited only during the summer months. We were thrilled to finally have a one-room log cabin to live in after sheltering beneath lean-tos made of branches for weeks and weeks. The lean-to that Papa and Maarten built offered no shelter at all when the rain poured down like it's doing today. *"But how wonderful this rain is for our crops,"* Papa would say, always finding rainbows in the storm clouds.

But I'm getting ahead of myself again. If I'm going to coax all these memories back to life like dying coals, I should be writing them down like the committee asked me to do. With nothing else to do on this dreary day, I sit down at my little desk and pull out my notebook, rereading the last page to see where I left off. Then I choose a freshly sharpened pencil and, as the memories pour down like the rain outside, I begin to write.

Geesje's Story

THE NETHERLANDS
50 YEARS EARLIER

I clearly remember the summer evening when my life changed once again. The day had been unusually hot, and I hurried through our simple dinner of bread and fish, hoping to leave our stifling apartment for a few minutes and walk down to the river, where the air always felt much cooler. I would have to ask Maarten to accompany me since my father still didn't want me to venture far from our house by myself. Papa always read from the Scriptures and prayed after we ate, but on this night the Bible remained closed on the table with Papa's ink-stained hands folded on top of it. The somber look on his face and the way he nervously cleared his throat told me he had something important to say.

"For several months now," he began, "I have been meeting with Dominie Van Raalte and some other men from our church to discuss the persecution we continue to experience. Added to those worries are our concerns about the blight that has struck our crops for two years in a row. After much discussion and prayers for God's guidance, we have reached an important decision. We feel that the Lord is directing us to leave the Netherlands and immigrate to a place where we can live and work and worship in peace."

"Papa, no!" I covered my mouth the moment I had spoken. I knew it was disrespectful to contradict my father, much less interrupt him. But Hendrik had just left for Utrecht, and I couldn't imagine moving even farther away from him.

My father didn't react to my outburst, continuing as if I hadn't spoken. "One place we have considered is the Dutch colony on the island of Java."

I squeezed my eyes closed to hold back my tears, remembering Hendrik's stories of the exotic lands in the Far East. It would take months and months of sailing to get there, with unimaginable dangers along the way. And in the end, Hendrik and I would be on opposite sides of the world from each other.

"However," Papa continued, "we discovered that we would face the same religious restrictions in Dutch-controlled Java as we do here. And so we have decided to go to America, where there is no state religion and all faiths are allowed to worship as they wish."

"No . . ." I said again, but in a whisper this time. America seemed as impossibly far as Java. The distance between Arnhem and Utrecht was already too far to be separated from the man I loved.

"America has good opportunities for workers and plenty of land waiting to be settled," Papa continued. "A state called Wisconsin is offering inexpensive land for sale. Good land, I'm told. The cost of traveling across the ocean has never been cheaper than it is now, and people from many other nations have already taken advantage of that fact. Dominie Van Raalte believes it's possible for us to settle in a place where we can live together quietly, farm our own land, educate our children, and raise them to love God. Most important, we'll be able to worship freely as a community."

Maarten grew very excited as Papa spoke, shifting on his wooden chair as if he could barely stay seated, his sturdy legs shuffling beneath the table. "I would very much like to immigrate with you, sir, if you'll let me."

"Of course, son. Of course." Papa offered Maarten a rare smile as he leaned forward to squeeze his shoulder. "You've been with our family through many tests and trials, and you are very welcome to join us. Some of the elders believe that the hardships we've been forced to endure these past few years were God's way of directing us to move on, just as the persecution that the early believers suffered in Jerusalem served to scatter them and spread the gospel around the world. And so, beginning tonight, our family will offer prayers for continued guidance in this matter."

I bowed my head and listened as Papa prayed for God's leading. But it was clear to me that he had already decided the matter and was merely asking God to prosper his plans. I felt sick at the thought of moving to America, thousands of miles away from Hendrik. Would I ever see him again? He had written two letters to me since moving to Utrecht, assuring me of his continued love. I made up my mind to remain here in the Netherlands, where he was, even if it meant saying good-bye to my parents.

Later that night I was unable to sleep—and not only because my room felt unbearably hot. I had moved back into my own bedroom after Hendrik and the others left, but I crossed the passageway to my parents' bedroom and knocked on their door. "It's me—may I come in?" I asked.

"Of course," Mama said. My parents were already in bed, but they both sat up, looking at me with concern. The sun went down so late on summer nights in Arnhem that there was enough light in the room to see them clearly. "What's wrong, lieveling?"

"I don't want to go to America. I want to stay here, in the Netherlands. Maybe I can move in with Anneke or Geerde and—"

"Your sisters are much too poor," Papa said. "They can barely afford to feed their own families."

I had been afraid he would say that, so I had another alternative ready. "Well . . . maybe I could ask the dominie to help me find a job. I could work as a house servant for a wealthy family, or—"

"Geesje, you're only seventeen years old," Papa said, "Besides, the people in our community of Separatists aren't wealthy. The few who do have money are also considering a move to America. And I doubt if any rich families who attend the State Church would hire you as their servant once they learn of your beliefs."

I didn't tell Papa, but I was so desperate to stay here with Hendrik that I would have considered returning to the old church.

"Geesje, why don't you want to go with your moeder and Maarten and me?" Papa asked. "The elders have prayed long and hard about this decision, and they feel it is God's will."

I had no choice but to tell them the truth. They would learn it sooner or later. I took another step closer to their bed. "I've been afraid to tell you but . . . but Hendrik and I are in love."

"Hendrik—the soldier?" Mama asked. "You barely know each other."

"Yes, we do, Mama. We talked about all manner of things when he lived with us this past year, and I've discovered that he's a wonderful man. Before he left, he told me that he loves me, too. He wants to marry me after he's discharged."

Papa groaned. Mama climbed from the bed and came to where I stood. "You can't marry him, Geesje. I'm sorry." She spoke softly, not angrily, wrapping her arm around my shoulder. "I agree that Hendrik seems like a nice young man, but you have very little in common with each other. A marriage works best when people share the same values and the same faith in God. It would be a huge mistake to marry a man who isn't a believer."

"But Hendrik is a believer. He wanted to make a profession of faith, but they sent him to Utrecht before he had a chance to talk to the dominie. Ask Maarten. He'll tell you. He was good friends with Hendrik, remember?"

"Even if Hendrik does become a Christian," Papa said, "and even if he joins the Separatists, how would he support you? He has no home or family, and work is very difficult to find these days.

That's why he joined the army, if I'm not mistaken. And the lack of jobs is one of the reasons we're leaving the country. I'm sorry, lieveling, but you are still so young. I can't allow you to stay here on your own, or marry a man who is nearly a stranger. Try to understand that."

I could no longer hold back my tears. "But I love him! Please, Papa! I want to be with him!"

Mama pulled me close as she tried to comfort me. "Listen, Geesje . . . listen to me." I could barely hear her above my sobs. "I would hate for you to have your heart broken, but you must understand that Hendrik no longer lives in our home or has Maarten to talk to about spiritual things. He won't be influenced by Dominie's sermons anymore. It will be much too easy for him to forget about God now that he is living with hundreds of other soldiers again. And his feelings for you might also change once he's away from you and living in the big city."

"No. That isn't going to happen. We love each other."

Papa climbed out of bed, too, and rested his hands on my shoulders. "You need to put this matter into God's hands, Geesje, and trust Him with it. If He truly intends for you to marry Hendrik, then nothing will stand in your way. Perhaps Hendrik can also come to America when he completes his service in the army. Maybe emigrating is the right answer for Hendrik, too. He could find work in America or buy land of his own within our community. Pray about it, and if this is the Lord's will for you, it will all work out. If not—then you must decide if you're going to obey God or go your own way."

I had a feeling that my parents didn't really believe that things would work out for Hendrik and me. They hoped this was a girlish infatuation that would fade once Hendrik and I were separated by thousands of miles. I knew it wouldn't.

I stayed up late into the night writing Hendrik a frantic letter, explaining what my parents and the others had decided, explaining that I had no choice but to go to America with them. I told him that he was welcome to immigrate to America, too, when he was discharged. I mailed the letter early the next morning, and for days I couldn't eat or sleep while I waited for his reply. What would he say? Was Papa right in believing that Hendrik would soon forget all about me? I wasn't sure if I was brave enough to defy my parents and run away to Utrecht if Hendrik asked me to join him there, but that's what I longed to do. Yet if I did that, I would not only be defying Mama and Papa, I'd be defying God.

That Sunday as people crowded into the print shop and stood outside near the windows and doors, I listened to the sermon from the kitchen, sitting beside Mama and a handful of other women. Dominie preached about the great heroes of our faith and how God worked in the lives of those who believed. Too restless to stay seated, I stood and moved to the window as he spoke about the faithful ones like Abraham who never lived to see the fulfillment of things that he'd hoped for in this life. Outside in our tiny yard, the sun shone on the clothesline where Hendrik had held me in his arms, and as I listened to the sermon, I knew that my faith wasn't strong enough to trust God's plan for me.

For the first time in my life, my heart was pierced by doubt. I had lived with my parents' example of unwavering faith in God and thought I believed everything they'd taught me. But now I began to wonder if what I'd learned about God was really true. With a huge, wide world to run, why would God even care if I followed my heart and married Hendrik? Why would He bring Hendrik into my life in the first place and watch us fall in love, only to cruelly decide that we shouldn't be married? Were we like insects to God who hovered over us, watching our every move, prepared to squash us and our dreams if we didn't follow His will?

Mama glanced at me with a worried look, but she was quickly drawn back to the sermon. Papa had said I must decide if I was going to obey God or go my own way. But did God really direct our lives if we prayed for guidance? How would I hear Him speaking? I felt as though we were all on a ship and God was our captain, standing at the rudder, choosing our direction and destination. We had no choice but to hang on to the rails as He took us through storms or allowed us to wallow in the doldrums—unless we decided to leap overboard and start swimming in our own direction. I knew enough to fear the chaos of the unknown deep.

My doubts widened and spread like the killing blight until I not only doubted God's goodness but also Hendrik's faithfulness. What if Papa was right and Hendrik's feelings for me began to change now that we were apart? Utrecht was filled with women who were much prettier than I was. And why would Hendrik even want to become a Christian knowing that he would have to submit to God's will and live by the Bible's strict rules and be persecuted for his beliefs?

Papa said I should trust God and put the matter into His hands. I wanted to do that, I really did. I wanted to believe that everything I knew about Him was true, and that He was a loving God who wanted only the best for me. Because if that wasn't true, then nothing in life had any meaning. If He didn't love us and have a plan for each one of us, then why bother living at all?

I didn't think I could ever be happy without Hendrik—but I knew that I couldn't endure life without God. When the sermon ended and it was time for prayer, I sat down at the table beside my mother again and bowed my head. I prayed, like everyone else, for God's guidance. I told Him that I wanted His will for my life, not my own will. I whispered *Amen*.

Then I held my breath and waited for Hendrik to answer my letter.

CHAPTER 10

Anna

HOTEL OTTAWA
1897

We've been at the Hotel Ottawa for nearly a week. It rained all day yesterday, keeping us inside the entire day, so today I'm eager to get back outside for my morning walk. I can tell that Mother misses her social life in Chicago and would like to return home, but I still need more time. "How much time?" she asks over lunch. I don't know the answer. Nor do I know the answers to the dozens of other questions that fill my head: Why am I so lonely and unhappy? Why was the life I had with William so unfulfilling? And did God truly have a different purpose for me?

I can't stop thinking about the woman I saw on Sunday with her little boy, the woman who had hair just like mine. I need to know what language she'd spoken. I'm not at all certain what difference the answer will make, but it somehow seems all wrapped up with who I am and who I'm really meant to be. As I walk along the pathway near the water, skirting the sandy puddles of rainwater,

I'm wishing I had stopped the woman and talked with her. I spot Derk striding toward the dock with an armload of gear. I watch him for a few minutes as he walks out onto the pier, his steps bold and certain as the wooden structure bobs up and down beneath his weight. The waves are choppy today after yesterday's downpour. Derk climbs aboard the hotel's sailboat, and I see that he's getting it ready for another excursion, checking the ropes and sails and all the other incomprehensible parts that make the ship sail. I've watched from the shore as he's taken guests on voyages around Black Lake, and as the boat glides across the water on the wind, the huge triangular white sail unfurled, Derk makes sailing look so simple, so gracefully beautiful, that I'm almost tempted to try it. Until the boat changes direction and tilts sideways, that is. Sailboats always do that, which is why I will never, ever set foot in one.

I watch him work for a few minutes, then eventually grow brave enough to walk out onto the pier and stand beside the boat. Several minutes pass before Derk finally notices me. "Good morning, Miss Nicholson. Have you signed up to go sailing today?"

"No, no. I just wondered . . . I wondered if I might ask you a question."

"Certainly. Ask away." He moves across the deck of the boat to stand closer to me, the ship rocking beneath him. I don't know how he can keep his balance, but he does.

"I–I don't want to get you into trouble if you have work to do." I am losing my nerve. It occurs to me how ridiculous my question will sound, especially if I mention my dream. "I can come back later if you're busy."

"I'm not. The boat is all ready to go, and I have a few minutes while I wait for my passengers. What's your question?"

I take a deep breath. "You mentioned the other day that you thought I looked Dutch. And that your own ancestors were Dutch."

"Right."

"Do you speak that language by any chance?"

"A little bit," he says, showing me an inch of space between his thumb and forefinger. "I used to be able to understand what my grandparents were saying, but I've forgotten a lot over the years. And I never spoke it very well, myself."

"Have you ever heard the word *lieveling?*"

His face brightens, as if I've said some magic word. "Sure. It's something you'd say to a loved one. Something like *darling*, I suppose."

"How did I know that?" I murmur. The dock feels unsteady beneath my feet, and I suddenly need to sit down. I feel myself swaying, and Derk leaps across the gap from the boat to the dock and grabs my arm.

"Are you all right, Miss Nicholson?"

"Yes . . . well . . . no, not really." Derk helps me off the dock and lowers me down onto the nearest bench. It's still damp from the rain, but I welcome the chance to sit. He looks concerned as he sits down beside me.

"You aren't going to faint on me, are you, miss? Shall I get some smelling salts?"

"No . . . but thank you." I've always disdained fragile women who swoon and reach for the salts at every minor disturbance. Yet I remember William's accusation, and at this moment I do feel as though I'm losing my mind. And yet I'm not! "I'm *not* crazy," I say aloud. "I *did* know what it meant. But where did I learn that word?"

I look up at Derk. He has a puzzled expression on his face. Perhaps he also believes I'm crazy. "Why don't you start at the beginning, Miss Nicholson, and—"

"It's Anna. Please call me Anna."

"Anna, then. I can see that you're upset, and I'm willing to listen if you'd like to tell me what's troubling you."

Derk isn't classically handsome like William, and certainly not as fashionably dressed. But I see so much compassion in his blue eyes and in his expression of concern that it makes him seem handsome. "That's what ministers do, I suppose. Console people."

"Well, I'm not ordained, yet," he says, smiling. "But you look as though you could use a friend."

A friend. I have been longing for a friend. I take a deep breath

83

to steady myself and let it out with a sigh—something Mother would abhor. "When the steamship from Holland docked here yesterday I overheard a woman talking to her little boy. She called him *lieveling*. Somehow, I knew what that word meant, yet I didn't even know what language she was speaking until you told me just now. The woman's hair looked very much like mine, and you said that I looked Dutch, and so I thought maybe you could tell me . . . I'm sorry. I'm probably not making any sense."

"Yes, you are. Go on."

"You've confirmed that it is a Dutch word, but I have no idea where I could have heard it or how I would have learned what it meant. I had a dream the other night that I was very young, like the little boy I saw yesterday, and Mama called me *lieveling* in my dream, just like the little boy's mother did. But I'm certain that my mother doesn't speak a word of Dutch."

"Hmm. That is a puzzle." Derk rests his hand on his smooth-shaven chin, massaging it as he thinks for a moment. "It's obvious that you and your family are people of means, so do you suppose it's possible that you had a nursemaid or a servant who spoke Dutch to you when you were little?"

I stare at him in surprise. He's brilliant. "Of course! That must be it. Thank you. I'll ask Mother about it as soon as I return to my room. Thank you."

He gives me a wide grin. "I'm very glad I could help."

"I was afraid I was losing my mind, you see. William told me to stop going to the castle church because it was making me crazy, and with all the dreams and nightmares I've been having lately, I was starting to wonder if he was right. But of course there's a simple explanation for it. Of course there is. Thank you."

"You're welcome." Neither of us makes a move to leave even though Derk has answered my question. "Is William someone special?" he asks.

"He's my fiancé . . . that is, he *was* my fiancé until he ended our engagement."

"I'm sorry . . . But I think I might understand how you feel.

84

There was someone I loved very much and wanted to marry, but she turned me down. She said she didn't want to be married to a minister, and that's what I'll be in another year."

"How odd," I say. "It seems that religion has played a role in ending both of our engagements. You see, I've been attending a church in Chicago these past few months—I've felt drawn there, in fact, as if by ropes and pulleys and—"

"Which church?"

"It was started by the famous evangelist D. L. Moody."

"Yes, I've heard of him. Sorry for interrupting. Go on."

"The way they talk about God there and about the Christian faith . . . they make it seem so real. The minister is always telling us how much God loves us, and that He has a plan for us, and I feel so peaceful whenever I go there. The church William and I attend isn't like that at all. Our minister makes God seem cold and distant, and there are a lot of dos and don'ts and 'Thou shalt nots.' I feel tied up in knots simply trying to remember all those rules. I have too many regulations in my life as it is with all the strictures of social etiquette and proper manners I'm required to follow. I know I can never measure up in God's eyes, and I certainly never felt that He loved me—until I found this new church."

I'm aware that I'm prattling on and on—and to a stranger, no less—but I can't seem to stop myself. Derk sits perfectly still and attentive as he listens, and I realize that William never truly listened to me. He never seemed interested in what I was feeling or thinking.

"I tried to talk to William about the differences between the two churches," I continue, "but he refused to listen. He told me to stop going to the castle church—that's what I call it—and when I didn't stop, he said I had chosen the church instead of him, and he ended our engagement."

"That doesn't sound very fair. But again, I think I know how you feel. Caroline gave me an ultimatum, too. I could marry her or I could be a minister. I couldn't do both."

"How selfish of her to demand her own way! She must not have loved you very much if she let you walk away from her."

For a moment, Derk looks as though the thought has never occurred to him. "Yes . . ." he says, nodding his head. "Yes, I suppose you're right. She didn't love me—at least not as much as I loved her. And the same things probably could be said about your fiancé. It was very selfish of him to give you that ultimatum. If going to a certain church makes you happy, why force you to stop?"

"William thinks they have radical beliefs at the castle church, but they don't."

Derk gives a short laugh. "It seems like nothing ever changes. I've been reading my Tante Geesje's memoir about emigrating from the Netherlands, and she says that the divide between the churches was what brought my ancestors to this country fifty years ago. She says her family broke away from the state church because it was too cold and lifeless—just like the one you described. And her ancestors were persecuted for wanting to worship differently. They made a lot of sacrifices in order to settle here in Holland and enjoy religious freedom. And it sounds to me that all you want is a small measure of religious freedom, too."

"Yes! That's exactly how I feel when I go to the castle church— like I'm finally free!" I stop and cover my mouth for a moment, ashamed of what I have just confessed. "I sound so spoiled and ungrateful," I tell Derk. "I have a wonderful life in Chicago with everything I could ever need or want. I'm not held captive in any way."

"I understand. But there's a difference between our physical well-being and our spiritual contentment." Derk's gaze is so intense and so sorrowful that I realize I'm showing no concern for him even though he shared the story of his heartbreak with me.

"What about your girlfriend—Caroline?" I ask. "Does she attend a different church than you do?"

"No, they're the same. But her father is a minister, and she says that he always puts his congregation before his family. He sometimes leaves in the middle of dinner or a celebration if a parishioner needs him. Caroline doesn't want to share her husband the same way she's been forced to share her father."

"But isn't that part of your job, comforting people when they need someone to talk to?"

"Yes. That's why we broke up. I couldn't promise her that I would never do what her father did."

The walkway in front of us is growing busier with guests coming outside for a stroll or to enjoy the beautiful summer day. I'm shocked to realize that I'm telling this stranger all the personal details about my breakup with William, details that even my parents don't know. Although, if Father has been talking to William, he has probably heard all the details by now.

"I should go," I say, rising to my feet. "Your passengers will be here soon, and I'm keeping you from your work."

"Wait. Do you have to go?" Derk asks, rising as well. "I feel as though we're just becoming friends. We have something in common, even if it is a broken engagement."

Again I realize how much I've been longing for a friend. But the social divide between Derk and me is too great. Mother would think it scandalous for me to befriend a hotel employee. "Yes, I'm afraid I must go. Thank you for your time, and for answering my questions."

"Not at all. You gave me a new perspective about Caroline. I enjoyed talking with you, Anna."

I walk back to the hotel porch where Mother sits with her friend Mrs. Stevens. I give a little wave and turn away from them, unwilling to overhear another embarrassing conversation about unfaithful husbands. Then I halt in midstride as another thought occurs to me. If Derk is right and it was a servant who called me *lieveling* as a child, might that servant also be my real mother? Since my parents adopted me as a newborn, might they have allowed my birth mother to stay as my nursemaid? And if that servant was Dutch, it would explain why I resemble Derk's friend Elizabeth and the Dutch-speaking woman I saw with the little boy yesterday.

I want to question Mother, but she spends the entire afternoon with Mrs. Stevens. We share a table with her and two other couples at dinner, and it would be impolite to casually raise the matter of my birth in conversation over the glazed ham and buttered peas. I ignore the boring chitchat and try to devise a crafty way to raise the matter later when I'm alone with Mother without arousing her suspicion. Or her defenses. My chance finally comes when she sits down in my room with me for a few minutes before we retire for the night.

"I've been thinking about my old nanny all day, for some reason," I say offhandedly, "but I can't recall her name."

"You mean Bridget? Bridget O'Malley?"

I have to hide my frustration at the obviously Irish name. "But I was old enough to go to school when Bridget took care of me, wasn't I? Didn't I have a nursemaid before her? When I was a newborn?"

"Bridget was with us for years. Until you turned eight, I believe." Mother might have fooled me into believing she was telling the truth if she hadn't looked away quite so quickly—or hurried to change the subject. "Oh, I nearly forgot, Anna. Your father tucked a letter for you in with the one he sent me today. Let me fetch it for you." She disappears into her room and returns a moment later with the letter. "Here, dear. I'm sorry I didn't mention it sooner." She gives a phony yawn and excuses herself, insisting that she's sleepy. I unfold the paper, dreading what I might read.

Dearest Anna,

I had a long conversation with William at the club yesterday, and he explained the details of why he ended your engagement. He believes that you betrayed his trust by behaving as you did, and I have to say that I agree with him. I see no reason at all for you to attend any other church than the one where we have been lifelong members. But you are still my dear daughter, and so I'm certain you would never do anything improper or shameful.

I firmly believe that a marriage between you and William would be a good one. Our families have much in common, and I couldn't ask for a finer husband for my only child. William is willing to reconcile if you can assure him that you will abide by his decisions from now on. It's what every husband expects of his wife, dear Anna. This is not an unusual request by any means. A husband is always the head of his own household. I told William that you aren't expected back for at least another week, so that will give you time to reconsider renewing your engagement. I sincerely hope that all the hard feelings between you and William will have healed by then, and that we can move forward with the preparations for your wedding.

Speaking of your return, I received your letter describing the storm you encountered on your way to the resort. Your mother agreed that it was unnerving. I'm sorry you were so badly frightened, Anna, and I understand why you wish to make the return trip home by train. I'll see what can be done about exchanging tickets.

That's all for now. But I urge you to think about William's good qualities and not allow any hurt feelings to stand in the way of your marriage to him.

I remain,

Your loving father

I read the letter through three times. If I hadn't talked with Derk earlier today, Father's words might have swayed me. But I'd clearly seen how selfish Derk's girlfriend had been to ask him to sacrifice his happiness, and William's demands seem equally selfish to me. If I married him, would I have to sacrifice my own wishes and my own happiness for the rest of my life?

I open the window, letting in a fresh breath of cool, evening air. Music drifts in from some distant dance band, the sound carried across the narrow lake. The waters of Black Lake mirror the evening sky—dark and dappled with starlight. I suddenly feel trapped in this room—and in my life. I don't know who I really am or what my purpose is supposed to be. Maybe if I could solve the mystery of my past and how I learned a simple Dutch word, it would help me figure out my future.

But until I do, I'm quite certain that if I marry William, my future will be swallowed up by his plans the same way the waves in my nightmare swallow up my mama.

CHAPTER 11

Geesje's Story

The weeks that it took for my urgent letter to reach Hendrik and for him to write back were a time of soul-searching for me. I thought long and hard about Papa's warning that I must choose between God's will and my own, and I prayed to be strong enough to follow God, even if it meant losing Hendrik. When his reply finally came, I ripped open the envelope, holding my breath.

> *My darling Geesje,*
> *I would gladly follow you to the ends of the earth, so why not to America? I can think of no reason for me to stay here in the Netherlands without you, and I believe we would have more opportunities over there for a good life together than we would ever have here. If I could buy a patch of land to call my own in Wisconsin and live there with you, I would be the happiest man alive.*

I'm so sorry that you will have to travel all the way to America without me for now. But will you wait for me over there until I can join you after I'm discharged from the army? I hope that your answer will be yes. In the meantime, the days and weeks and months until we can be together again will seem very long.

Your loving soldier,

Hendrik

I wept with joy as I read his letter and quickly wrote back to him, promising to wait. Leaving Hendrik behind with a vast ocean between us was going to be the hardest thing I'd ever done in my life. But I had trusted God so far, and I decided to trust Him to bring us together again.

"I'm so happy for you, lieveling," Mama said when I told her the news about Hendrik. "The next time you write to him, you can send him this list of provisions that the shipping company recommends for the trip." The amount of food we were advised to bring seemed absurd, totaling 160 pounds per person! This included meat, flour, rice, potatoes, peas, bread, cheese, butter, sugar, coffee and tea, as well as household items like kettles, plates, pots, and tin water cans. My family didn't pack nearly that much because Papa also needed to bring some of the equipment he would need to start a new printing business in America. We weren't wealthy people, so we had very few clothes and other belongings to pack.

During the next few weeks, our family's plans seemed to move forward with great speed. We said a tearful good-bye to Geerde and Anneke and their families, knowing that we would probably never see them again on this side of heaven. Then on September 24 my parents and Maarten and I joined Dominie Van Raalte and about fifty other Separatists and set sail from the port of Rotterdam on the brig *Southerner*. The vessel looked huge to me with its boxy wooden hull and three towering masts. Our little congregation was filled with faith for our future as we launched out to sea with a litany of psalms and prayers. We sailed only as far as the Dutch port of Hellevoetsluis when our first calamity struck. A fire broke out, starting in the cook's galley and quickly spreading to the upper deck of our ship. Thick smoke found its way into every stateroom and passageway, sending us fleeing up from below, coughing and choking, our eyes stinging. What a terrifying sight to see flames consuming our wooden ship! Papa, Maarten, and all the other men quickly pitched in with the crew to form a bucket brigade. Thankfully they managed to extinguish the flames, but not before the fire burned a hole through the upper deck. The experience left everyone badly shaken. "What if the fire had happened while we were at sea," I asked Papa, "instead of in port?"

"Our lives are in God's hands, lieveling, whether we're on land or at sea," he replied. "We must learn to trust Him."

I had never been fearful before, but now I began to worry about all of the hindrances that might keep Hendrik and me apart. For the first time in my life I had a plan for my future but the obstacles that stood between me and the fulfillment of that plan seemed enormous.

Our voyage was delayed for a week because of the fire, and we remained in Hellevoetsluis until our ship could be repaired. A local church invited Dominie Van Raalte to preach on Sunday and we crammed into the sanctuary with so many other parishioners that we couldn't have fallen over if we'd tried. Everyone agreed that Albertus Van Raalte was a spellbinding preacher. His sermon filled all the passengers with courage, including me. "God is able to use all manner of obstacles to accomplish His purposes," Dominie assured us, "including the blight on the potato crop and the fire aboard our ship." I left the service reassured that everything would work out for Hendrik and me in America.

At last we sailed out into the North Sea, passing through the English Channel and into the Atlantic Ocean. My mood, as changeable as waves on the water, went from the heights of hope to the trough of despair. I can't begin to describe the melancholy I felt as I watched the shoreline of my homeland disappear from sight, knowing I would never see my beloved Netherlands again. America was so huge and distant and unknown. Would it ever feel like home to me the way Leiden had? I had sent one last letter to Hendrik before we'd departed from Hellevoetsluis, knowing it would be many, many months before he would receive another one from me, and even longer before I would receive one from him. He would have no way of knowing where to address a letter to me on the other side of that huge ocean until after we'd landed and gotten settled. Those months of silence would be excruciating to endure.

The other immigrants in our traveling party were filled with anticipation and excitement, knowing they were beginning a brand-new life in a new country with God guiding their every step. But each passing day on the featureless ocean took me farther and farther from the man I loved. Hendrik had assured me of his love in his last letter. Nothing could keep us apart. He promised to join me in America as soon as he could. I read that letter again and again until the paper became limp and the ink blurred from the salty air and my lovesick tears.

During our first day at sea, I spent as much time as I could on the passenger deck, fascinated by the intricate workings of a sailing ship. I loved the sound of the waves slapping against the bow as the ship plowed through the water, the call of the sailors as they signaled to each other, the snap of the sails in the wind. I was just getting my "sea legs" and adjusting to the feel of the rolling deck when a second calamity struck. A strong wind began to blow, and it soon swelled into a powerful storm. Sky and sea turned black, illuminated by spears of lightning that stabbed through the darkness. Rain and wind and waves pummeled our helpless vessel. Even the sailors had difficulty standing on the pitching deck, and they ordered all passengers to take cover below. Every door and hatch in the ship had to be closed up tightly to prevent the waves that rolled across the deck from pouring inside. The wooden-hulled *Southerner* seemed no match for the storm. I was certain we would all die.

For the next week, the storm refused to free us from its grip. Everyone on board was struck with violent nausea and vomiting, including the crew. The relentless pitching and rocking made it difficult to walk and impossible to keep even the smallest bites of food in our stomachs. Our stash of recommended supplies went uneaten. Mama, Papa, and I took turns nursing each other even though we were all equally sick. Maarten also tried his best to care for us, but he was deathly ill, too. By week's end, so much weight had fallen from his sturdy frame that his round face looked pale and haggard. Everyone prayed and hung on tightly to God and any railing or handle or post that we could find. Then, at the end of the week, Jesus finally calmed the wind and waves, and the convulsing sea became tranquil once again.

"Our prayers have been answered," Maarten said as he brought me some bread and tea on that first calm morning. He was out of bed and back on his feet before my parents and me, and he prepared a simple meal to help restore our strength even though he was still so shaky that he had to cling to the walls and furniture to remain upright.

But not all of our prayers had been answered. Tragedy struck for a third time. We learned that two of our fellow passengers had died, a young bride not much older than me, and a two-year-old child. I stood beside Maarten during the funerals beneath the billowing sails and miles of ropes and rigging, the canvas snapping and cracking in the wind above our heads like gunshots. Gripping the rail on the swaying deck, we watched the crew drop the bodies into the sea. "Why does God allow these terrible things to happen?" I asked him. "How can He see such tragedies and look the other way?"

"I can't answer your questions, Geesje," Maarten replied. "God's ways are not our ways."

I'll never forget the sound of that child's tiny, shroud-wrapped body splashing into the fathomless water. Or how inconsolable his mother's grief was. She would never be able to visit his grave or set up a marker to remember him by. I would think of that grieving mother again years later when I buried my own child.

Dominie Van Raalte conducted the funeral service for the families, reading Jesus' words as he tried to reassure us. "'I am the resurrection and the life: he that believeth in me, though he were dead, yet shall he live. . . .'" But after he'd prayed and the service ended, I still had unanswered questions.

"Was God punishing those two people for some reason?" I asked Maarten. "One was an innocent child, the other a new bride. Didn't we all obey God's will and leave our homeland? Why did this have to happen? It makes no sense."

"The Bible says that all of our days are written in God's book before one of them comes to be," he replied. "And remember, our life here on earth isn't all there is. We have the promise of heaven awaiting us. And resurrection. That mother will see her child again, the husband will see his bride. Do you believe that?"

"I do . . . But it still doesn't seem fair." For the second time in my young life, my faith was battered by a storm of doubt as I questioned God's goodness. If He could cruelly snatch the young bride from her husband for no reason, the child from his mother, might He snatch Hendrik from me, too?

CHAPTER 12

Geesje's Story

AMERICA
50 YEARS EARLIER

We spent more than seven weeks crossing the Atlantic Ocean before reaching America. Thankfully, none of those weeks was as bad as the first one. I couldn't help feeling bored during those long months, weary of living in such a cramped space. We arrived in New York City on November 17, 1846, a frigid day beneath gray, wind-scoured skies. The port looked even busier than the one in Rotterdam had with sailing vessels and steamships coming and going in all directions. Dozens more vessels waited offshore, their spiky masts poking the cloudy sky. We docked at the Castle Garden Immigration Depot on the lower end of Manhattan Island and wobbled ashore, relieved to set foot on firm land once again.

People from all over the world jammed the interior of the building, waiting to enter America. As we huddled together to avoid getting lost, a group of young men from who knows what other country seemed intrigued by us, pointing at us in our striped skirts and white poke bonnets, our men in their baggy trousers and black caps. Most of us wore wooden shoes, the only ones we owned. I had made friends with two other girls my age on the ship and as we stood talking together, a half-dozen bearded young men inched closer. They seemed to be flirting with us, laughing and babbling in their foreign tongue as they tried to communicate, kissing their fingers and tossing imaginary kisses in our direction. I found them amusing and wasn't frightened at all, but Maarten and the other young men in our group hurried over to stand guard as the foreigners continued their pantomime.

Minutes passed as we all wondered where to go and what to do next. Then a group of Dutch Americans arrived, amazing us by speaking our own language. They'd come to Castle Garden from Dominie Thomas DeWitt's Dutch Reformed Church to greet us and help us through the immigration process. "New York City was first settled by our countrymen from the Netherlands hundreds of years ago," their leader told us. "It used to be called New Amsterdam." Our Dutch-American hosts also explained what the dark-haired strangers had been saying. "They think your women are very beautiful. They've never seen such fair skin and blond hair before. You must be very careful to protect your young women. From now on you must all stay close together and ignore any strangers who approach you." Maarten stuck even closer to my side after that, until it seemed that with every step I took, there he was underfoot. The strangers had seemed harmless to me, and I didn't understand why we couldn't return their gestures of friendship. No one except Hendrik had ever told me I was beautiful.

After several hours of waiting in the immigration depot, the American authorities finally allowed us to leave. Our hosts arranged transportation and lodging for us, and we set off through the busy city streets for our first glimpse of America. What I saw of New York City was very disappointing to me. It seemed dirty and smelly and overcrowded, with none of the lovely old buildings and canals and tree-lined streets I remembered in beautiful Leiden. If I could have reboarded the ship and returned to the Netherlands, I would have gladly done it, no matter how long the return journey took or how seasick I might become. I tried to hide my weary tears as I undressed for bed that night in the boardinghouse, but Mama saw them. "What's wrong, Geesje?"

"The voyage took so long, and I'm so tired of traveling, and we're not even to Wisconsin, yet, Mama. I miss our home. And I miss Hendrik."

"I know, I know . . ." she soothed. "But the Lord has wonderful blessings in store for us. You'll see."

"Do you and Papa regret our decision to come?" I asked, blowing my nose.

"No. I miss your sisters, of course, and my grandchildren. But no, we have no regrets."

"Do you think Anneke and Geerde and their families will decide to join us once we're settled?"

"Only the Lord knows. The important thing is that we're following God's leading to create a *kolonie* where we'll be free to worship Him and raise our families to follow Him. The sacrifices we make for Him will lead to blessings for future generations. You'll see."

Thankfully, we didn't stay in New York City very long. The following day we boarded a steamship and traveled up the Hudson River to the city of Albany, and my enthusiasm and my faith were renewed. What a beautiful trip that was! The Netherlands is mostly flat and featureless, so I had never seen mountains before. These stunning, tree-covered hills seemed to grow right out of the banks on both sides of the river, becoming higher and higher as we traveled north up the gently winding Hudson. "Have you ever seen such beautiful countryside, Geesje?" Maarten asked as he stood shivering beside me on the deck in his thin coat and vest.

"No, never! Why can't we live here? Do you think it will it be this lovely where we're going?"

He shrugged then said, "Our people want to purchase farmland. This part of America is already well-settled and the land is very costly." Snow dusted some of the mountaintops and the air was very cold, but I stood out on the deck beside Maarten, basking in the beauty all around me until I felt too frozen to stay outside a moment longer.

At last we reached Albany, another dirty, smoky-gray city, and were greeted by Dominie Wyckoff from one of Albany's Dutch Reformed churches. I can't describe the relief we felt to find friendly Dutch-speaking Americans to help us along the way. No one in our group spoke English, although Dominie Van Raalte had taken a few lessons from our ship's captain on our journey across the sea. Dominie Wyckoff distributed funds that the area churches had collected for us, and the kindness of these Christians amazed us. They didn't even know us, yet they treated us just like family. The weather in Albany was very cold, with a swirl of dirty snow blowing across the frozen ground from a bitter wind off the river. We crowded into Dominie Wyckoff's sitting room for warmth, leaving our wooden shoes lined up by his doorstep, while he arranged lodging for the night. "Your faith is like Abraham and Sarah's," he told us. "You've left the land of your fathers to go to a land God will show you, following wherever He leads."

We had been a tightly knit group since leaving Rotterdam, but now our bonds began to unravel as a few of the families, exhausted by the long journey and running out of money, chose to stay behind in Albany. They would look for work there for now but promised to rejoin us in the springtime. Dominie Van Raalte also left us, traveling ahead by train to make further arrangements for our journey to Wisconsin. Like many in our group, my family couldn't afford the train fare so my parents and I—and faithful Maarten—loaded all of our goods on a barge, and we traveled across New York State on the Erie Canal. The narrow ribbon of water, forty-five feet wide, took us through dismal mill towns and luscious open countryside dotted with farms and orchards. I counted more than fifty locks that we had to pass through on the canal. We could travel no faster than the plodding pace of the mule team as they walked the tow road beside the canal, pulling our barge. Some of the men in our party got out and walked alongside from time to time whenever we docked or changed mules. The animals rested on the barge in a special pen, then traded places every so often with the team doing the towing. But as much as I longed to get off the barge and stretch my legs, the weather was much too cold for walking. With little sunshine to warm the air on the seven-day journey, I remained inside the barge's small enclosure to escape the cold.

On one rare, sunny afternoon, I ventured outside to stand near the front of the boat and watch the barren trees and frozen farmland slip slowly past. Within moments, Maarten came to stand beside me. After all these weeks of travel, Maarten had lost most of his shyness around me. Today his cheeks were red from the cold air, not bashfulness. "Beautiful day, isn't it?" he asked.

"Yes . . . for once."

"If they holler, 'Low bridge!' take them seriously and duck down, Geesje. Our barge barely squeezes beneath some of these bridges, and you could get your skull bashed in."

I didn't reply. Maarten had hovered close beside me, watching out for me, ever since we arrived in Castle Garden. I wondered if he was doing it for Hendrik's sake, as his friend, or because he still hoped to win my affection. Some days I grew annoyed when Maarten trailed after me like a duckling behind its mother. Other days, his hulking presence comforted me. Today, for some reason, I felt smothered. "What's wrong, Geesje?" he asked when I didn't respond. "You used to be so talkative back in the Netherlands, and now you barely say a word. Are you homesick?"

I decided to tell him the truth. "The longer we travel, the greater the distance grows between Hendrik and me. The ocean is so vast, America so huge, that sometimes I fear we'll never find each other again."

His breath fogged the air as he took his time replying. "Don't worry. Hendrik is very smart and resourceful. He'll find you." I thought I heard admiration in Maarten's voice, not jealousy. Still, I wasn't convinced that his words were true.

"I never imagined there would be so many perils and dangers along the way or that it would take so long. I guess I thought it would be like traveling from Leiden to Arnhem or from Arnhem

101

to Rotterdam. America is still so wild and uncivilized in places. I feel lost here, don't you?"

"Our God knows exactly where we are and where we're going. We can trust Him to lead us and watch over us."

I nearly lashed out, impatient with Maarten's God-talk. I wanted to talk about Hendrik, whose handsome face was already starting to fade in my memory. But I controlled my tongue, realizing that my attitude toward Maarten was unkind. He had left his entire family behind and would probably never see any of them again. We were the only family he had now. "Do you ever regret your decision to come to America?" I asked him.

"Never." He answered without hesitation. "This trip has been exhausting at times, but I keep thinking about what Jesus told His disciples: 'No man, having put his hand to the plough, and looking back, is fit for the kingdom of God.' I want to keep looking forward, not back. This is a new beginning for all of us, Geesje, a chance to work together to create a new community, to settle down and build homes and churches and schools."

His words pricked my conscience. I needed to stop looking back and begin looking forward, too. From now on I would follow Maarten's example and work hard so that everything would be ready by the time Hendrik came. That's when my new life would finally begin.

Our canal voyage ended in the city of Buffalo, New York, but our journey was far from over. Once again, a few more families chose to remain behind until springtime while the rest of us boarded a steamer to cross Lake Erie to Detroit, stopping in Cleveland along the way. By now we had been traveling across America for weeks and it seemed as though we should be on the other side of the world by now. But we weren't. Dominie Van Raalte gathered our group together on the evening after we arrived in Detroit to tell us some disappointing news.

"I am sorry to say that even though we still have two more huge lakes to sail across to get to our destination in Wisconsin, we can travel no farther for now. The captain has informed me that the

LYNN AUSTIN

lakes have become icebound, and they closed the port of Detroit right after we arrived. We won't be able to set sail again for the remainder of the winter."

His words were met with weary groans. As tired as we all were of traveling, none of us relished the idea of being stranded in a foreign city, far from our destination for the remainder of the winter. "What are we going to do, Dominie?" someone asked.

"The local church leaders will help us find places here in Detroit where our families can stay. And if any men are willing to work, our ship's captain knows of a shipyard that is looking for laborers during the winter months."

Papa had developed a nagging cough aboard the canal barge and felt too ill to do hard labor. But Maarten cheerfully set off to work with the other men, traveling to the small city of St. Clair, some sixty miles north of Detroit while we remained behind. As much as it had bothered me to have him underfoot these past months, I found that I missed Maarten and his cheerful optimism. He had been a real asset to us on this journey, toting bags, nursing us through seasickness, and helping us keep our eyes on our goal. And now, thanks to him, my family would be able to afford food and housing from his earnings at the shipyard. I was grateful for his help, but I feared we would be forever indebted to him.

Staying in Detroit for a few months meant that I could send letters to Hendrik and perhaps one of his might find its way to me in return. I mailed the packet of letters I had been writing to him during our journey, telling him all about my travels and assuring him of my love. Then I waited, hoping his letter to me would be able to make the long return trip across sea and land to our rented rooms in the Detroit boardinghouse before the frozen lakes melted and we moved on.

Shortly before Christmas, Dominie Van Raalte left our group to travel by train across Michigan to Chicago, then north to Wisconsin to purchase land for us. When he returned near the end of January, he gathered us together to worship in the apartment he'd rented for his family and told us his news. "I have been exploring

103

the western part of Michigan all this time and have found good land that we can buy from the government for only $1.25 an acre. The officials here in Michigan want their new state to grow, and they would like very much for us to settle here. I explained to them what our needs are—that we want room to spread out and create farms and communities, separated from people of other religions and beliefs so we can maintain our unity and live by our religious principles. These officials assured me that western Michigan offers the seclusion we're seeking, yet it is still a place of great economic opportunity."

The men murmured amongst themselves, nodding and clapping their hands together to show their enthusiasm. I didn't care about seclusion or farmland or economic opportunities. I simply wanted to settle in a town somewhere—anywhere—so Hendrik could find me after he was discharged from the army. I wanted to marry him and feel his strong arms around me for the rest of my life and see his handsome face every morning when I awoke. I hadn't heard from him since leaving Arnhem last September, more than four months ago. So much might have changed for him back in Utrecht during that time.

"Right now," Van Raalte continued, "the land I scouted near Black Lake is sparsely occupied by native Indian tribes. A Christian missionary and his family live nearby and have led most of the Indians to faith. There are no roads or railroads there, but the abundant rivers and nearby Lake Michigan will provide shipping and transportation in the future. The forests will supply lumber for building houses. The soil is good for farming and the climate is favorable for growing fruit trees."

"Sounds like the Promised Land," Papa murmured beside me.

I wrote to Hendrik before going to sleep that night, then begged Papa for a few pennies to mail the letter the next morning, praying that it would reach him. I told Hendrik about our change in plans; that we were going to settle in the western part of Michigan, not Wisconsin. I gave him the address of our current boardinghouse as a way to contact me, then begged the proprietress to save any letters that arrived for me. I would let her know my new address as soon as we were settled on the other side of the state. The process of communicating over such vast distances was arduous. With so many perils such as shipwrecks and train derailments and fires, I cried myself to sleep some nights, despairing of ever seeing Hendrik again in this life.

In early February of 1847, Maarten rejoined us in Detroit, and we set off by train with Dominie Van Raalte and the other settlers for our new home in western Michigan. The rail line came to an end in the town of Allegan, a small settlement of wood-frame houses perched above a river. I wore every pair of socks I owned inside my wooden shoes as we stepped off the train, but they offered little warmth in the deep snow. Steam from the locomotive froze in the frigid air and hung in an icy fog above our heads. How did people survive such cold? I huddled on the wooden platform between Mama and Maarten, waiting for directions. I had never seen so much snow or so many thick forests, or felt such bitter weather. We sometimes had snow back home in the Netherlands and the wind off the North Sea could be frigid during the winter months, but the snow never lasted for very long and didn't pile up in huge drifts the way it did here.

The dominie had arranged housing for us ahead of time with friendly families, and so late that afternoon I crowded together with my fellow immigrants in the home of a stranger. Our hosts didn't speak Dutch, and trying to make ourselves understood or to understand them proved frustrating for everyone. We were stuffed into rooms that were much too small to hold all of us, rooms where we had to sleep and cook our meals and wash ourselves and our clothes.

"This is only for a short time," Dominie assured us the next morning. "A few of us will now go ahead to the land we purchased and build a log cabin large enough to house everyone. We will return to Allegan for you when it's ready."

Maarten and Papa stayed behind. I watched from the window that afternoon as Maarten ventured out into the snow with some of the children from our group, frolicking with them and sinking up to his knees in the snow. He was laughing when he came back inside, his round face ruddy with cold. "You are so tiny, Geesje, I will have to carry you through the drifts or you will disappear! How will we ever find you?" His childlike delight brought a rare smile to my face. I had felt myself sinking lower and lower, not into the snow but into a state of gloom. I was careful to weep only when no one was looking, but in such crowded conditions it was hard to find the solitude I craved. I didn't turn away quickly enough after my smile faded, and Maarten noticed my tears. "Geesje, what's wrong?"

"Life in America isn't at all what I thought it would be. It's hard not to look back at everything we left behind and wish . . ." I couldn't finish. Maarten pulled me close the way Mama or Papa might have done, and let me cry against his chest.

"We're almost there," he soothed. "Just a few more weeks, and we'll reach our new home." At the time, neither of us could know that the final few miles of our journey would be so difficult. Maarten treated me so kindly that day, that I remember thinking he deserved a sweet wife, one who would appreciate his gentle nature.

Three weeks later Dominie Van Raalte returned to Allegan to collect us, and we set off for our "promised land." There were no roads or pathways through the dense, dark forest, only blazes cut into tree trunks to show us the way. We trudged mile after mile through the deep snow in the dead of winter with all our belongings. Maarten thought the snow looked beautiful as it clung to the bare branches beneath a cloudless blue sky. I found the forest endless and foreboding. We had to stop twice to rest and build a fire, warming our feet to keep our toes from freezing. When at last we reached the log house the men had built for us, a roaring fire blazed inside. The cabin was very crude and dark inside, yet large enough to house our group until our families could build shelters of our own.

"We're here at last," Maarten said as he set down his burdens. He had carried a large pack on his back and a satchel in each hand. I could see by the way he dropped them onto the dirt floor that they had been very heavy. "Just think," he said, looking all around. "Someday this land where we're standing will be a thriving village filled with homes and shops and churches. . . , What's wrong, Geesje?"

I couldn't stop my tears. "This isn't a village, it's . . . it's a wilderness! There's nothing here—no roads or houses or shops—and it will take years and years of hard work until it looks anything at all like the villages back home."

He moved to try to comfort me again, but I turned away this time. How many months had it been since I'd last heard from Hendrik? I had no idea if he had received any of my letters or if he even knew where in the world I was. This rough-hewn cabin made of logs wasn't going to provide a permanent address where Hendrik could send letters to me. How could I receive mail way out here in the middle of nowhere? I longed to see my name in his handwriting on an envelope from him, to learn that he was all right. And that he still loved me.

In spite of the cold, I fled outside to the little clearing in front of the cabin and sank down on a ragged tree stump as large as a table. Virgin forest with towering trees surrounded me on all sides—taller than any building I'd ever seen, taller than the ship's soaring masts. It would take four people, holding hands, to encompass some of those tree trunks.

And the silence . . . the silence of this lonely forest was more terrifying than any sound I had ever heard.

Geesje

HOLLAND, MICHIGAN
1897

I can't write any more. The loneliness I felt fifty years ago seems to surround me all over again. I stuff the notebook and pencil in my desk drawer and go out to the kitchen to make tea. Most days I don't mind living alone in my snug little house with just my tabby cat for company. But today, after unearthing memories and emotions from my past like so many potatoes and turnips, I find myself wishing for someone to talk to.

No sooner does the kettle boil than my wish is granted, and Derk walks through my back door. "You're just in time," I tell him, reaching for another teacup and the cookie tin. He gives me a hug and bends to kiss my forehead before pulling out a chair. I love to see his long legs sprawled across my kitchen floor.

"I hope you have more of your story for me to read," he says. "I can't stop thinking about it. I'm dying to find out what happened. . . . Well, I suppose I know *some* of what happened," he adds with a grin, "but not all of it."

I fetch my notebook with the newest pages and silently hand it to him, then sit down across the table from him with my cat on my lap, drinking tea and watching him read. Derk devours my handwritten pages as quickly as he devours my cookies, and when he reaches the last page he looks up at me in surprise. "That's all? Where's the rest of the story?"

"I haven't written any more. In fact, I finished those pages just a few minutes before you came."

He groans and shakes his head in dismay, but he's smiling. "You're keeping me in suspense, Tante Geesje. What an adventure that must have been, moving halfway around the world! I've barely been out of Michigan."

"Be careful what you wish for, dear. God just might move *you* halfway around the world someday." His laugh is delicious, rumbling like welcome thunder on a hot, sticky day. "I never imagined you would be so interested in my silly ramblings, Derk. All I do is go on and on about falling in love."

"That's what I like best about it. Your story gives me a lot to think about. Who we fall in love with and choose to spend our life with is such a huge part of everyone's story, isn't it? Our choice affects the rest of our lives."

"And our children's lives, too."

"Yes. And sometimes our faith gets entangled in our love stories. Caroline broke up with me because of my commitment to God. And I met a woman at the hotel the other day who told me her fiancé ended their engagement because of the church she wanted to attend. It's part of your story, too," he said, patting the notebook. "Your parents never would have allowed you to marry Hendrik if he didn't share your faith."

"That's true." I take another sip of tea and ask, "Why is it that young people often fall in love with the wrong person?"

"Like Samson falling in love with Delilah? And David with Bathsheba?"

"Right," I say, laughing.

"When I was talking with this guest at the hotel—her name is Anna—I started to see that even if Caroline had agreed to marry me, she never would have been the partner I'll need in my work. I would always feel pulled between her and my church, and guilty for ignoring one or the other. I just hope I can find a wife who'll share my work with me—and who'll share me with my congregation."

"You will, Derk. My son Jakob's wife, Joanna, is a wonderful helpmate to him. If I've learned anything at all about marriage and romance, it's that God will give us the perfect partner if we ask."

"Well, when I do find her, will you teach her to make these cookies the way you do, Tante Geesje?" he asked, biting into another one.

"I'd be delighted, my dear boy."

CHAPTER 13

Anna

It's another lazy day at the hotel. The sun is shining around the edges of my window shades when I wake up, so I know it has already risen well above the eastern shores of Black Lake. Yet here I am, still in bed. Ever since I arrived here in the storm, I've had the most disconcerting dreams. The first few nights I suffered through a repeat of my childhood nightmare of nearly drowning in a shipwreck. Then I dreamt about Mama giving me the peppermint and calling me *lieveling*. Last night I had another odd dream: Mama and I were sitting in the castle church, and she was wiping her tears again with the white handkerchief embroidered with blue flowers. But this time when the sermon ended and the music began to play, she took my hand and walked with me up the long aisle to the front of the church. She knelt down in front of the altar, her arm around my waist. After a moment, the minister came and put his hand on her head to pray for her.

110

I can't imagine my mother doing such a humbling thing in real life, but I think I know what prompted that dream. I was rereading my diary yesterday, and it reminded me of the day when Reverend Torrey preached such a powerful sermon that I nearly walked up the aisle myself when he invited people to come forward for prayer. Fear held me back. I watched others go forward, but I remained in my pew, knowing how appalled William would be if he ever found out that I'd surrendered my life to God in such a public way. Now I have missed my chance.

I climb out of bed and wash my face, then dress and brush my hair, which has become much curlier in the lakeside humidity. I love the simplicity of my morning routine here. If I never have to sit still again while Sophia, our maid, yanks and twists and pins my hair into submission, it will be fine with me—not to mention being squeezed into a stiff corset until I can barely breathe. Mother's room is already empty, so I head downstairs to join her for breakfast. The more I ponder the mystery of how I knew what the word *lieveling* meant, the more certain I am that Mother is hiding the truth from me. She must know more about my birth and my family's ancestry than she's willing to admit. Why else would she change the subject every time I bring it up? How will I learn the truth if she won't tell me? Perhaps I could try to track down my nanny, Bridget O'Malley, and ask what she knows. But I'm not a detective, and besides, Bridget is likely married by now, with a new name.

I find Mother's table and sit down across from her, ordering toast and jam and strong tea. She looks as serene and elegant as a queen despite our humble surroundings, as if she might rise at any moment and glide off to rule over her kingdom. Prying any information from her about my nanny will be as difficult as unlocking the vault in William's bank. I wish I could recall the names and faces of some of the other servants we had when I was a child but I'm embarrassed to admit that I never paid much attention to them. They labored in the background of my life, useful yet invisible, and of no more interest to a spoiled child like myself than the draperies or plant stands. Now I wish that I had paid attention. Surely one of them must have spoken to me in Dutch.

"You look very pensive this morning," Mother says. "Have you reached a decision about reconciling with William?"

I shake my head, then remember my manners. "No, I haven't."

"Would it help at all if we talked about it?"

"I don't think I'm ready to talk about William yet." I want to change the subject, but Mother persists.

"I realize that he hurt your feelings, but you may have hurt his, Anna. The mature thing for both of you to do is to forgive and forget."

Her advice reminds me of the conversation I overheard between her and Honoria Stevens—Mother had counseled Mrs. Stevens to forgive and forget her husband's unfaithfulness, as well. Mother had made it sound simple, but surely forgiving a sin as great as adultery couldn't possibly be easy. And what about William's refusal to consider my wishes, his insistence on having everything his way? Would that become the pattern if we married?

"William is willing to try again," Mother continues, "so why not go home and pick up where you left off? You have a beautiful wedding to plan, and a wonderful life with William to look forward to." When I don't reply she adds, "You love him, don't you?"

I ponder her question for a long time before saying, "I really don't know." Did I ever love him? Or was I merely in love with the idea of marrying a man who was as handsome and charming and as determined to succeed as William—a man who could have chosen any woman in Chicago's high society for his bride, but had chosen me. After talking with Derk, I now view William differently. He seems selfish and demanding, with little regard for my happiness and no respect for the choices I made.

Mother removes the linen napkin from her lap and sets it beside her plate. I can tell by the way she lifts her chin and purses her lips that she is trying not to lose patience with me. "Listen, Anna dear. This may sound harsh, but it's time for you to stop moping."

"I'm not moping. What makes you think I'm moping?"

"Well, the way you've let yourself go, for one thing. Your hair, your clothes . . ." She leans across the table and lowers her voice to ask, "Do you even have a petticoat on?"

"It's too hot to wear a petticoat."

"And your posture, Anna. You know better than to slouch in your chair that way."

Years of obedience make me sit up straight at my mother's rebuke, my back erect, my chin held high.

"That's better. I worry that if we stay here too much longer, these bad habits will become ingrained."

I agree to take a stroll with Mother after breakfast to the sandy beachfront on Lake Michigan. The sun feels wonderfully warm on my face and bare arms, but Mother insists I wear a hat and carry a parasol to shield my skin. "You wouldn't want to ruin your beautiful complexion, would you?" Her question renews my curiosity about my heritage. Except for our Swedish maid, no one I know has skin as fair as mine. But I decide not to spoil our walk by raising the subject again.

When we return to the hotel, Mrs. Stevens invites Mother to play canasta with a group of guests on the wide front porch. Happy to be on my own, I make my way to the dock. I watch Derk distribute rowboats and oars to a group of enthusiastic hotel patrons. He steadies one of the boats as a young couple climbs aboard, then pushes them away from shore with a hearty shove. He's the closest thing I have to a friend here, and I feel drawn to him. When he turns and sees me, he smiles and comes to stand beside me.

"Good morning. Beautiful day for a sail, isn't it? The wind is just right, if you're interested."

I shake my head. "No, thank you. But I have another question for you . . . if I'm not keeping you from your work, that is. I can come back at a better time."

"Why don't you sign up for a sailboat ride with me or an excursion in one of these rowboats? We would have hours to talk."

"Thank you, but no. I will never step aboard a ship again as long as I live."

"Never? How will you get back to Chicago?"

"I plan to take the train."

He looks as though he's about to laugh, thinking I've made a joke. Then he sees that I'm serious and says, "There's really no reason to be frightened. Look how calm the water is today." He gestures to the sparkling expanse of Black Lake. "We could easily cross over to the Macatawa Hotel and back. I could promise to hug the shoreline if it will make you feel better."

"Again, thank you, but no."

He must hear the coldness in my voice because he quickly apologizes. "I'm sorry, Anna. I shouldn't tease you. What was it you wanted to ask me?"

I feel foolish now for disturbing him, but I plow forward. "It's a hypothetical question, really. But if your lady-friend, Caroline, decided that she wanted to reconcile with you, would you do it?"

He scratches his chin thoughtfully. He doesn't wear a beard or a mustache and the stubble on his face looks as though someone sprinkled him with gold dust. "She would have to change her mind about being married to a minister or there would be no point in starting all over again." I try to stifle my sigh, but he must have heard it anyway because he asks, "Why? Does your fiancé want to renew your engagement?"

"I haven't spoken with him yet, but my father has. He says William is willing to forgive and forget if I promise never to go back to the castle church."

"Are you going to do it?"

"My parents are pressuring me to. They think William will make a wonderful husband and that we're well-suited for each other."

"But . . . ? I sense your hesitation, Anna."

"I don't know. . . . What if I still feel like something is missing from my life?"

Derk scratches his chin again as he ponders my question. "I'm no expert on marriage," he finally says. "My mother died when I was very young, and my father never remarried. But I've been reading my Tante Geesje's memoirs, and when she fell in love she thought about the man she wanted to marry day and night. There was no doubt in her mind that they were meant for each other. I think that's the way I want to feel, too, when I fall in love again."

"Did they attend the same church?"

"Not at first. But my aunt was very firm in her beliefs, and the man she loved seemed willing to adopt her faith so they could be married."

"Were they happy together?"

"I don't know," he says with a shrug and a sheepish grin. "I haven't gotten to the end of the story yet, and she won't tell me. She was already a widow when I met her. But listen, Anna, maybe you need some answers to all the questions you have about religion before you commit to something as important as marriage. You need to be sure you're making the right decision before you agree to give up that church."

"That's good advice. And I do have a lot of questions. I started reading the Bible before I came here, but it was our old family Bible and much too big to bring with me on this trip."

"I can give you a Bible to read if you'd like."

"Yes, I would like that. Thank you." We have both noticed another couple approaching the dock, as if interested in taking out a rowboat. "We'll talk again," I say, then hurry away to sit on the nearby bench so Derk can do his job. I see him gesturing toward the eastern end of Black Lake, presumably giving directions and advice before helping the couple climb into a rowboat. The oars make loud splashing sounds as the man tries to maneuver the paddles, and I hear the woman giggling nervously. More patrons come and go—rowing seems to be a popular activity today—and I can tell that Derk is going to be much too busy to talk again. I head across the lawn to the hotel, and as I step onto the porch, I'm surprised to see that my mother isn't playing cards with the others.

"Do you know where she went?" I ask Mrs. Stevens.

"She decided not to play with us after all. The poor dear has a headache."

I go upstairs to check on her, and as I open my door, I'm surprised to see Mother standing near my bed. She quickly stuffs something into the drawer of my nightstand, but it gets stuck and the drawer won't close.

My diary. My mother has been reading my diary.

I stand frozen in the doorway in shock. "W-what are you doing?" How much of it has she read? I try to calculate how much time I spent talking with Derk and sitting on the bench. Was this the first time she's read it, or has she been invading my privacy for months? I step into the room and close the door behind me. "That's my diary!"

"Yes. I'm sorry. I've been so worried about you, Anna, and I didn't know what else to do. You won't talk to me. I'm simply trying to understand you."

At least Mother didn't compound the injury by lying to me, but I'm no less outraged. "How could you?"

"Your father told me that your breakup with William had something to do with religion, and I thought if I understood your feelings I could help you. You seem so confused and unhappy—"

"And so you read my private thoughts?"

"I did. Forgive me, darling. And please believe that I did it out of love and concern for you."

"You had no right!" I turn to leave again. I'm much too angry to talk to her.

"Wait! Don't run away." Mother hurries across the room and stops me. "Talk to me, Anna, darling. If you're really as lonely and unhappy as you say you are in your diary, then I want to help you. Tell me what I can do."

"Nothing . . . There's nothing you can do except stay out of my business. I'm a grown woman. I can figure out these things for myself." I try to shake off her restraining hand, but she tightens her grip on my arm.

"Anna, I'm as confused by all of this as William is. We've given you everything you could ever want—and yet it isn't enough? Even our church isn't good enough for you?"

I huff in frustration, knowing she will never understand. "The castle church is very different from ours. They make God seem so . . . so real. If you would come there with me when we get home, then maybe you would see for yourself."

"Are you ready to go home? Shall we see about tickets? Your father misses you and so does William, I'm sure."

I quickly shake my head. "No. I'm not ready to go home." I sound like a petulant child. I know Mother will never agree to attend the castle church with me, and if I leave Michigan now, she and Father will pressure me even harder to reconcile with William. I want to take Derk's advice and look for answers to all the questions I have about God before I agree to stop attending the castle church. Before I agree to marry William. Maybe Derk can help answer some of them. After all, he said he was studying to become a minister.

"Anna, dear, tell me what I can do. How can I help?"

I start to shake my head again, then I do think of something. "I want to know about my past, where I came from. And this time, don't change the subject. Tell me everything you know about my parents."

Mother is quiet for a long moment before saying, "I don't know anything about your real parents. I'm sorry, but that's the truth."

"Does Father know?"

"Neither of us does."

"What about my original birth certificate? That should have information about my family."

"You didn't have a birth certificate."

"How is that possible? Doesn't everyone have a birth certificate?"

"I'm sorry, but you didn't. Our lawyer arranged to have one made for you, listing us as your legal parents. We could only guess at your age and your birthday."

"Well, where did I come from? I didn't simply fall out of the sky and land on your doorstep, did I?"

I can tell that Mother is reluctant to say more, but I wait, needing to know the truth. She owes me that much. "You were abandoned,

Anna," she says softly. "No one knew who you were or who your mother was. We tried to find out, but we didn't succeed. Your father and I had longed for a child for years, so when you came to us, you were like a gift from heaven."

"I was a newborn?"

"You're our precious daughter, in every possible way." Mother pulls me into her arms, but I remain rigid, still too angry to hug her in return. "Please say you'll forgive me for reading your diary, Anna. I did it with the very best of intentions."

I'm still angry, but I finally say, "I forgive you."

She holds me close, the way she did when I was a child. I finally wrap my arms around her, and I feel like a child again as my tears fall against her soft shoulder. "I love you, darling Anna," she murmurs.

"*Ik hou ook van jou*, Mama." I whisper in return.

"Hmm? What did you say?" she asks.

What *had* I said? Where had those words come from? "I-I said, I love you, too." Somehow I know that's what those words mean. But how? And if these were phrases I remember from my childhood, where had I learned them? Someone had once wrapped her arms around me as Mother had just done and had whispered, *"Ik hou van je, Anneke."* I remember squeezing her tightly in return and saying, *"Ik hou ook van jou."* I love you, too. Was I losing my mind?

I couldn't go back to Chicago yet. Not until I solved this mystery. I needed to talk to Derk again.

CHAPTER 14

Geesje's Story

HOLLAND, MICHIGAN
50 YEARS EARLIER

When we arrived in America, we had no idea how difficult it was going to be to create farmland and a town in the Michigan wilderness. We might not have come if we had. We staked our claim in the virgin forest not even knowing how to chop down a tree properly. We Dutch are a hardworking, persevering people, but the difficulties we faced that first winter in Michigan were nearly more than we could bear. We all shared a crude one-room cabin, sleeping on beds made of hemlock boughs covered with blankets. The men took turns keeping the fire going at night, but the wind and the cold still seeped through the cracks between the logs.

No roads existed from where we lived to the neighboring villages of Allegan, Saugatuck, Singapore, or Grand Haven. In order to get supplies, the men from our settlement had to follow narrow Indian trails through the woods to one of those nearby towns, following the markings carved into tree trunks, then carry our supplies home again on their backs. There was talk of starting a community store in which each settler would own a share, but that endeavor would require a lot of organization and hard work. Back then, only a shallow stream connected Black Lake to Lake Michigan, so any goods shipped to our settlement had to be unloaded on the shore of Lake Michigan, dragged across the sandbar to Black Lake, reloaded onto flatboats, and then paddled to our settlement and dragged inland. Until more settlers came, none of the men could be spared for such a daunting task. Nor did they have the energy for it, existing on such meager food rations. We ran out of staples like flour and potatoes long before winter ended, leaving us hungry and miserable.

But I think the lowest point came when Mrs. Willem Notting became seriously ill. She had traveled every step of the way from the Netherlands with us and was one of Mama's closest friends. The hunger and exhaustion that affected all of us compounded her illness. In spite of our fervent prayers, Mrs. Notting died. As we dug the first grave in this unforgiving land, many of us wondered who would be next. And why God wasn't listening.

Our closest neighbors were the native Ottawa Indians, who lived on the shores of Black Lake not far from us. I had glimpsed them from a distance several times. The first time was when a group of braves stood outside the Old Wing Mission when we stopped there on our trip from Allegan. Later, Papa showed me their village of log buildings and huts clustered along the lakeshore. I stared at the squaws and their little ones in fascination and fear. Their way of life seemed so primitive, yet Reverend Smith from the mission assured us that the natives were Christians like us. Every now and then I'd glimpse one of their braves slipping between the trees outside our cabin like a shadow, familiar with the paths and forest trails that had once been theirs. But I had never encountered an Ottawa Indian up close until one night during our first winter in Holland, when we were all shaken from our sleep by a furious pounding on our door.

Papa and the other men hurried to answer it while Maarten

lit a lamp. When they opened the door, there stood an Indian brave armed with a rifle, leaning against our doorframe. His leather and fur clothing hung in tattered shreds soaked with blood. More blood ran down his face from deep gashes in his flesh. One of his arms was badly mangled. I quickly looked away from the gruesome sight. The brave was taller than Papa by several inches, but he fell forward into Papa's arms, as if unable to stand a moment longer. The men lowered him to the floor in front of the hearth.

A great commotion followed as Maarten stoked the fire and Mama and the other women hurried to tend his injuries. "From the look of these wounds, I'd say he encountered some sort of wild animal," Papa said. Mama took needle and thread and stitched some of the worst of the gashes closed, while I helped prepare bandages and dressings.

"Do you think he'll live?" Maarten asked.

"He's in the Almighty's hands," Dominie replied, then he led the rest of us in prayer, beseeching God to spare the life of this man who had come to us for help.

Eventually, I fell back to sleep. At dawn the Indian still lay beside the fire, moaning softly from time to time, but Papa and the other men were gone. They had decided to follow the bloody trail in the snow that the Indian had made to see if any more braves were in need of help. We were alone in the cabin with the injured man, but I could see that he was too badly hurt to do us any harm. He looked young, no older than Maarten, with black hair and high cheekbones and skin the rich color of mahogany. When the men returned, they were dragging the skin of a huge black bear with them.

"It looks like this Indian fellow put a bullet into the creature," Papa told us, "but the wounded bear must have attacked in return, putting up a savage fight before it died."

"The area where we found the bear was trampled and covered with blood," Maarten added. "It looked like wolves and other scavengers got there before us during the night."

"If the Indian hadn't made it to our door," Papa said, "it's likely the wolves would have killed him, too."

The Indian stayed with us for nearly two weeks until he was strong enough to be moved. A group of his people came for him, showering us with gifts of venison and hides to show their gratitude. I wasn't quite as afraid of the Ottawa Indians after that, but I never got over my fear of bears! The incident underscored the dangers of this wilderness place, so different from the civilized world where I grew up in Leiden.

At last the long winter ended and spring arrived. The snow melted, turning the ground into mud and marshland that was nearly as difficult to travel through as the snow had been. Living conditions slowly improved as more and more immigrants arrived to help us clear the land and build houses. More than forty people now lived in our little settlement. We held worship services outside in a clearing, sitting on logs for pews. I dutifully sang psalms of faith and praised God with the others each Sabbath day, hoping that my flagging spirits would revive, and praying that we would survive this ordeal. Things would be better when Hendrik came, I told myself—although the thought of him suffering hardship along with us filled me with guilt. Was it fair to ask him to make the long journey here for me, knowing the adversity he would face?

"Maarten and I are going to choose a patch of land to buy today," Papa told us one bright spring day. Mama and I and some of the other women were heading down to the creek to wash our filthy winter clothing and socks. We would hang the clean laundry on the still-bare branches to dry, hoping the wind didn't blow them into the trampled mud that surrounded our communal cabin in every direction. "Once we find a place of our own," Papa said, "we'll build a log house and clear the land and—"

"Wait! Are we going to move away from everyone else?" I asked in alarm. The forest was frightening enough in the company of the other settlers. I couldn't imagine living all by ourselves, far from our nearest neighbors.

"Of course we are, lieveling. Everyone wants a house and farmland to call his own. Dominie Van Raalte has arranged to purchase land from the State of Michigan, and he's going to show us which lots are available to buy."

"Not near the Indians, Papa. Please!"

"They mean us no harm, Geesje," he said, chuckling. "Besides, their settlement is on the shores of Black Lake. I would like to live farther inland, where the center of town will be."

"Dominie says our community will have a newspaper one day," Maarten added. "That means the town will need a printer."

I couldn't imagine it. Nothing in this vast wilderness resembled a town. A newspaper was ludicrous. It would take years and years until we even came close to having the civilized life we left behind in Leiden and Arnhem.

"What about wild animals?" I asked. "The women we stayed with in Allegan told me that bears and wolves and wildcats live in these woods."

"I don't think you need to worry about animals," Maarten said. "The biggest danger is getting lost." If his words were meant to comfort me, they didn't. I watched the two of them set off, their wooden shoes sinking into the soft forest floor. They quickly disappeared, swallowed by the thick trees.

Late that afternoon, the last of our laundry was finally dry, and Mama and I took it down from the tree branches. "Look at this," Mama said, wiggling her finger through a hole in one of Papa's woolen socks. "Nearly every pair of socks we own has a hole or two that needs to be patched. We'll have mending to do this evening."

"Maarten's are even worse than Papa's." I showed her one with the heel completely worn away. "But where will we get yarn to mend them? Or to knit new ones?"

"We'll manage, Geesje," she replied with a smile. Mama steadfastly refused to be discouraged no matter our circumstances. I often wondered if she truly had that much faith in God and in our future here, or if she was merely pretending to in order to keep up our spirits. "We can always unravel one of the worst ones and use the yarn from it to fix the others," she said.

"We need a lot of other supplies, too, besides yarn," I grumbled. I couldn't remember the last time I had felt full after eating a meal.

"How spoiled we were back in the Netherlands," Mama said. "How mindlessly we took it all for granted. Maybe God is teaching us to be more thankful for all His gifts to us."

Papa and Maarten retuned before sunset, telling tales of the wonderful plot of land they had decided to purchase. I shook my head at them. "How can you tell if it's wonderful? The forest looks exactly the same in every direction—just trees, trees, and more trees."

"We chose a piece of land on slightly higher ground, away from the marsh," Maarten told me. "It has a stand of pine trees we can use to build a sturdy cabin, and a good-sized area we can clear for a garden." His excitement made him more talkative than usual, and as he described the land we would soon own, I saw Maarten as if for the first time in months. Now that he was no longer swaddled in winter clothes, I realized how thin he had become over the winter. His once-sturdy body and large, square hands had shriveled until it seemed that his bones were about to poke through his skin. His round face looked sunken and pale. Did I also look that thin and pale? It was hard to tell without a proper mirror.

Mama was beaming at the news. "This is what we've waited for, worked for, and come all this way for—land of our own."

"Is it far away from everyone else?" I asked. "You were gone all day."

"No, lieveling," Papa said, patting my shoulder. "It isn't far at all. A short walk from here. About the distance from our shop in Leiden to your sister Geerde's house—maybe a little farther." But of course there wouldn't be paved streets to walk on to get there or shops to peek into along the way. We wouldn't pass a single soul we could greet or stop and chat with for a while. We couldn't watch the clouds chase across the blue expanse of sky above the river since our view would be blocked by a dense thicket of tree branches that barely let in the sunshine. And once we arrived, Geerde and her children wouldn't be there to welcome us.

"The reason we were gone all day," Maarten explained, "is

because we spent the afternoon cutting marks on the trees so we could find our property again—and so no one else would claim it."

"When can we move there?" Mama asked. "Shall I start packing our things?"

What things? I wanted to ask. Our hole-filled socks? Our threadbare coats? Our dented pots and chipped plates? We had so very little to call our own.

"Maarten and I need to build some sort of shelter or lean-to, first," Papa said. "It should only take us a few days. Then we can all move there together."

The first temporary hut Papa constructed out of tree branches was so flimsy that water poured inside every time it rained. And it rained a lot that spring. The woods were very dark, especially at night, and filled with terrifying sounds—trees moaning in the wind, owls hooting, insects whirring and buzzing, coyotes howling. It was very frightening to a city girl like me. I cried myself to sleep at night, shivering beneath my damp blanket and wishing I had defied my parents and run away to Utrecht to marry Hendrik.

Then—a miracle! Maarten walked to the town of Allegan for some much-needed food supplies one day and returned with a letter from Hendrik, the first one I had received since leaving home more than six months ago. He had sent it to our boardinghouse in Detroit, and they had kindly forwarded it to the home where we had stayed in Allegan. At last, at last, it had made its way to me! I went into our hut by myself to open it. What if Hendrik had found someone else by now? What if he'd decided he didn't want to make the long journey to America after all, and I never saw him again? After all these months, I could barely picture his handsome face or remember how it felt when we'd kissed. I began to read, trying to see his words through my tears.

> *My darling Geesje,*
>
> *It has been months and months since I've seen your beautiful face or held you in my arms. I miss you so much! I can't even imagine how far away you are or comprehend the huge*

distance that now separates us, but please know that I still hold you very close in my heart. I have been receiving all your wonderful letters and waiting for the day when I could send one to you in return. At last, that day has come.

As I've read your letters I've felt as though I was traveling with you that long, long way. What an adventure you are having! I am envious of all the places you've been and the things you've seen and the people you've met. Meanwhile, my life here in Utrecht has been very routine and boring. I've been unable to attend services in any church, let alone a Separatist one, and I sometimes fear that I will forget all of the things Maarten taught me. It's very hard to be a soldier in a city like Utrecht with its many temptations, but I am trying to remain strong for your sake. You are such a pure, God-fearing woman, and you deserve to marry a man whose faith is as strong as yours. I know I have much to learn before I am that man, but I hope you will be patient and willing to teach me when we are together at last.

The good news is that I will be discharged from the army at the end of the summer. I've been saving all of my money for the passage to America and I hope to have some left over to buy land. Does it really cost only $1.25 an acre? I want to buy acres and acres for you! I contacted the emigrant aid society you mentioned about the possibility of joining with some other Dutch families who are going to America in the fall, and they assured me that it won't be difficult to do. Dozens of Dutch families are making plans to move to America because of the famine and the lack of jobs here.

Soon, Geesje. Soon the distance between us will disappear, and we will be together again. My love for you hasn't diminished in the least. I hope that yours for me hasn't, either.

I love you with all my heart.

Hendrik

His letter made me ashamed of my whining attitude during all our hardships and of my lack of faith. Hendrik called me a God-fearing woman, but after reading his letter I felt like a hypocrite. How could I dare to teach him the things he longed to know about God and about living by faith when I had set such a poor example all these months? I knew I needed to change. The following Sunday, I confessed all my sins to God and asked forgiveness for my selfishness and grumbling lack of faith. Then I joined in all the hard work with a new attitude and sense of commitment. Together, my family and Maarten and I cleared enough land to plant a garden. We finished building our tiny cabin, filling the cracks between the logs with mud to keep out the wind and rain, and cutting shingles out of bark for the roof.

A few weeks after Hendrik's first letter arrived, I received a second one from him, brought from Allegan by one of the Dutch families who had stayed behind in Albany, New York. They were finally rejoining us. Hendrik had received my letter about our decision to settle in Michigan instead of Wisconsin. He would be able to find me here! And he now had firm plans to travel with a group of Dutch settlers leaving from Rotterdam in October. By the time he arrived, more than a year would have passed since we last saw each other. But I could endure any hardship now, knowing that Hendrik was coming. He was coming! And I was receiving letters from him again. My spirits soared. I tried to remain cheerful even when the deer and squirrels and chipmunks and quill pigs invaded our newly planted garden and ate our crops faster than we could grow them. And when the foxes made a meal of Mama's new chickens, just when we were starting to get fresh eggs to eat.

Later that first summer, the men began building a log church so we would have a place to worship when the cold winter months returned. They chose a patch of high ground, up the hill from Dominie Van Raalte's home on the creek. Land surveyors arrived and plotted the streets of our future town, nestled between Black

Lake and a bend in the swampy Black River. River Avenue would run north and south, parallel to the lake shore. Cross streets were given numbers for names—First Street, Second Street, and so on. A market square was planned where people could gather together someday to buy and sell their goods. Someone had started calling our settlement Holland, after our homeland, and the name stuck. New settlements with Dutch names like Graafschap and Zeeland were sprouting up all around us. But these ambitious plans still seemed very far in the future to me. The woods surrounding us remained forbidding, the tiny cabins few and far between, the roads nonexistent. When Hendrik finally did arrive six long months from now, he would see nothing resembling a civilized town. Even so, I remained optimistic throughout that summer, and filled with faith for our future, trusting in a loving, benevolent God.

And then the rains came, and with them swarms of mosquitos. . . .

HOLLAND, MICHIGAN
1897

I pause when I see the mailman coming with a letter for me. We chat for a minute before he continues on his way, wiping sweat from his brow with his handkerchief. I look down at the return address on the letter, and my stomach does a slow, sickening turn. It's from my nephew in Leiden. He has never written to me before. I delay opening it, walking to my kitchen and making myself a cup of tea, first. If it is bad news, I can postpone facing it for a few minutes longer. If someone has died, they will remain alive to me until I read it in black and white.

When I finally slit open the envelope, the letter does contain tragic news. My sister Anneke has passed away. She and I have kept in touch these past fifty years, knowing that we would never see each other again on this side of heaven. Now she has gone to paradise ahead of me. I let my tears fall as I absorb yet another loss, added to the many I've endured over the years. The number of loved ones waiting for me on heaven's shore has become quite a multitude.

I can't write any more today. My grief is too great.

CHAPTER 15

Anna

I stop at the hotel's front desk as I do every morning after breakfast to see if there is any mail from home. The clerk hands me a book-sized parcel wrapped in brown paper. "Package for you, Miss Nicholson." I thank him and sit down on the front porch to open it. Inside is a Bible. It must be the one Derk promised to bring me. I leaf through it, excited about the prospect of reading it. Back home, I had just finished reading the Gospel of Matthew, so I turn to the book of Mark, starting with chapter one. I'm in the middle of an intriguing story about a group of men who cut a hole in the roof so Jesus could heal their paralyzed friend, when I see Derk getting the boats ready down by the pier. I hurry across the dewy grass to thank him for the Bible and to ask him about the Dutch phrase I had remembered—at least I assume it's Dutch. Maybe it's gibberish.

"Good morning, Derk. Thank you so much for the Bible," I say, holding it up.

"You're welcome. Beautiful day, isn't it? The wind is perfect for sailing." The boat he's standing in rocks back and forth as he gestures broadly to the cloudless blue sky. The motion doesn't seem to faze him.

"Yes. It is beautiful." I don't want to talk about the weather. I can make inane conversations anytime I want to, back home. "I need to ask you something. Can you spare a moment?"

"Of course." He steps off the tottering boat and onto the dock, never faltering or losing his balance. It seems like an appropriate picture of a man of faith, able to stand firm when rocked by the storms of life. I long for that certainty and stability. "What's your question?" he asks.

What I want to ask him seems silly now, but I plunge ahead just the same. "I remembered another strange phrase yesterday, and I wondered if it might be Dutch: 'Ik hou ook van jou.'"

He grins and his tanned cheeks turn faintly pink. "I love you, too."

"I knew it!" I fairly shout the words. "But how? Where did I learn to say it? I asked my mother about the nanny who raised me when I was small, and she said her name was Bridget O'Malley."

"Definitely not Dutch."

His grin makes me smile briefly in return. "I've thought and thought about who might have taught me those words, but I can't think of a soul. I was never very close to any of our servants—and none of them would have said 'I love you' to me or called me 'darling.' It's a mystery that keeps growing, and it bothers me more and more. William said the castle church was making me crazy, and sometimes I wonder if he was right."

"He isn't, Anna. When people lose their minds, they don't suddenly start speaking a foreign language. You must have learned those phrases somewhere. But I agree that it's a mystery. I don't suppose many people in Chicago speak Dutch, do they?"

"No one I recall meeting." I hear shouts and children's laughter

131

behind me and turn to see two young boys hurtling toward the dock. They ignore their father's order to slow down, and Derk barely manages to catch one of the boys before he tumbles into the swaying rowboat. I move away to let Derk do his job and sit down on the bench near the water to continue reading the Bible. I'm so intrigued by the story of how Jesus healed a man with a withered hand that I don't notice Derk approaching until he halts beside me.

"I'm sorry we were interrupted," he says. "Things get really busy for me when the lake is this beautiful."

"I understand. Can I ask you something else?"

"Of course."

"I've been thinking about the advice you gave me the other day, that I should find answers to all my questions before I commit to marriage. The problem is, I can't even put my questions into words. I mean . . . I don't understand how the two churches in Chicago can be so different if they're both Christian. The one my family attends makes God seem distant and a little scary, while the castle church insists that He's kind and loving. In our church, God seems to treat us the way my father treats our servants, making sure they do what they're told and that they measure up to his standards if they want to win his approval. In the castle church, the pastor insists that God loves us the way my father loves me, that he hopes I'll do the right thing but is quick to forgive me when I do something wrong. Which picture of God is the right one?"

Derk scratches his chin. I can tell that he wants to sit down beside me while we talk, but he glances over his shoulder at the dock and decides not to. "Well, maybe a little of each. I believe that God is a father who loves us, but that doesn't mean we should just live any way we want to. We show that we love Him in return by obeying what the Bible teaches us. Jesus said that if we love Him, we'll keep His commandments. He paid a huge price, suffering and dying in our place so we could be adopted into the family of God."

The word *adopted* unnerves me. Ever since yesterday, I've allowed the anger I felt toward my mother for reading my diary to distract me from the terrible truth she revealed. *I was abandoned.*

132

My real mother abandoned me. Whoever she was, she didn't want me. No one knows where I came from—or who I really am.

"Anna? . . . Anna, are you all right? Did I say something wrong?"

I look up at Derk through my tears. "No . . . no, you didn't. I . . . I just need some time to think. Thank you again for the Bible." I clutch it to my chest as I struggle to my feet and hurry away. I end up walking all the way to the sandy beach on Lake Michigan without stopping. I have no blanket or chair to sit on when I get there, so I sink down in the soft, warm sand and stare out at the rippling lake without really seeing it.

Does William know that I am adopted? And that my mother abandoned me? Would it change his opinion of me if he did?

I sit motionless for a long time as if in a trance, oblivious to the laughter and activity all around me or the gentle shushing of the waves. The spell is finally broken by a piercing whistle as a train arrives at the station behind the hotel. In a moment, passengers will pour onto the platform to spend a day at the lake or to stay at the resort. I've watched them do it every day at lunchtime. The beach will soon be crowded with vacationers, the hotel will house hundreds of new guests for the night—yet I feel utterly alone. *Abandoned.*

I remain where I am for a while longer, waiting for the crowds to disperse from the train platform, picturing Derk and the other porters scrambling to help guests with their baggage. The locomotive blasts its whistle a second time as it prepares to follow the shoreline of Black Lake back into Holland. I finally rise and return to my room, quietly unlocking the door in case Mother is napping.

I hear voices coming from her room. One of them is a man's. For a moment, I can't seem to breathe. Then I recognize my father's voice, talking in hushed tones. I quietly tiptoe to the adjoining door to listen, aware that it's wrong but not really caring. Didn't Mother invade my privacy yesterday?

"Anna is asking a lot of questions," I hear Mother say. "She's curious about her parents. Perhaps it's time you told her." My heart races faster.

"Told her what?" Father says. "I don't know anything about her parents, you know that."

"You could tell her how you found her. How she came to us."

"I don't think that's wise. Look, the important thing is for all of us to return home and straighten things out with William and his family."

"But Anna still isn't sure she wants to marry him. I don't want her to be unhappy."

"I don't, either, of course. But there's a problem, Harriet. I've had some unfortunate business losses. I need to stay in the bank's good graces if I want to come through this crisis in one piece."

"What are you saying?" Mother's voice is shrill with fear. "You're scaring me, Arthur!"

"Now, now . . . I don't mean to frighten you." I picture him patting her hand to soothe her. "It's just that my finances are a bit tight at the moment. I need William's family to continue extending credit to me, and I'm worried that they may not do it if there are hard feelings about this broken engagement."

"Would they do that?"

"Who knows what might happen? I'm certain that my business can weather this storm provided I can get special consideration from the bank. Anna's marriage to William would ensure that."

"Arthur! You wouldn't use our Anna this way."

"I'm not using her! She told us she was in love with William. They were engaged to be married. What happened between them is just a silly misunderstanding. I'm simply trying to get the wedding back on track. I know Anna will have a wonderful life with William. You know it, too."

"Yes. That's true. But the other day when she was out of her room I had a chance to read her diary. She is unhappy about a lot of things right now, Arthur. I'm not sure we should pressure her to marry."

"I'm not pressuring her. But our daughter is immature and naïve. We've spoiled her a bit too much, and she can act very childish at times. She needs to grow up and settle down. William and his family will give her everything she could ever dream of. And more. Isn't that what we want for Anna? Isn't that what every parent wants for the child they love?"

"You're right, you're right. . . . Listen, we should go find her and tell her you're here. She'll be so surprised."

I back away from the door as quickly as I can and leave my room so they won't know I've been listening. I race down the steps and sink into the first empty chair I find on the front porch. Then I try to look surprised when Mother finds me and says, "Anna, look who came to see us."

"Father!" I go to him and feel his strong arms surrounding me. His embrace reminds me of my nightmare and the reassurance I always feel in my dream when he keeps me safe above the surging waves. I inhale the scent of cigars on his linen suit coat. "What are you doing here, Father? I didn't know you were coming."

"I decided to visit for the weekend so I could escort you home. Since you'll be returning by train, I traveled that way, too, so I could help you make all the right connections."

He would never tell me the truth about why he really came or confide in me about his financial problems the way he had with Mother. Even so, I love my father, and I know I need to help him. For my parents' sakes, I need to marry William.

CHAPTER 16

Geesje's Story

I can't remember a summer that was as cool and rainy as our first one here in Holland in 1847. Everything in our cabin stayed damp and clammy all the time, including our blankets, so we tried to keep a fire burning most of the time. It was easy to do since we were surrounded by a forest. The days were gloomy and cheerless. Thick, low-hanging clouds covered the moon and stars at night, making the woods so dark I was afraid to walk to the privy alone.

Meanwhile, new settlers arrived from home every day. Cabins and lean-tos and bark huts now dotted the forest, and the settlers began clearing patches of land. At first the new immigrants lived in the communal house or in the log house that the Ottawa Indians had built on the shores of Black Lake; Dominie Van Raalte made arrangements to purchase the log house and an acre of land from Chief Wakazoo. The natives migrated to their hunting grounds farther north during the summer months and weren't using it.

When those living conditions became overcrowded, Papa invited a young, newly arrived family named Van Dijk to stay with us while they built a cabin not too far from ours. The young couple had two small boys: Arie, who was three years old, and Gerrit, who had just turned one. Food was still very scarce since animal pests continually invaded our garden, and the Van Dijks generously shared their provisions with us in return for sharing our cabin. Mama loved those two children as if they were her own grandchildren, and the Van Dijks filled a place in her heart that had been left empty after leaving my sisters and their children behind in the Netherlands.

The cool weather made it easier for the men to work during the day, but the constant rain and flooded marshland along the nearby Black River created perfect breeding grounds for mosquitos. Thick, humming clouds of them hovered around us during the day and hummed incessantly around our heads at night as we tried to sleep. Their bites created itchy welts on every patch of our exposed skin. Mrs. Van Dijk daubed mud on her children's faces and arms to keep the mosquitos from biting, turning the boys into little mud babies. But the itching wasn't the worst of it. We soon learned that the mosquitos carried a disease called malaria, and it struck every home in our settlement.

Mama was the first one of us to be felled by the disease. Fever and chills left her bedridden and wracked her frail body, which was already weakened by our poor diet during the winter. Mama had always been a tiny woman, but vomiting and diarrhea quickly reduced her to skin and bones. I soaked cloths in cool water to bathe her feverish skin, then fed the fire and covered her with blankets when she shivered with chills. And I prayed. How I prayed!

Mrs. Van Dijk fell ill next, and I took over her duties, as well, cooking for all the men and caring for her two small children while nursing both women day and night. "The illness is everywhere," Papa told us. "Every home and family in our community has been affected."

"Why would God tell us to move to such a terrible place?" I asked. Papa ignored my question. His faith in a loving God filled every inch of his soul, leaving no room for doubt to gain a foothold. Nor could he comprehend how I could ever distrust the God he knew and loved.

"We must learn, like the Apostle Paul, to be content in whatsoever state we are in," he said. "Paul knew how to be abased and how to abound; to be full and to be hungry; to abound and to suffer need. All for the sake of the Savior he loved."

The next day Papa fell ill, too. In spite of all his efforts to remain strong and keep working with Maarten and Mr. Van Dijk to clear the land, the raging fever toppled him like one of the huge trees they were cutting down on our property. I watched helplessly as Papa shook with chills. All around us, people began to die from malaria. Every day Maarten whispered the news to me of another death among our fellow settlers. The oldest, the youngest, and the weakest were the first to pass away.

In spite of my prayers, the illness continued to infect our cabin until every one of us fell ill, some worse than others. I seemed to have a milder case than my parents and the Van Dijks did, so I took the two children into bed with me so their parents wouldn't know how ill they were. Every time I drank a sip of water, I made sure the children drank some, too. Maarten kept filling the wood box and fetching fresh drinking water for everyone, even after he became sick himself. In between bouts of shaking and chills, he tended the fire and tried to cook a little porridge to help us recover our strength. The people in our community who were lucky enough to stay well or who had already recovered went from house to house with Dominie Van Raalte to help care for the sick, comfort the grieving, and, when the time came, bury the dead.

I remember sitting beside Mama in the damp darkness of our cabin late one evening, listening to the rain pattering on our roof as I tried to persuade her to eat something. She looked up at me with fever-bright eyes and said, "He keeps all His promises!"

"Who does, Mama?"

"Jesus. Our Savior. He said He would never leave us or forsake us, and He's here, Geesje. He's right here beside us."

"Where, Mama?" I looked all around, wondering if the fever was making her hallucinate.

"Can't you feel His presence, lieveling?" Her smile seemed to light up the dingy cabin. I didn't want to tell her that in my darkest moments of sickness these past few days I had felt totally abandoned by God.

"Please don't die, Mama!" I whispered.

"I'm not afraid of dying," she said, smiling. "I followed Him on this journey to America, and I'll gladly follow Him to heaven if He asks me to."

I set down the bowl and spoon and gathered her fragile body in my arms. "Don't leave me, Mama! Please don't leave me!"

"If He calls my name, I want to obey. But Jesus will always be with you, Geesje, just like He's with us right now. Can't you feel Him? This is a holy place."

The next morning I awoke to find two men and a woman from our settlement standing in the doorway of our cabin. Maarten came over and knelt beside my bed, tears streaming down his fevered face. "Geesje . . . Geesje, I'm so sorry. Your mother went to be with our Lord during the night."

I insisted on getting up and helping prepare Mama's body for burial, my tears wetting her beloved face for the last time. She looked peaceful, but I had never felt such despair. Papa and I were both too weak and too sick to attend her funeral. They buried her in the ever-expanding graveyard on the hill near the new log church.

That afternoon Dominie Van Raalte returned to our cabin with medicine that had just arrived from Kalamazoo. It was supposed to cure malaria. "The entire kolonie has become a sickbed," he told us. "I'm sorry that I'm forced to use this medicine sparingly, but I have so little to spread among so many people."

I wanted to rage at him for coming too late to save Mama. I turned away when he offered a dose to me. "Give it to my father and the others. And the children. Their fevers are much worse than mine." We dissolved some of the medicine in water, and Maarten and I held little Arie and Gerrit on our laps as we forced them to drink the bitter liquid.

"Why would God allow this to happen?" I asked Maarten after Dominie was gone. "How can God expect us to have faith in Him when He puts us through such hardship? We left home at His command to start a community because we longed for religious freedom. Now we're dying in this terrible place!"

Maarten gently stroked Arie's sweaty hair. The child had fallen asleep in his arms. "The Bible says that 'faith is the substance of things hoped for, the evidence of things not seen.' The godly men and women in Scripture all walked by faith, and most of them never received the things they hoped for—at least not in this life."

"Don't quote the Bible to me," I said angrily. "There is no good reason in this world why Mama had to die. She trusted God!"

Papa died that evening, less than an hour after reciting the Twenty-third Psalm and the Lord's Prayer with me as I bathed his burning forehead. Over the next few days, Mr. and Mrs. Van Dijk also died, lying side-by-side on the same pine-bough bed, their hands entwined. The cart that circulated through our settlement came to collect their bodies, adding them to all the others. Maarten and I and the two children were the only ones in our cabin who survived.

"There are so many orphans in the kolonie," Maarten told me one evening, "that the elders have decided to build an orphanage to house them all. But I think we should take care of Arie and Gerrit ourselves. What do you say, Geesje? These little ones shouldn't be all alone. They need us."

I readily agreed. The children had lost their parents just as I had. They needed love. Caring for them gave me a reason to go on living as I waited for Hendrik to arrive. Maarten and I also agreed to let a middle-aged widow named Mrs. Van den Bosch and her twelve-year-old son move in with us after her husband and young daughter died of malaria, too.

At last the rain stopped. The terrible summer and the plague of malaria finally came to an end. Maarten and I were sitting outside our cabin on a fall afternoon as the leaves began to turn colors, when I looked up at him and said, "I'm not sure I believe in a loving God anymore."

Maarten didn't flinch at my scornful words. "Even so, Geesje, He believes in you. Nothing can separate us from the love of God which is in Christ Jesus—not tribulation nor famine nor persecution nor death. Not things present nor things to come—"

"I don't believe that. I feel abandoned by Him. Forsaken."

"I've felt that way at times, too, these past few months," he admitted. "But it isn't true. We're His, and He's hanging on tightly to us. Nothing and no one can pluck us out of His hand."

"But where's the meaning in all these deaths?"

"We couldn't understand God's purposes even if He explained them to us. Could little Gerrit understand us if we tried to explain malaria to him or tell him how a tiny mosquito caused it? When we forced him to drink the bitter medicine that saved his life, Gerrit simply had to trust us and believe that we were doing it because we loved him."

"Where's the proof that God loves us? Show me, Maarten."

He didn't reply. I'm not sure I would have listened to him if he had.

HOLLAND, MICHIGAN
1897

My tiny house is much too hot for me to sit inside it all day. Derk finds me on my front porch that evening when he arrives home from the hotel. "Beautiful evening, isn't it, Tante Geesje?" he asks.

"It's wonderful! There's a nice breeze off the lake that's keeping the mosquitos away." He bends to kiss my forehead, and I smell pine trees and lake air on his clothing. "Your skin has turned very brown from being in the sunshine all day," I tell him. "You're starting to look like one of the Indians who used to live down by Black Lake, except that your hair has bleached nearly white."

He runs his fingers through it making it stick up on end. "I'm hoping you have more of your story for me to read," he says as he flops down on one of my porch steps.

I'm reluctant to show him what I've written. In fact, I considered ripping out the last few pages right after I wrote them and burning them in my stove. In the end I decided not to. Derk needs to know what despair and heartache look like. His congregation will ask him many hard questions someday, like the ones I asked Maarten. Derk will need to help his parishioners find strength in God the way Dominie Van Raalte helped us during that terrible time. Sooner or later, sorrow and tragedy are part of everyone's life. Besides, I haven't written about the greatest sorrow of all, yet.

I fetch my notebook, and we sit on my front porch as he reads it. The sun sets so late these midsummer days that the sky remains light for a long time. When he finishes, Derk slowly closes the notebook and turns to me. "So much loss," he says, shaking his head. "It must have been hard for you to go on."

"Yes. . . . And now you know the truth about all my doubts. They outweighed my faith, at times."

"And yet you weathered them, like a sturdy ship battling a storm at sea."

"What I've written doesn't shock you?"

"No," he says. "No, I'm not shocked. I nearly gave up on God, too, remember? After my mother died? You're the reason I didn't, Tante Geesje. You had just lost loved ones, too, and yet you told me you didn't hate God. You said you had decided to cling to Him like a lifeboat, and you encouraged me to do the same. You helped my father and me through that terrible time."

"There were many people who came alongside me. And taking care of you helped me with my own grief, the same way taking care of Arie and Gerrit helped me after their parents died. Our burdens are lighter when they're shared."

"I like the words Maarten said that came from John's Gospel," Derk says. "'Nothing and no one can pluck us out of His hand.'

God held on tightly to both of us after the *Ironsides* sank, and even grief couldn't pluck us out of His hand."

I hear the emotion in his gravelly voice. I'm surprised by the tears that suddenly fill my eyes as he refers to my favorite Bible promise. *No one can pluck us out of God's hand.*

"When my parents were gone and God was all I had," I said, "I discovered that He is enough. I survived malarial fever, so I knew He must have a purpose for me on this earth even though I couldn't see it. I kept moving forward, one tiny step at a time, clinging to Him in faith. And isn't that the definition of faith—moving forward through the darkness, clinging to God?"

Derk rises from his seat and gathers me into his warm, sun-browned arms. "I love you, Tante Geesje," he murmurs.

"Ik hou ook van jou," I tell him. *I love you, too.*

CHAPTER 17

Geesje's Story

I still remember the early fall afternoon when I received my final letter from Hendrik. One of the other settlers had made a trip into Allegan and had returned with it. The pages were filled with good news, and I could feel Hendrik's excitement in every sentence. Weeks had passed since he'd mailed it in the Netherlands, and by now he was on his way to America. I probably wouldn't hear from him again until he walked out of the woods and into my arms.

> *My darling Geesje,*
> *I have been discharged from the army and have finished all my preparations to come to America. I will be traveling with a group of Dutch emigrants who plan to settle in the state of Wisconsin. We will set sail from Rotterdam tomorrow. I feel like one of my ancestors must have felt as he prepared to sail the seas. I could leap and dance with joy and anticipation.*

I will travel with them across the ocean to New York City, then sail up the Hudson River and go by way of the Erie Canal to Buffalo, like you did. It will be early enough in November that the American shipping lakes should still be navigable, and we will be able to board a steamer to cross Lake Erie and into Lake Huron, then down to Sheboygan, Wisconsin on the western coast of Lake Michigan. From there, I will take another steamer across the lake to the port of Grand Haven, which I'm told is some twenty miles north of you. They will give me directions to your settlement from there. If I have no delays, you and I will be together at last by the end of November.

I have saved enough money to buy several acres of land in America. If you agree and if your parents allow it, we will be married right away. I would build a palace for you if I could, grander than the king's palace in Den Hague. Geesje, I'm filled with hope for our future together. Soon! Soon I will be able to hold you in my arms. Soon we will be together for the rest of our lives.

I love you so much,

Hendrik

He was coming to be with me at last! He was already on his way and would arrive in just a few more weeks. We would be married as soon as we could. The anticipation helped ease the terrible grief I felt at the loss of my parents. Hendrik didn't know they were dead. He didn't know the challenges he would face in this wilderness. But at least we would face them together.

Every day I mentally charted his progress, counting the weeks he would spend crossing the ocean, checking off the days in my mind, praying that God would keep him safe from storms. I pictured him arriving at Castle Garden in New York City like I did, traveling up the beautiful Hudson River to Albany. The plodding mule trip along the Erie Canal would seem endless to him, and I imagined him walking along the towpath with the mules to hurry them on their way.

The days and weeks of waiting seemed interminable to me. I took care of Arie and Gerrit and worked beside Widow Van den Bosch to store up what little food we had managed to harvest for the coming months. We prepared our cabin and mended our clothing and knit warm socks for winter. Every day, from the middle of November onward, I watched for Hendrik to step out of the woods into the clearing that surrounded our cabin and into my waiting arms. Every day brought disappointment.

"He should be here by now," I said as I stoked the fire to make pea soup. Widow Van den Bosch was kneading dough for bread. "Today is the first day of December already. I can't imagine why he isn't here." It wasn't true. I could easily imagine all sorts of disasters. My stomach ached so badly from fear and worry that I could barely eat. "I hope he isn't lost in the woods."

"You said he was a soldier, didn't you? I'm sure he can take care of himself." The widow gave the dough another thump with the heel of her hand. I didn't say so, but her bread was always tough and dry, not at all like Mama's. "What are your plans after he does arrive?" she asked. "Will you continue living here once you're married?" I knew she was trying to distract me from my fear by helping me think about our future together.

"I feel like this is Maarten's cabin, since he worked so hard to build it and clear the land. But I hope he'll let Hendrik and me live here until spring. Hendrik will probably want to buy land farther out of town. He plans to clear several acres for farmland."

"Maarten may take a bride of his own one of these days," the widow said, lowering her voice and giving me a sly wink. "Have you noticed that young Johanna Van Eyck seems smitten with him?"

I hadn't noticed. I'd focused solely on myself these past months. "Is that right?" I said, feigning interest. "Is he smitten with her, too?"

"He seems to be. Haven't you seen them talking after church?"

146

I didn't want to admit that I barely paid attention to the people or the sermon or anything else at church—so totally consumed was I with my prayers for Hendrik. "I hope Maarten finds a good wife and that he's happy," I said. "He's so good with the little boys. He'll make a wonderful father."

"Will you adopt them when your Hendrik comes or will Maarten?"

I stopped chopping carrots and looked down at Gerrit, napping in his little wooden bed by the fire. Maarten had made the bed for him so he would be off the damp dirt floor. Widow Van den Bosch's question was one I had never considered. "I'm not sure who the boys will live with. I need to wait and ask Hendrik what he thinks."

I had grown to love Arie and Gerrit as if they were my own children. They even called me Mama. I couldn't imagine giving them up. But Maarten loved them, too. He and the other men in our settlement had sold the trees they'd felled to a lumbering company, and Maarten used some of his proceeds to buy more chickens, a pig, and a dairy cow so the boys would have milk to drink. I had no idea how Hendrik would feel about raising someone else's children. We had never talked about such things. We had known each other for barely six months before Hendrik had been transferred to Utrecht. The vast distances our letters had to travel and the weeks it took for them to arrive limited what we'd been able to talk about. But once Hendrik and I were together again, we would have the rest of our lives to get to know each other. We would grow as close as my parents had been. Mama and Papa had known each other's moods and thoughts without asking and could communicate with a simple look or gesture. It would be that way for Hendrik and me someday.

When the first snowflakes began to fall, I could no longer disguise my worry. I remembered watching the two burials at sea in the middle of the Atlantic and doubting God's goodness. I had asked myself the question: *If He could cruelly snatch the young bride from her husband for no reason, the child from his mother, might He snatch Hendrik from me, too?* He had also taken my parents. Fear of God's seeming capriciousness consumed me.

Hendrik was all I ever talked about. "He should have been here weeks ago," I told Widow Van den Bosch as we trudged up the hill over the frozen ground one Sunday morning. The men had finished building the log church, and it felt warm inside when we arrived. I unbundled Arie and Gerrit and hung up my own coat.

"There are always unexpected delays," she assured me. "We will pray for him this morning." We settled beside each other, flanked by her son and the two young boys.

I could see that something was wrong the moment Dominie Van Raalte stepped behind the pulpit that Sunday. He had been our pastor for a long time, and I had seen him weather every crisis imaginable: suffering from seasickness on the Atlantic, from exhaustion after trudging through snow up to his waist, and sorrow after tirelessly nursing his congregation through malaria. I'd seen him weep as he buried men, women, and children who had followed him faithfully to this new land. But I'll never forget the pallor on his face when he stepped behind the pulpit on that Sunday in December and read the news.

"There has been a shipwreck," he said in a trembling voice.

My heart dropped like a dead weight in my chest. I wanted him to stop talking. I covered my mouth to keep from crying out and wished I could also cover my ears. I trembled as I waited, as if I had malarial fever all over again.

"A steamer called the *Phoenix* caught fire and sank in Lake Michigan nearly two weeks ago on November 21. The ship carried many of our countrymen from the Netherlands, some two hundred eighty men, women, and children who were immigrating to Wisconsin. There were many casualties."

When he paused to swallow and regain his composure, Widow Van den Bosch grabbed my hand and held it tightly. As Dominie continued reading, every word he spoke felt like a blow to my heart.

"The *Phoenix* set sail from Buffalo, New York, crossing Lake Erie into Huron, then into Lake Michigan. Five miles from their destination of Sheboygan, Wisconsin, the ship caught fire. Out of more than three hundred passengers, only forty-three survived. Seats in the two lifeboats were given to the first-class passengers, not the poor Dutch immigrants." He folded the paper in half and looked up at us. "Entire families were lost with many small children. I know that some of you have family members coming. . . ."

I didn't wait to hear the rest. I lifted Gerrit off my lap and thrust him into Widow Van den Bosch's arms, then ran from the church into the cold morning air, not bothering to grab my coat. My stomach heaved. I thought I would be sick. I ran blindly down the hill on the frozen pathway, my heart screaming soundlessly.

Not Hendrik. Please, God, not him. The *Phoenix* couldn't be his ship. And even if it was, he would find a way to survive, I know he would. He would grab a seat in the lifeboat. Or he would swim. Hendrik was young enough and strong enough to endure the lake's icy water until he was rescued. I refused to believe he was dead.

My tears blinded me, and I tripped over a tree root and fell to my knees on the path. I remained there, weeping and shivering and praying with all my heart, my breath fogging the air. "Please, God! Please let Hendrik be alive, please!" I wanted to bargain with God, to promise Him anything and everything, but I had nothing to offer in exchange for Hendrik's life.

I heard footsteps behind me, but I didn't turn. A moment later someone draped a warm coat over my trembling shoulders. I thought it might be Widow Van den Bosch, but it was Maarten who crouched beside me. He pulled me into his arms, rocking me, letting me cry. "Geesje, I'm so sorry. What can I say? What can I do?"

"He's alive, I know he is. . . . Hendrik made it out alive. He'll come for me. We'll be married. . . ."

Maarten said nothing.

I don't know how long we sat there before Maarten finally helped me to my feet and walked with me back to our cabin. He stoked the fire and wrapped me in a blanket. "I'm going back to get the boys," he said. "Will you be all right?"

I stared into the flames, rocking back and forth, shivering. Hendrik would come. He would.

But he didn't.

Nearly three months after the shipwreck I awoke to a blizzard outside our cabin. The forest was frozen in sorrow along with my heart, dead and white and featureless. I went outside to fetch more wood for the fire, and as I watched snow piling on top of snow all around me, I understood the truth: Hendrik wasn't coming. He was dead. As dead as the frozen world that stretched as far as I could see. A drift had buried the block Maarten used to split firewood. More snow buried all traces of the path to our neighbors' cabins. I wished it would bury me. My despair felt as deep and cold as the winter snowdrifts, my grief as wide and vast and bottomless as the lake that had swallowed the man I loved. I had reached the end of all my hopes and dreams, my parents' hopes and dreams. Mama and Papa were gone, and now Hendrik was gone, as well. I was miles and miles from home, trapped in this wilderness, living in a shack. All hope was buried. I saw no reason to continue living. I wanted to die and join everyone else I had ever loved in heaven.

I heard the cabin door open and close behind me. A moment later Maarten rested his hand on my shoulder and gently turned me around. "Come inside, Geesje. I'll get the firewood. The children need you. They are clamoring for breakfast." I did what he said. Taking care of Arie and Gerrit was the only thing that kept me going.

Late that afternoon when the blizzard finally stopped, I bundled up the boys so they could go outside and play in the snow with Maarten. I watched from the window and listened to their laughter. They adored Maarten, and he adored them. Six months had passed since their parents died, and the children's grief was ebbing. Would mine, as well?

Their cheeks were red with cold when they finally tumbled inside. I dried them off and fed them soup and got them ready for bed. Maarten told them stories in front of the fire, stories from back home in the Netherlands and from the Bible. I held baby

Gerrit and rocked him to sleep, then tucked him in his little bed. When Maarten went out to the lean-to to take care of our cow, I followed him.

"I want to go home," I told him.

He stopped chipping the ice in the watering trough. "To the Netherlands?"

"Yes. I don't care how far I've traveled or how long it takes me to get there, or how much it costs, I want to go home. Will you help me make all the arrangements?"

Maarten stared at me. "By yourself?" I nodded. In truth, I was terrified of traveling by myself, let alone boarding another steamship after the *Phoenix* disaster. Hadn't our sailing ship the *Southerner* caught fire, too, on the way here? Fortunately for us, we had been in port and not five miles out to sea. But I wouldn't let fear stop me.

"I want to go home to Leiden. I'll live with one of my sisters."

"Things will get better here—"

"How?" I shouted. "How will things get better? Can you really promise me that?" I lowered my voice, not wanting Widow Van den Bosch or the children to hear me. "And when? In a year? Two years? Will we have everything we left behind in Leiden by then? I've lost everyone I ever cared about!"

Maarten looked away. I could see I had hurt him. "What about Arie and Gerrit?" he asked. "Will you take them back to Leiden with you?"

"I don't know. . . . Please help me figure out a way to go home, Maarten. I'm afraid I'll go insane if I can't hang on to the hope of going home."

He exhaled, creating a cloud of icy steam with his breath. He started chipping at the frozen water again. "I'll talk to Dominie Van Raalte—"

"No! Don't do that. He'll ask me why I've lost hope, and I don't want to talk about God or faith or any of those things right now." I hadn't attended church since the morning Dominie had told us the news about the *Phoenix*. I had nothing to say to God, and I didn't want to hear what He might have to say to me. "There's no explanation he could possibly give for why God took my parents. Or those two innocent children's parents. Why are we suffering in this place when all we wanted to do was obey God and follow where He led us?" Maarten didn't try to reply, too beaten down by my doubts. "Can you or Dominie Van Raalte or anyone else tell me why God took Hendrik," I asked, "when he was coming here to learn more about Him and try to serve Him? Or why God took an entire boatload of families with little children, people who loved Him and trusted Him?"

My questions hung in the frozen air. The cow shifted positions, stomping her feet and bumping against me. I pushed her away. When Maarten finally replied, his words surprised me. "I'll try to figure out how to get us home, Geesje. Can you wait for a few more months, though? The lakes won't thaw until spring. And I'll need to earn some money for our passage back across the country to New York, then across the ocean." He stroked the cow's muzzle as he continued talking, almost to himself. "I can sell your father's land and this cabin. And I can probably find farmwork in the spring to earn a little more money for our fares."

"I'm not asking you to come with me, Maarten. Just help me figure out how to get home."

He shook his head. "I promised your father I would take care of you. I can't let you travel all that way by yourself."

"I'm not afraid. If I can survive *this* terrible place . . ." I couldn't finish, my throat choking at the memory of how these violent woods and lakes had taken the people I loved. Yet I knew Maarten was right. A pretty young woman like me had no business traveling alone. I didn't speak English. Strangers had leered at me at Castle Garden when I was with an entire group of people. I would be much safer if Maarten went with me.

"We'll go together," he said. "We'll take Arie and Gerrit with us."

"Do you want to go back home, too?" I asked. He hesitated. "Tell me the truth, Maarten."

"I want you to be happy. I feel so sorry for all that you've gone through. . . . I'll talk to Dominie Van Raalte in the morning about selling this land. We'll see what he says."

Maarten left home to walk to the dominie's cabin as soon as morning chores were finished. I had no idea how he would find his way there and back through the snow with the trails all buried. I was half afraid the dominie would march back here with Maarten and try to talk me out of it, but Maarten returned alone. "What did he say?" I asked before Maarten had a chance to stomp the snow off his wooden shoes and come inside the cabin. "Can he sell this land for me?"

"Yes . . . selling the land isn't going to be the problem."

"Well, what is?"

He came inside and closed the door behind him, taking a moment to ruffle Arie's thick blond hair. The boy had run to Maarten and was clinging to his leg, making it hard for him to move. Maarten kept his voice low. "He said it wouldn't be right for us to travel alone together since we aren't related to each other. And we can't adopt the boys or take them with us for the same reason. He said we should take more time to pray about our decision, and he would pray about it, too."

"But what other choice do we have? I want to go home!"

Widow Van den Bosch looked up from where she sat sewing beside the fire, letting down the hem of her son's outgrown trousers. "What do you mean, *home*?" she asked. "Not to the *Netherlands*?"

"Yes. As soon as the snow melts I'm going home. I hate this place!"

"But don't you remember the famine? And how there were no jobs for any of the men?"

"I'd rather die back home in Leiden than in this uncivilized place."

Neither she nor Maarten said another word as we all returned to our chores. But I pondered what to do throughout the day. It would be very unwise for me to travel all that way alone. I wanted to accept Maarten's offer to come with me but traveling together wasn't proper. And I was devastated to learn that I couldn't take Arie and Gerrit with me. I'd grown to love them and couldn't imagine leaving them behind in this godforsaken land. They needed to stay with Maarten and me.

As I was changing Gerrit's diaper that afternoon, a solution to all of these problems suddenly occurred to me. If Maarten and I were married, he could take me home. And we could keep the children. But could I go through with it?

Married. To Maarten. Not Hendrik. Unthinkable.

And yet I knew I needed him. I had been dependent on Maarten to do all the work a husband did ever since my parents died last summer. He had shown me endless kindness and patience. I knew he had once loved me. He probably still did. And I did care for him as one might love a brother or an old friend. I would be helpless without him. We had endured everything together since the persecution first began back in Leiden, when that first brick had been hurled through our window. He had always been faithful to God and to me and to my family, never complaining, watching out for me.

I heard him outside chopping firewood, the powerful *thunk* and *thwack* penetrating the silence. I put on my coat and an extra pair of socks.

"I come, too?" Arie asked when he saw me dressing.

"No, I'm coming right back, lieveling. You stay inside where it's warm." I closed the door behind me and crossed the snow-covered yard.

Maarten stopped working when he saw me. "What's wrong?"

"Do you still want to marry me? . . . We could travel home together, and we could take the boys if we were husband and wife."

His gaze met mine in the meek winter sunlight. Minutes seemed to pass before he replied. "I love you, Geesje. I always have. I would do anything for you."

I had to look away. "And you're my very best friend. . . . But before you decide if you want to marry me, I need to be honest with you. I don't think I will ever love anyone the way I loved Hendrik."

"I know. I know." He looked down at his large, square hands, gripping the axe handle.

"Maarten, look at me." I waited until he lifted his head. "You deserve so much more than me. You deserve a wife who loves you with all her heart. A wife who has as much faith in God as you do. My faith has withered away to nothing. Don't say yes unless you truly want to marry me."

"I wouldn't be marrying you with false hopes," he said. "I know you loved Hendrik. I know I could never take his place in your heart. . . . But still, I would be happy to take care of you for the rest of my life. And little Arie and Gerrit, too."

Sweet Maarten. He had been with me for as long as I could remember, a comforting shoulder to lean on in my grief. He'd protected me from danger, cheered me when I was sad, encouraged me when I was afraid, helped me when I was sick. He'd walked into town for food when he must have been starving and exhausted himself from the hard work of building this cabin and clearing the land. Now he would make another sacrifice for me, leaving everything he'd labored so hard for here in America in order to take me home to Leiden. He was willing to marry me, knowing I didn't love him, knowing he would always live in Hendrik's shadow. He would sacrifice his own happiness for mine. The least I could do for this gentle, loving man was to try to be a good wife to him in return.

The only man I would ever love was dead, and I would have to spend the rest of my life without him. I was not quite nineteen years old, and as I gazed into the future at all the years that stretched ahead of me, I knew I didn't want to feel this aching loneliness forever. I didn't want to be alone. I wanted the contentment and security of a husband and family. If I could never be with Hendrik, then why not spend my life with Maarten, who I had known since I was ten years old? He was all I had left from my old life. I couldn't imagine finding a better husband than him. And he had promised to take me home. I took his hand, red and chapped with cold, and held it between mine.

"I'll do my very best to be a good wife to you. Let's ask Dominie Van Raalte to announce the banns in church."

"Are you sure, Geesje?" I saw naked hope in his eyes.

"Yes. Are *you* sure, Maarten?"

"I am." He smiled, and his hope changed to joy. I could tell he wanted to hold me in his arms, but he just squeezed my hand in return, then released it. "Well, then. It's decided?"

"It's decided."

We told Dominie Van Raalte our decision, and when one of the elders read the banns in church that first Sunday, I saw Johanna Van Eyck rise from her seat and quietly leave through the back door. I remembered that she had hoped to marry Maarten. Now I had destroyed her hope.

Three weeks later, Maarten de Jonge and I were married in a quiet ceremony in the log church on the hill. We returned to our cabin with our adopted sons, Arie and Gerrit, to begin our new life together as a family. And to plan our trip back home to the Netherlands.

CHAPTER 18

Anna

"I've decided to marry William," I tell Father that evening as we eat in the hotel's elegant dining room. All day I have felt the weight of father's financial problems as if I now carried them on my own shoulders.

"Are you sure, Anna?" I see the guarded hope in my father's eyes. He seems to be holding his breath.

"Yes. I'm sure—if William is willing to take me back, that is."

"Of course he is. I talked with him about it, and he cares for you, Anna. I know you'll have a wonderful life with him, with everything a girl could ever dream of." Father's relief is palpable.

I look down at my plate, carefully cutting my broiled whitefish into tiny pieces. Jesus' question suddenly echoes through my mind. *"For what shall it profit a man, if he shall gain the whole world, and lose his own soul?"* I had read this verse from the eighth chapter of Mark earlier today and remembered hearing the pastor

157

at the castle church quote it in his sermon. Was I sacrificing my soul for this marriage? I needed to finish talking with Derk. I felt certain that he could answer my questions. He planned to become a minister, so he should be honest enough to tell me if I was at risk of losing my soul.

I look up at my parents again. "I think you and Mother should go back to Chicago without me on Sunday. I would like to stay here for another week."

"But why, darling?" Mother asks. "We have a wedding to plan and—"

"Travel alone?" Father interrupts. "Out of the question."

"I'm a grown woman, Father. I'm not afraid."

"Well, you should be."

"Why do you want to stay?" Mother asks again. "I've had the impression that you were becoming bored here."

"Not at all. I find it very refreshing to be out of the hot city during the summer and away from all the noise. You must admit, Father, that it's much cooler here than in Chicago."

"What about William? What will I tell him when he asks why you haven't returned?" Father appears worried again, the creases in his forehead deepening.

"I'll write a letter to William—tonight, in fact. You can deliver it to him as soon as you arrive home. I'll tell him how sorry I am that we quarreled and that I would very much like to marry him." I know Father is right—William will provide me with a wonderful life. He is a good man. A very wealthy man. He will build a lovely mansion for me on Prairie Avenue, and I will give him a son to inherit his fortune.

Out of nowhere, another verse I'd read in the Gospel of Mark suddenly comes to mind: *"It is easier for a camel to go through the eye of a needle, than for a rich man to enter into the kingdom of God."* The words stuck with me because I didn't understand them. Jesus had been talking with a very wealthy young man who had asked how he could inherit eternal life. "Sell everything you have and give the money to the poor," Jesus told him. The young man couldn't do it—any more than William or my father could ever give away all of his wealth to the poor. Would Jesus really ask for such a sacrifice? Maybe Derk can explain what Jesus meant to put my mind at ease.

"Why not come home and tell William yourself?" Father asks, interrupting my thoughts.

"Because . . . because I like it here." I don't dare to explain my true reasons. "I would like to stay for just one more week. Please, Father?"

"I cannot let you travel alone, Anna. It isn't right."

I turn to my mother, pleading silently with her. I know she is bored and ready to return to her fashionable life in Chicago. But I also know she owes me a favor after violating my privacy and reading my diary. She knows it, too.

"If it would make you happy, Anna, I'll stay one more week with you. Your father can write down all the instructions for returning by rail—is that agreeable to you, Arthur?"

In the end, Father reluctantly agrees. It's in his best interests to keep me happy. I stay up late that night composing a letter to William, begging for a second chance. I tell him how sorry I am for not honoring his wishes. I say that as his wife, I will submit to him as the head of our household from now on. If he can forgive me for my stubbornness, I hope we can start all over again and renew our engagement. I assure him that we will have a happy life together.

I reread the letter before sealing the envelope, and I realize that I haven't said a single word about loving him. Do I still love him? It doesn't matter. I am marrying William for my parents' sakes. It is hardly a sacrifice. Becoming one of Chicago's wealthiest women couldn't possibly be considered a sacrifice, even if I'm not in love with him.

I recall thinking that if I married William my future would be swallowed up by his plans the same way the waves always swallow Mama in my nightmare. But if I don't marry him, my father's business may fail, and our future would change in unimaginable ways. I may not be certain of my love for William, but I am certain of my love for my parents.

The next morning I slip out of my room before breakfast and hurry outside to search for Derk. I find him tending the boats down by the dock as usual, dragging the beached rowboats and skiffs closer to the water so they'll be ready when the hotel patrons finish their breakfasts. "You're up early this morning," he says when he sees me.

"Yes. I have a few more questions for you. Is there a time later today when we can talk, perhaps at the end of the day so I won't interrupt your work?"

He suddenly appears shy as he looks down at his feet, his tanned cheeks turning faintly pink. I wonder if I've been too bold, imposing on his time this way. After all, I'm practically a stranger. But Derk smiles when he looks up again and says, "I finish work at four o'clock. I'll meet you on that bench over there where you usually sit." I worry, briefly, that Mother might see us talking and misunderstand, but I don't want to make any more demands on Derk than I already have.

"Thank you. I really appreciate all the help you've given me." I hurry away, wondering how I would explain the situation to Father if he happened to look out of his bedroom window and see me talking with a good-looking hotel employee—especially after I've begged to stay for an extra week.

But he hasn't seen us. Later that morning I give Father my letter for William and bid him farewell as he boards the train to Holland. From there, he will make connections back to Chicago. I wonder why he doesn't take the more direct route across the lake by steamship the way Mother and I did, but I don't question him. My thoughts are preoccupied with the letter he's carrying. Once he delivers it, I will be committed to marrying William. In the meantime, I have one more week to find the answers to all my questions so I can keep my promise never to return to the castle church.

The first thing I tell Derk when we meet near the bench later that afternoon is precisely that. "I have only one more week to get all of my questions answered."

"One week?" he asks with his usual grin. "I've been studying at the seminary for quite a while now, and I still haven't found answers to all my questions. What's the big hurry, Anna?"

I glance around, worried that Mother might see us together and misunderstand. "Would you mind if we walked toward the beach while we talk?" I ask.

"Not at all. Whatever you want." We follow the shoreline of Black Lake, then take the path along the edge of the channel that connects that lake to Lake Michigan. I don't take Derk's arm, and I'm careful to keep a proper distance between us. I notice that a steady stream of sailboats is heading down the channel alongside us, one right after the other. The crews of each boat call good-naturedly to each other as they sail out to Lake Michigan.

"Goodness, I've never seen so many sailboats all at once," I say.

"I believe there's a race. The owners sometimes arrange a spontaneous event on a summer afternoon like this one when the weather is nice. They'll head out to Lake Michigan and race around a course marked with buoys. In fact, if you look out there," he says, pointing past the mouth of the channel, "you can see where they've set up the course."

I stand still for a moment, watching, and I can't help feeling a little thrill of excitement as I watch the billowing sails unfurl and catch the wind.

"I've agreed to marry William when I return home," I finally say. "That means I won't be able to go back to the castle church ever again. My family's church doesn't seem to encourage questions, especially the kind that I have."

He looks at me with a puzzled expression. "It's probably none of my business—and feel free to tell me so—but what made you decide to marry him? I thought you'd concluded that he was asking too much of you."

161

I don't reply right away as I begin walking again. I decide to trust Derk with the truth. "I learned that my father's business is in financial trouble. He needs the family connections with William and his bank in order to survive the crisis. I love my father. I would do anything for him and Mother. They wouldn't know how to survive if they lost all their money."

"Do they know that's why you're making this sacrifice and marrying William?"

"No. But it's hardly a sacrifice. William is a good man from a fine, churchgoing family. I'll be a wealthy woman. I'm sure he'll let me give generously to the poor. I can do a lot of good as his wife."

"So your decision is made." Derk makes it a statement, not a question.

"It is."

I wait for a sailboat filled with laughing young people to pass us on the channel before continuing. The late afternoon sun is still warm, and I draw a deep breath as I prepare to launch my first question. I'm surprised yet grateful that Derk hasn't tried to talk me out of marrying William. "I've been reading your Bible and—"

"It's yours now. You may keep it."

"Oh, but I couldn't—"

"Consider it an early wedding gift."

"Well . . . thank you." The mention of my wedding is discomforting. It takes me a moment to gather my thoughts. "The other day I read where Jesus said it was easier for a camel to go through the eye of a needle than for a rich man to enter the kingdom of heaven. I'm going to be a very rich woman after I marry William, so I'm wondering what Jesus meant. Will I be excluded from the kingdom of heaven because I'm wealthy?"

Derk scratches his chin as he ponders his reply. "Well . . . Jesus had just told the rich young ruler to sell everything he had and give the money to the poor, right? The young ruler couldn't bring himself to do it. He was too attached to his money to give it all away."

"I can't really blame him. I know how hard it would be for my parents or for William to lose everything, much less give it away voluntarily."

"Jesus was making the point that to a lot of rich people, their wealth means more to them than following Him. That's what He wanted the young ruler to see for himself. But then Jesus said, even though it may be hard for a rich man to stop trusting his wealth and trust in God, it wasn't impossible. God can change anyone's heart if he allows himself to be changed. Jesus said that all things are possible with God."

"So there are good rich people who serve God?"

"Of course. And—"

"I could still enter the kingdom of heaven, even if I'm rich?"

"The young man in the story walked away from Jesus, not the other way around. But the point is that we have to be willing to obey Him and follow Him, even at a great cost to ourselves and to the things we love."

"Is that why you gave up marrying the girl you loved instead of giving up being a minister?"

Derk gives me a funny look that I can't quite interpret. I don't know him well enough. He seems surprised that the conversation has shifted to him instead of about me and my problems. "Yes," he finally says. "I suppose it is." We hear a shout, and Derk turns and waves to someone aboard one of the passing boats. "Hey! Good luck in the race!" he shouts back.

"We could use you on our crew, Derk," the fellow calls.

"Next time," he says, laughing.

I have to admit there is a sense of excitement and energy and freedom among the racing teams that I envy. And joy. Then another thought occurs to me. "I hope I didn't keep you from racing this afternoon."

"Not at all. He's a friend of mine from college. We used to sail together a lot before we graduated and our lives got busy. Most of my friends took jobs right away and many of them married and started families. I started my studies at the seminary."

"Because you believed that's what God wanted you to do?"

"Yes. God asked the prophet Isaiah, 'Who will go for me? Who can I send?' and Isaiah replied, 'Here I am. Send me.' I gave God the same answer."

"So . . ." I say after exhaling deeply, "will I be turning away from Jesus if I marry William and stop going to the castle church? What does it mean that someone could gain the whole world but lose their soul?"

He looks out at the lake for a moment, as if deep in thought. I wonder if he is praying. "I think . . . I think that 'losing your soul' means walking away from God the way the rich young ruler walked away from Jesus. It means making other things more important than Him and worshiping those things. Living your life apart from Him. It's hard for wealthy people to turn to God for all their needs because they're used to relying on their money. God wants a relationship with us, one where we talk to Him in prayer, where we love Him and love our neighbor, and where we try to live the way Jesus taught us to."

"If I do those things, will it compensate for giving up the castle church? Will I be able to still keep my soul?"

Derk sighs. "I can't answer that question for you. Time and a hundred daily distractions can slowly turn us away from God before we even realize it's happening. But I urge you to keep reading your Bible. Jesus said if you seek Him you will find Him, if you search for Him with all your heart. He's with us everywhere we go, Anna. He's not just in a church building."

"Reverend Torrey said that in one of his sermons. He said, 'Seek and ye shall find; knock and the door will be opened.' He said we should always keep seeking God. But I'm not sure how to do that. God seems so near to me whenever I go to that church. That's why I kept going back. But I promised William that I wouldn't go anymore, and this time I need to keep my promise."

"God is everywhere, Anna. Jesus said He'll never leave or forsake us. My tante Geesje taught me that. I felt all alone after my mother died, but Geesje told me that Jesus was with me always."

164

"And was He? . . . Is He, still?"

"Yes," he says simply. "I don't feel alone anymore."

I want what Derk has, what Tante Geesje has. We have reached the end of the channel, and we stand on the sandy beach for a few minutes watching the sailboat race. When I glance up at Derk, he has his hand raised to his forehead, shading his eyes. I notice that he's smiling broadly.

"What do you enjoy about sailing?" I ask.

"The challenge of it, wrestling the wind and the waves, making the boat go where you want it to. And I like being part of a team, working together, having fun together."

"I always feel so alone," I tell him. "Abandoned." That was the word Mother used when she told me that she and Father had found me all alone, without parents. *Abandoned*. But I had been a newborn. I couldn't possibly remember being abandoned. And I had been lovingly cared for by my parents all my life, for as long as I can remember. I clear my throat to push away my inexplicable sorrow and tell Derk, "William never seems to listen when I try to talk about God or faith or things like that. He doesn't understand what I mean when I tell him that I feel like something is missing, in here. . . ." I lay my hand over my heart.

Derk turns to look at me, leaning a little closer as he listens. I see so much compassion in his eyes that I want to weep. His eyes are the same color as the sky above us and the lake before us, his hair the same warm gold as the sand. "Isn't there anyone back in Chicago you can talk with or who can answer your questions?" he asks.

"Not in my social circle. Those friendships are very superficial, the topics of conversation inconsequential. I've been longing for a true friend for a long time. That's another reason why I felt so drawn to the castle church. It felt like home to me. I never feel as if I belong when I'm with all the other wealthy young people my age. I've always felt . . . different. As though a piece of me is missing."

"I don't mean to give glib answers, but why don't you pray and ask God for a friend to walk beside you, someone you could talk with about these things? Someone your fiancé would approve of."

"I'm not very good at praying. That's something else I was trying to learn at the castle church."

"There's no mystery to it. Just talk to God the same way you're talking to me. Tante Geesje taught me that, too. She told me that whenever I felt alone or afraid or angry, I should tell God all about it—and then I would feel better because I would know that He'd heard me."

"Did it work?"

He nods and gives a crooked grin. "One time, I was thinking about the special *pannenkoeken* that my mother used to make—pancakes, in English. I told God I was mad at Him for taking my mother away because my father didn't make them right. That very night, Tante Geesje brought us a meal, and guess what she had cooked."

"Pancakes."

He laughs and nods his head. "God did a lot of little things like that to let me know He was there and that He was listening to me. So don't be afraid to pray, Anna. You can tell Him anything and everything."

"Thank you. I'll do that. . . . We should probably go back now."

"Are you sure? The race isn't over yet."

"Yes, I believe so." Derk has answered some of my questions and given me a sliver of hope. But as we walk back toward Black Lake I see the slowing activity all around me as the afternoon winds to an end, the rowboats returning to shore, the bathers walking toward the hotel from the beach, the porches and croquet lawn emptying, and the feeling that time is running out for me is so suffocating that I can hardly breathe. Once I return to Chicago, once I marry William, I will no longer be able to do whatever I wish. I will have to be circumspect in my actions and keep my thoughts and feelings to myself. I do believe everything Derk has told me about prayer, and I loved his charming little story about the pancakes. But the whirling social world that I'll soon be part of again, with hundreds of parties and social calls and events, will leave little time in my life for God, apart from the hour-long church service on Sunday morning. It truly does seem hard for a rich man—or woman—to enter the kingdom of heaven. I worry that waves of duty and obligations and expectations will swallow me, just like the waves in my nightmare swallowed our lifeboat, and that I'll lose my soul.

"Do you think I'm making a mistake by marrying William?" I ask. "I admit that I'm marrying him for his money. Is that a terrible sin?"

"Do you love him?"

"I once thought I did. But now I worry that it might have been a girlish infatuation. I was dazzled by him. And amazed that he'd chosen me. We have nothing of importance to say to each other, and I feel as though I barely know him. Is it a sin to marry him if I don't love him?"

"I don't believe it's a sin. Breaking your marriage vows to him would be a sin."

I think of Mother's new friend, Honoria Stevens, and her sorrow over her husband's affair. Mother said that such dalliances were more common than most people realized, yet why doesn't our minister point out this wrongdoing or call the men who do it sinners?

"Tante Geesje married a man she didn't love and—"

"Was it a terrible mistake? Was she unhappy all her life?"

"I don't think so. I haven't finished reading her story, yet. She married him after her true love died in a shipwreck, but I know they had children and grandchildren and a good life together. I believe she was happy with him. I wish you could meet her, Anna. She could answer your questions about marriage much better than I can. She hasn't had an easy life, but she's a godly woman who considers Jesus her best friend and constant companion."

"She sounds amazing."

"She is. And I find it interesting that her faith wasn't always as strong as it is now. For a time she was very angry with God for causing so much sorrow and loss in her life."

"I would love to meet her." We've returned to the bench where our walk began.

"Maybe you can. Would you have time to make a trip into Holland before you go back to Chicago? I'm sure she'll be willing to talk with you. You could take the steamship—"

"Or the train. There's a train into Holland, isn't there?"

"Yes. There's also the train," he says with a grin. "I forgot that you've vowed never to step foot onto a boat again. Let me talk with Tante Geesje and see if she would be willing to help answer your questions."

"Thank you. And in the meantime, I'll figure out a way to travel into Holland and back without my mother knowing about it. She would never approve."

"I think you and Tante Geesje would get along great. Like you and I do, Anna."

"You're so easy to talk to. And very patient with all my questions." I feel so comfortable with Derk.

Maybe too comfortable.

I see the intensity of his gaze as he gives me his complete attention and suddenly realize that our easy familiarity is wrong on so many levels. I'm engaged to marry William. Why am I confessing things to a hotel employee—a good-looking, unmarried one, at that? I shouldn't be talking to any young man without a chaperone present.

I begin backing away. "I need to go. Thank you for your time. And for the Bible. I can't tell you how much I appreciate all your help."

"It's nothing. . . . You're welcome." He seems dazed by my abrupt departure. "Anna?"

I have already turned my back on him but I look over my shoulder to face him again. "Yes?"

"I'll visit my aunt tonight and ask if she'll meet with you."

"Thank you. That would be good." I keep walking away, forcing Derk to call after me in order to continue the conversation.

"I'll let you know what she says. Should we meet here again tomorrow after work?"

"If it isn't too much trouble." Why is my heart racing at the thought of talking with Derk tomorrow? I stride toward the hotel as fast as my dainty shoes will allow, wondering why I am suddenly in such a hurry to flee from this kind, gracious man.

CHAPTER 19

Geesje's Story

April of 1848 brought more changes than just melting snow and the rebirth of spring. Widow Van den Bosch married a widower from our kolonie, and she and her son moved to his cabin. More and more settlers were arriving from the Netherlands, causing our community to grow. And Maarten had good news for me one night as he sat at our table by lamplight, counting his earnings. "I think we have enough money for our passage back to the Netherlands," he told me. He had been working as a laborer every day, helping one of our wealthier settlers clear his land, since there was no longer any reason to continue clearing our own. "Once we sell your father's land and this cabin, we should have enough money to go home."

Home. I was going home. I rose from my chair to hug him tightly. "That's wonderful news, Maarten! Thank you, thank you!" I had news of a big change to tell him about, too, but I had been waiting for the right time. I sat down on his lap, the first time I had ever made such an affectionate gesture, and put my arms around his neck. "That means our child will be born in the Netherlands instead of here."

"Our child? . . . You mean . . . ?"

"Yes."

The joy on Maarten's face brought tears to my eyes. I couldn't remember ever seeing him as happy as he was at that moment. But as he hugged me tightly, I knew I didn't share the full measure of his joy. God forgive me, but I was still thinking of Hendrik, wishing they were his arms surrounding me, his child growing inside me.

After Maarten left for work the next morning, I decided that the mild, sunny day would be a perfect one to wash some of our clothing. I was bent over the outdoor fire pit, piling on wood to heat the water, when Arie ran up to me and said, "Mama, there's a man coming."

A man? Had Maarten forgotten something? I stood and watched a tall figure weave his way through the dusky woods following the narrow path. There was something familiar about the way he walked.

When he saw me, he began to run. His cap blew off his head, and a shaft of spring sunlight shone down through the trees onto his golden hair, his handsome face.

Hendrik.

Was I imagining things? Was he a ghost? A wave of dizziness washed over me, but there was nothing to grab on to. The trees twirled in circles around me, and I felt myself falling. Then everything went black.

When I opened my eyes again, Hendrik was kneeling beside me, holding my head on his lap, calling my name. "Geesje . . . Geesje, are you all right? Say something . . ."

"Are you real?" I whispered. I touched his face and felt his bristly whiskers. There was a vivid scar on the side of his face and neck that hadn't been there before, as if his skin had melted.

"Yes, Geesje! Yes, I'm real, and I'm finally here!" He pulled me close, holding me so tightly I could barely breathe. "I've dreamt of this moment for so long," he murmured. "Oh, thank God . . . thank God!"

I wept as I held him tightly in return. I never wanted to let go. I was afraid I was dreaming, and I didn't want to wake up. "I thought you were dead!" I told him. "When we heard that the *Phoenix* sank, I thought you must have been on that ship. And that I'd lost you!"

"I was on that ship. Didn't you get my letter?"

"What letter?" I pulled away and sat up to look at him, my insides making a slow, sickening turn.

"I wrote right away to tell you I was alive, but that I would be delayed. My hands were badly burned trying to put out the fire." He held one of them out for me to see. It looked misshapen, the new skin shiny and pink, stretched tightly over his bones. I lifted it and kissed it, letting my tears fall on his mangled fingers.

"Your letter never came. I thought I'd never see you again."

"It took time for my burns and frostbite to heal. I couldn't do any work until they did. After that, I needed to find a job so I'd have money to get here. I needed to start all over again and earn enough to buy land and to support us."

I struggled to comprehend what he was saying. Hendrik was here! But how could he be? He had drowned when the *Phoenix* sank. And yet he hadn't! I still felt so dizzy that I thought I surely must be dreaming. I touched his face again to reassure myself that he was real.

"Geesje, all of my money burned up with the ship. But that wasn't the worst of it. Watching all those people die . . ."

His voice choked, and he covered his eyes as he began to weep. I held him close, letting him cry. "That must have been so horrifying for you." And yet he had survived. He was here! I was holding Hendrik in my arms.

"I can't describe what it was like. . . . A scene from hell! It was only by the grace of God that I lived when all the others didn't. . . . So many men and women, wonderful people who I had grown to know and love! Little children!"

I could see how deeply the experience had scarred his soul along with his hands. Maybe telling me about it would help release some of his pain. "Tell me, Hendrik. Take me there so I can share the burden of what you went through."

His story slowly emerged, and with it, his enormous pain and horror as he relived that night. "We encountered two terrible storms along the way, with winds and waves that beat against our ship, tossing us like driftwood. Conditions were so bad that the ship's captain took a terrible fall on the heaving deck and shattered his knee. There were moments when we all believed we would die. I huddled below deck with the other Netherlanders, praying and begging God for mercy. And He answered our prayers. We found shelter on the leeward side of an island, where we waited until the storm blew itself out. Two days later when it did, we pressed on.

"Geesje, I thought the worst was over. I thought surely God wouldn't punish us any more than He already had after we'd endured those two storms and such paralyzing fear. The women and children had been so terrified. All of us had been, even the crew. And it seemed, at first, that God had heard our pleas. After crossing the huge Atlantic Ocean and sailing through the Great Lakes, traveling thousands of miles, we were nearly there at last." He paused, wiping his tears with his fist. I noticed that Hendrik's hand no longer closed all the way because of his scars.

"Along with our group of immigrants, the ship also carried cargo that needed to be delivered to a port about thirty miles north of Sheboygan, Wisconsin, which was our destination. It took longer than we'd hoped since the lake was still very rough, and we didn't arrive in that port until close to midnight. The crew unloaded the cargo, but since the waves were still bad, the captain decided to wait until they settled down. He let the crew go ashore." He paused, drawing a deep breath as if gathering his strength. "Some of the other survivors said the sailors were drunk when they came back to the ship. If it's true . . . if that's why they foolishly let the ship's boilers overheat, they'll be accountable before God for all those innocent souls."

He rested his cheek against my hair for a long moment until he could go on. When he did, I felt his entire body tense. "I managed to sleep for an hour or so while we were in port, but when the whistle blew to summon the crew back, I woke up. I went up on deck, and even though it was November and the night was very cold, the lake had miraculously calmed and the skies had cleared, and I could see the stars. Millions and millions of them. Geesje, they were so beautiful that I stayed up on deck, overwhelmed by the glory of that sky.

"We set out again, and after a while, it seemed to me that the sound of the ship's engines changed. I had been hearing their familiar thumps and hisses ever since leaving Buffalo, but now they sounded different, somehow. But what did I know? Then I noticed an odd glow on the water just below the rail where I was standing, and I realized that it was flames, coming from the windows of the engine room. The ship's boilers had overheated and caught fire.

"Everything was a blur of frantic activity after that. The engine room was in the center of the ship, and the heat and smoke awakened all the passengers and drove them upstairs. I could hear the little ones crying and screaming, the women praying as the crew got out the fire hoses and started the pumps. I joined a bucket brigade with some of the other passengers but the heat was so intense . . . it was like battling the fires of hell.

"We did our best. We tried . . . I heard someone say that we were only five miles from shore and heading that way. But then the ship's engines burned out and died, leaving us dead in the water. The pumps stopped, too, and the hoses could no longer put out the fire. It raged out of control.

"The crew finally gave the order to abandon ship, but Geesje, there were only two lifeboats—*two*, for more than three hundred passengers! Each boat could hold maybe twenty people at the most, even if they were overloaded." Hendrik paused again, too overcome to continue.

"Until the day I die," he said in a choked voice, "I'll never forget the horrible moment when I realized that all of those families . . .

men and women I had traveled with from Rotterdam, people I had prayed with and grown to know and love . . . they were all going to die! And so was I."

I could feel Hendrik's body shuddering with sobs as I held him tightly. "It wasn't fair!" he cried. "It wasn't right!"

I wept with him, remembering that I had felt the same anger and confusion when my parents had died of malaria, and when Arie and Gerrit's parents had died. And so many, many others. Why had God abandoned us? What possible reason could He give that would explain those senseless deaths? I didn't know. I doubted if I ever would.

"The first-class passengers were given all the seats in the lifeboats," Hendrik said when he could continue. I heard the edge of bitterness in his voice. "Some of the gentlemen gallantly offered their seats to our immigrant women and children. Most did not. One of the American gentlemen who stayed behind worked until the very end to help people climb over the side, clinging to anything that would float. Later, I saw him jump overboard, holding two small Dutch children, trying to save them. . . . None of them survived.

"By now, the roar of the flames was like an inferno. But as the two lifeboats were lowered into the water, I could hear mothers pleading with the first-class passengers to take their children aboard, begging them to have mercy so their little ones could be saved. One woman threw her baby down into the lifeboat, but I never found out what happened to him.

"For those of us left behind, we no longer had any place to go to escape the terrible heat and flames. The fire was arching out from the sides of the ship and meeting above in a tower of flames that must have been two hundred feet high. A piece of flaming debris struck my face and set my hair on fire. I burned my hands trying to put it out. People began leaping overboard into the icy water, parents gripping their children, even though few of us knew how to swim. Our choice was to die in the fire or drown in the lake. There was no alternative. So I jumped.

"The shock of that frigid water sucked the breath from me. When I recovered, the horror still hadn't ended. The surface of the water all around me was crowded with people, coughing and crying and screaming, praying and begging for mercy, all of us searching for a piece of debris to hold on to, trying to stay afloat. The worst were the cries of the children. . . . So many, many children!

"Some people tried to grab the lifeboats as they floated near us, and I'll never forget . . . I'll never forget how the people in those boats beat at those poor souls' hands with the oars to drive them away, refusing to help them stay afloat for fear the lifeboat would capsize. When they couldn't hang on any longer, their fingers smashed by the blows, they fell away beneath the water. . . . Dear God . . . How could people be so cruel? I'll never understand it. . . . Never!

"I tried to help as many people as I could, finding pieces of debris to help keep them afloat, telling them that they would make it, that help was surely on the way. But those who survived the flames couldn't survive the cold. Our clothing was soaked and the icy water chilled all the way to our bones. Little by little the voices and cries and prayers all around me dwindled away into silence."

Hendrik paused again, and I was aware of the sound of birdsong and cawing crows filling the forest. The wind rustled through the leaves of the trees, high above us like whispers. I wondered if Hendrik heard any of it—or if he was still hearing the screams.

"Somehow, I survived," he said when he could speak. "I clung to a piece of wreckage I had found and pulled as much of my body as I could onto that scrap of debris, out of the freezing water. Gradually the glow of the flames began to die down as the ship burned to the water line. I drifted away from the ship, and I could see the beautiful night sky again, the millions of stars. The surface of the water was littered with bodies and debris, and in the eerie quiet I did my best to pray and confess Jesus as my Savior as I prepared to die. The flesh had been burned from my hands and the pain was so intense, I didn't know how much longer I could hold on.

"I looked up at the star-filled heavens and thought of you,

Geesje. If I was going to die—and I feared that I would—then I wanted my last thoughts to be of you. I imagined holding you in my arms the way I'm holding you now. I pictured how happy we would be when we could be together at last. My will to survive was gradually failing, and it would have been so easy to close my eyes and fall asleep and wake up in heaven. . . .

"I think I did close my eyes—I don't know for how long—but I opened them again when I thought I heard a sound like oars dipping in and out of the water. Were the lifeboats finally returning from shore to rescue us? Then, in the distance, I heard the sound that a ship's boilers make when running under a full head of steam. I thought I was imagining these things, but when I gazed in the direction of the sound, I saw the lights of an approaching ship. Then a second ship. I waited until they drew nearer, then began waving my arm, calling for help. I didn't know if they would be able to hear my voice or not above the sound of the engines on that vast lake. But they sent out crews in lifeboats, and they found me.

"They told me later that I was one of only forty-three people who had survived—forty in the lifeboats and only three of us among the wreckage. I was treated for severe burns and for frostbite from the cold water. I had inhaled a lot of smoke and lake water, and had lost everything I owned—but I was alive. . . . And now I'm here."

Hendrik was really here! When he finished telling his story, I held him tightly, at a loss for words after hearing the horror he had endured. "We're together now," I told him. "We'll never be separated again."

"Yes." The word sounded like a sigh of relief.

I had been completely unaware of Arie and Gerrit standing beside us, watching and listening all this time, until I heard Arie's voice asking, "Mama, what's wrong? Don't cry, Mama." I released Hendrik and beckoned to them, and as they climbed onto my lap, all of the color seemed to drain from Hendrik's face.

"Are . . . are these your children, Geesje? You promised you would wait for me."

177

"No, my darling, no. They were orphaned and I adopted them. But . . ." I couldn't tell him the truth. I couldn't tell him that I had foolishly married Maarten. I felt the panic a trapped animal must feel as it fights to free itself from the snare. I battled to quell that panic, to hide my distress from Hendrik. He and I would run away together. We would leave before Maarten returned and go someplace else to live—and never come back.

But what about Maarten? I knew the devastating grief of losing someone I loved. I remembered how I had suffered when I thought Hendrik was dead. I couldn't put Maarten through that. Not after everything he'd done for me. But what other choice did I have? I wanted to spend the rest of my life with Hendrik. I thought of the impossible choice Hendrik had faced—dying in the flames or drowning in the frigid water—and like him, I didn't know which way to leap.

"Geesje, what's wrong? Please tell me what's wrong."

"Let's go," I said, scrambling to my feet. I lifted Gerrit in my arms. "I hate it here in this place. Let's leave together, right now, and never look back."

Hendrik stood as well, and I saw him gaze all around in confusion as I hurried toward the cabin door. "Leave? You mean, today? I'll do whatever you want, Geesje, but I have very little money. . . . How would we live? Where would we go?"

I remembered my longing to return to Leiden, but I could never ask Hendrik to make that perilous return voyage. Not after what he'd endured to get to America. And not when it had been Maarten who had earned the money for my passage home. I would stay in Michigan, then. Or maybe go back east somewhere. "I have a little money," I told Hendrik. I knew where Maarten kept his earnings. I would borrow some from him. We would pay him back when we could.

Hendrik followed me into the dark, damp-smelling cabin. "What about these children?" he asked.

I would leave them with someone . . . maybe Widow Van den Bosch. But how could I abandon Arie and Gerrit and leave them motherless for a second time? Yet it would break Maarten's heart if I took them with me. He loved the boys as if they were his own. I didn't know what to do.

I set Gerrit down on the cabin's dirt floor and blindly rummaged through my things, trying to decide what to pack. My shocked mind was unable to think clearly. My instincts screamed at me to run, to leave everything behind and disappear with Hendrik before Maarten arrived home, so that's what I decided to do.

"Where are your parents, Geesje?" Hendrik was looking all around the cabin as his eyes adjusted to the dim light.

"They died several months ago. Of malaria."

"Geesje, I'm so sorry. Your parents were wonderful people and—"

"Should I pack food?" Hendrik had said he had no money. I didn't wait for his reply, just grabbed an empty sack and blindly stuffed supplies into it. Gerrit crawled across the floor toward me, crying pitifully, upset by my distracted confusion.

"You've been living here alone all this time?" Hendrik asked. "With these two children?"

I didn't answer him. I couldn't tell him. When I'd married Maarten I had betrayed the only man I would ever love. Yet if I ran away with Hendrik, I would betray my marriage vows—vows I had made to God as well as to Maarten. I had found contentment with Maarten these past months, but I didn't love him. I probably never would. The simplest thing would be to leave without any explanation at all. Give Arie and Gerrit to Widow Van den Bosch, letting her think I would return shortly, and simply disappear with Hendrik. We could run away, and Maarten would never know what had happened to me. Let him think the woods had devoured me. But it would mean walking away from God. Committing adultery. Living a life of sin. At that moment, I didn't care. Hendrik was alive! He was here! I continued my hurried packing, desperate to escape with him.

Then I remembered that I was expecting Maarten's child.

I remembered the look of joy on Maarten's face last night when

I'd told him the news. How he'd held me and tenderly kissed me this morning before he left. How he'd gone off to work with a smile on his face. I wished I had never told him. He would be inconsolable. And I would suffer from guilt for the rest of my life every time I looked at Maarten's child.

I felt so nauseated I thought I would be sick. Yet Hendrik was alive! Alive! I hadn't lost him after all. He loved me and I loved him, and now we could be together for the rest of our lives.

I was so lost in my tangled thoughts that I no longer heard Gerrit crying, or noticed that Arie had begun to cry, too. I didn't hear Hendrik calling my name until he gripped my shoulders and turned me around and said, "Geesje! What's wrong? Please tell me what's wrong!"

"Nothing . . . I-I need to get ready to go. We need to go!"

"Go where? Isn't this kolonie the place where we planned to live? Can't we get married and live in this cabin? I'll have to work for someone else until I can earn enough money to buy land of our own, but at least we'll finally be together."

I shook my head, trying to erase the future he was drawing. We couldn't live here. I could never divorce Maarten. The people in our community lived their lives according to the Bible, and they would never condone a divorce. Neither would God. Our only hope was to run away together. To simply disappear. Hendrik was everything to me, my whole world, and now that I had him back, I had everything I would ever need.

"What shall it profit a man, if he shall gain the whole world, and lose his own soul?"

The words came to mind, unbidden. I couldn't breathe.

"Geesje, please answer me. Tell me what's wrong. Don't you love me anymore?"

His question shattered my heart, like a rock thrown through a glass window. I flung myself into his arms, nearly knocking him off his feet as I held on to him with all my strength. "Yes, Hendrik, yes! I love you, I love you! I could never love anyone but you! Please take me away from here! Please! Let's leave right now."

"But . . . what's the hurry? I don't understand. I'm not going anywhere until you tell me what's going on, why you want to leave."

And so I told him. I told him what I had done, the mistake I had made out of grief, anger at God, and a selfish desire to return home to the Netherlands. As the truth spilled out along with my tears, I clung to Hendrik and explained that my parents had died and I was all alone. That his last letter had never arrived. That I believed he was dead. Marrying Maarten had been my only choice once I made up my mind to go home to the Netherlands.

Hendrik freed himself from my grip and held me at arms' length. I watched as he absorbed the truth, and something inside him seemed to die before my eyes. He may have survived the fiery shipwreck and icy water, but the truth of what I'd done destroyed something in his heart that day. "Now do you understand why we have to run?" I asked. "Please, Hendrik. Let's just go. We can disappear."

It took an eternity for him to reply. "I'm not a thief," he said, slowly shaking his head. "I won't steal something that doesn't belong to me. And I can't rob Maarten, of all people."

"But I don't love him. I love you, don't you see? And Maarten knows the truth. He knows I never would have married him if I'd known you were still alive. He won't force me to stay."

"That may be true, but we owe it to him to wait and give him an explanation. You can't just vanish, Geesje. He'll never give up searching for you. I know I wouldn't."

"No," I begged. "No, please! Let's run away!"

I was unable to convince him. Hendrik proved more honorable than me. He waited alone outside our cabin all afternoon until Maarten returned. I stayed inside with the children, unwilling to see Maarten's face when he found Hendrik sitting on a log in the little clearing in front of our house. I could easily imagine his shock and dismay. I stayed inside, sick with dread, listening to the mumble of their voices as they talked. Neither of them argued or shouted. They never even raised their voices. How could the happiest day

181

of my life—the day I learned that Hendrik was alive—also be one of the worst days of my life?

In the end, neither Maarten nor Hendrik would choose to hurt the other man by claiming me. Nor would either one offer to surrender me to the other. "The decision is yours alone to make, Geesje," Maarten told me. "You have to decide what you want to do, who you want to be with." They didn't try to pressure or persuade me. And so I was forced to choose between the two of them.

If I ran away with Hendrik, carrying Maarten's child, I would live with the sin and guilt of adultery for the rest of my life. I couldn't deliberately disobey God and then ask for His forgiveness. But if I gave up Hendrik and kept my vows to Maarten, sacrificing the man I loved, I would live with regret and resentment and sorrow every day of my marriage.

"The decision is yours alone to make, Geesje."

Impossible. I had no idea what to do.

HOLLAND, MICHIGAN
1897

I stop writing and drop my pencil as if it's on fire. I close the notebook and stuff it into my desk, remembering the mistakes I made, the tragic choices I faced, and the people I hurt in the process. The memories cause me immeasurable pain. Even now. Even after all these years.

CHAPTER 20

Geesje

I'm still sitting at my desk when Derk arrives at my front door. He must have just come home from work because he hasn't bathed, and he's still wearing his sweaty work clothes. He's worried about something, I can tell. I stand and offer him a drink of lemonade and some cookies, but he refuses both, telling me instead about Anna, the woman he met at the hotel.

"She's getting married to a man she doesn't love, and she asked for my advice. I didn't know what to tell her. She needs more help than I can give her, Tante Geesje. Would you be willing to talk to her? I'm afraid she's making a terrible mistake."

I sit down in my chair again. I doubt if I'm the right person to offer advice about marriage. Derk hasn't read how Hendrik walked out of the woods one day like a ghost and turned my plans and my life upside down. "Tell me about her," I say, stalling for time. "What is she like?"

183

"Very pretty—some might even say beautiful. I think I already mentioned that I mistook her for your granddaughter, Elizabeth, the first time I saw her. But she's a more sophisticated version of Elizabeth. Anna comes from a wealthy Chicago family, and so the way she talks and walks and all of her manners are very proper and . . . what's the word . . . ?"

"Genteel?"

"Yes, that's it. She's way out of reach of us ordinary folks." As Derk talks about her, his eyes dance, his cheeks flush. He is enamored with her. It reminds me of the way Maarten used to react when I would deliberately tease him by parading in and out of Papa's print shop in Arnhem. I hope this Anna isn't toying with Derk the same way I used to toy with Maarten.

"Yet I feel very sorry for her," Derk continues. "The only reason she's marrying this rich man is because her father is in some sort of financial trouble, and she wants to help him. He needs the boyfriend's money to bail him out."

"Oh, dear. That's not a very good start to a lifelong commitment." I should know. I'm ashamed when I recall my selfish motives for marrying Maarten.

"Anna also has a lot of questions about the Bible. The church her family attends is very formal from the sounds of it, but lately she has been drawn to a gospel-preaching church, and the differences confuse her. She asked me what it means to gain the whole world and lose your soul."

The verse he quotes sends a stab of pain to my heart. I had recalled that verse earlier when I was writing my story. I press my fist to my chest to ease the tightness, hoping Derk won't notice my distress.

"Don't be surprised if Anna asks you about your faith as well as about marriage. She's just starting to pray and read her Bible and things like that, but she doesn't know much about it. And she says there's no one back home in Chicago she can ask."

"How fortunate for her that she met you this summer."

Derk grows flustered. His blush deepens. "Um . . . well . . . as I said, she has a lot of questions. And she knows I'm studying to be a minister. Most of all, she's wondering if she's making a mistake by marrying a man she doesn't love. She even asked me if it was a sin. I wasn't sure whether I gave her the right answer or not, so I was hoping you could advise her."

"Because I married a man I didn't love?"

"Well . . . yes."

I lean back in my chair, at a loss. What would I tell this woman? What words of advice would I have given myself the day I stood at the altar in the log church and married Maarten, a man I didn't love? When I don't respond, Derk says, "May I bring her here to talk with you, Tante Geesje?"

He wants so much for me to meet her, yet his admiration for me is misplaced. I'm not the saint he believes me to be. Before his lady-friend comes, I need to finish writing my story so Derk can read what I've done, the terrible decision I was forced to make. He needs to know what a selfish woman I really am, the people I've hurt, the lives I've injured. The pain in my chest deepens when I remember the even bigger mess I made of things years later, when my daughter told me she'd fallen in love. That weight of sorrow waxes and wanes with time, but it never goes completely away. Nay, I'm not qualified to advise anyone about marriage.

"Ya, I'll talk with her, dear," I finally say. "But I need to finish writing the next part of my story, first. I want you to read it before you bring your lady-friend here."

"I'm very eager to read it. I'll do so right now, if you have more pages for me. I can't imagine what it must have been like to lose the man you loved. I hope you eventually found happiness with Maarten." He gives me an impish half-smile and adds, "I already know that you never moved back to the Netherlands or else you wouldn't be here. But I'm curious to read the rest of your story and see why you changed your mind and decided to stay."

"I know you are. But it's easier for me to write about it than to talk about it. Come back tomorrow, and I promise I'll have more for you to read." Derk isn't going to want me to meet his friend after he reads about the poor decisions I made. But I don't tell him that. "We'll settle on a time when I can meet your friend after you read my story. Go home and get some rest, Derk. You look tired."

"I am. I had a long day today. When the weather is this nice, everyone wants to go out on the water. You know how much I love to sail, but all that wind and fresh air and wrestling with sails tires me out."

"We'll talk again tomorrow, dear."

I don't rise from my chair as he bends to kiss my forehead before leaving. It is suppertime, and I have some ripe tomatoes in my garden that I was going to pick and eat, but I'm not hungry. I remain seated, stewing over my past, sifting through the memories until the pain in my chest gradually goes away. Would I make the same choices today that I made back then? Or have I grown wiser with the years? Do I have the right to advise this rich young woman?

I'm still sitting at my desk, doing nothing, when Derk bursts through my front door for a second time, startling me. I was so deep in thought I didn't hear him coming. His distress is written all over him, plain to see. His impish grin is gone, his body is tense, and his hair is rumpled as if he's been running his sweaty hands through it. He still hasn't bathed or changed out of his work clothes. "Derk, honey? What's wrong?"

"I got a letter from Caroline. Read it." He thrusts the pages at me, and I see that his hand is trembling slightly.

"Is Caroline the woman you hoped to marry?"

He nods and remains standing while I read the letter.

Dear Derk,

The longer we've been apart, the unhappier I've been. All of the things I once found pleasure in are no longer the same because something is missing—like a gourmet dish with a forgotten ingredient. It has taken me all these months to realize that what's missing is you. I saw a sailboat gliding across Black Lake the other day, and for a moment I felt happy inside when I imagined it was you and that you were coming to take me sailing the way you used to do. Then I

*remembered that you weren't coming back, that I'd sent you
away, and tears came to my eyes.*

*I miss you, Derk. I miss your smile, the way you make me
laugh out loud, the way you always made me feel pretty and
treasured. My life isn't the same without you. I think I may
have made a huge mistake when I ended our relationship. And
so if you can forgive me—and if you haven't found someone
else by now—I would like to know if we can try again.*

I stop reading and look up at Derk in alarm. "Oh my. This is a
surprising turn of events."

"Keep reading," he says. I turn to the second page.

*I still can't picture myself being married to a minister, and
I hate the thought of constantly shoving my own needs aside
to share you with a demanding congregation, but I don't
want to lose you, either. So I've thought of a compromise that
might work for both of us. What if you found a position as a
religion teacher at the academy or at the college? Or maybe
you could work as a chaplain there. The students could be
your congregation and you would still be in the ministry, but
there wouldn't be as many demands on your time as there
would be as a full-time pastor of a church.*

*I want you back in my life, darling Derk. I'm convinced
that together we can make this relationship work. If you are
as sorry as I am that we're no longer together, and if you
would like to give our love another chance, please come
to my house on Wednesday night, and we can figure out a
compromise. I know I may not have said it often enough,
but I do love you. I realize that now. And I'm sorry that I
turned down your marriage proposal. I only hope that this
letter hasn't come too late.*

With love,

Caroline

I let my hands fall to my lap, still holding the letter. I exhale. I've been holding my breath while I've been reading without realizing it. I look up at poor Derk and ask, "What are you going to do?"

"I don't know . . . I don't know what to do."

It occurs to me that he does know what he should do, deep in his soul—just as I had known, deep down, whether I should stay married to Maarten or leave him to run away with Hendrik. Back then I wasn't listening to that still, small voice and neither is Derk.

"What do you think I should do, Tante Geesje?"

I want to ask him why he isn't turning cartwheels on the front lawn at the idea of having a second chance with the woman he loves. Why he isn't racing to her house right now if her offer of a compromise seemed right to him, unwilling to wait a moment longer to see her. Instead, he's pacing in my front room, biting his thumbnail, his brow furrowed. And he's asking my advice instead of seeking God's—the same mistake I made. But Derk isn't ready to hear all of that just now.

"Her letter must have come as a great shock to you," I say. But not nearly as shocking as seeing Hendrik walk out of the woods like a ghost. "You had written 'the end' to the possibility of marrying Caroline and buried all your hopes and dreams. Give yourself time to think before you resurrect them from the grave."

"I was in love with Caroline. And you're right, it felt like a death to me when she left me. Now I have a chance to have her back, to be with the woman I love. She's willing to compromise . . . but I just don't know."

"Are you interested in teaching or becoming a chaplain, as she suggests?"

"I don't know. It's a new idea that I haven't thought much about."

"Why don't you talk with one of your religion teachers or the college chaplain about the work they do. See if it resonates with you. I'm concerned that if you give up the ministry before knowing what the new job entails, you might resent Caroline in the future because of it."

"I wouldn't be giving up the ministry entirely. Just taking a less demanding position."

I don't reply. He hasn't heard me. He's trying to make Caroline's solution fit into the hole in his heart, like squeezing the wrong puzzle piece into the place where you want it to fit in order to complete the picture. Again, I want to ask him why he isn't dancing for joy if this compromise is the perfect solution for them.

"Caroline said that if I wanted to patch things up, I should come over to her house Wednesday evening—and that's what I plan to do. But before I see her, I'd like to know what you think I should do, Tante Geesje. Your opinion matters to me."

"My dear, I'm so flattered. But I've never met Caroline. I'm not in a position to judge whether or not she's the right wife for you. There are some decisions in life that only you can make, and I believe this is one of them. But I have two pieces of advice for you before you see Caroline, besides talking with the chaplain. First, ask your friend Anna at the hotel what she thinks you should do. Isn't she facing a similar dilemma and trying to repair a broken engagement? Perhaps she'll see a side to this decision that an old woman like me doesn't see."

Derk smiles faintly for the first time since showing me Caroline's letter. "That's a great idea. I'll talk to her tomorrow."

It's clear that he's smitten with Anna. I'm hoping he'll notice that some of his love for Caroline has faded, and that other women can attract and fascinate him, even if a wealthy woman like Anna is way out of reach for a small-town preacher like Derk. In his heart, he knows it, too.

"What's the second thing?" he asks.

Derk won't like this idea as much as the first. "Make sure you talk over your decision with God before you decide if you still want to marry Caroline."

"Of course, of course. I pray about all my decisions. You taught me that." But Derk isn't smiling anymore.

"There have been times in my life, Derk, when I haven't wanted to pray about a decision because I already knew what God would

189

say about it—and I didn't like His answer. And there have been other times when God didn't give me a clear answer to the question I asked."

"That happens to me, too. Why do you think that is?"

"Well . . . I've thought about it a lot, and I've decided that it's because He knows our mind is already made up. We won't obey Him if He does answer. And then our deliberate disobedience will cause a rift in our relationship with Him. If you know you're doing something wrong, it often seems easier to keep doing it than to swallow your pride and turn back to God."

"If marrying Caroline turns out to be a mistake, I can't divorce her. And my friend Anna can't divorce her husband, either, if it's the wrong decision."

"If my own story teaches you nothing else, Derk, I hope it shows you the importance of not making important decisions in haste."

"Were you unhappy with Maarten?"

"Come back tomorrow, and you can finish reading my story." I hand back the letter from Caroline.

"Thanks. I'll do that. See you tomorrow, Tante Geesje." He walks out of my door with heavy steps, shoulders slumped. I want to tell him to go home and look in a mirror. A man who has just been given a second chance with the woman he loves shouldn't look so dejected.

CHAPTER 21

Anna

HOTEL OTTAWA
1897

I don't know what it is about this hotel room or this bed that causes me to have such strange dreams, but I had another one last night. It wasn't exactly a nightmare, but it had the power of one. I awoke from it trembling and upset, and I had to stand at the window for a while and gaze down at the moon's reflection on the lake until my heart slowed and I could breathe again. In my dream, I stood in my familiar bedroom back home in Chicago. Everything was exactly as it has always been for as long as I can remember. I saw my canopied mahogany bed and mirrored dresser, the blue-and-yellow flowered wallpaper, the creamy silk draperies on the window that overlooks our back garden. I was crying inconsolably and calling for my mama—yet she was right there! Mother had tears in her eyes as she tried to take me into her arms and console me, but I kept pushing her away, sobbing, "Mama! Mama!" as if my heart would break.

Some people attach a great deal of meaning to dreams and what they might signify. One girl I knew at the ladies' school I attended paid a gypsy woman to decipher her dreams and to read her palm and tell her the future. But it isn't hard to figure out where my dream originated. I am still upset and angry at Mother for violating my privacy. I'm hesitant to fully trust her, yet I miss the easy companionship we once shared. Instead of turning to her, I've been confiding in Derk—a virtual stranger—telling him things that I've never shared with Mother.

I need to shake the unsettling feeling that the dream leaves behind, so I decide to spend the morning with Mother, walking the hotel grounds and sitting in canvas chairs on the beach, showing her all the lovely little places I've discovered. After eating lunch together, I join her on the porch where she enjoys sitting, and we watch the boats sailing on the lake. We chat with Mrs. Stevens and the other friends she has made during our stay. I play a game of croquet on the lawn with three of their young daughters. The day seems to pass very slowly as I wait to speak with Derk again.

When it's time to meet with him, I quietly slip away from the gathering on the porch and walk down to the bench near the lake. I won't stay long—I won't even sit down. I'll just see if Derk has made any arrangements for me to meet his aunt. I'm still not sure it's a good idea to talk to a stranger about love and marriage, especially since I've already made up my mind to marry William. But to avoid my growing attraction for Derk, perhaps it's better if I talk with his aunt from now on instead of with him. I still have many questions about the Bible that I would like her to answer.

Derk is already sitting on the bench when I arrive. My heart betrays me by speeding up. I remain standing, planning to keep the conversation short. "Hello, Derk."

"Hi. I was worried that you couldn't get away." He has no smile for me today. He looks upset about something. Before I can ask what it is, he says, "Do you have a minute? I could use your advice today."

"Mine?"

"Yes. Please, have a seat."

My knees do feel strangely weak, so I sit down on the bench, careful to leave a respectable space between us. I can't imagine why Derk would need my advice, especially since he knows what an embarrassingly confused and indecisive person I am. "What's wrong?" I ask.

"When I got home from work yesterday, there was a letter waiting for me from Caroline."

"The woman you wanted to marry?"

He nods. He looks serious today. I miss his warm smile. "She said she misses me. That she may have made a mistake in refusing my marriage proposal. She wants to know if I'll give her a second chance."

"Just like William and me," I mumble.

"Yes, I thought of that."

"But didn't Caroline say she didn't want to marry a minister? Has she changed her mind?"

"She seems to be softening a little when it comes to that. She asked if I would be willing to compromise, and maybe take a position as a religion teacher or work as a chaplain at the college. She said the students could be my congregation and there wouldn't be as many demands on my time."

"Are you going to do it?"

"I don't know."

"Then I'll ask you the same question you asked me about William. Do you love her?"

He exhales as if he's been holding his breath for days. "I don't know that, either. I was convinced that I was madly in love with her before she turned down my proposal—to the point of distraction, in fact. I didn't think I could ever love anyone as much as her. But now I feel . . . wary. I don't know if it's because she hurt me so much or if my love for her has faded a little."

"Maybe once you see her again it will help you decide."

"Or maybe it will make things worse. She's beautiful and charming and a little mysterious, and when I'm with her I can't seem to think straight. I want to decide with my head, not just my heart. She's offering to compromise, and I suppose being a chaplain would be pretty much the same thing as being a church pastor . . ."

I listen patiently as Derk thinks out loud, fighting a ridiculous prickle of jealousy as I hear him talk about Caroline. But I'm glad to be able to repay him for all the time he spent listening to me and answering my questions. I just wish I knew what to say to help him.

"It's hard to know if Caroline's offer is a test of my commitment to God or if it's His way of steering me in a different direction than where I've been headed. It's like when I'm sailing and the wind suddenly changes. I have to adjust the sails if I want to stay on course . . . or else go with the wind and maybe find a new and better destination." He sighs again. "What do you think I should do, Anna?"

His direct question surprises me. The truth is, Caroline seems very selfish to me for making demands on Derk's career. I don't think he should marry her. But I hesitate to give my opinion since I'm very confused where love and marriage are concerned. And William has proven to be just as selfish, yet I'm marrying him.

"It seems to me," I reply carefully, "that your situation is quite different from mine now that Caroline has suggested a compromise. William was never willing to do that. I'll have to concede to his wishes and give up my own desires when I marry him. He'll be happy and I'll . . . I'll make the best of it, I suppose, for my parents' sake. But in a compromise, both people need to sacrifice something for the sake of the other person, and hopefully they'll both be happy with the outcome in the end. You're giving up being a pastor, but I'm not sure what exactly Caroline will be giving up."

"Well . . . she . . . um . . ." He scratches his chin. Runs his hand through his hair. "I see your point. . . . So you don't think I should do it?"

"I didn't say that. I just don't think her compromise is a very fair one unless you're happy with the idea of teaching or being a chaplain. To tell you the truth, I'm not even sure what a chaplain is or does." I laugh a little as I confess my ignorance and finally—finally—Derk manages a smile in return.

"I don't either, Anna. Tante Geesje suggested I talk to the chaplain at Hope College before I decide."

"That's very good advice. When do you need to give Caroline an answer?"

"She invited me to her house on Wednesday night to talk."

"Will she try to pressure you?"

"She can be very persuasive," he says with a crooked grin. "In the past, I was so in love with her that I couldn't say no to her. She seemed very surprised when I finally did and I refused to give up the ministry. She's going to want an answer on Wednesday night, and if I don't have one, I'm afraid she'll accuse me of stalling in order to hurt her and get even."

Manipulative. That was the word that came to mind to describe this Caroline. I don't dare say so to Derk since I've never met her. But I've met girls like her when I was in school, girls who used their beauty or a false air of mystery to toy with members of the opposite sex, just for fun, and then break their hearts. "Did Caroline say what made her change her mind?" I ask. "You know why I changed mine."

"She said she missed me. That her life wasn't the same without me. She said she loves me."

"I can't argue with any of those reasons. But since you aren't in a rush to get married, I think you should take your time deciding. I would still be dithering over whether or not to marry William if I hadn't overheard my father talking about his financial situation."

"I'm very sad for you, Anna. You deserve a loving husband and a happy marriage."

"You don't need to feel sorry for me. Many marriages in our social circle are matters of convenience, not love. I'll find a charitable cause to champion, one that William approves of, and I'll throw myself into my work. That's what Chicago's other grand matrons do."

I haven't been paying attention to the people who have been

strolling past us on the walkway while we've talked, but someone suddenly halts beside the bench, casting a shadow over us. I look up—and it's my mother!

"Anna. What do you think you're doing?" I know by the icy tone in her voice that she is furious, even though she speaks calmly and quietly. Derk leaps to his feet as if he's done something wrong, making the situation worse. Mother appraises him from head to toe, taking in his tanned skin, his sweaty work clothes, his rumpled hair. I can tell by the way she lifts her chin and turns away that she has judged him in an instant and found him lacking—and her dismissal enrages me. I scramble to my feet, longing to defend him. She can't see his kind heart, his gentle nature, his eagerness to obey God.

"Mother, I'd like you to meet Derk . . ." I hesitate, embarrassed that I cannot recall his last name. He comes to my rescue.

"Vander Veen. Derk Vander Veen, ma'am."

"Derk, this is my mother, Mrs. Arthur Nicholson."

"How do you do," Derk says.

Mother nods ever so slightly. She says nothing. He is beneath her notice. She turns her stern gaze on me. "Is this what you've been up to when you've gone wandering off by yourself?"

"What? . . . No, I—" I start to deny it but realize I would be lying. I *have* been wandering off to see Derk.

"Is he the reason you wanted to stay longer?" she demands.

Again, I stumble for a reply, unwilling to lie. "It's not what you think, Mother. Derk is studying to be a minister. He has been kind enough to answer some of my questions about the Bible."

"Without a chaperone present? You would risk ruining your chances for a good life with William for this boy? I thought I could trust you, Anna."

"And I thought I could trust you! But instead, you invaded my privacy and read my diary, and now you're following me around to spy on me? Derk and I weren't doing anything wrong. Tell her, Derk." I hate throwing him into this, but I'm confident he can handle my mother.

"Ma'am, this is all a big misunderstanding," he says gently. "She's telling you the truth. We have simply been talking as friends."

Mother doesn't look at Derk, doesn't acknowledge him, addressing all her words to me. "Respectable young ladies know better than to have friends of the opposite sex. It couldn't possibly have escaped your awareness, Anna, how improper such a friendship is. And with an employee of this hotel, no less. I'll see that you are fired immediately, young man. Come, Anna."

I grab her arm to keep her from leaving. "Don't do that, Mother. It isn't his fault. It's mine. I kept asking him questions, and he has been kind enough to take time out of his busy day to answer them."

"I'll bet he has. What questions?"

"I told you. About religion and faith. I've been reading the Bible, and I don't always understand what Jesus means when He says certain things. Derk is studying to be a minister—" I begin to flounder in my panicked efforts to explain, and Derk comes to my rescue again.

"Ma'am, we've always talked right out here in the open, the way we were when you found us. Anna is—"

"So, it's 'Anna' now, is it? I'm sure the hotel management explained the impropriety of calling guests by their given names."

"Yes, ma'am, they did. But Anna—I mean, Miss Nicholson—asked me to call her—"

"I've heard quite enough. Come, Anna."

"No, Mother. I won't."

Her face registers shock, as if I've said a curse word. "Anna!"

"I've never defied you in my life, but I'm doing it this time. I won't let you treat Derk this way. He has done nothing wrong, and neither have I. You need to sit down and listen to me."

"I will not discuss this any further out here." Mother tries again to leave, but I refuse to let her go, holding tightly to her arm and digging in my heels. Derk looks embarrassed and uneasy, as if he'd rather be anywhere else than here. I admire him for not taking the easy way out and slinking off, leaving me alone with my irate mother. But I don't want him going home thinking he won't have a job to return to.

"Sit down, Mother. I need to say what I have to say." I wait for her to sit. "You read my diary. You know I've had questions. And as I said, Derk is studying to become a minister. If he and I were going to sneak around and do something improper, we wouldn't be sitting out here in the open, would we?" My mother owed Derk an apology. I would have liked to tell her so, but she has too much pride to admit she was wrong. She would never do such a thing.

"Derk has a girlfriend. Her name is Caroline," I continue. "And I'm engaged to William. The first time Derk and I spoke it was because he mistook me for someone else, a Dutch woman. And so later, when I heard a woman talking in another language that I somehow could understand, I asked him if that language was Dutch. And it was."

Mother lifts her chin, shakes her head. "You're changing the subject."

"I'm not. I'm telling you why Derk and I have been talking. Everything is connected, don't you see? I want to know more about God and figure out who I am and who God wants me to be before I marry William. William forbade me to go back to the castle church where I can find some of those answers, so I turned to Derk. And I also need to know about my past, and why it is that I understand a few words of Dutch, and who I was before you adopted me—"

"You didn't tell me you were adopted," Derk interrupts. "That changes everything."

"Didn't I? I guess I never thought to mention it. My parents adopted me as a newborn."

"I will not sit here in such a public place and have this discussion." Mother starts to rise, but I stop her.

"See? You're changing the subject right now, just like you always do whenever I ask questions about my past. You evade them."

"I certainly do not."

"Can you explain to me how it's possible that I understand a few Dutch phrases?"

Mother's face is pinched with fury, her lips pressed into a tight line, her hands balled into fists on her lap. But she is too much of a lady to release her anger. "I have no idea. Someone from your school spoke it, perhaps. A friend or a teacher. I don't see how it matters."

"You said my parents abandoned me, but you never told me where you found me or how I ended up with you and Father or—"

"You can discuss those things with your father when we get home. Not here, not now. You're trying to create a distraction to steer my attention away from your abominable behavior with this boy. I'm appalled at your lack of judgment, Anna."

"And I'm angry and hurt that you don't believe me. Have I ever lied to you before, Mother?"

"I don't know. Have you?"

I hesitate, remembering that I did lie so I could sneak away to the castle church. If she has read that entry in my diary, she knows. I draw a steadying breath. "I am not lying now. If you want me to marry William, you have to let me stay for another week. You have to let me talk to Derk and his aunt so I won't need to go back to the castle church. There's no one else who can answer my questions."

"Our church has highly qualified ministers."

"It's not the same. They don't talk as though God loves me and considers me His child."

"Now you're being ridiculous."

I don't know how to reply. The discussion has taken so many twists and turns that I've lost track of them all. Mother is adept at redirecting a conversation. In the momentary lull, Derk says, "Ma'am, I don't mean to interfere—"

"Then don't."

I admire Derk for rowing on. "But I just want to say that I've made arrangements for Anna—um, Miss Nicholson—to meet with my aunt Geesje because I know she has a lot of experience and wisdom to offer. She is a fine Christian woman who helped me walk through some very hard places in my life. Geesje has walked through them, too, and I know she would be much better at giving advice than I am. One of the reasons your daughter and I met here today was to try to figure out a time when she and my aunt could meet. Anna is telling you the truth when she says this is the reason that she wants to stay for an extra week."

Mother doesn't reply. I lay my hand on her arm, pleading with her as she rises gracefully to her feet. "Please, Mother. You can't have Derk fired. It isn't fair to him. I don't care if you're angry with me, but he isn't to blame for any of this. He was simply trying to be helpful."

Mother isn't anywhere near as tall as Derk is, but with her straight spine and imperious gaze she seems to be. "Very well. But in the future, Anna, you need to find a more appropriate way to satisfy your religious curiosity. Now, kindly come with me." She turns and glides away, seeing no need to address Derk again or bid him good day.

"I'm so sorry about this," I tell him as I follow her, walking backward away from him.

"Me too," I hear him say. "Me too."

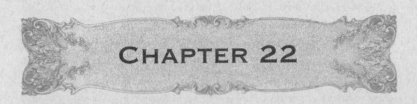

CHAPTER 22

Geesje

It's late in the afternoon and I'm weary as I walk home from the ramshackle jumble of houses in Holland's poorest district. Yet there's satisfaction along with my weariness, knowing I have offered a "cup of cold water," so to speak, in the Savior's name. It's been nearly two years since my friends from church and I began helping Holland's neediest families. Heaven knows I understand what it's like to be poor and cold and hungry. Our town has four furniture factories now, not to mention the basket factory and several other new industries that have sprung up, so the number of laborers and their families who have moved into town has also multiplied. My friends and I do what we can to help—collecting clothes and warm bedding and household items, delivering food, comforting the sick, sitting with those who ask us to pray with them.

I arrive home too tired to cook a big meal for myself. Besides, it's too hot. I'm mixing flour and eggs to make pannenkoeken for my supper when Derk comes through my door, shoulders slumped, head hanging. He looks so pitiful that I pull him into my arms as I did when he was a child and hug him tightly. "Oh, my dear boy! What happened? Tell me what's wrong."

"Do I really look that bad?" he asks, trying to smile.

"Yes. That invisible load on your shoulders looks awfully heavy. I'd love to help you with it if I can."

He flops onto a kitchen chair, his long legs sprawled across the tiny room. "Well, I've had Caroline on my mind all day . . . and then right after work I met with my friend Anna—I mean, Miss Nicholson—to ask her what she thinks I should do." He pauses and heaves an enormous sigh. "I don't think she'll be coming into town to talk with you, Tante Geesje. And she probably won't be able to talk with me ever again, either. Her mother found us sitting on a bench together this afternoon and completely misunderstood. She said it wasn't proper for us to be talking without a chaperone or for a lady of Anna's stature to speak with a lowly hotel employee like me. She threatened to report me to my boss. I may not have a job to return to tomorrow."

"Oh, dear. I'm so sorry. No wonder you look so forlorn."

"Anna did her best to stand up for me—and for herself. But her mother is . . . I mean, her whole way of life is . . ." He shakes his head. "It's so different from ours."

"And intriguing, I'm sure."

"Anna is such a complex woman. She has everything a person could ever want, but her life isn't her own—you know what I mean? I get to decide if I want to marry Caroline or not, or be a minister or a teacher or a chaplain, but Anna's choices are so few. She feels as though she has to marry this rich man for her family's sake, even though she doesn't love him. And there's still a mystery about who she really is that she hasn't solved yet. It turns out that she knows a few phrases in Dutch, of all things. And she has no idea how she ever learned them. I thought maybe she had a Dutch nanny or a servant when she was young, but she told me today that she was adopted, so now I'm wondering . . ." He trails off, waving his hand as if erasing a chalkboard. "I guess I'll never know the answer to that riddle. I doubt if I'll ever see her again."

I stand beside his chair and rub the spot between his two shoulder blades to comfort him, wishing I could rub strength back into him. But maybe it's for the best that their friendship has ended. They come from two different worlds, and Anna will soon return to her life in Chicago. "And Caroline?" I ask. "Have you decided how you'll answer her?"

"That's what Anna and I were talking about today before we were interrupted. I asked her what she thought I should do. She said I shouldn't give Caroline an answer right away. She liked your idea of talking to the chaplain, first. And she posed an interesting question. She said Caroline was asking me to compromise and give up being a minister, but what was she giving up in return?"

"Ah. That is a good question."

"I'm still planning to go over to Caroline's house and talk with her Wednesday night. But I want to read the rest of your story, first. You said it might help me decide. Have you finished it?"

"The important parts are done. If you feel like reading it now, I'll go get it for you."

"I do. I need to think about something else for a while after the day I've had."

I retrieve the notebook from my desk and skim through it to find the place where Derk stopped reading. It was where I had just accepted the fact that Hendrik was dead and I'd asked Maarten to take me home to the Netherlands. We had gotten married. "Here," I say, handing him the open pages. "This is where you left off."

He settles back in the chair and starts reading. I watch him from across the table, too nervous to sit down, too distracted to continue cooking. When he gets to the part where Hendrik walked out of the woods, he sits upright in his chair and looks at me, startled. "Hendrik *survived*?"

"Yes. Keep reading," I tell him. I watch him turn the pages, faster and faster. He has always been fascinated with shipwrecks and disasters at sea, so I know he's intrigued by Hendrik's firsthand account of the *Phoenix* tragedy. He looks up again a few pages later and says, "Maarten and Hendrik forced you to choose between them?" I nod. "Wow! I thought I had a tough decision to make."

"It was an impossible one. Go on," I say, gesturing for him to continue. "There isn't much more to read. I just finished writing these last few pages today."

Geesje's Story

HOLLAND, MICHIGAN
49 YEARS EARLIER

Choosing between Hendrik and Maarten was the most agonizing decision I have ever faced. I knew which man I loved, which man I wanted to spend the rest of my life with—Hendrik, of course. The anguish came from knowing it was wrong to leave Maarten. I had made a vow before God to forsake all others and cleave to him until death parted us. I still believed in God, even though I was furious with Him for the way He chose to run the universe. And I still believed that the Bible was God's truth and that I would endanger my eternal soul if I deliberately disobeyed it. But what should I do?

Two full days passed. I couldn't eat, couldn't sleep. I performed my daily tasks in a fog of indecision and anger and grief—preparing meals, feeding the children, changing Gerrit's diapers, washing them. Hendrik and Maarten went about their work, too, while they waited for my decision—hauling water, chopping wood, getting our garden ready to plant.

Hendrik was in many ways a stranger to me. We'd known each other for less than a year before being separated and forced to communicate through letters. But he was my first love, my only love. The stolen kisses and love-sick promises we'd shared were as precious to me as silver and gold. In a way, we still barely knew each other. Yet when he'd walked out of the woods two days ago and held me in his arms again, I knew I belonged with him. He had traveled thousands of miles to find me, endured so much to be with me—and I had betrayed him.

Maarten, on the other hand, had been part of my life for nearly ten years. His mannerisms and thoughts and beliefs were as familiar as my own. We'd worshiped together, prayed together, traveled together, suffered hardship together. He'd taken care of me when I was seasick and when I had malaria. He'd watched over me and protected me during the long journey here. He'd labored in the shipyard in St. Clair and then shared the money with my family and me. He'd helped us clear our land and build this cabin. But should I stay with him just because I owed him so much? Would obligation make a good foundation on which to build a marriage? Shouldn't love be part of it?

How could I decide something as complicated as this? No matter which path I chose, it would lead to heartbreak.

The fact remained that I was married to Maarten in the sight of God. We'd made a commitment to raise Arie and Gerrit together as our sons. If I believed in a God who had created me and loved me and had given me the Bible to guide my life, then obeying Him was the very least I should do. In spite of the deep longing of my heart, I reached the reluctant conclusion that I needed to make the morally right yet painful choice to stay with Maarten. And I needed to tell him and Hendrik soon—before I changed my mind.

I was in our cabin with the two children, who had just fallen asleep for their naps, when Maarten ducked through our open door. Widow Van den Bosch was with him. I felt a chill. Had she come to persuade me to take Maarten's side? Neither Hendrik nor Maarten had tried to do that in the days since Hendrik arrived. I stopped singing the lullaby, but kept patting Gerrit's back, needing the contact with his softness and warmth.

"I need to tell you something," Maarten said. "I-I have a ter-

rible confession to make. It might help you decide what to do."
I couldn't breathe, waiting for him to begin. "The missing letter
from Hendrik? . . . It came—"

"What!"

"I-I didn't know what to do with it . . . I didn't know whether
I should give it to you or not."

"Of course you should have given it to me! It was mine!"

"I know, I know. But by then you believed Hendrik was dead. We
all did. He couldn't possibly have survived. And so I thought . . . I
thought he must have mailed the letter from New York or Buffalo
or somewhere else along the way. I was afraid that it would hurt
you too much to read something he had written just days before
he died. You had finally begun to heal from your grief."

The chill I felt burrowed deeper into my bones. "When did the
letter come?"

"On the day you asked me to help you return to the Netherlands.
You seemed so strong and clear-minded. It was the first day in
weeks that I hadn't heard you crying. I didn't want to cause you
grief all over again when you saw his handwriting and read his
last words to you. . . ."

"That wasn't your choice to make!"

"I know, I know. I didn't open the letter, Geesje, so I had no way
of knowing that he was still alive and that he had mailed it from
Wisconsin after the shipwreck. . . . I showed it to Widow Van den
Bosch and asked her what she thought I should do."

"And when he showed it to me," the widow said, "I grabbed it
out of Maarten's hand and threw it into the fire. I told him you
would never heal if we kept poking at your wounds."

"You had no right!" The shock and anger I felt left me barely
able to draw a breath, let alone speak. "No right!"

Widow Van den Bosch burst into tears. "Oh, Geesje . . .
Geesje . . . I'm so sorry! If I had only known what the letter said . . .
I can't tell you how sorry I am!" She moved forward as if to embrace
me, but I held up my hands, stopping her.

"Don't! Stay away from me!" I wanted to strike her. She had

ruined my life and all she could say was she's sorry? I could never forgive her. Never.

"I'm so sorry, too," Maarten said. "I swear I didn't know she would burn it. And when she did . . . at the time I thought it might be for the best."

"Blame me, Geesje," the widow begged. "Don't hold it against Maarten. It wasn't his fault or his decision to burn it. If I had only known all the heartache it would cause . . . Oh, Geesje, I wish I could go back and undo my mistake, but I can't, and I'm so very, very sorry. I don't deserve your forgiveness—but even so, I hope you'll find it in your heart someday to forgive me."

I couldn't answer her, couldn't look at her, overwhelmed by the hatred I felt toward both of them. "Go away and leave me alone," I said, my voice shaking. "Get out!" Thankfully, they did. I sat on the dirt floor in the gloomy cabin until the boys woke up from their naps, unable to move, too angry and too stunned to cry.

Maarten's confession changed everything. He was entirely to blame for causing this miserable dilemma, and it would serve him right if I deserted him. He had brought about his own grief. If he had done the right thing and given me Hendrik's letter, none of this would have happened. His actions were inexcusable. I would never forgive him. He deserved to have me leave him for Hendrik. And that's what I now intended to do.

I lifted Gerrit onto my hip and took Arie's hand and walked outside with them to search for Hendrik. I found him out on the little plot of land that Maarten had cleared last year for our garden. He was crouching down, crumbling the sandy soil in his fingers, admiring the texture of it the way Mama used to admire the fine, imported silks and brocades in the market stalls in Leiden. He stood up when he saw me coming and brushed his hands together to dust them off. I could barely contain my fury as I told him what had happened to his letter.

"It arrived here from Milwaukee but instead of giving it to me, Maarten showed it to Widow Van den Bosch. They threw it into the fire, unopened."

"*They* did this to us?" Hendrik was as outraged as I was. It was on the tip of my tongue to tell him I had made up my mind to leave Maarten and to run away with him. It would serve him right. But before I could get out the words Hendrik said, "You mean to tell me that Maarten threw away my letter and then had the gall to ask you to marry him?"

Even through the red haze of my anger at Maarten, I knew that picture wasn't an accurate one. "No, no . . . It wasn't exactly like that. . . . No, I asked Maarten to marry me. I'm the one who proposed marriage. But I need to explain why—"

"You don't have to. I understand." He turned away from the garden area and started walking toward the clearing in front of the cabin. "You were all alone, your parents had died. You had no choice."

I knew that wasn't true, either. I followed Hendrik until he halted and sat down on one of the fallen logs that still littered our yard, but I was too upset and fidgety to sit. I set Gerrit down to play in the sand beside his brother as I struggled for words. As angry as I was with Maarten, I couldn't let Hendrik believe a lie.

"It was my own fault for rushing into marriage with Maarten. I proposed to him, not the other way around. I did it because I wanted to go home to Leiden. I knew I could talk Maarten into taking me home if I married him. I didn't ask him what he thought of the idea or even if he wanted to go back to the Netherlands. I didn't care about him at all. I took advantage of the feelings he had for me in order to get my own way."

As I spoke the words and confessed the truth, I saw the ugliness of my actions, the selfishness in my heart. And I realized that I still wanted my own way, regardless of anyone's feelings. After manipulating Maarten so I could return home, I now wanted to compound my selfishness and leave him so I could run away with Hendrik. And in the middle of this tug-of-war were two little children who had grown to love me as their mother and Maarten as their papa. Whether I left them with Maarten or took them with Hendrik and me, they also would suffer because of my selfishness. I sank down on the log beside Hendrik, my body heavy with the load of guilt I carried. I realized, too, that no one had forced Maarten to confess the truth about the destroyed letter. Yet he had done the right thing.

"I had the greatest respect for your mother and father, Geesje," Hendrik said as the silence between us grew. "If they were still alive, what would they advise you to do?"

I folded my arms across my middle where Maarten's child was growing. My stomach ached with sorrow and regret. The unborn baby was another link in the chain that forged Maarten and me together. "On the night that my parents told me we were moving to America, I begged them to let me stay behind with you. I told them I was in love with you and I wanted to stay in the Netherlands and marry you. Papa said that I needed to put the matter into God's hands and trust Him with it. He said if God truly intended for you and me to marry, then nothing would stand in our way. Papa suggested that you should come to America, too. 'Pray about it,' he said, 'and if this is the Lord's will for you, it will all work out.' If not—then he said I had to decide if I was going to obey God or go my own way."

Hendrik picked up a fallen acorn, and I watched him absently toss it from one scarred hand to the other. The children's chatter blended into the background of birds twittering and a blue jay's strident call. "When I thought you were dead, I was overwhelmed with grief. I didn't pray about whether or not I should marry Maarten or even if I should return to Leiden. I wanted my own way, and I didn't care what God said I should do. I was furious with Him for taking your life. I even stopped going to church. Yes, it's Maarten's fault that your letter was destroyed. But it's my fault for not praying about my decision before rushing into marriage."

Hendrik lifted his arm and threw the acorn as far as he could into the distance. "Have you prayed about your decision now?" he asked.

I closed my eyes and shook my head. I hadn't. I still wanted my own way. I wanted to be with Hendrik. I knew what God's answer would be. Divorce contradicted His teachings. So did adultery. Innocent people would be hurt if I insisted on my own way. This dilemma was so unfair to Hendrik, the one person I loved the most. My selfishness had hurt him the most. I had broken my promise to wait for him.

"Then maybe you should pray about it," he said quietly. "I'm still new at all this. I'm still not sure how people hear from God. I know they say that He guides them. Some of the men I talked with on the ship said they'd heard God telling them to come to America. But when the *Phoenix* burned . . . I-I couldn't understand it. Had they heard wrong? Why did He let them all die? I wish I understood."

"I wish I did, too," I said miserably. "My parents were convinced they'd heard from Him, yet they died of malaria in this godforsaken place. I haven't prayed about what to do now because I'm pretty sure what His answer will be. I made my vows to Maarten in His presence."

Hendrik looked up at me, and I watched as tears filled his blue-gray eyes. I couldn't bear it. I wrapped my arms tightly around him and hid my face on his chest. "If you would just ask me to run away with you, Hendrik, I would do it. I would leave everything behind and go away with you—I wouldn't even care where we went. But please don't make me decide what to do. Beg me to go with you, please. I wouldn't refuse anything you asked of me."

He hugged me briefly in return, then his arms fell slack. "I can't do that," he said quietly. "I remember how your family lived in Arnhem, the integrity and faith and grace they showed to me and the other soldiers. That's what drew me to you—and to God. I can't ask you to turn away from everything you believe in. The decision has to be yours."

"No . . . no . . ." I still clung to him as I wept and I felt his body shaking with silent sobs. "I wish I'd died of malaria when my parents did! I wished they'd lived instead of me!"

I felt Arie tapping my arm, pressing his body close to mine. "You going away, Mama?" he asked.

I loosened my grip on Hendrik and faced my child. "No," I whispered. "No, I'm not going anywhere, lieveling."

Hendrik slowly stood, rising to his feet as if he were a hundred years old. He had no bags to pack, nothing to gather together for his trip. He had walked out from the woods two days ago with nothing, and his arms were empty now. I watched him walk away from me, following the narrow path through the woods until he disappeared from sight. He didn't look back.

HOLLAND, MICHIGAN
1897

Derk reaches the end and slowly closes the notebook. He looks up at me. "You stayed with Maarten even though you loved Hendrik?"

"That was the only choice I could make and not walk away from God. The child I carried is our son Jakob. Our daughter Christina was born four years later. Maarten and I gave Arie and Gerrit our name and raised them as our own sons."

"Do you know what happened to Hendrik after he left?"

I've been waiting for this question. I nod, swallowing hard, not sure I can speak. "He went off to work in Kalamazoo for about a year, and when he returned he brought his new bride with him."

"He came back?"

"He had earned enough money to apply for a mortgage on fifty acres of land in Zeeland, six miles away. He turned it into a prosperous farm. He and his wife raised four children together." I pause, steadying my voice, anticipating his reaction when I finally put all the pieces together for him. "Your mother was his only daughter."

"My-my mother . . . ? Hendrik is my grandfather?"

"Yes."

"But . . . but that can't be! His name wasn't Hendrik, it was . . ."

"Hank. He adopted the American name Henry, but people called him Hank."

Derk has never been good at disguising his emotions, and

they are all there on his face for me to see—shock, disbelief, then slow understanding. "I-I knew my grandfather had been ship-wrecked. . . . I remember the scars on his neck and his hands. . . . But he never told me the details."

"He never talked about it to anyone after the day he told me."

"I can't believe it! Hendrik . . . is my grandfather? I don't understand why he stayed here under the circumstances."

"He told me before we left the Netherlands that he wanted his own farm someday. It was his dream, and he accomplished it. He didn't have to watch his family starve or die of illness the way his parents and siblings had back home. And he was sincere in wanting to live a life of Christian faith. What better place to do that than here?"

"His farm is still in our family. My uncle runs it now. I used to love visiting there when I was a boy."

"Hendrik did very well for himself. And I think he was happy with his life." I can see that Derk is still trying to digest the truth. He shifts on his chair, runs his hand through his hair, making it stick up, making me smile. "You look so much like him, Derk. And now you're going to be Dominie Vander Veen. Who would have imagined such a thing when the Dutch government billeted four soldiers with a family of Separatists all those years ago?"

He lets his breath out with a *whoosh*, shaking his head. I can almost hear his mind spinning with more questions. "Did you ever regret your choice to stay married to Maarten?"

"Dozens of times, especially in the beginning. Until one day I realized that regret from the past was keeping me from living well in the present. And it was robbing me of a future. We had a good life together with our children."

"I wish I had known Maarten."

"I wish you had, too. You would have liked each other. I always thought he would have made an outstanding dominie. He had the heart of a shepherd, so compassionate and caring. But his family had been poor back in the Netherlands, so he became my father's apprentice in our print shop instead."

"I wish I had gotten to know my grandfather better, too."

I suddenly picture Hendrik the way he looked the last time I'd seen him, still handsome after all the years, though his shoulders were a little more stooped and his fair hair had turned to silver. All the blue had faded from his eyes, but they still reminded me of the river in Leiden on a cloudy day. My eyes tear up at the memory of him.

"If Hendrik had turned into a bad man, a drunk, a wife-beater," I tell Derk, "it would be easy for me to look back on the choice I made and say that God was trying to spare me from a terrible marriage. But it wasn't true, of course. Your grandfather was a quiet, distant man—scarred, I think, by what he had endured on the *Phoenix*. He carried an enormous load of guilt for surviving when so many others died. It weighed on him for the rest of his life. It was almost as if he felt obligated to live well and fully here in America for the sake of all those people aboard the *Phoenix* who never had a chance to live." I pause to swallow my tears, and when I speak again my voice catches. "I know that my betrayal wounded him deeply, although he never showed any ill will toward Maarten or me. Hendrik became a good husband and father, a good Christian man. He attended his church in Zeeland faithfully. He even became an elder."

Derk sighs. "It broke his heart when my mother drowned. I remember I saw him leave our house after her funeral, and I ran outside to follow him. I found him leaning against the back fence, all alone, sobbing as if he would never be able to stop. The force of those sobs terrified me. I had never heard a grown man cry like that before. My father grieved for my mother in private, trying to remain strong for me, I suppose. I hid beneath our back porch that day so my grandfather wouldn't see me, and I cried all by myself. Now I wish I had gone to him. Maybe we could have comforted each other."

"When your mother's ship sank, Hendrik knew better than anyone else the horror his daughter must have endured in those last moments. I think that's what broke his heart. It was a cruel twist of fate that his daughter and mine both died in the same shipwreck."

Derk is quiet for a long moment, and when he speaks again he has changed the subject. His heart shattered that day, too, and he doesn't like to dwell on the memory of losing his mother. "Why didn't you and Maarten go back to Leiden?" he asks. "You had saved up enough money, hadn't you?"

"Because I felt it was a fitting punishment for me to stay here where life was so hard. Maarten had only agreed to go back in order to make me happy, but I knew that deep in his heart he wanted to stay. God had called him to come to America, and he had worked hard to build a new life here. So we stayed and built a life together." I was telling Derk the truth, but not the complete truth. I had also chosen to stay because Hendrik was here in America. I wanted to be near him so I could find out how he was and maybe see him once in a while. "Maarten and I both lived with the guilt of our mistakes. He never forgave himself for letting Hendrik's letter burn instead of giving it to me. He regretted it our entire married life, even though I assured him countless times that I had forgiven him. I lived with my guilt for manipulating Maarten into marrying me. If I hadn't insisted on my own selfish desire to go back to the Netherlands, he might have married Johanna van Eyck, instead. That's why I couldn't blame Maarten or Widow Van den Bosch or God or anyone else for keeping Hendrik and me apart. I had done it to myself."

"Was it hard for you and my grandfather when you saw each other?"

Oh, yes. I close my eyes, unable to choke out the words. I remember our conversation after Christina's funeral as if it were yesterday. "We rarely saw each other," I finally say.

"That's sad."

"If the *Phoenix* hadn't sunk, if Widow Van den Bosch hadn't burned the letter, if I hadn't demanded my own way, Hendrik and I would have married. And then you would be my grandson."

He looks up at me with a smile that warms my heart. "I call you *tante*, but you'll always be so much more to me. You saved my life!"

I reach over to smooth his rumpled hair with my fingers. "Well . . . anyway, now that you've read my story you know how unqualified I am to speak with your rich lady-friend or anyone else about love and marriage."

"You aren't unqualified. I admire you more than ever for making such a difficult decision. For following God's Word instead of your heart."

"Do you see now why I advised you to seek His guidance before you talk to Caroline? Make sure the choices you make are His will for you."

"I wish my friend Anna could read your story. I believe more than ever that she'll be making a mistake if she marries this man she doesn't love. Her father's financial problems aren't her fault. Why should she sacrifice her future happiness for his mistakes?"

"Have you told her your opinion?"

"No . . . do you think I should? I hate to see her settle for a loveless marriage—although you didn't love Maarten, and you still had a happy life together, didn't you?"

"Yes, we did."

Derk shifts in his chair again and picks up my notebook from the table. He hands it to me. "I think you should keep writing the story of your life, Tante Geesje. This doesn't feel finished to me. I think there's an even bigger story than what I've read so far."

"I don't know about that," I say, shaking my head. "I've lived a very unremarkable life."

"That's not true. For as long as I've known you, you've been a woman of great strength and faith. But how did you get there? How did you keep on believing and growing and serving God after all the incomprehensible hardships in your life? How did you and your husband get past your guilt and your mistakes and build a life together?"

I shrug. "One day at a time."

"I want to know more, Tante Geesje. You lost everything, but you didn't give up on God. Tell me how you managed it."

I hold the notebook close, then lay it down again as if it's made of glass. The memories inside it are just as fragile. "I'll think about it," I tell him. I turn to the stove and my bowl of unfinished pancake batter. I lift the stove's iron lid and nudge the coals back to life. "I have more than enough batter to make pannenkoeken for the two of us. Can you stay and eat with me, Derk?"

"I'd love to." He stands and envelops me in his embrace. He's still holding me tightly when he says, "You loved my grandfather very much, didn't you?"

I can only nod in reply, unable to speak. Even after all these years.

CHAPTER 23

Anna

HOTEL OTTAWA
1897

The fight I had with Mother keeps replaying in my mind, circling around and around like a boat on a small lagoon. We retreat to our separate rooms, the air between us prickly with hurt and distrust. Unable to relax or nap, I pick up the Bible Derk gave me and go downstairs to read it on the wide front veranda. The view of Black Lake through the porch's arched opening resembles a picture postcard, with blue sky and sparkling water and lazy sailboats drifting by. I watch other guests stroll past, laughing and at ease, men in their straw boaters and women in summer skirts and cotton shirtwaists. Most of the ladies carry parasols or wear wide-brimmed hats to protect their skin from the sun. I love the feeling of the warm summer sun on my face, but I don't dare indulge in it. I can't return to Chicago with my complexion as sun-browned as Derk's is. I'm still thinking of him and the unhappy way we parted as I open the Bible to where I left off in the Gospel of Mark. Something inside me slowly uncoils as I read.

Mother finds me late that afternoon, still reading in my chair on the veranda. She looks rested from her nap. "What are you reading, Anna?" Her tone is friendly and offhand, and she cocks her head to try to see the book I'm holding.

I lift it to show her. "It's the Bible."

"Oh."

She sounds annoyed, as if she has caught me reading a cheap dime romance novel or a sleazy murder mystery. I can't resist saying, "Derk gave it to me." All the anger I felt earlier after the infuriating incident near the dock comes roaring back, making my ears hum. Mother sits down on a chair beside me but remains perched on the edge.

"I don't understand this sudden fascination of yours with the Bible or with that strange church on LaSalle Street," she says.

"There's nothing odd about wanting to learn more about God. Shouldn't everyone know what the Bible says? Isn't that why we go to church and listen to sermons—so we'll know how we're supposed to live?"

"Even so, I see no reason to become so . . . *fanatical* about it. And why would you allow religion to come between you and a very good man who loves you?"

"I don't know how to explain it to you, Mother. . . . I just don't. And I don't want to argue with you anymore."

"You can always come to me with your questions instead of going to a stranger. I've been a church member all my life."

Without another word, I find the Bible passage I just read, the one that stopped me cold and gave me so much to think about. "Someone asked Jesus which commandment was the most important one," I tell Mother. "Jesus replied with these words: 'Thou shalt love the Lord they God with all thy heart, and with all thy soul, and with all thy mind. This is the first and great commandment. And the second is like unto it, Thou shalt love thy neighbour as thyself.'"

218

I turn in my chair to face her. "That sounds so . . . *fanatical*, doesn't it?" I ask, using Mother's word. "Imagine loving God that much—with all our heart and soul and mind and strength. How do we do that? How do we show Him that much love? It seems as though there are so many other things that take precedence in our minds and hearts, like all the social events that are on our calendars, and which gown we should wear, and how to make certain our home is just as stylish as the next person's."

"Don't diminish the importance of what we do, Anna. The women we know serve on the boards of some very important services and charities."

I barely hear her. I'm not finished. "And how do I love my neighbor as much as I love myself? *Myself!* I've been spoiled and pampered all my life. Even if Jesus means only loving the people who live next door to us, we barely even know them, let alone love them!"

Mother reaches across my lap and closes the Bible, then takes my hands in hers. "Anna, dear. You're getting all worked up over things you don't understand. This is precisely why it's a mistake to try to read the Good Book without proper training. We aren't meant to understand it. We must leave it to our ordained ministers to interpret Jesus' words for our current times and situations."

"But that's exactly why I asked Derk for help. He's studying at a seminary to become a minister. Working here at the hotel is only his summer job."

"But he isn't a minister yet. Listen, we all do the best we can every day to live as we should. God knows none of us is perfect. Now," she says, releasing my hands and rising to her feet. "I believe it's nearly time to freshen up and dress for dinner. Shall we go upstairs?"

I stop at the desk for my room key and the clerk hands me a folded note. It's from Derk. I quickly stuff it inside my Bible so Mother doesn't see it. I wait until I'm alone in my room to read it.

Dear Miss Nicholson,

I apologize for any trouble I caused today between you and your mother. I feel terrible about the abrupt way we had to part. There is more I would like to say to you, and I know you still have questions for me that I never had a chance to answer. If it isn't proper for us to meet again, I think you would find my Tante Geesje very helpful and easy to talk to. I'm sure she will meet with you if you are still interested—if that's even possible now, under the circumstances.

I begin work tomorrow morning at 8:00 (unless I've been fired), but I will make a point to arrive an hour earlier if you would like to talk one last time—if you are able to or interested in talking, that is. If nothing else, I would like to say a proper good-bye and wish you all the best in your future. I'll understand if you're finished with me and don't want to see me again, but on the off-chance that you do want to talk, I'll be waiting in our usual place at 7:00 am.

Sincerely,

Derk Vander Veen

I refold his note and tuck it inside my Bible again. I don't understand why my heart is thumping along like a carriage with a broken wheel at the prospect of seeing him. I don't need to stop and consider whether or not it is wise or proper to meet with him again. I already know that I'll be awake early tomorrow morning, and that I will go out to speak with Derk. I tell myself it's because I need to apologize for Mother's rudeness and thank him for all his help. But it's also because I want to see him one last time.

I arrive at the bench before he does the next morning. The wood is damp with dew so I remain standing, shivering a little in the cool morning air. The water on Black Lake is motionless, the hotel grounds nearly deserted, and I feel as if the new day is holding its breath, just like I am. The morning is so quiet I can hear my heart pounding in my ears. At last I see Derk approaching, his fair hair bright in the sunlight. When he sees me he breaks into an easy jog.

"Thanks for coming, Miss Nicholson." He is grinning and breathless from the run.

"Derk, I need to apologize for Mother's rudeness yesterday." He tries to brush it off. "No, that's not necessary—"

"Yes. It is. She was very rude to you for no reason at all, and I want you to know how sorry I am. You didn't deserve it. And I insist that you stop calling me Miss Nicholson and call me Anna like all my other friends do."

His grin widens. "Thank you . . . Anna."

I glance around nervously, as a few early morning fishermen and hotel workers begin to appear. "Listen, in light of yesterday's unfortunate incident, I don't believe it would be wise for us to speak here. If we were to go for a stroll somewhere, I would be able to tell my mother I have been out walking."

"Are you sure? I mean, would it be proper for us to . . . ?"

For some reason, I feel rebellious. "I'm a grown woman," I tell him. "I can do whatever I please. Where shall we go?"

"Have you hiked up Mt. Pisgah yet?" he asks, pointing to the sand dune behind the hotel, partly covered with trees and bushes and dune grass. A row of private cottages perches near the base of it.

"I haven't. And I hear it offers a beautiful view."

"It's a rigorous walk—"

"Lead the way," I say, taking his arm. We follow the wooden walkway through the hotel grounds, then continue along the board-walk as we slowly climb the dune. We pass lovely, whitewashed cottages with breezy front porches and gauzy curtains blowing from open second-story windows. No one seems to be up this early, and the only sounds I hear are birdsong and the distant call of gulls.

At first Derk is quiet, but as I pause a moment to catch my breath and look back at how far we've come, he finally says, "There's something I feel compelled to speak to you about, Anna. I know we don't know each other very well, but . . . but it's been bothering me." I wait. Derk looks unusually serious as he scratches his chin and rakes his fingers through his fair hair. "I don't think you should marry William," he says. "I think you would be making a mistake."

I don't know what I was expecting him to say, but it certainly wasn't this. "Why?" I ask.

"Well, for two reasons. First of all, you don't love him, and I believe that love is a very important ingredient in a marriage. And second, a husband is the spiritual head of the family and should encourage his wife to grow in her faith, not hinder her."

Derk is adding to my already considerable doubts about William. But I can't let him talk me out of marrying him. I start walking again. "Thank you for your concern," I say primly, "but I believe I've already explained that my father is having financial difficulties, and he needs my help. I have decided to marry William for my parents' sakes, so they can continue living the only lifestyle they've ever known."

Derk keeps up with me and takes my elbow again. "Your father's problems are of his own making. He shouldn't use you or ask you to sacrifice your future happiness in order to solve them."

"He isn't using me. He doesn't know I overheard him. He doesn't know that's why I agreed to marry William. And I love my parents very much." But even as I profess my love for them, I recall the conversation I overheard and the enormous emptiness I felt as I listened:

"She's curious about her parents. Perhaps it's time you told her."

"Told her what? I don't know anything about her parents, you know that."

"You could tell her how you found her. How she came to us."

"I don't think that's wise."

I had been too afraid to ask how they had found me—nor did I know how to raise the question without admitting I'd been listening at their door. Even now an appalling feeling of rejection washes over me as I remember that my real parents abandoned me as a newborn baby. No matter what I learn about them, whether they left me on a street corner or in an orphans' home, it won't diminish the hurt and shame I feel. I was unwanted. Father and Mother were kind enough to give me a home. "I have to help them," I say aloud. I hope Derk drops the matter, but he doesn't.

"This country has been in a financial depression for four years," he says. "People of all incomes have felt its effects. Yes, your marriage might well improve your father's finances, but at what cost? He'll be back on his feet and you'll be stuck in a loveless, unfulfilling marriage for the rest of your life. Or what if your marriage doesn't solve his problems? You'll still be stuck. The only reason you should marry William or anyone else is because you love him. No other reason is good enough."

I find it hard to breathe, whether from the gradual climb or the conversation, I can't tell. "It's too late. I already gave William my word for a second time. I can't go back on it again."

"Fine, then. Even if you do marry him, I think he should allow you to attend any church you want to. Tante Geesje and her family were persecuted in the Netherlands for wanting to worship God freely. They came here to Michigan when it was nothing but a wilderness and endured great hardship to carve out a town where they could have that freedom. The same story has replayed throughout America's history, starting with the Pilgrims. Thousands of people came here for religious freedom, and so now, at the turn of a new century, it's outrageous for a husband to forbid his wife to attend a perfectly acceptable Christian church where she feels close to God. It's just not right. I know you must see that, Anna. And when you add in the fact that you don't really love him—"

"In the social circle I come from, marriages are very often mere alliances between families and businesses. They are rarely motivated by love. It's nice when the two parties are attracted to each other and enjoy being together, as William and I did before we argued. But people don't consider marrying for love. No one expects it as the norm."

"And they live together for years and years anyway? Like strangers?"

I recall the conversation I overheard between Mother and Honoria Stevens. *"Your husband isn't the first gentleman to have a little fling, nor will he be the last. It's much more common than one might imagine."* I can easily imagine the hurt and rejection I would feel if I learned that my husband was unfaithful to me. And yet, according to Mother, it is a very real possibility. Anger makes my voice sound clipped, my replies to Derk seem cold. "The couples I know certainly don't live like strangers. They share a home, a family. They attend social events together and have genuine respect and affection for each other. Yet each person leads his or her own life with its own set of social expectations." I'm too embarrassed to add that the couples I know also have separate bedrooms.

"Pardon me for asking, but what about your own parents?"

I pause as we reach the end of the wooden walkway. From here, the steep, narrow path is sandy and crisscrossed with tree roots, bordered by weeds and beach grass as it winds its way to the top. "In many ways, yes, that does describe my parents. They lead mostly separate lives. But there is no doubt in my mind that they both adore me. That's why I would do anything for them, including marry a man I'm not sure I love." I step off the walkway and begin to climb, letting anger and uncertainty propel me. I've never hiked on such a crude, steep path before, and I'm forced to cling tightly to Derk's arm, praying I don't twist an ankle. Only stubbornness keeps me from turning back. "Besides, I believe that love can grow between two people as the years go by and as they raise their children. Didn't you say your aunt Geesje married a man she didn't love? How did that turn out?"

He exhales as if reluctant to concede the point. "They were together a long time and raised four children. She says they were happy—"

"There. You see? I'm certain I will be happy as well. I'll have a great many privileges in return for marrying a powerful, important man like William—a beautiful home, dozens of servants—"

"I can't believe you'd be content with that life. There is so much more to you than those superficial things. Am I wrong, Anna?"

I recall my diary entries and the emptiness I've felt, the nagging sense that I don't belong. "It's the only life I've ever known or expected," I say, avoiding the truth. "It's the only role I know how to play. Rich or poor, every woman has expectations she must fulfill. When you marry, won't there be certain obligations that your wife will be expected to meet? Obligations that go along with your career and way of life?"

"Yes, I suppose so. She'll have to help me with my work as a pastor, care for our home and our children, be part of a church community where we pray for each other and celebrate together and sometimes grieve together—"

"She'll cook your meals, wash your clothes, change your children's diapers?"

"Well . . . we might be able to afford to hire a girl to help—"

"I wouldn't know how to cook a meal or be part of a church community like yours any more than Caroline would know the rules of etiquette in my world." For some reason, I'm fighting tears. "It seems to me that Caroline analyzed her future as a minister's wife and decided she didn't want it."

"Yes, and you should do the same, Anna. Before you marry William, look into your future and decide if that's what you want and if it's how you want to live. That's all I'm saying."

My vision blurs, and I stumble over a large rock in the path. Derk grabs me to keep me from falling, and I cling to him in return. For a long moment we are in each other's arms, closer than if we were dancing partners. I'm aware of his warmth and the scent of his soap, the bare skin of our arms touching. I find my balance and pull away to catch my breath, pretending it never happened.

"I appreciate your concern, Derk. It's kind of you to offer your advice. Now if you would care to hear my opinion about your life, I'll be happy to share it with you." I sound stiff and formal and don't know why.

"Go ahead. I would like to hear your opinion." Derk folds his arms across his chest. He looks cross.

"I don't think you should marry Caroline. I think you should

pursue your intended career as a minister, not as a teacher or whatever else it was that she suggested. You told me when we first met
that God had called you to be a minister. I don't quite understand
what it means that He 'called' you, but it seems to me you should
do what God says. You once made the difficult choice to give up
Caroline to become a minister, and I think you should follow
through on it. I don't think her compromise is a fair one at all."

"Thank you for your advice." Now he sounds reserved and
formal. I'm sorry that we have annoyed each other, but I plunge
on up the hill, continuing the conversation.

"When do you see her again?"

"Tonight."

"And will you have to give her an answer tonight?"

"I'm sure she'll be expecting one. She won't like it very much
if I make her wait."

I halt and look up at him. "Do you realize how manipulative
that makes her sound? I'm surprised you don't see it. Perhaps
you're blinded by these feelings of love you keep touting so highly."

"Have you ever been in love, Anna? If so, you would understand
why it's such a hard decision to make."

At last we reach the top of the hill and the view steals what little
breath I have left. Lake Michigan fills the horizon in front of us,
reflecting the blue sky above my head. A passenger ship steams
toward the channel that connects the two lakes, the lighthouse at
the entrance looks like a toy. Below us on the left I see the sprawling Hotel Ottawa on the shores of Black Lake. More hotels and
cottages dot the lake's opposite shoreline. A sailboat is already
taking advantage of the mild breeze to glide across the pristine
water. The scene is so beautiful from up here that I can barely recall
the noise and busyness of Chicago. Nor can I imagine returning
to the life I just described to Derk, spending my days planning
and attending parties and events, ordering clothes and making
social calls, a life where my every move is scrutinized and gossiped
about by my neighbors and peers. A life where thoughts of God or
what my purpose in life might be are rarely considered, let alone

discussed. This idyllic place on the shore of Lake Michigan isn't the real world, merely a brief escape from it. In a few days, I'll have to leave it all behind.

I look up at Derk. I'm still loosely holding his arm. "You and I are opposite sides of the same coin, don't you see? You want to marry for love because you consider it all-important. You're willing to compromise and possibly sacrifice your future for the sake of true love."

"I haven't decided yet—"

"And I don't expect love at all. I believed I had a measure of it with William in the beginning, but now I'm not so sure. A secure future is more important to me, so I'm willing to sacrifice love in order to get it."

"Why can't we have both?" he asks heatedly. "Why can't we marry for love and still have a good future? I could fall in love again with someone else who doesn't mind being a minister's wife. And surely there are other rich men you could fall in love with and marry, men who could help your father financially but who would still let you worship wherever you wanted to. You're a beautiful woman, Anna. You can easily find a man who is more sympathetic and understanding than William is."

I feel tears welling again and look away. "In an ideal world I suppose we could have both. But my world is hardly ideal. There's a price to pay for the wealth and status my family enjoys. The truth is—and I'm realizing it just this moment—if I don't marry William after announcing our engagement at a huge party, I'm not likely to receive a proposal from any other gentlemen in our social circle. William and his family are at the very top when it comes to prestige and prominence. They are highly respected, powerful, and perhaps a bit feared. Few men would risk the stigma of marrying William's castoff fiancée. It would be assumed that something was wrong with *me* if our engagement ended, not the other way around, because no woman in her right mind would reject 'perfect' William."

"You're trapped."

"Don't feel sorry for me!" I say angrily. "I'll have servants and a mansion and more money than I can possibly spend in one lifetime."

"A beautiful bird in a gilded cage."

"Listen, Derk, if you start giving away parts of your future to please Caroline, you'll end up just as trapped as I am. Once she learns that she can manipulate you, she'll never be satisfied with anything less than her own way from now on."

"Caroline isn't as bad as you seem to think she is."

"And William isn't as bad as you think, either. . . . And yet we've both advised each other not to marry them."

"What do you make of that?"

"I don't know. . . . But I think we'd better go back to the hotel now."

He takes my arm again as we head down the hill, our shoes slipping on the sandy path. We don't speak except to say things like "Watch your step!" I'm curious to know what will happen when Derk talks to Caroline tonight, and I long to ask him to tell me all about it tomorrow. But I have no right to know. The friendship we've briefly shared has come to an end, and now we must return to the lives we had before we met. Somewhere deep inside, I'm very sad about that.

"Thank you for the walk," I say as we part. "It was very invigorating."

"You're welcome." We're back to speaking politely, distantly. The warm relationship we shared seems like only a dream.

"Good-bye, Derk. I wish you well with Caroline."

I turn and start walking back toward the hotel. Behind me I hear him say, "Good-bye, Anna."

CHAPTER 24

Geesje

I'm washing my supper dishes at the kitchen sink when I see Derk loping across my backyard from his house next door. I dry my hands and open the screen door for him. He's so tall that his head barely misses the top of the frame. "I can't stay. I'm on my way to see Caroline," he says. "Tonight's the night."

"You look like you're on your way to a funeral." He's wearing his best Sunday suit, and his blond hair is tamed and slicked with Macassar oil. From the expression on his handsome face, one would think doomsday has finally arrived.

Derk tries to smile but doesn't quite manage it. "I had an upsetting talk with my friend Anna this morning. I asked her to meet with me one last time because I wanted to explain why she shouldn't marry her fiancé. She didn't take my advice very well and proceeded to tell me why I shouldn't marry Caroline. We

229

both gave our reasons . . ." He shrugs helplessly, hopelessly. He has fallen for this Anna harder than he realizes.

"So she's still going through with her marriage after she returns to Chicago?"

"Yes. And now I feel very foolish for meddling. I have no right to get involved in her life. I don't know anything about the high-society world she lives in." He collapses onto a chair as if his legs have given up hope of carrying him any farther. "What upsets me the most is that she doesn't think love is all that important in a marriage. I didn't know how to convince her that it is. . . . What do you think, Tante Geesje?"

"About love? Well . . . I think the human heart is a very fickle thing. I've seen people who married for convenience end up deeply in love. And I've seen couples who were once deeply in love allow those feelings to die over the years. I've often wondered what my marriage to Hendrik would have been like if things had worked out differently. I have no way of knowing, of course. The truth is, we didn't really know each other very well in spite of the powerful attraction we felt. Would that have been enough to sustain us through the rough times? I don't know. We would have had a lot to learn about each other in order to make it work."

"But you do know me very well. I stopped by on my way to Caroline's house to see if you had any last words of advice for me."

I take a long moment to consider his question. "Ask her why she loves you. Why she wants to marry you. Listen carefully to her reply. Then listen to your own reply if she asks you the same thing."

After Derk hauls himself away again, I decide to take his advice and continue writing the story of my past. It's not so much a decision as a compulsion. It has been interesting to relive my past from the vantage point of fifty years. And I've been surprised to find that putting my thoughts into words has helped liberate many dormant emotions. I've been sitting on those feelings all these years, keeping them safe and hidden away. And now, like baby birds that have finally hatched, they are free to fly from their nesting place in my heart. Yet I know there is still much more for me to work out. What went wrong with Christina, for instance? How and why did I fail with my daughter? What might I have done differently? I ache to have that final loose end between God and me tidied up and settled.

I sharpen a pencil and sit down at my desk, gazing at the family photograph we all posed for years ago and Christina's playful smile. It takes me a while to figure out where to start writing, but at last I begin.

Geesje's Story

HOLLAND, MICHIGAN
49 YEARS EARLIER

There are times in life when we must leave the past behind without looking back, the same way we did when we said good-bye to our loved ones in the Netherlands and left our homeland forever. We must set out in the direction God is leading us and sail forward in life from that day on. That's what I had to do after Hendrik left. My journey back to wholeness and peace, one painful step at a time, seemed as long and arduous as the trip across the ocean to America had been. I needed to ask forgiveness from the people I had hurt. I needed to ask God to forgive me. I needed to lay aside the bitterness I felt toward Him for all the losses in my life and begin trusting Him again, believing in His goodness and in His love for me. I hoped that if I did all of those things, I would have a fresh, clean start.

My adopted sons Arie and Gerrit taught me about starting fresh. As Maarten and I walked up the hill to the log church with them one bright Sunday morning in November, I realized how happy and content they were. They had suffered the loss of their parents just as I had, yet they now embraced their new life with Maarten and me with energy and curiosity. And hope. I needed to do the same thing, learning all over again the importance of embracing the community of believers I lived with and worshiped with.

I paused partway up the hill to rest and rub my aching back. I carried the extra weight of our soon-to-be-born first child. The town we'd named Holland was rapidly growing, and the view from the rise near the church revealed spreading patches of cleared land and columns of smoke rising from numerous chimneys to curl into the clear fall sky. The people who lived here were my sisters and brothers, my family. We had suffered persecution together in the Netherlands and endured all the trials of the journey and the taming of this land. There wasn't one woman from among the original settlers who didn't know about Hendrik and me. I had talked about him every step of the way and dreamed aloud with the young women my age about being married and having homes of our own. We had shared each other's grief when so many of our loved ones died of malaria. They tried to share my grief when I believed Hendrik was dead, many of them coming to mourn with me as I wept. But I had turned away from them, so overwhelmed by my anger at God because of Hendrik's senseless death that I stopped going to church. I refused to talk to Dominie Van Raalte when he tried to comfort me. I didn't tell anyone of my decision to return to the Netherlands with Maarten for fear they would try to talk me out of it. Several women did come to talk to me after the elders read the banns announcing my upcoming marriage to Maarten. One of Mama's friends even stood outside our cabin door after I refused to let her inside and begged me to take more time to grieve before marrying so hastily. I didn't listen to her. Now, as Maarten and I tried to move forward in our marriage, I finally realized how much I needed the community's help and support.

"You all right?" Maarten asked as I stood looking down at our settlement. He scooped up Gerrit, whose little legs had grown tired, to carry him the rest of the way.

"Yes. I just need a breather." I saw Maarten's look of concern and added, "The baby will come soon, but not today." We started walking again.

Maarten had always been very involved in our community, helping the other settlers any way that he could, sharing the hard work and the suffering with them, even during the months when I stayed away from church. I wasn't the only one in our kolonie who grieved the death of a loved one, but by isolating myself from everyone, I had missed out on God's comfort. He used other people to extend His compassion and care, but I had refused it. That sense of love and Christian community was what had attracted Hendrik to our faith years ago. Now I knew that I needed my fellow church members beside me through my baby's birth and to help me raise and educate my children. And to learn to love my husband the way I should.

The log church was wonderfully warm inside with fires blazing on the two hearths. We removed our coats and hats and found our places on the wooden benches. I clearly remember the sermon that Dominie Van Raalte preached that morning, because he might have written it especially for me. The text was Jesus' commandment from the twelfth chapter of Mark to love thy neighbor as thyself. Dominie said that loving our neighbor didn't necessarily mean we must feel loving emotions toward them, but that we must speak lovingly to them, rather than in anger or derision. And we must do acts of lovingkindness and compassion, deliberately and frequently, demonstrating the undeserved grace God shows to us. If we spoke loving words and did loving acts, then genuine love for our neighbor would have an opportunity to grow and flourish.

I didn't love Maarten, but I needed to obey the Bible's command. Perhaps my love for him would grow, as Dominie promised, if I spoke loving words and did loving acts. It would be a tragedy if Maarten lived his entire life wondering if I loved him, wondering if I was thinking of Hendrik every time I held him or kissed him.

I was still thinking of the dominie's sermon at home later that afternoon, after the children had been fed and put down for their naps. The Sabbath day when we rested from our daily work would be a good time for me to begin all over again with Maarten and share my heart with him. The November day was sunny and warmer than usual, so we bundled up and sat side-by-side in the sunshine on the low front step of our cabin. "I don't think I ever asked you this," I began, "but why did you leave the Netherlands and come here? How did you reach the decision to emigrate?"

Maarten clasped his hands around one upraised knee as he pondered his reply. "At first it was like catching a fever. Everyone was talking about emigrating and constantly discussing it, and their excitement became contagious. Then at one of the meetings that I went to with your father, Dominie Van Raalte advised each of us to pray individually and ask God to clearly reveal His will. He explained how hard emigrating was going to be and the difficulties we might face. He said knowing that we were obeying God's call might be the only thing that would help us through all of those trials."

"So you were certain that you were called to come?"

"Yes. As I was praying about it and reading my Bible early one morning, a verse in Genesis seemed to jump off the page: 'Get thee out of thy country, and from thy kindred, and from thy father's house, and unto a land that I will shew thee.' God was speaking to Abraham, of course, but I heard Him speaking those words to me, too. Abraham hadn't been able to worship God in the land of his ancestors, and neither could I."

I shivered with a sudden chill as the sun disappeared behind a cloud for a moment. "And yet you were going to disobey God and take me back to the Netherlands?" I asked quietly.

Maarten shrugged his wide shoulders. "Dominie tried to talk me out of it, but . . ." He didn't finish.

He would have disobeyed because he loved me. I felt ashamed that I had misused his love to make him sacrifice his convictions. Now I was glad that he hadn't taken me home.

"You never felt God's call to come here, did you, Geesje?" he asked after a moment.

"No, because I never prayed about it or asked about His will

234

for me. I was too caught up with being in love. Faith in God had been so important to my parents—and to me at one time. But I wanted my own way, not God's. At first I begged my parents to let me stay behind. Then when Hendrik agreed to move to America, I figured that must be what God wanted for me, too."

A cardinal swooped down and landed on the bare ground in front of us, flashing his scarlet feathers. He cocked his head inquisitively, as if asking me a question, then flew away again. I stared at the tiny prints left behind in the sandy soil. "I know I've drifted far from God. I want to get back to that place of certainty and closeness to Him, but there are so many questions and doubts blocking the way. I keep thinking about my parents' deaths, and I can't make sense of it. What a cruel waste after they'd traveled so far. And what about all those other Christians who followed God's call and then died on the *Phoenix*?"

Maarten drew a deep breath, as if preparing to scale my mountain of doubt. "You weren't in church during the weeks that followed the malaria plague or after Dominie read the announcement about the *Phoenix*, but he talked about all those deaths. He said we shouldn't try to analyze God's will or look for reasons to rationalize it or explain it. He read us the verse from Isaiah where God says, 'For my thoughts are not your thoughts, neither are your ways my ways . . . as the heavens are higher than the earth, so are my ways higher than your ways, and my thoughts than your thoughts.' Dominie admitted that reading a verse or two of Scripture doesn't stop our sorrow and grief—"

"Or our anger," I added. "I was so angry with God for taking Mama and Papa."

He looked at me as if he couldn't comprehend my anger. "But your parents are in paradise, Geesje, in the very presence of God. So are all the believers who died on the *Phoenix*. If we could only grasp what heaven is like, we wouldn't cling so tightly to this life. It's like . . . it's like this baby you're carrying in your womb. The only world he has ever known seems safe and warm and secure to him. Leaving it to be born must seem like a death to him, and a very painful one. But the new world he'll suddenly enter is filled with light and air and sound and color and loving arms to hold him. It's so much more glorious than the dark, cramped life he knows now. He would never choose to remain there—or to return to it. Our life here on earth isn't all there is either, any more than our life in the womb was. Dying wasn't the end of your parents' lives. It was only the beginning."

Tears filled my eyes as I remembered holding my mother's hand as she lay dying. "Mama told me she felt God's presence near the end. She said He was right there beside her. She wasn't afraid of dying." My fingers and cheeks felt icy, my tears warm as I wiped them away. "I miss my parents so much."

"I miss mine, too. But in a way, having them with us makes it too easy to be carried along on the current of their faith instead of developing a vital faith of our own. It's easier to ask their advice and trust them to guide us than it is to study His word and listen for His voice ourselves. If I always carried Gerrit on my shoulders, he would never develop the strength to walk by himself or learn to find his own way through the woods."

That's what I had done. I had let Mama and Papa carry me, pray for me, advise me. Now I needed to grow up and walk on my own. I felt the baby kicking strongly inside me, running out of room. I lifted Maarten's hand and rested it on my belly so he could feel the movement, too. I watched his face as he experienced the wonder of it and saw tears form in his eyes.

A week later on a cold Sunday afternoon, our son Jakob Maarten de Jonge was born. The love I felt for him nearly overwhelmed me, and I knew it was just a small taste of the love that Father God had for me. I had done nothing to deserve such love, just as little Jakob had done nothing to deserve mine, and had, in fact, caused me great pain. But I loved my son enough to give my life for him, simply because he was my child. As I fell asleep with exhaustion, holding the miracle of tiny Jakob in my arms, I felt my faith and trust in God begin to sprout and grow once again.

CHAPTER 25

Geesje's Story

HOLLAND, MICHIGAN
49 YEARS EARLIER

When we first settled in western Michigan, the canopy of trees overhead was so thick I could barely glimpse the sky through the tangled leaves. The silence of that vast wilderness terrified me, especially at night or when I was alone with the children. At first we shared the forest with the native Ottawa Indians, our closest neighbors. They taught us to make a sweet, honey-like syrup and crumbly blocks of crude sugar by collecting sap from certain local trees each spring and boiling it down. But as more and more settlers arrived in the coming years, we squeezed the natives out as we slowly tamed the forest they depended on for their livelihood. They eventually migrated north to a less-settled part of the state. Reverend Smith and his family, who had worked with the Indians at the Old Wing Mission, moved along with them.

Gradually, the silence of the wilderness yielded to the constant noise of construction: the *thunk* of axes as we chopped down the great forest of trees; the groan of splintering wood as trees toppled; the whistles and whips of the teamsters as they worked their oxen to move logs and uproot tree trunks; the pounding of hammers and rasp of saws as our community slowly rose up from the forest.

In the spring months after Jakob was born, the town elders decided to start a Dutch-language newspaper. Maarten went to a meeting at Dominie Van Raalte's house to discuss the details. I was excited for him. The newspaper would require a printer, and Maarten would finally be able to return to the work he loved and was skilled at doing. I couldn't stop peering out of the cabin door as I waited, watching for him to return. When I finally saw him walking up the path, his shoulders were slumped and his head hung so low I couldn't glimpse his face. I stood on our doorstep, waiting, fearing bad news.

"What happened?" I asked when he finally looked up at me.

"Geesje . . . Hendrik is back."

"He's here? In Holland?"

Maarten nodded. "He arrived just as our meeting was about to end. He wanted to talk to Dominie Van Raalte about purchasing farmland. Hendrik asked me to stay while they discussed it because I could vouch for him. Dominie suggested that he look at some parcels in Zeeland where a lot of newcomers are farming."

I swallowed and tried to speak. "Is that what he decided to do then? Settle in Zeeland?"

Maarten exhaled as he nodded again. Then he added, "I thought you should also know that Hendrik is married now."

"Yes . . . Well. So am I."

I spoke matter-of-factly, but the news hit me very hard. I had watched Maarten and the other men chopping down the forest, and I always felt such a devastating loss at the moment when a towering tree started to fall over. A beautiful living thing had been killed, falling with a crash. It would never live again. That's how I felt when Maarten told me the news about Hendrik's marriage. All hope for Hendrik and me was gone and would never live again.

Maarten followed me as I turned and went inside the cabin. As if sensing my sorrow, he scooped up our two older boys and took them outside, leaving me alone with the sleeping baby. I don't know how long I sat near the hearth, gazing into the empty fireplace, feeling sorry for myself. Eventually, the sound of Maarten splitting logs outside broke through my grief. I stood and watched him through the window, chopping wood as if he was furious with the logs. It was selfish of me to ignore my husband's feelings while I wallowed in my own. I thought back to all the ways I had seen my parents show their love for each other, and I walked outside, took the axe from his hands, and held him tightly in my arms.

"You never told me what Dominie Van Raalte said about the newspaper. Have they decided to go ahead with it?"

He sighed, like a locomotive releasing steam, and hugged me in return. "Yes. And they asked me to print it. They're going to help me secure a loan so I can purchase the equipment I'll need and set up a shop where the town center will be one day."

I lifted my head from his chest and looked up at him. I could see how quietly happy he was, and I was sorry that the news about Hendrik had diluted his joy. "Will the equipment be hard to find?"

"I don't think so. I may have to travel to Kalamazoo to see about ordering a press. And it will have to be shipped here from Chicago, somehow. I suppose by freighter across Lake Michigan, then dragged over the sandbar and put on a flatboat for the trip up Black Lake to Holland. The leaders are still trying to figure out how to open a deeper channel between the two lakes."

"We'll need to build a shop where we can set up the printing press, won't we?" I added. "I don't think it will fit in our cabin."

"No, it won't. But we can start small and simple, at first."

I felt pleased that he had included me. "I'd like to help you with the business," I said. "I watched you and Papa all those years, and I helped out now and then when Papa had a large order to fill. And I can help with the bookkeeping the way Mama sometimes did. We'll do it together, Maarten."

"Maybe our three sons will join us, too, someday. I'll hang a big sign in front—'de Jonge and Sons, Printers.'"

He rested his hands on my waist. They were so huge he could nearly encircle it with his fingers, especially now that I was getting my figure back after Jakob's birth. I knew Maarten was acting cheerful to disguise his own pain, pretending to be brave as he pushed his fear and sorrow away. We both were. I laid my head on his chest as I tried to erase the picture of Hendrik with another woman—his wife. Holding her. Kissing her.

"I remember the first time you held me in your arms, Maarten. It was on the night in Arnhem when that gang of ruffians smashed all our windows with bricks and stones. You came up to my bedroom to see if I was all right. Remember?"

"I do. You felt so tiny and helpless. And you were so scared. I could feel your entire body trembling when I held you. That's when I knew I wanted to protect you and take care of you for the rest of my life. And I always will, Geesje. For as long as I live."

I was sorry that Hendrik had returned, and yet at the same time I was glad. I wouldn't have to wonder what had become of him. I would know where he was and maybe hear about him from time to time. Maybe see him. I was vain enough to wonder if he'd returned to this area to be close to me.

I looked up at Maarten again and said, "You've given the children and me a very happy life here. I'm so grateful for that." I could tell by the tender way he held me, the soft way he looked at me, that he loved me. I didn't ever want him to feel unloved in return. I had never spent a single day of my life feeling unloved, and I vowed that if it was within my power, Maarten wouldn't either. "The life we have is a very good one," I told him.

"I know. I thank God every day for it."

I heard Jakob fussing in his cradle inside the cabin, ready to be nursed. Maarten and I released each other and I went back inside. My love for him would grow one day at a time, I told myself. One loving act at a time.

CHAPTER 26

Geesje's Story

Dominie Van Raalte understood the importance of a shipping channel to connect Holland with the Great Lakes and the rest of the nation, but at first only a shallow, unnavigable creek connected Black Lake to Lake Michigan. He petitioned the American government for help in digging a deeper canal, and when his efforts stalled, the men of our community took picks and shovels and proceeded to dig out the channel themselves. Maarten joined the other workers, leaving me to tend the children and the farm animals and the garden by myself. In the end, it was worth the effort even if sand continued to fill the new waterway year after year. Maarten was able to use the open port to get our printing business up and running after the delivery of a secondhand printing press from Chicago, along with the other supplies we needed. Our new shop occupied one end of our property where the city street would one day be, and we built a new wood-frame house on the other end with lumber from Holland's new planing mill. Our old log cabin became our barn.

I sat at the dinner table one evening with my husband and three little boys, savoring the scents of newly sawn wood and the fresh pea soup I had made. While the others bowed their heads to say grace, I surveyed my cozy home and thought, *Look what God has given me. Look how rich I am.* God had blessed me with a good husband who loved me and with three precious sons. It would be selfish and ungrateful to want more. And I would be insulting God if I wished for anything different than the life He'd given me. Yes, we had been poor at first and had suffered tragic losses, but thanks to God and our community of hardworking people, the town was growing and prospering. And I was content. My only wish was that my parents had lived to see their dream fulfilled.

Nearly four years after Jakob was born, our daughter Christina joined our little family. I had suffered a miscarriage in between the two births so we thanked the Almighty when she was born safe and sound. Jakob had been a contented child with Maarten's easygoing nature and his tender heart toward God. Our adopted sons Arie, who was nine, and Gerrit, who was seven, continued to be quiet, eager-to-please boys. They attended the Pioneer School now, where they enjoyed their lessons and were learning to speak English. Our community believed in educating our sons and daughters to find their places in life, armed with faith, to become beacons of light in a dark world. All was peaceful.

Then Christina burst into our lives, healthy and strong and wailing for attention. She was demanding and headstrong and knew her own mind from a very young age. Yet she was such a delightful and charming and affectionate child that her three doting brothers raced to grant her every wish. Christina was a mystery to me her entire life. Instead of glorying in her unique position as our only daughter, she followed her three brothers everywhere they went, determined to be just like them. She was as rough-and-tumble as they were, catching frogs in the creek and shooing rabbits out of our garden with a homemade slingshot. I despaired of keeping her dresses and pinafores clean and mended. She would have gladly worn Jakob's outgrown clothes if I had allowed her to. She chafed at having to work alongside me at home the way I had worked alongside my mother, insisting she preferred her brothers' chores. She hated sitting still in church, grew impatient and bored when Maarten read from the Scriptures every evening after dinner, and rebelled at having to observe a day of Sabbath rest each week. She required more stern discipline on my part than the other three children combined. Yet she was the delight of my life.

By the time Christina was two years old, our community had outgrown the log church on the hill, so we constructed a beautiful new one on Ninth Street near the heart of the growing village. It was a handsome wood-frame building with six tapered white pillars adorning the portico in front—and referred to informally as Pillar Church. It contributed a great deal to helping our town look like one of the civilized cities I had left behind in the Netherlands, yet the village still had a rickety impermanence to it. If only they would build with brick or stone instead of wood, I remember thinking as I walked to the cobbler's shop with Christina one morning when she was four years old. And if only the streets were paved with cobblestones or bricks so we didn't have to slog through a sea of mud every spring or inhale lungsful of dust on hot summer days whenever a heedless vehicle swept past.

We were nearly to the cobbler's shop when a wagon drew to a halt near us in a choking dust cloud. I was thinking unkind thoughts toward the driver when I heard someone call my name. "Geesje? . . . Geesje, is that you?" I looked up at the man who had stepped down from the wagon to tie his horse to the post.

"Hendrik!"

"I thought it was you, Geesje. How are you?" I froze in place, fighting a powerful urge to run into his arms and hold him tightly, letting him lift me, laughing, off my feet. He seemed taller than I remembered, stronger and sun-browned and still handsome. He lifted his hat for a moment and ran his fingers through his golden hair, and the once-familiar gesture nearly left me undone.

243

"I'm good . . . very good," I stammered. In the years since Hendrik went away I thought I'd reached a full measure of contentment with my life—but it vanished in an instant as I stared up at the man I loved. I had made the wrong choice half a dozen years ago. I should have run away with him instead of staying married to plodding, boring Maarten.

Hendrik walked around to the other side of the wagon and lifted a woman and a little girl about Christina's age down from the wagon seat. "Geesje, I'd like you to meet my wife, Nella, and our daughter, Rosie."

"I'm pleased to meet you," I said, trying to smile. "This is my daughter, Christina." I didn't want to take my eyes off Hendrik for a moment, but I forced myself to be polite and face his wife. She was about the same height and build as me, the same age, and as fair-haired and blue-eyed as I was. We might have been sisters. "I understand you live near Zeeland," I managed to say.

"We do. We have a farm there."

Hendrik and I chatted for a few minutes, our conversation stiff and formal. He told me about the land he'd cleared, the crops he'd planted, the barn and frame farmhouse he had built for his family. I told him about Maarten's print shop and how it reminded me of the shop Papa had owned in Arnhem—the one where Hendrik and I had met. A flood of memories threatened to overwhelm me as we talked, and I found myself gazing at him so intently that I finally had to force myself to turn to Nella and ask what had brought them into town. I have no idea how she replied. I wasn't listening. Instead, I was trying to think of a way to meet Hendrik alone later, remembering how we had often snuck away to meet in secret in Arnhem. I wanted to feel his arms around me, ask if he was truly happy with Nella, and confess to him how lonely I often felt when Maarten was busy with work or his obligations at church. I wanted to tell Hendrik that I loved him and hear him say that he still loved me.

As we talked our two little girls played together outside the cobbler's shop. They became instant friends and stood with their arms entwined, their laughter bubbling up like spring water. It was the first time I had ever seen Christina so engaged in play with another little girl. She usually wanted nothing to do with girls and ran off to play with the boys, instead.

The loss I felt when Hendrik and I finally said good-bye was as if my heart had been ripped away. I didn't know when—or if—I would ever see him again. I went inside the cobbler's shop, barely able to recall why I was there, and finished my errands in a daze. I returned home to my plain clapboard house feeling desolate and unable to cope with Christina's whining demands. She had fussed at having to separate from her newfound friend and continued to nag me about wanting to play with Rosie until my own raw emotions made me lose my temper with her.

I decided not to tell Maarten that I had run into Hendrik, but later, as the six of us sat down to dinner, Christina began fussing again, this time nagging her father. "Can I play with Rosie again, Papa? She's my best friend in the whole world. Will you take me to visit her tomorrow?"

"Rosie who?" he asked with a mouthful of potatoes. "Who are you talking about?"

"The girl we met at the cobbler's shop today. Mama said I can't play with her again but you'll let me, won't you Papa? Please?"

"Who is she talking about, Geesje?"

I had to explain or Christina would pester her father to distraction. She was accustomed to getting her own way and aware that Maarten was like warm butter in her hands. "We ran into Hendrik Vander Veen and his wife outside the cobbler's shop today," I told him. "Their daughter, Rosie, was with them. I hadn't met his wife before so we talked for a few minutes."

"And I played with Rosie. She was so nice, Papa, and I want to play with her again, but Mama won't let me."

I couldn't help snapping at her. "I told you, Christina. They live in Zeeland, not Holland!"

"But you'll let me see her again, won't you, Papa?"

Maarten's face darkened as he struggled to control his emotions.

"You need to obey your mother," he finally said. "And don't come running to me when she says 'no.' Understand?" He was upset, but not at Christina. Maarten was usually very even-tempered, but he strode off to his meeting that night in a sour mood. As soon as he was gone, Christina threw a temper tantrum. It was the last straw for me. I came dangerously close to venting my grief and sorrow on my daughter.

Just in time, Arie came to my rescue, scooping Christina up in his arms and soothing her as he chatted with her in English. They were nine years apart in age, but there had always been a close bond between them. Arie and Gerrit were learning the American language in school and Christina thought it was a great treat to talk with her brothers in a language that her parents still didn't understand very well. Arie carried her off—I don't know where—leaving me alone with only my thoughts for company.

I couldn't get Hendrik out of my mind, how tall and muscular and handsome he still was. I loved everything about him, including the way his hair stood on end after he'd run his hand through it and the way his tanned skin crinkled at the corners of his eyes when he squinted into the sun. What would my life be like if I had run away with him years ago? I was fond of Maarten, and I had a good life with him, but I didn't love him. The rush of passion I'd felt for Hendrik today revealed what was missing from my marriage. How could I go through the rest of my life without feeling that breathless, intoxicating emotion?

I knelt down on my bedroom floor and dug in my steamer trunk for the tin box I'd brought with me from the Netherlands. Inside were all of Hendrik's letters, tied in a bundle with a wide pink ribbon. I loosened the ribbon and began reading through them as tears of regret and loss washed down my face. As my mind spun once again with plots to somehow meet with Hendrik in secret, I understood the temptation that my ancestor Eve had faced as she'd doubted God's goodness and the truth of His word. How easy it was for a lie to turn contentment into dissatisfaction and sin. Unlike Eve, I had resisted temptation the last time and

246

had obeyed God. I'd stayed with Maarten—and ended up with second-best.

I was still reading through Hendrik's letters, still wandering down the dangerous road of bitterness and self-pity, when Arie and Christina returned. I hastily shoved the pages into an envelope as Christina burst into my bedroom, happy again, her tantrum forgotten. She threw her arms around my neck and gave me a kiss. "Arie said I have to say 'sorry,' Mama." I hugged her in return, too filled with emotion from Hendrik's letters to reply. Christina spied the box and asked, "What's that, Mama?"

"They're letters, lieveling. From someone I knew a long time ago in the Netherlands."

"Can I have that box for my things? It's pretty."

"Then I wouldn't have a place to keep my letters."

She picked up the pink ribbon a moment later and said, "May I have this, then?"

"All right. Shall I tie it in your hair?" Christina nodded, and I loosened her braids, which were already coming undone. I tied the ribbon in a bow around her thick blond hair. It was so unlike her to let me fuss with her hair that she surprised me.

"Rosie wore pretty ribbons in her hair, didn't she, Mama?"

"Yes, lieveling, she did." Hendrik's daughter had resembled a little porcelain doll with every hair and pleat and bow in place— just like her mother. His wife, Nella, was much prettier than I was. I pulled Christina close so she wouldn't see my sudden tears.

As I lay in bed beside Maarten later that night, I was aware that I had sinned. Jesus said if we even looked with lust at someone who wasn't our spouse, we'd committed adultery in our heart. Maarten didn't know how I still longed for Hendrik—but God did.

I needed to pray for forgiveness. I needed to erase Hendrik from my heart and mind all over again and burn his letters in the fireplace. The stakes were high if I didn't repent and flee tempta- tion: the loss of my faith, my soul. I needed to return to a place of contentment and gratitude for everything God had given me; to believe that He loved me and wanted what was best for me. I lay awake for several hours, praying to be forgiven, vowing that tomorrow I would begin again.

The sky wasn't even light yet when someone knocked on our back door. For a wild moment I thought it might be Hendrik coming to beg me to run away with him. I wrapped a shawl over my nightgown and followed Maarten to the door. Pieter Visser from church stood on our step, looking pale and distraught. He removed his hat when he saw me and held it over his heart. "Geesje, can you come? It's Johanna—"

"Is her baby coming? Is it time?" Johanna and I had become good friends, and I'd offered her advice and reassurance during her pregnancy—her first. I had suffered my miscarriage the same week that Johanna's mother had suddenly died, and together we'd shared our bewilderment at God's incomprehensible ways. "Have you sent for the midwife?" I asked Pieter.

"Yes . . . she has been with us all night." Tears filled Pieter's eyes. "The baby was stillborn, Geesje."

"Oh, no!" I covered my mouth as grief for my young friend welled up.

"Johanna wants you. She asked if you would come."

"Of course. I'll get dressed."

I prayed to find words of consolation as I hurried to Johanna's bedside in the pale predawn light. None came to me. When I arrived, all I could do was hold my friend tightly and weep with her, a silent companion in her grief. The midwife let her hold her child for a few minutes—a perfectly-formed baby boy, as gray and cold and colorless as the dawn sky—before taking him away for burial. He had died inside her womb without ever drawing a breath.

"Why does God allow such terrible things to happen?" she asked. Her arms were empty, and she hugged herself tightly, rocking in place. I sat on the bed beside her, holding her, weeping with her.

"I don't know," I said simply. "But it isn't right. And I'm very angry with God right now."

"I am, too," she whispered, as if afraid to say the words out loud. She swallowed and said, "I wanted you to come, Geesje, and no one else because I knew you would take my side. You won't tell me everything will be all right or that I can have another baby to take his place. You won't say that this was God's will and I must accept it or that God must have needed my little one in heaven. When terrible things like this happen, I've heard people say that we must examine our lives and repent of our sin, but I know I didn't do anything to deserve this, and neither did my baby."

"Don't listen to the stupid things people say, Johanna. They're wrong. And you have every right to be angry with God right now. I was furious with Him when my baby died, and I didn't try to pretend that I wasn't. Besides, He already knows exactly how we feel."

"But you didn't stay angry. And right now I feel like I'll never be happy again. Help me, Geesje. Tell me how to make sense of this. You're such a strong woman of faith."

I didn't reply. I was glad she couldn't see my face or read my heart and see the rebellion I'd felt toward God only yesterday after seeing Hendrik.

"How can I ever trust God again after He took my baby?" she asked.

I squeezed her tightly and said, "No matter what, don't ever stop trusting Him. I believe that God is as grieved over your baby's death as we are. He created us and gave us life on this beautiful earth because He wanted us to live here for eternity. But death entered this world when Adam and Eve sinned. Now we feel pain and grief each time a loved one dies because we know it isn't right. God knows it isn't right, too. That's why He sent His Son to die in our place, so that death would be destroyed and we would have eternal life. Keep your eyes on the cross, Johanna, and you'll know that you can surely trust Him."

"Is that how you keep going, Geesje? By waiting for heaven?"

"In a way . . ." I said, stroking her hair. "But Jesus also taught us to pray for God's kingdom to come now and for His will to be done now, here on earth, as it is in heaven. He has work for us to do, Johanna. A life to live for Him now. When I felt the way you do right now, I asked God to let me know He was still beside me.

249

To show me that He loved me and that His ways were good and right. Then I watched and waited for His replies. . . . Slowly, little by little, He let me know in dozens of everyday ways that He was near me and that He loved me. He'll do the same for you if you ask."

I stayed with Johanna until she fell asleep, exhausted from her ordeal. After promising Pieter I would come back as soon as I could, I hurried home to my family. I needed to be with Johanna when the other women came to offer comfort, shielding my friend from any hurtful words.

My house was quiet inside. The jumble of dishes and dirty pans in my kitchen told me that Maarten had fed the children and sent the boys off to school. I found Christina with him in the print shop. She wore the pink ribbon tied around her tousled hair, and I smiled at the thought of Maarten struggling to tie it in a bow with his large, thick fingers while our daughter bounced and wiggled on his lap. God forgive me, but when I'd wallowed in self-pity last night I had called him "second-best." He wasn't. Maarten was a loving husband to me, a wonderful father to our children.

Christina ran to me when she saw me and hugged my legs. The overwhelming love I felt for her, for all my children, was one of the convincing proofs God had offered me when I'd challenged Him to show that He loved me. I would lay down my own life for them, which was exactly what He had done for me.

The pink hair ribbon also reminded me of Hendrik. Today I would begin the difficult task of forgetting him all over again. But I still couldn't bring myself to burn all of his letters in the fireplace. I simply couldn't. They remained in the little tin box, hidden away in my steamer trunk.

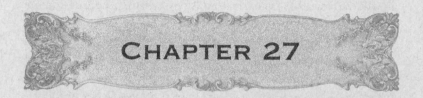

CHAPTER 27

Anna

It seems as though my hike up Mt. Pisgah with Derk happened weeks ago instead of just this morning. I've been mulling over the advice he gave me ever since, pushing it around in my mind the way I pushed my scrambled eggs around on my plate at breakfast. Derk said I shouldn't marry William, and he gave me two reasons why. The first was that I didn't love him. Derk had insisted that love was all-important, and I'd insisted that it didn't matter to me, justifying my opinion with a lengthy discourse about how love wasn't expected in my social circle. But as I sit here on the veranda watching young couples walk past arm-in arm, gazing into each other's eyes and talking animatedly, I long to feel that same breathless passion for William. I used to secretly read romance novels at school—all the girls did—and we would dream of the mysterious excitement of falling in love, the unbounded joy of knowing we were loved in return. I've brought my diary downstairs with me, and I spend a few minutes rereading the passages where William kissed me, trying to remember what I had felt for him then and wondering what he had felt for me.

I also reread several diary entries about the castle church and how I had found a missing piece of myself there. They remind me of the second reason Derk gave for not marrying William. He said I should be free to attend any church I chose, and that William had no right to take away that religious freedom. Even if William did allow me to attend the castle church, I can well imagine what all the other ladies I know would say about it. I would be ostracized if I dared to talk about the Bible or bring up Jesus' teachings as a topic of conversation over tea. All mention of religion is taboo in my circle. It's considered *fanatical*, to use Mother's word.

I open my Bible to the place I left off and read the story of Jesus' arrest in the Garden of Gethsemane. All His disciples scattered and deserted Him. Peter adamantly denied knowing Him—not once, but three times. I suddenly wish I had never met Derk Vander Veen or talked with him about Jesus. I feel as though I, too, will be denying Christ when I return to Chicago and my old way of life.

I hear brisk footsteps and look up to see Mother approaching, armed with a stack of fashion magazines. She sits down in the empty chair beside mine. "You promised we would look through these together, remember? We need to give our seamstress plenty of time to sew your wedding gown and trousseau." She lays one of the magazines on top of the open Bible in my lap as if she hasn't noticed it and begins leafing through another magazine on her own. "Oh my, just look at these gorgeous dresses! And the new hats they're wearing! Honoria Stevens told me this magazine was the best one with the very latest fashions, and she was right."

I lean over to peer at the page she is studying. "What's the purpose of those huge, puffy sleeves?" I ask.

"They don't need a purpose. They're in fashion this season."

"They look hideous. Who would want arms that looked like that?"

Mother calmly turns to the next page and then the next. "One might say that the look you've chosen during your stay here is equally unsatisfactory." Her voice is tight with barely controlled restraint. "You don't wear gloves or petticoats, you stopped fixing your hair. . . . I see now that it was a mistake to leave our lady's maid at home. You've developed some very bad habits while we've been away."

I gaze into the distance at the rippling blue water, the emerald trees, the cotton-puff clouds that float above the grand hotels on the opposite shore of Black Lake. "Don't you ever get tired of having to look pretty and wear the latest clothes?" I ask. "And having to listen to boring conversations as we sip tea and nibble cucumber sandwiches?"

"The conversation isn't at all boring to me. The other women are my friends. We enjoy each other's company. And don't reduce our life in Chicago to something trivial, Anna. The women in our social circle accomplish a great deal of good for the community."

"I don't have a close friend." That's the problem, I realize. None of the girls I knew back home would ever engage in frank discussions like the one Derk and I had as we'd climbed the dune. My time with Derk had ended unsatisfactorily, but at least we had been honest with each other.

"If you want friends, Anna, you need to stop being so bashful and talk to people. Invite them to go places with you. I'm sure you would find that you have a great deal in common with other girls your age if you simply tried harder."

I'm not so sure. I can't think of a single girl I know who would be willing to visit the castle church with me or read the Bible.

"What about William's sister?" Mother asks. "Jane is nearly your age, isn't she? You'll have plenty of time to become friends while your new home is being built and you're living with William's family."

"I suppose," I reply. But how can I talk frankly about love and marriage with my husband's sister? And Jane has never shown any interest at all in religion, much less in discussing the Bible. I sigh without realizing it, and Mother slaps her fashion magazine closed.

"Anna, listen to me. You simply must shake off this gloomy attitude of yours. Moroseness is not an endearing quality for anyone to have. I understand why you felt sad when we first arrived and your engagement to William had ended so abruptly. I thought if you spent a week at the lake it would improve your disposition and you would be able to move forward again, but it seems your time here has only made things worse. Now that you've reconciled with William and all is forgiven, you have everything in the world to look forward to—a future that is the envy of all the young ladies your age. Yet you continue to mope around as if you want something more. I simply don't understand it."

"I don't understand it either!" I reply in exasperation. "I know I should be happy, and I want to be—I truly do. But . . . but coming here has raised even more questions in my mind."

"What questions?" She seems truly baffled, even though she has read my diary and knows all my private thoughts. We are worlds apart, Mother and I. She doesn't understand me and I don't understand her. I don't understand how she can blithely sail through life without ever questioning the things that happen to her. Or how she can be content to leave every decision to my father. Why is she satisfied with shallow, superficial friendships, and stiff, formal religious services that keep God at a distance? I am nothing like my mother. I want answers to my many doubts and questions. I want to feel God's love when I worship Him. I want to know what my purpose is in life. I glance at the serene façade Mother presents and wonder if the rebellion I feel is in my blood, something I've inherited from my real mother along with my blond hair.

"I have a lot of questions, Mother—such as where did you find me? Was I left on your doorstep? In an orphans' home? You told me I was abandoned as a newborn, but where and how did it happen? What were the circumstances?" If I keep bringing up the subject, maybe she'll finally weaken and give in and tell me what I want to know.

Instead she says, "Why are you asking this now, Anna? Why all of a sudden after all these years as our beloved daughter?"

"I'm not sure. Maybe because I'm getting married soon, and I'll have children of my own someday. . . . I guess I've always wondered about my real parents, but I didn't want to hurt your feelings by asking about them. And I've been a little afraid to learn the answers before. But now I need to know."

I can see that Mother is losing patience with me. Perhaps she feels rejected because I'm asking about my "real" mother. When she finally replies, her tone is cold and clipped. "Your father was traveling on a business trip when you were found. I wasn't with him. You need to ask him the details."

"But where was he traveling to? Where did he find me?"

She shakes her head, her chin lifted, her mouth pinched in a firm line. "Don't ask me again, Anna. You need to hear the story from him."

"But I must have had a real mother and father—"

"Of course you did. And we tried very hard to locate them. Your father contacted the proper authorities, put announcements in all the newspapers . . . I don't know why your family never came forward to claim you, but they didn't. In the meantime, we both grew to love you very much, so we began making arrangements to adopt you."

"No one wanted me."

"You're wrong." Mother is close to losing her temper, but proper ladies don't indulge in tantrums, especially in public places. "Your father and I wanted you very badly. If you only knew how much we worried that your family would be located and that we would lose you. . . . When the adoption was finalized and you became ours, we were overjoyed."

"But where—?"

"Let your father tell you the story, Anna. You owe him that much."

I was sorry I hadn't asked him while he was here. Now I would have to wait until I returned to Chicago. I had reached a dead end once again. But I still had questions for Mother. Derk had made such a fuss this morning about marrying for love that I found myself asking, "Were you in love with Father when you married him?"

"Where did that question come from?"

"I know you met Father through Uncle Robert. You told me they had been friends in college and that they both worked for your father for a while."

"Yes, my father gave Arthur a start in business. He gave him his first loan and helped his business become a success."

Had my father used his marriage to Mother to get ahead, the same way he now wanted to use my marriage to William? I adored my father, but this new thought made me see him in a different, less flattering light. "Were you madly in love with each other when you decided to marry?"

"Listen, Anna—"

"I'm getting married soon, and I don't want to talk about trivial things like puffy-sleeved dresses and hideous hats for my trousseau. I want to talk about marriage, and how I'll know whether or not I'm in love with William, and if love is really important for a successful marriage or not!"

"Anna, hush!" She glances all around after my outburst, horrified that I've raised my voice. She lowers her own voice to a calm murmur. "First of all, you must understand that I'm very uncomfortable discussing such personal matters. One must avoid letting one's emotions spill out for everyone to see. Part of growing up and becoming a mature woman is learning to control your feelings rather than allowing them to control you. Women who indulge in histrionics and have to take laudanum pills are from an entirely different class than we are."

"I can't help how I feel, can I?"

"Of course you can. You must learn to take control of yourself, Anna. You have always been a very emotional child, what people refer to as high-strung. I feel partly responsible for indulging your moodiness for as long as I have, and I'm sorry if it sounds cruel, but it's time for you to stop."

She opens her magazine and erects a barrier of dignity like a brick wall. "Now, about these gowns. If you don't like the sleeves on that one, perhaps you'd prefer this one, instead."

She is avoiding my question. It can only mean that she wasn't madly in love with Father when they married—and still isn't. A woman in love wants to talk about the details endlessly, the way one of the girls at my school did after she fell in love. Yet my parents seem content with each other. Perhaps I will learn to be content, too.

I do what Mother asks and dutifully page through the fashion magazines, choosing several gowns for my trousseau. Mother complains that they're much too plain, but the ones she prefers look fussy and confining and purposeless to me. They remind me of my life. When we finish leafing through the last magazine, I lean back in my chair and watch the activity on the lake. There is a brisk breeze today, which evidently makes it perfect for sailing, because Black Lake is dotted with white triangular sails. I wonder if Derk is sailing one of them. They skim the surface of the sparkling water so freely and effortlessly that it almost looks inviting—but a sickening feeling writhes in the pit of my stomach at the thought of venturing out on the deep, cold water.

I have another strange dream that night. Mama and I are on a train that is stuffed full of working-class people. Their simple clothing is well-worn and patched—no puffy sleeves or voluminous petticoats for them. They carry baskets with homemade lunches that smell of sausage and garlic and raw onions. I hear shouts and loud laughter as two rough drunks begin fighting. Mama holds me close, whispering, "Shh, shh. It won't be much longer and we'll finally be far away from all this. We'll be safe. We'll live in a place with beautiful trees where it's peaceful and quiet."

When we finally get off the train, we're near the waterfront where dozens of ships are moored, their sails rolled up, their empty masts poking into the darkening sky. We walk until I grow tired and ask to be carried, but Mama has her hands full as she struggles with our bags. We stop several times to rest before reaching the steamship office. Mama asks for two tickets and dumps out a purse full of coins to pay for them. The clerk points toward a ship docked at the pier. The sun is setting behind our backs, and the water stretches out in front of us as far as I can see, all the way to the gently curved horizon. Panic floods through me at the thought of boarding that ship. I can't breathe. I begin to scream. "No . . . !"

I wake up sweating, tangled in the bedsheets, relieved that it was only a dream. I rise and open the window, gulping in the moist, clean air. The waves are shushing in the distance like Mama's soft shushing in my dream. Lights from the other hotels across the lake sparkle and twinkle.

Am I so terrified of marriage that it's giving me nightmares? Is it truly a fear of the deep, unknown water—or of surrendering my life to a future that has already been mapped out for me?

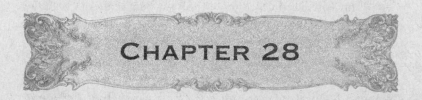

CHAPTER 28

Geesje

Something compels me to keep writing my story. I know the committee only asked me to write about the early years of our kolonie, which I'm well past now, but if I want to tell my story properly I need to write about the War Between the States and how it changed all of our lives. I drag a wooden chair to the attic trapdoor and teeter on tiptoes to climb up. Beneath the eaves, the cramped attic is hot, filled with cobwebs and discarded possessions. Dust motes shift and float in the dead air, making me sneeze as I move things around in my search. I'm looking for the box of letters Arie sent home to us when he was away at war.

I move aside a broken rocking chair, an old bureau with a missing drawer, a crumbling box of books. Why do I keep so many useless things when I obviously no longer need them? My family left nearly everything behind when we emigrated from the Netherlands, so I know I can live just as well without all these things.

259

Success at last! I find the old tea tin with Arie's letters and carefully lower myself down from the attic again, praying that the chair doesn't topple over and take me with it. The front of my apron is smudged with dust, and I have to shake the cobwebs out of my kerchief before tying it over my hair again. I'll read the letters outside in my chair on the front porch, where I can listen to the birds chirping and the bees buzzing in my flower garden.

As I page through these precious, ink-stained pages, I remember the fear that filled me during those suspenseful years and my many, many prayers, not only for Arie but for all of the young men from our community. Arie's letters are relentlessly cheerful at first as he describes his many adventures—a deliberate ruse, I suspect, to disguise his own fear and to attempt to minimize ours. I hear Christina's voice in my mind as I read them, not Arie's. She loved to read his letters aloud to us, over and over again, as we sat around the fireplace.

"Arie is so lucky," she would sigh when she finished. *"He gets to go so many places and do so many things!"*

Later that afternoon when I've finished reading through all the letters, I finally sit down with my pencil and notebook to continue writing my story. I decide to begin with the day that Arie raced home from the print shop with the news . . .

Geesje's Story

HOLLAND, MICHIGAN
36 YEARS EARLIER

"Our nation is at war, Mama!" Arie burst into my kitchen one April morning in 1861, breathless with the news. "They asked Papa to print a special edition of the newspaper. The Confederates opened fire on our Union soldiers at Fort Sumter near

Charleston, South Carolina. They're demanding that we surrender the fort."

I had to sit down to take in the news. Ever since Abraham Lincoln was elected president last November, the southern states had been seceding from the Union, one by one. Now this deliberate act of war, only a month after his inauguration.

"Papa will bring a copy of the paper home later, but he thought you'd want to know, Mama."

"Tell him thank you for telling me."

Arie was halfway through the door when he turned back again. "I almost forgot. Papa said to tell you not to worry. He said God is in control." I smiled at him and shooed him away. Arie was seventeen and had decided not to continue his education and go on to college with his friend Dirk Van Raalte, the dominie's son. The original Pioneer School had grown into the Holland Academy, and a few years earlier Dominie Van Raalte had deeded five acres of land to create a college campus. The college's first building had been completed two years ago in 1859, a square, three-story brick building known as Van Vleck Hall. It housed offices, classrooms, and dormitory rooms for students.

But Arie had no interest in attending college there or anywhere else. He loved working with his father in the print shop. The dream Maarten had when he'd hung the sign above his shop—*de Jonge and Sons, Printers*—had finally come true. Well, at least one of his three sons had decided to join him. It was too soon to tell what fifteen-year-old Gerrit or thirteen-year-old Jakob would decide. They both helped out in the print shop whenever they were needed, but becoming part of the family business was a choice they would be free to make in the future. Maarten would never pressure them.

That evening Maarten brought home the newspaper—it was still printed in our Dutch language—and we read about the Battle of Fort Sumter. Our adopted country was at war. For now the fighting seemed very far away and had little to do with our everyday lives. Dominie Van Raalte had long been an outspoken opponent of slavery, and we agreed that the institution was evil and needed to be abolished. When the war began that April day, we naively believed that the hostilities would last only a few weeks before the divided nation would be sewn back together again. We were wrong.

President Lincoln called for seventy-five thousand troops. Later, in July, Congress voted to increase that number to five hundred thousand. In September of 1861, twenty-six young men from our community volunteered to fight, enlisting in the Michigan cavalry. The war that had once seemed very far away inched closer as we read newspaper reports of the battles and of General McClellan's Peninsula Campaign. I remember looking at our three young sons gathered around our table and praying in earnest that the war would end before they each turned eighteen. My prayers went unanswered.

A year after that first battle at Fort Sumter the war was no closer to ending. Our son Arie turned eighteen, and when Dominie Van Raalte's two sons, Ben and Dirk, enlisted in the 25th Michigan Infantry in August of 1862, Arie decided to join them. He and about three hundred other area boys went off to war together, marching past Dominie Van Raalte's home and up the hill past Pilgrim Home Cemetery, then on down the road to Kalamazoo. I wasn't the only mother in the crowd who wept to see her son go. A group of women presented the soldiers with a silk flag, emblazoned with the motto *God is Our Refuge*, and Dominie prayed for them, saying, "May all this shaking bring us nearer to God, may it make us strangers and pilgrims; may it make us holier." I tried to pray as well, but my prayers were sometimes hindered by memories of God's seeming capriciousness in taking my parents, the innocent immigrants aboard the *Phoenix*, and my friend's stillborn baby, along with so many, many others. Yet I also knew that those times of great "shaking," as Dominie phrased it, had also brought me closer to God. In wrestling with Him, I had learned to hear His voice more clearly and experience His love in a greater way. My faith had grown through each trial, and it would weather this time of testing, too.

Arie cheerfully relayed the news of his travels in his letters.

We arrived in Kalamazoo where they will try to make soldiers out of us for the next month. We're going to wear out our new boots with all this marching and drilling. . . .

October 1: They loaded us into railroad cars, and we headed south. We passed through Michigan City and New Buffalo, then into Indiana where there is plenty of good farmland. We saw the fine capital city of Indianapolis, then crossed the border into Kentucky and arrived in Louisville. This is where we'll be stationed for the next few months as we scout the countryside south of Louisville for Rebels and perform routine guard duty. Kentucky is a border state between North and South, so we're guessing we'll see lots of action with our Rebel neighbors from Tennessee or Virginia.

The entire community mourned when we received news of our first casualty, a young man named Ary Rot who died in Louisville—not from battle injuries but from one of the many diseases that swept through the army camps that cold winter. In December Arie wrote that they were leaving Louisville and marching south through the state of Kentucky to the city of Bowling Green. *The weather is cold and snowy. The fences throughout the countryside are disappearing as they're turned into firewood. But after living in Michigan all my life where the weather is much colder and snowier than down here, I'm not bothered by the winter weather at all.*

Nine-year-old Christina wrote to her brother nearly every day, even when there was nothing new to say. She told him every detail of her life at school and at church and even what Maarten was printing that day in the shop. I feared we would go broke paying for postage but Arie insisted that Christina's long-winded letters cheered him and the other Holland boys. One payday, Arie sent money home to his sister, writing, *I was thinking of you today and remembering how we used to walk over to the store on Eighth Street to buy a handful of penny candy. Tell Jakob to take you there for me so you can enjoy a little treat.*

Arie's regiment stayed in Kentucky for nearly a year. He described how mountainous the region was compared to the flatlands of Michigan and told about the earthworks they had built in the woods above the Green River to prevent the Confederates from crossing it. *We can't let the Rebels through*, he wrote, *or they'll be able to take control of our main Union supply line and attack Louisville*. On the Fourth of July in 1863, the Rebels attempted to do just that. We read in the newspaper that a battle had taken place, but it was nearly a week before we received a letter from Arie describing the fight. The suspenseful days in between were a test of our faith and led to several sleepless nights. He described the battle this way when his letter finally arrived:

> *The Rebs thought we'd be easy targets with only two hundred of us against more than two thousand of them. We saw their cavalry coming at sunrise and we opened fire. They answered with an artillery bombardment, wounding two of our men. A short time later they had the nerve to send their officers forward waving a flag of truce, telling us we'd better surrender and stop the bloodshed since we were outnumbered ten-to-one and certain to lose. Of course we refused, and not long afterward when the fighting started up again, our Michigan sharpshooters were able to take out their gun batteries. The Rebs attacked us seven or eight times over the next three hours—believe me, it felt like three days to us—but we kept sending them back. They finally gave up and waved the white flag again, asking if they could pick up their wounded and bury their dead. We let them do it, then they turned around and headed south. That was the last we heard of them. Colonel Moore says we have a right to be proud of ourselves, fighting so hard against a force that was ten times the size of ours.*

Arie and the other Holland soldiers thanked God for their victory. Thirty-one of them took up a collection and sent the money home with a note to Dominie Van Raalte: *With gratitude to God for sparing them in the battle of Green River, the undersigned send a contribution to Kingdom causes.* The Battle of Green River was of great interest and importance to our little community, but it was overshadowed in the national news by a horrific series of battles that had taken place at the same time in a little Pennsylvania town called Gettysburg.

As the war dragged on and on into another dreadful year, casualties among our area men began to mount. Every day brought news of Union setbacks and victories, with more and more deaths and appalling injuries. Every day we gathered with other worried families on a downtown street corner not far from the print shop to listen to the news as it was read aloud, holding our breaths as we waited to see if one of our Holland boys was listed among the wounded or dead. Whenever a local boy's name was read, the outbursts of grief nearly broke my heart. These bereaved mothers often begged me to come home with them and pray with them. I'm not sure why they always asked for me. Perhaps because they knew I didn't expect them to keep up a façade of unwavering faith and trust when they were hurting. In the privacy of their bedrooms and kitchens and parlors, I gave them the freedom to weep and mourn and ask, "Why my son? Why would God take one so young, so full of life and promise?" When we attended church and countless funerals, we were all obliged to be courageous and present a picture of steadfast faith. But when we were alone, we helped each other find strength in God and in a sense of His nearness. I can truly say that He was always with us. Always. We emerged with our faith forged stronger, the façade no longer a false front.

Our boys in the 25th Michigan Infantry continued to make their way south, and by mid-July of 1864 they were within sight of Atlanta, Georgia. Arie complained of the terrible heat in his letters and the continuous bombardment of Rebel shells. After much anticipation and worry, the Battle of Atlanta was finally fought on July 22. We rejoiced in the news of a Union victory, but it had come at a terrible price—more than 3,600 Union casualties.

Our community waited in suspense for the list of names to be read. Maarten and I were standing on the street corner listening together, when we heard our son's name—Arie de Jonge—listed among the wounded. We had no way of knowing how seriously he had been injured. I collapsed into Maarten's arms.

"We must stay strong," he said as he helped me walk home. "Arie's life is in God's hands now, and that's the safest place to be."

I trembled for such a long time that I didn't know how I would be able to make supper. With no information about Arie's wounds, my fearful heart imagined the worst. I would need the support of my friends more than ever to remain strong. Then another worry occurred to me. "How will we tell the children?" I asked Maarten. "They'll be home from school soon. You know how Christina adores her brother."

"I'll walk to the school and meet them," he replied. "I'll tell them as much as we know. We'll pray together as a family. God is merciful."

"I'm worried about how this will affect Christina's faith. She's been praying for her brother's safety, and now she may feel as though God has let her down. It's hard enough for me to understand God's ways—and she's just a child."

"Even children need to learn to respect God's sovereignty," Maarten replied. "Yes, He hears our prayers, but He isn't manipulated by them. She needs to understand the difference."

"Maarten, I'm not sure *I* always understand the difference. We've taught Christina that Jesus can do miracles. That God can do the impossible, that He answers prayer. How will we explain this to her?"

"We'll do the best we can. Her faith will be tested, just like ours is being tested. And I imagine Arie's faith is being tested, too."

A few agonizing days later, we received a letter from our son's commanding officer with more details. Arie's left knee had been badly shattered by a Confederate musket ball, and he had been moved to a hospital in Marietta, Georgia, for surgery. Another week passed before we finally received a short letter from Arie, his handwriting shaky and uneven, saying that he was still alive and that he loved us. But I read his despair between every line when he told us the doctors had been forced to amputate his leg.

Weeks passed with no word from him. We all felt sick with dread. Christina wrote countless letters to him and prayed so hard that I feared her faith would shatter if Arie didn't survive. At last another letter arrived, but it was addressed only to me. The handwriting wasn't Arie's. I had to sit down to read it as the strength drained from my body.

Dear Mama,

A volunteer is writing this letter for me since I'm too weak to do it. I've been transferred by train to Jefferson General Hospital in Port Fulton, Indiana. It's just across the Ohio River from Louisville, Kentucky, where this long war began for me. I'm sorry to say that my leg isn't healing right, and I have a fever that I can't seem to shake. I'm in so much pain that I don't think I can go on this way much longer. I'm not sure I want to. Please don't let Christina read this. I don't want her to know that I'm in a bad way. Don't grieve for me, Mama. I'm not afraid to die. I'm much more afraid to live the rest of my life this way. I love you and Papa so much. Tell Gerrit and Jakob and Christina that I love them, too. And tell Christina she will always be my favorite girl.

Love,

Arie

There are no words to describe the helplessness I felt. I ran to the print shop to show the letter to Maarten. When he finished reading it, he stumbled over to the chair behind his desk and sank down on it. He closed his eyes for a long moment. When he opened them again, he gazed sightlessly toward the window that faced the street. "What are we going to do?" I asked him.

He didn't reply. The only sound was the rhythmic thumping of the printing press, like an urgent heartbeat. "We can't let Arie die all alone down there, Maarten. We need to go to Indiana to see him, to be with him."

Maarten finally looked up at me. "We can't just drop everything and go. Besides, it won't change the outcome if we're there. God holds Arie's life in His hands, and we have to trust Him to know what's best."

I was so angry I wanted to strike him. "How can you abandon our son this way?"

Tears filled Maarten's dark eyes as he stood and took my hands. "I'm not abandoning him. I'm as devastated by this as you are. The only things I know to do are to keep praying and to keep working. Arie loves this print shop. It's his future, God willing. I need to make sure it's thriving when he gets home."

Maarten would find comfort in his work, but I knew I would find none in mine. If I returned home, every little thing would remind me of Arie—the chair at the table where he sat, the empty hook where he hung his coat, his narrow bed, still neatly made up the way he had left it, the book he'd been reading still lying on the bedside table. I couldn't recall feeling this despondent since hearing that Hendrik's ship had sunk.

Maarten and I were still standing together when the door to the print shop opened and the little bell above it jangled. Maarten released my hands, and I turned around. Hendrik stood in the doorway. Was I imagining things? I couldn't take my gaze from him, afraid he would disappear. It had been years since I'd last seen him, but he looked unchanged, still as tall and golden and muscular as the first time he'd walked through our print shop door in Arnhem.

"Hendrik. Good to see you," Maarten said, walking past me to greet him. "What brings you here today?"

"I read in the newspaper that your son was wounded. I came to see how you were doing and if you needed anything."

"Yes, yes he was wounded," I stammered. "They moved him to

a military hospital near Louisville, but . . ." I wanted to take three steps forward and move closer to Hendrik, but I stayed rooted in place.

"I imagine the news has hit you both pretty hard."

"It's the uncertainty," Maarten said. "The waiting. Yet I know God hears our prayers."

My tears, which had remained so close to the surface these past weeks, spilled over and rolled down my face. "Arie lost his leg, and he doesn't want to live," I said. "I feel so . . . so helpless!"

Hendrik shook his head in sympathy. "That's a terrible feeling. But Louisville isn't that far. Is it possible to travel to the hospital to see him?"

Maarten spoke before I could. "We would like to, but we can't leave the shop. We're very shorthanded with all the young men off fighting the war."

"I understand. It's been hard for me to find good farmhands, too."

"We can trust God while we wait," Maarten said. "Arie is safe in His hands."

"Yes," Hendrik said. "That's a comfort."

I wiped my tears as they continued to fall. Hendrik was here, right in front of me, talking to me—to us. Yet I felt numb to his presence and the love I once felt for him, my mind and my heart on my dying son. I felt like something inside me was slowly dying along with him.

"I should go," Hendrik said. "I have some errands to run in town, but I wanted to let you know you're in my prayers."

Maarten reached to shake his hand. "Thank you. It was very good of you to come."

It occurred to me that Hendrik had come to see Maarten, not me. He couldn't have known that I would be in the shop. He paused in the doorway before leaving and looked at me. "Please let me know if you need anything."

I walked through the next few days feeling numb. My fear for our son crushed me like an enormous weight as I prayed for him.

Everywhere I looked, something reminded me of Arie. I needed to escape, so on a cool September day I went outside to dig the potatoes from our garden. The work was tiring, and I knew I should let Maarten or one of the boys do it, but stabbing the ground with the shovel and turning over the sandy earth to reveal the newly grown potatoes helped me deal with my warring emotions. I longed to go see my son, but my husband said we couldn't. Seeing Hendrik again made me realize the importance of every word we spoke to our loved ones, every decision we made concerning them. Our time on earth with these dear ones was so fleeting.

The more I thought about it, the more I realized that if I didn't go see Arie and something did happen to him, I would regret it for the rest of my life. And I already had too many regrets. I abandoned the shovel and the half-filled basket of potatoes in the garden and went inside the house. I washed my face and hands, took off my dirty apron, and rebraided my hair before pinning it up. Then I calmly walked to the print shop and said to Maarten, "I've decided to go to the military hospital to see Arie. If I don't, I'll regret it for the rest of my life."

He gestured to the laboring printing press, working at full speed to print the latest news of the war. "No one else knows how to operate this machine without me."

"I know. I know you need to stay here and run the shop. But I need to be with Arie. Help me get there, Maarten. That's all I'm asking." I held my breath and waited as Maarten thought it over in his slow, deliberate way. I wanted to remind him of how much Arie had already suffered in his short life, how he'd lost his parents at the age of three, how he'd nearly died of malaria along with them, how we'd nursed him through a host of bruises and falls and childhood ailments. I wanted Maarten to remember how we had held Arie close through the very worst of times and dried his tears, so he would understand that I needed to do it all over again. "If the Almighty decides to take Arie away from us, Maarten, I want to hold him one last time."

Maarten must have recognized my fierce determination. He

nodded slowly and said, "If that's what you need to do, I'll see about purchasing a railroad ticket for you."

"Thank you." I went to Maarten and held him tightly in my arms. The weight of his sturdy body, the feel of his bones and muscles and arms, and the strength of his embrace were wonderfully familiar and comforting to me. In that moment, I think I loved Maarten more than I ever had before.

CHAPTER 29

Geesje's Story

HOLLAND, MICHIGAN
36 YEARS EARLIER

Maarten began making arrangements for my trip to Jefferson General Hospital in Port Fulton, Indiana, the next morning. I went with him to the railway office, and it didn't take long for me to realize that I couldn't speak or read English well enough to travel all that way by myself. I would be in trouble the moment the southbound train left Holland's village limits. "Maybe I should take Gerrit along to help me," I told Maarten as we walked home from the station again. Gerrit was nearly eighteen, and as worried about his brother as the rest of us.

Maarten heaved an enormous sigh. "I need Gerrit's help in the print shop, Geesje. We are shorthanded as it is with all the young men away fighting in the war. That's why I had to say no to you the first time you asked to go."

"What about Jakob, then?" He was almost sixteen.

"I'm sorry, but I can't spare him, either. If I don't get my printing orders finished on time, my customers will take their business someplace else."

In the end, Christina decided the issue for us. "I'm going with you, Mama," she told us at dinner that evening. "I'm the one who needs to take care of Arie. You know I have to go. He'll get better when he sees me. He will." If anyone could charm Arie and make him smile or restore his will to live, it was Christina. "Besides, my English is just as good as Jakob's and Gerrit's," she said. In fact, it was probably better. It seemed as though Christina had done more talking during her eleven short years than all three boys combined. She had overheard Maarten and me worrying about the cost of the trip, so her final argument seemed most convincing: "You'll save money on my train ticket since I'm only eleven." She was a tiny little thing with thick, golden hair and deep blue eyes and a determination that was as fierce as my own.

Christina and I left together a day later. It was the first time I had been out of the state of Michigan since arriving here with my parents nearly twenty years earlier. Christina had never traveled outside of the Holland area in her life, let alone ride on a train. We began the three-hundred-fifty-mile trip south with a great deal of enthusiasm and energy, and although my fear for Arie still made my stomach churn with worry, it felt good to finally take this step.

The journey was long and tiring, our passenger train often side-tracked and delayed to allow the more important army supply trains to pass through. We nibbled food from the bag we had brought with us and slept on train seats and in stations along the way that were crowded with soldiers in transit. We passed through broad stretches of farmland in Indiana, dotted with barns and wood-frame farmhouses; through villages and towns with tiny railway stations and single main streets; and through the prosperous city of Indianapolis with its tall brick buildings and church steeples and paved roads. The trees were just beginning to change color from green to vivid shades of yellow, orange, red, and rust. Their beauty was mostly wasted on me. A powerful sense of urgency

273

propelled me, and I never stopped praying, all along the way, that Arie would be able to hang on until we arrived.

We traveled the entire length of Indiana and arrived at Port Fulton on the Ohio River just as the sun was beginning to set on the second day. Christina helped me hire a carriage to take us to Jefferson General Hospital. I only understood snatches of the conversation as she talked with the grizzled driver, but from his grim look and wagging head, I gathered that he didn't think the military hospital was a proper destination for a delicate lady and her young daughter. "Tell him I need to see my son, Christina. . . . Tell him!"

They talked some more then she turned to me again. "He says it's an enormous place with nearly thirty hospital buildings. He thinks we'll get lost inside."

"Just get us to the main door. Someone will help us find our way." The driver finally agreed, and the carriage lurched forward as the horse began to move. I rummaged through my bag as we rode through Port Fulton's streets and found Arie's letter with the return address and building number on it. When we arrived at Jefferson General Hospital, it was indeed an enormous place with dozens of long, white-painted hospital wards radiating from the central buildings like the spokes of a wheel. Later we learned that it housed nearly one thousand patients in various stages of recovery. I remember wondering how much longer this terrible war was going to last, how many more young men would end up maimed and wounded in hospitals like this one—or worse, in their graves. I still believed that slavery was wrong and needed to be stopped—hadn't we come to America ourselves for freedom? But what a terrible price the young men of America were paying for that freedom.

The sun had already sunk below the horizon when I walked through the hospital's main door carrying our bags in one hand and holding Christina's hand in the other. The outside of the complex had been daunting enough, but the inside was overwhelming, with the sound of chattering voices and the bustle of urgent activity all around me. I stopped the first person I saw and said in my clumsy English, "Are you able to help us?" I showed him the envelope with Arie's address on it. When the man mumbled something in return then walked away, I looked at Christina.

"He said he'll find someone to show us the way." It turned out to be a young man not much older than Gerrit, wearing a torn undershirt and dirty Union trousers. His arm was in a sling. He led us back outside the building and across the broad hospital grounds in the center of the "wheel" to one of the long, white buildings. The moment we entered Arie's ward and faced row after row of men, pale and maimed and skeletal, Christina began to cry. Tears sprang to my eyes, too. The smell of urine and sickness and rotting flesh so overpowered me that I whirled my daughter around to lead her back through the open door, deeply regretting my decision to bring her to such a dreadful place. "We need to leave, Christina. I had no idea—"

"Mama, no!" She yanked her hand free and squirmed away to prevent me from pulling her through the door. "We can't leave. We have to find Arie. We have to help him."

"Are you sure, lieveling?"

"I'm sure." I took her hand again, and we continued on. I longed to hold my handkerchief over my nose and mouth as we walked down the long, narrow ward together, but Christina didn't cover her eyes or look away. With tears still streaming down her face, she slowed her steps so she could look each man in the face and offer him a smile. "Hello," she said again and again. "Hello, I'm Christina de Jonge. Do you know my brother, Arie?"

After wandering among the rows for a time, our guide finally halted beside Arie's bed. I thought he had made a mistake. This frail, hollow-eyed ghost wasn't Arie. Christina stared in disbelief, as well. He was asleep, and his large, square hands were the only things I recognized. I could see that he was gravely ill. He looked as though he hadn't eaten in weeks. He lay on his back, his body covered with a gray sheet that showed all the contours of his thin frame. Below his left knee, Arie's leg and foot were missing.

He didn't wake up when Christina sat on the bed beside him and lifted his hand, holding it between hers. An hour passed, but she didn't move, didn't let go, staring at Arie's face until he finally opened his eyes. He blinked at her in the ward's dim lamplight. "I wondered how long you were going to sleep, lazy bones," she said with her teasing smile. "It's very rude of you to take a nap after we came all this way to visit you."

"Christina?" he whispered. "Is that really you?"

"Of course it is. And Mama is here, too."

She stood to let me sit beside him on the bed. I gazed at my son for a long moment, then carefully gathered him in my arms, holding him as if he might break. If I could have let the life flow out of me and into my child, I would have gladly done it. I remembered the beautiful towheaded boy I had held in my arms this way years ago, and how he and Gerrit had slept beside me when they burned with malarial fever. I loved Arie every bit as much as the two children I'd given birth to, and that fierce mother-love helped me forget the horror around me and believe that my son would survive. "You're going to get well now," I told him. "I promise you."

In the days that followed, Christina's method of cheering him included cajoling, pestering, and admonishing him. "You will get well! You will live! Don't you dare go and die on me, Arie de Jonge! I forbid it!" She sat on his bed and held his hand while his fever raged and he tossed in delirium. When he was awake, she told him stories and sang Dutch songs to him and talked about all the things they would do together when they got home. Her happy chatter and bubbly laughter made Arie and all the other men in the neighboring beds smile. The hospital matron directed us to a nearby boardinghouse where the proprietress, Widow Jansen, not only rented us a room but allowed us to use her kitchen after the supper dishes were washed and put away so we could prepare some of Arie's favorite foods for him. He longed for my homemade bread and Dutch pea soup.

Christina and I stayed in Indiana with Arie for nearly a month until the color returned to his cheeks and the fever went away and the stump of his leg began to heal. The doctor assured us one bright October morning that Arie was no longer in danger. He would live. It would be another few months before he would be well enough to travel home, but it was time for Christina and me to return to Michigan.

With worry and fear no longer clouding my vision, I gazed out of the train windows on the journey home, absorbing all the sights. As we slowly chugged through the city of Indianapolis, Christina pointed to the stately buildings. With all the passion and drama of an eleven-year-old she said, "Holland is so backward! Why can't we live in a big city like this one?"

"Your papa and I used to live in a pretty city in the Netherlands called Leiden. But we chose to move to America so we would have more freedom."

"But it's free everywhere in America. It's such a big country, and yet we never leave home!"

"Why would we leave? We have everything we could ever need or want—a warm house, our pretty church, people who know us and love us. Why would we want to live in a place with so many strangers?" The train pulled to a halt at the station where crowds of people swarmed the platform, waiting to board or to greet arriving passengers.

"I'm sure all those people are very nice, too, if we got to know them," Christina insisted. "Wasn't Widow Jansen at the boardinghouse nice? And look at all the Christian churches they have here. See the steeples?"

"The people who live here come from different backgrounds than we do, with different beliefs—and some of them have no beliefs at all. They speak a different language, too."

"Not me. I speak English," she said with the pride of youth. Christina loved the excitement of the cities we traveled through, and I really couldn't blame her when I recalled how much I had loved city life in the Netherlands. Our journey gave Christina her first taste of the world beyond our tiny, sheltered community, and afterward, she was no longer content with our life in Holland.

In the years that followed, she felt a mounting restlessness, insisting she felt deprived and isolated in our poky village with its old-fashioned ways. She longed to be part of America instead of remaining stuck in a backward settlement where the majority of people still spoke and acted like the foreign Dutchmen we were. As I reflect on that time and our journey together, I'm thankful that I made the trip. I credit Christina with saving Arie's life. Even the doctors agreed that she single-handedly restored his will to live. Yet at the same time, I'm truly sorry we went. I saved one child's life and lost another's.

Maarten and Jakob met us when we finally stumbled off the train at the station, hungry and weary and travel-worn. Maarten looked so worried and gaunt that I wondered if he had eaten at all since we left. His round cheeks were sunken, his broad forehead creased with worry lines. "We're finally home," I said, smiling to reassure him. I hugged him tightly. "Arie is going to be fine, Maarten. The doctors assured us that he would recover. You mustn't worry about him. Christina cheered the life back into him."

"I know. You told me so in your letters. It isn't Arie I'm concerned about, Geesje—it's Gerrit. He left home a week ago to enlist."

HOLLAND, MICHIGAN
1897

I lay down my pencil and close the notebook, remembering all too well the way my limbs turned to lead that day when Maarten told me the news about our son Gerrit. I clung to Maarten's arm all the way home, leaving Jakob to carry my bag. Christina couldn't hold back her emotions, and she sobbed as if her little heart would break. She had witnessed the reality of war at Jefferson General Hospital. She now knew better than to envy Gerrit's adventures.

For years I wondered if Gerrit would have run off and enlisted if I had been home to reason with him. Who can say? Maarten worried that I blamed him for not stopping Gerrit, although I did my best to convince him that I didn't. Christina clung to her brother Jakob, who was nearly sixteen and begged him not to run off to war and leave her, too.

Remembering those years brings a storm of sorrow now. Instead of indulging it, I decide to get out and go for a walk. My house is only a few blocks from the main street, which bustles with wagon traffic and people. I take my time strolling down Eighth Street, greeting several people I know along the way, stopping to chat with a friend for a while. My walk ends at the tidy brick building on River Avenue that houses the print shop.

Arie is seated behind his desk when I enter, but he rises to greet me, leaning on the arms of his chair for support. "Moeder! What brings you here?" He envelops me in a hug. The familiar *thump* and *whoosh* of the printing press in the background, the smell of ink and fresh newsprint, always transport me back to my childhood days in Leiden. Arie's assistants continue working while we talk.

"You haven't come to scold me for not visiting you, have you?" he asks with a worried look.

"No, of course not. I know how busy you are."

"We've been working long hours on an order for the Hotel Ottawa. They need a steady supply of stationery and menu cards and advertising pamphlets and things like that. The hotel is very good for business, but it takes a lot of my time."

"I know, dear. Both my father and yours were printers, remember?" I shake my head as he offers me his chair. "No, I won't stay long. You sit, dear." He gets around well on his crutches, but I know he prefers to hide his missing leg behind the desk. Arie has never married. He lives in an apartment behind the print shop and looks much older than his fifty-three years, his light brown hair turning gray at his temples, the silvery strands spreading through his mustache and beard.

"You were on my mind today," I tell him, "so I decided to pay you a visit."

"Do I dare ask what brought me to mind?" he asks.

"I dug out all the letters you wrote home to us during the war and spent the morning reading through them."

"You've kept them all these years?"

"Of course. You know how sentimental I am about things like that. I've been thinking about the past a lot lately, ever since the Semi-Centennial Committee asked me to write down my memories of the early days when we first came over from the Netherlands to settle here. They're asking all of us old-timers to tell our stories so they can put them in a book for the town's fiftieth anniversary. I don't suppose you remember much from those early days, do you? You were barely three years old when you came over on the boat."

Arie leans back in his chair, linking his hands behind his head. "I remember living in a log cabin with a dirt floor. And I remember walking with you and Papa through the woods every Sunday to go up to the old log church on the hill. I don't remember the voyage across the ocean at all."

"How fortunate for you. Ours was a terrible trip. We were all seasick."

"I remember when Jakob was born." His expression turns serious. "And Christina."

Hearing her name brings tears to my eyes. "I've been thinking about Christina a lot, too. I still have the last letter she wrote to us, saying she was coming home."

"The prodigal daughter."

"Yes . . . I often wonder what she was coming home to tell us. She said she needed to tell us in person, and that she would understand if we turned her away. But of course I could never turn her away. Not my own daughter."

Arie sees my tears and stands to embrace me again. "Losing her was one tragedy I'll never understand."

I savor the warmth of his arms before pulling away again to look up at him, wiping my eyes. "I've always worried that you blamed me that she left. Maybe I was too hard on her, too strict. You and Christina were so close, and when she ran away—"

"I never blamed you, Mama. Never. Christina was strong-willed

280

from the day she was born. I don't see how you could have done anything differently to make her stay. The same is true for Gerrit. They both would have left us no matter what any of us said or did."

"Well . . . thanks for saying so. I suppose I'll always wonder, though, if I should have handled things differently." I take both of Arie's hands in mine and squeeze them before letting go. "I'll let you get back to work. You're welcome to stop by my house anytime, you know, and have dinner with me. You don't even have to stay long."

"Maybe I'll do that. . . . Listen, would you like a ride home, Mama? It's awfully hot outside. Almost as hot as the summer we besieged Atlanta."

"No, thanks, dear. I enjoy walking." I start to leave, then turn back as I think of something else. "But I would like to take a ride up to the cemetery one of these days. Can you give me a lift there sometime?"

"How about tomorrow afternoon?"

"Perfect. I want to put some flowers from my garden on the graves."

Two of those graves belong to my parents. One of them is Christina's. One is Maarten's, God rest his soul. And one of the graves belongs to our son Gerrit, who died in the Battle of Petersburg in Virginia at the age of nineteen. The War Between the States ended less than a month later.

Chapter 30

Anna

I'm awakened by a storm during the night. Thunder crashes and booms, echoing off the surrounding dunes. Flashes of lightning pierce the sky, illuminating my room. The trees carry the sound of the wind in their leaves, and I hear the distant roar of waves on Lake Michigan crashing against the shore. I go to the window and part the curtains to watch the storm, knowing I won't be able to go back to sleep until it's over. Rain pours down in sheets as if there's a veil outside the glass. The dock and the beached rowboats reappear with each stab of lightning, the view as bright as daylight.

I'm trembling not only from the storm but from the dream I had before I awoke. In it I was lying on a lumpy mattress in a tiny room, my blanket thin and threadbare. The room stank of urine and mildew and rotting wood. A large water stain marred the ceiling above my bed. Angry voices came from the room next door, and I sat up in fear. Men shouted and argued, a woman screamed at them to stop. I heard sounds of a fight—glass breaking, furniture smashing, grunts and blows—and I feared the men would crash through the flimsy wall next to my bed with its peeling, yellowed wallpaper. Mama pulled me into her arms and held me tightly, humming a melody to soothe me and drown out the noise. "Don't cry, darling," she murmured. "I'll find a way to get us out of this terrible place, I swear I will."

As I wait for the thunderstorm outside to pass, I ponder what the dream might have meant. The two arguing men must represent William and Derk, fighting over whether or not I should marry William. Mother has tried to reassure me that I'm making the right decision, just as she tried to soothe me in my dream. But where did that horrible room come from? Does it represent my lonely and confused state of mind? Is that what Mama was promising to rescue me from?

At last the storm blows past. The rumbling thunder grows more distant, the lightning dims. But rain still lashes the windowpanes as I pull the curtains closed and return to my bed. There is no water stain on the ceiling above my head. My hotel room smells fresh and clean like ironed linen and lavender soap. I fall asleep trying to remember the tune Mama had hummed in my dream. Was it one of the hymns they always sang at the castle church? And had she called me *lieveling*? "*Don't cry, darling . . .*"

In the morning the air outside is cool and refreshing, washed clean by the storm. I take a walk before breakfast and the sun shines brilliantly in the sky as if the storm had never happened. Puddles of rainwater dot the pathways, broken tree branches litter the grass. The surface of Black Lake churns and seethes with angry waves, lashing the dock and the shoreline, and I can hear the surf on Lake Michigan roaring in the distance. I doubt if anyone will want to go sailing or rowing today.

I don't see Derk anywhere. Again, I wish we had never spoken yesterday. I wish we hadn't gone for a walk or that I hadn't felt his arms around me when I stumbled, because now I can't forget what it felt like when he held me. I'm more confused than ever about marrying William. I never should have written him that letter, promising to renew our engagement. I should have waited until my mind was more settled about everything. I wish I knew if I loved him.

But what am I thinking? I can't stand by and watch Father lose his fortune. I need to forget Derk's speech about marrying for love, and remember that I'm one of the most fortunate women in Chicago to be marrying William. I wonder if Derk is going to marry Caroline. I wonder what answer he gave her last night. The two of them may be engaged now, just like William and me.

The morning passes much too quickly. My time at the resort is drawing to an end too soon. When I see a steamship docking at the pier after lunch, I watch the passengers disembark, then freeze in stunned disbelief when I spot a man who looks exactly like William. I blink, certain I must be seeing things. It can't be him. What would he be doing here?

The man walks closer, striding toward the hotel entrance, a servant trotting behind him with his bag. I see the man clearly now, tall and self-assured, his stride confident. He looks handsome with his closely trimmed beard, his shoes shining, his beautifully cut clothes unwrinkled, every glossy dark hair in place.

It is William.

A woman in love would run down the path to meet her beloved, but I feel a ridiculous urge to run inside the hotel and hide. Before I can move, William sees me and hurries the rest of the way up the path to take both of my hands in his and kiss my cheek. "Anna! I wondered how I would ever find you in such a huge hotel—and here you are."

"What are you doing here?" He looks out of place in a coat and necktie, even though it's a casual linen jacket with summer trousers.

"The woman I adore is staying in this hotel, so I decided to visit her and see why she finds this place so charming." He glances all around and adds, "It seems very peaceful and well appointed."

"It . . . it is peaceful." I'm at a complete loss for words.

"Since you only have a few more days here, I decided to purchase a round-trip steamer ticket so I could accompany you and your mother home on Sunday."

"But I'm not returning by steamship. I'm taking the train."

William smiles. It's more a tightening of his lips than a true smile. He is still holding one of my hands, and he pats it as if I'm a child. "Your father told me about your little sailing phobia. But surely you'll feel safe with me beside you, won't you? I had a very pleasant voyage here. And traveling by steamship is so much easier than changing trains at various stations and coping with all the grit and smoke. You have to agree that it will be much faster and more convenient to sail straight home across the lake."

I have to agree? I shake my head and try to smile. "I still prefer to take the train."

"Why? Because you had a bad experience with a storm on the way here? You still arrived safely, didn't you?"

I hesitate, afraid to mention my childhood nightmare, knowing it will make me seem immature and naïve. "It was quite a frightening experience, William. All of the passengers were terrified, not just me. The way the waves washed over the deck . . . The fear of sinking to the bottom of the lake is still very fresh in my memory."

"Don't be silly. There have been some spectacular train wrecks, too."

I don't reply. I am inexplicably close to tears as William's forceful personality starts to engulf me, just as I feared it would. I know I'm wrong to feel this way. William is in no way abusive. But I don't know how to stand up for myself when we disagree. In fact, I'm not supposed to contradict him. I'm expected to remain silent and trust his judgment. Yet as I watch the massive steamship bob up and down on the leftover waves from last night's storm, I feel numb with fear at the thought of getting aboard a ship again and crossing Lake Michigan.

"I'm going to see about my room and freshen up," William says. "Decide what you would like to do afterward, darling. I'm all yours for the next few days."

The next few days. He leaves me while he goes inside to get settled. My time of peaceful soul-searching and Bible reading has come to an end. I still have so many unanswered questions, and now it won't be possible to talk about them with Derk or his Aunt Geesje. I would have liked to meet her. I gaze at the cottages and hotels on the other side of Black Lake as I mourn my loss of solitude. The sky is impossibly blue and cloudless, as if trying to atone for last night's fury.

William rejoins me an hour later and suggests a walk. "Why don't you show me your favorite places to stroll," he says. I wouldn't dare suggest the hike up Mt. Pisgah that I took with Derk yesterday—was it only yesterday? William would never manage it in his polished shoes. And he would be appalled to learn that I had ventured up such a rugged trail. I take his arm as we walk toward Black Lake, remembering Derk and feeling sorry for the awkward way we parted. He had become a friend. But maybe it isn't possible for two people who are as different as Derk and me to have an enduring friendship.

"I've forgotten how beautiful you are, Anna," William says. "Even dressed the way you are."

I look down at my simple cotton skirt and shirtwaist. My hair isn't pinned up and I'm not wearing a petticoat or a corset or stockings or gloves. I stammer an apology. "I-I didn't know you were coming, or I would have worn something different." Mother has been nagging me about my appearance for days, and I realize too late that I should have pulled myself together while William was freshening up. I could have at least pinned up my hair and put on a nicer shirtwaist. We must look like a gentleman taking a stroll with his chamber maid.

"I've never seen you with your hair down before. I always imagined it would be beautiful—and it is."

"I'm so sorry . . . Shall I go fix it?"

"No, leave it for now." He is being kind and considerate, saying all the right things. I'll have a good life with William. He isn't an ogre.

We reach the end of the walkway, and William decides to turn toward the rowboats. I glimpse Derk's fair hair as he tends the boats, and I try to steer William away from the water to walk in a different direction. He gently pulls me back. "Wait, I would like to walk down by the boats. Perhaps we could go rowing in one of them."

Derk glances up as we approach, and I see him surveying William from head to toe. I nod slightly, and I can tell Derk understands that this is William. It seems snobbish of me not to introduce him to William, but I don't dare—for all manner of reasons. Not only would William consider Derk to be beneath him, but I dare not even hint that I'm friends with another man and that I know his name—let alone a man who is an employee of the hotel. If Mother was outraged by my friendship with Derk, William would be even more so. It wouldn't matter in the least that Derk is a college graduate and a seminary student. He is still a nobody to William.

"Excuse me, are these boats for use by hotel guests?" William asks him. "Might I rent one?"

"Yes, sir, they are. You can sign up for them with the hotel's concierge."

"Let's do that, Anna," William says, turning to me. "Let me take you rowing."

My stomach writhes in panic. "I-I think we should wait for another day. The lake is usually much calmer than this. We had a bad storm last night."

"Nonsense." He turns to Derk and asks, "What's your name?"

"Derk Vander Veen, sir."

"Listen, Derk. I'm staying in Room 201 in the annex. Kindly run up and tell the concierge to add the rental fee for one of these rowboats to my account."

"I'm not allowed to leave the boats unattended during the day, sir. It's against hotel rules. I'm sorry."

I'm appalled when William digs into his pocket and pulls out some money. "I'll make it worth your while to bend the rules just this once."

I tug on William's arm to keep him from offering the money to

Derk. "I don't want to go rowing, William. Not when the waves are this choppy. Please, can't we wait for a better day?"

"I want you to see that there's nothing to worry about. Don't you trust me?"

"Of course I trust you, but I still don't care to go out on the water when it's this rough."

"We're taking the steamship home, remember? And after our wedding I'm taking you to Europe on our honeymoon. How will you ever cross the Atlantic if you're afraid to board a ship? And I want to take you to Venice, Italy, where they have canals instead of streets and people travel from place to place in water taxis. You'll find it charming, Anna. But first you need to overcome this irrational fear of the water." He tries to tug me onto the bobbing dock.

"But I-I—"

"You can't let fear govern your life, dear. I would never put you in danger."

I'm on the verge of tears when Derk says, "Excuse me, sir, but the lady seems genuinely frightened. And you're going to find it very challenging to keep your balance as you step in and out of these boats today. Another day might be better for the lady's first time out."

I want to hug him in gratitude. William appears calm, but I can tell he is furious—with both of us. "This is none of your business," he tells Derk.

"Excuse me again, sir, but these rowboats and the safety of their passengers are my business. I already canceled two sailing excursions that were scheduled for today because of the rough waves."

"Let's go, William," I say before he can respond. "Please. I want to show you the beach." He is too much of a gentleman to argue further with Derk or with me, so we move on. But I'm worried that William will speak with the concierge about this incident and get Derk into trouble. I'll probably never have a chance to talk with Derk again—and maybe that's a good thing. I know exactly what he would say about my marriage now that he has met William. I tell myself that it doesn't matter what Derk thinks. I still plan to marry William. I just wish there was a way to ask about Caroline, to find out if he decided to marry her.

I take extra care with my clothing and hair before meeting William for dinner later that evening, hoping to please him. I need to make it up to him for my stubbornness earlier that day. My stomach feels as uneasy as the water on the storm-tossed lake. Will it always be this way throughout our married life? Will I always be forced to give in just to please him?

We enjoy a lovely candlelit dinner together in the hotel's dining room, and I'm encouraged by how charming William is, how much I enjoy being with him. Afterward we stroll the grounds beneath the stars and he pulls me into the shadows to steal a kiss. The softness of his lips against mine, the caress of his fingers as he cups my face, send a thrill through me as if I've touched a frayed electrical wire. Perhaps I'm in love with him after all.

Then, as he says good night to me at the door of my hotel room, he squeezes my hands and kisses my cheek and says, "Don't forget, darling, we're going rowing together in the morning."

I feel like I can't breathe.

CHAPTER 31

Geesje

HOLLAND, MICHIGAN
1897

"Why is being in love so hard?" Derk asks. He sits slumped at my kitchen table, the untouched tin of cookies in front of him. I have no answer for him. It's late at night, but he saw my kitchen light on and needed my consolation. "I went to see Caroline last night. I told her that I couldn't give up the ministry to become a chaplain."

"What did she say?"

"She burst into tears and told me to leave. She said I must not love her since I don't care about her feelings. But she's wrong. I do love her."

I pause before saying, "I think you made the right decision, Derk."

He rakes his fingers through his hair. The Macassar oil he applied before last night's visit is gone, and he looks more like himself again. "I don't know, Tante Geesje. Now that it's over I'm having second thoughts."

"Really? Why?"

"My dad never remarried after Mama died. He said he could never love anyone as much as he loved her, so it wouldn't be fair to marry another woman. What if I can never love another woman as much as Caroline? What if I regret losing her for the rest of my life?"

"I think you'll regret it even more if you give up becoming a pastor."

"I know, I know . . . But why can't I have both? When Caroline wrote that letter saying she still loved me, I was sure that nothing would stand in our way. Now we're right back where we started."

"No, I think you're farther along than you were. You told her you loved her and still wanted to marry her, right?"

"Yes."

"But that you were still going to become a pastor?"

"Yes."

"So now the decision is hers, not yours. If she doesn't love you enough to respect your calling from God, then you should be relieved that she didn't marry you. Caroline needs to find God's plan for her life, too, and it may not include being married to you."

Derk props his elbow on the table and rests his forehead on his fist. "Why is being in love so hard?" he asks again.

"Listen, dear. I have no doubt at all that you'll fall in love again. I thought Hendrik was the one and only love of my life but he wasn't."

Derk looks up in surprise. "You fell in love again?"

"And while your father's love for your mother is very admirable, I just wonder if he was motivated by fear as much as by love. It must have been devastating for him to lose your mother. Perhaps he didn't want to fall in love again and risk going through such terrible pain a second time."

"I guess I can understand that."

"I know Caroline hurt you, but I hope you'll risk giving your heart away to someone else. Love is well worth the risk."

Derk gives a weak half-smile and asks, "So who did you fall in love with after my grandfather?"

"With someone wonderful," I reply, returning his smile. "I'll write about it in my notebook and let you read it. But for now you need to understand that there's a difference between the giddy euphoria of falling in love the way you did with Caroline, and the deep joy of loving someone for an entire lifetime and being loved in return. The excitement and passion of first love often wears thin as you journey through all the waves and storms of life. But the deep, abiding love and commitment that replaces it is far more satisfying. You'll find that kind of love someday, Derk. I know you will."

He leans back in his chair and exhales. "Thanks for listening, Tante Geesje. I should let you go to bed."

"You may come over and talk to me any time, dear. You know that."

After Derk leaves, I begin to wonder why he hasn't confided in his father and shared his romantic woes with him. Is it because his father set such a high standard that Derk feels there should be only one woman for him, too? The love I once felt for Hendrik was so deep and powerful that I didn't believe I would ever fall in love again, either.

But I did.

Geesje's Story

HOLLAND, MICHIGAN
26 YEARS EARLIER

Maarten's grief after the death of our son Gerrit was as bottomless as my own. We had shared all the joy and hard work of raising our four children together, and now we shared our aching sorrow, as well. We both had a difficult time accepting Gerrit's death, so we comforted each other as we talked and wept and prayed. "Why would God take him?" I asked Maarten one night as we lay curled together in bed. Our long habit of clinging to each other for a few minutes each night before going to sleep had become even more important to both of us after this tragedy. "Gerrit was so young, with his whole life ahead of him. Isn't it bad enough that God took his parents at such young ages when all they had wanted to do was worship Him freely here in America? Did He have to take Gerrit, too?"

"I'll be honest," Maarten replied. "I've struggled to find a reason for his death. God doesn't owe us an explanation for what He does, of course—and we may not understand His reasons even if He did try to explain them. And yet . . . and yet as I kept asking God why, He finally offered me a measure of comfort in the words that Dominie Van Raalte said at Gerrit's funeral: He said that Gerrit gave his life for the cause of freedom—remember?"

"I think so."

"Geesje, we came here to America so we'd have the freedom to worship. But this country won't remain free unless we're willing to safeguard our freedom. Our family agreed that it was a crime against humanity to keep the Negro race enslaved. They deserve freedom as much as we do. So even though we miss our Gerrit, his death does have meaning. He died so all those former slaves—along with our children and grandchildren and great-grandchildren— could enjoy freedom for generations to come."

I hugged my husband tightly, savoring the familiar, solid shape of him. "I don't know what I would ever do without you," I whispered.

"Nor I you."

The outpouring of love and consolation from our community of believers, along with the assurance that Gerrit was with his heavenly Father in paradise, slowly helped Maarten and me to heal. I had glimpsed Hendrik and his wife, Nella, at Gerrit's fu-neral, but we didn't speak. Only Maarten truly understood how I felt, and so I leaned on him. Then Hendrik came to our door one morning soon after the funeral, while Maarten was at work. I didn't answer it. Instead, I hid in the shadows, pretending I wasn't home. Something had changed inside my heart, and it seemed wrong to let Hendrik console me. When I chose to remain with Maarten years ago, it was partly because I had also chosen to be a mother to Arie and Gerrit. My grief at my son's death should be shared with Maarten, not Hendrik. And so I sat in Gerrit's darkened bedroom alone, waiting for Hendrik to leave. Together, Maarten and I slowly healed.

Our kolonie was now a thriving town of about 2,400 people. Arie became a full partner in the printing business with Maarten after the war and learned to maneuver expertly on his crutches. Jakob finished his degree at Hope College and enrolled in the newly founded Western Theological Seminary to become a minister. And Christina turned seventeen, the same age I was when I left the Netherlands to come to America. We had a family portrait taken of us by a traveling photographer who visited Holland. Christina was a beautiful young woman, friendly and vivacious and as attractive to the young men in our church as my flower garden is to the honeybees. The summer before her final year of high school she worked as a maid for the Cappon family, one of Holland's most prosperous families. That fall she announced at dinner one evening, "I've decided to move to Chicago and work for a wealthy family after I graduate."

"Chicago!" Maarten thundered. "Heaven forbid!" He was usually so soft-spoken. I had never heard him thunder before. Neither had Christina.

"I need to get out of this town and see a little bit of the world, Papa. When Mama and I visited Arie in Indiana, I saw that there's so much more to America than tiny, little Holland, Michigan. I want to see some interesting, exciting places before I settle down and get married."

Before Maarten could respond again, Arie spoke up. "Those places only appear exciting on the surface, Christina. You have no idea how blessed we are to live here in this community."

"If you're not ready to get married and settle down yet,"

Maarten said, "why not continue your education and become a teacher?" Christina shook her head, staring at the tabletop.

In the weeks that followed I noticed that she stopped sharing her plans with us and became more secretive. I missed the close relationship we'd once enjoyed. Christina went for long walks in the evenings after her chores were done and seemed to spend a lot more time with her friends than at home. She even begged us to let her sit with them in church instead of sitting with our family.

On a warm Sunday morning in September, one of the elders pulled Maarten and me aside after the church service and said, "May I have a word with you please, Mr. and Mrs. de Jonge?"

"Yes, of course," Maarten replied. We sent Jakob and Arie ahead of us with the carriage, telling them we would follow them home on foot in a few minutes. Christina wasn't with us. For the sake of peace, Maarten had allowed her to sit with her friends, and she always walked home with them afterward. We stood outside on the church steps with the elder, the stately white pillars framing a view of the changing fall leaves.

"I'm sorry to have to tell you this news," he began, "but I'm concerned about your daughter, Christina. Perhaps it is nothing—I hope it is nothing—but for the past three Sundays I've seen her get up and leave before the service ended. I thought she might be changing seats or using the facilities. But today I happened to be standing in the back of the sanctuary when she rose from her seat. I watched through the window as she left the church grounds altogether and hurried west on Tenth Street. I believe your home is in the other direction, isn't it?"

My heart felt like an iron weight inside my chest. I looked up at Maarten and saw him briefly close his eyes. "How long ago did she leave today?" he asked.

"At least an hour ago. Maybe an hour and a half."

"Thank you for letting us know," he said.

"If I can help in any way . . ."

"Thank you." Maarten was suddenly in a hurry to leave. My arm was still linked to his, but he quickly turned and plunged down the stairs as if he'd forgotten, pulling me, stumbling, along with him. My husband was a godly man, and I knew that if anyone possessed the good judgment and wisdom to handle this situation, it was him. I remained silent for as long as I could on that aching walk home, aware that Maarten needed time to think and pray in his slow, deliberate way. I longed to do something that very minute, to chase after Christina and drag her home, to convince her to be the loving, trustworthy daughter we once knew. When we turned onto our street, I could no longer hold back my tears. I tugged Maarten's arm to slow his marching pace.

"Before we get home, we need to talk about what we're going to do," I said.

"I don't know what to do, Geesje . . . I don't know what to say to her." I heard the raw emotion in his voice. Christina's deception had hurt him deeply. The fact that an elder at church had known about it before we did shamed us both. I struggled for words to make things better.

"Maybe she's just restless, Maarten. Christina has hated to sit still in church all her life. Don't you remember how she used to act up when she was small? No amount of punishment has ever worked. Maybe there's a good explanation for why she walked out."

Maarten wiped a tear with his fist. "We trusted her and allowed her to sit with her friends, but she betrayed our trust."

"Christina has always chafed at the rules and at our way of life. She thinks we're too strict and unyielding. I'm worried that the more we restrict her and punish her, the more she'll rebel. It's like holding sand too tightly in your hand—it will all slip away."

"I fear that she has already slipped away from us. I'm not sure she even believes what we do anymore."

"She does . . . of course she does." But a prickle of doubt made me uneasy. Christina had never wholeheartedly embraced our faith the way her three brothers had. There had been many times when I felt she was simply going through the motions, saying the right things to placate us.

We walked the rest of the way home in a daze, struggling to control our shock and grief. Christina arrived home just as I was putting Sunday dinner on the table. She was as lively and cheerful as usual while we ate, as if nothing at all was wrong. I felt too sick to eat, and Maarten didn't seem to have an appetite, either. When the meal ended, Maarten read from Scripture and prayed like he always did, but when Christina rose to help me stack the dishes, he cleared his throat and said, "Everyone remain seated, please." She sat down again. I laid my hand on top of his as I looked up at him, silently asking if he intended to expose Christina in front of her brothers. Maarten understood me perfectly and gave a slight nod. We were a family and we would deal with her behavior together.

"Christina, would you kindly explain to us where you have gone these past three weeks when you have left the church service early?"

Her mouth fell open and a blush crept up her cheeks. But she quickly recovered and raised her chin in defiance. "Who told you that lie?"

"Someone who has no reason in the world to lie."

"That's what I hate about that church and this stupid town. Everyone is so nosy! Everyone has to know everyone else's private business. I'm so sick of it! That's why I'm leaving the first chance I get and going someplace else to live."

She started to rise again, but Maarten said firmly, "Sit down, Christina, and listen to me." She sat. "You can leave home and leave Holland, but you can't escape God's watchful eye—or His love for you. As for despising our church, we all need those 'nosy' brothers and sisters for our own protection, to keep us from going astray. We depended on each other for our very survival in the early days, and we still depend on each other today. The Bible says 'Two are better than one . . . For if they fall, the one will lift up his fellow: but woe to him that is alone when he falleth; for he hath not another to help him up . . . a threefold cord is not quickly broken.'"

Christina didn't respond. She stared at the tabletop, her body tensed as if ready to leap up the moment Maarten excused her.

"You haven't answered my question, Christina," he said. "Why have you been leaving church?"

"Because it's boring. I'm tired of all the rules and laws. I'm tired of being told I'm a sinner just because I can't possibly obey all of them. Nobody lives a perfect life, and if anyone says he does, he's a hypocrite. There's a world full of interesting people beyond our city limits if we ever bothered to go meet them, but the narrow-minded people in this town are all dead set against anyone who isn't Dutch or who doesn't belong to their church."

Christina's bitter words struck me like a slap in the face. I started to react, but Maarten squeezed my hand to stop me. How could he remain so calm? "Where have you been going after you leave the service?" he asked her.

"Nowhere. Just walking around." She looked away, her cheeks turning crimson. She was lying. I remembered the long walks she had also been taking every evening and her outburst suddenly made sense to me—she was meeting someone in secret. Someone who wasn't Dutch.

Arie spoke up first. "Are you still seeing that boy you met last summer? Tell us the truth, Christina."

She shot him a look of fury from across the table, and her blush deepened. "I confided in you, Arie. You said you wouldn't tell on us!"

"I have to tell. I'm trying to save your life, Christina, the way you once saved mine. Nothing good can come from a relationship with an outsider, especially if you have to tell lies and sneak around behind Mama and Papa's backs to see him."

I had done the same thing with Hendrik, meeting him in secret to hold hands and share a few stolen kisses. I could only hope that Christina had done nothing more than kiss. Our church had dozens of wonderful young men to choose among, but like Eve in a garden full of beautiful trees, Christina was drawn to the only one she couldn't have, the forbidden fruit—an outsider. Just as I had been drawn to Hendrik.

"Christina, listen," Maarten said. He still sounded calm, not

298

angry. "You must stop this behavior before you ruin your reputation and destroy all your chances of marrying a fine Christian man from our community—someone who shares our faith and who values the same things we do. Your mother and I made sacrifices and worked hard to establish a fellowship of faith for you and for your children after you. I believe that God has a husband in mind for you here—"

"How do you know Jack isn't His choice for me? You haven't even met him!"

"Is he a Christian?" Maarten asked. When she didn't reply he said, "He can't be God's choice if he isn't a believer. Scripture says, 'Be ye not unequally yoked together with unbelievers: for what fellowship hath righteousness with unrighteousness? And what communion hath light with darkness?' Marriages work best when the couple has the same values and traditions and share the same faith in God."

"I love him! You don't understand how I feel!"

But I did understand. Should I tell her? Should I give her the same speech that Papa gave me about choosing God's will or my own? "Tell us about him, Christina," I said. The room was silent for a moment.

"His name is Jack Newell, and he's from Toledo, Ohio." Her angry look dissolved as she talked about him, and her face glowed with love, like a fire burning brighter. "He left home on foot with barely a cent in his pockets, determined to make something of himself. And he has! He was passing through Holland on his way to find work in Chicago, and he found a really good job at the Cappon Bertsch Tanning factory. He's going to work his way all the way to the top and own his own factory someday."

Christina must have met him last summer when she worked for the Cappon family. Their home wasn't far from the tannery. "What about his family?" I asked.

"His father started drinking too much after his mother died. He didn't want to stay in that home anymore."

Part of me wanted to grab my daughter by the shoulders and

shake some sense into her for getting involved with a homeless, penniless drifter with an alcoholic father. But Hendrik hadn't been a believer either, at first, and he had come to faith through our family's Christian example. Surely Maarten was thinking of Hendrik as well when he said, "Why don't you bring him home so we can meet him?"

"No. I don't want him to come here." Her angry defiance returned.

"Are we an embarrassment to you with our accents and our clothes and our humble home?" Maarten asked.

She lifted her chin. "Jack wouldn't care about any of those things. But I know you would judge him and condemn him and try to make him feel guilty because he isn't religious like you. You would start preaching to him and telling him he was a sinner." Again, I thought of my parents who had preached to Hendrik by their way of life rather than with words.

"We are all sinners, Christina," Maarten replied. "I could overlook the fact that your friend isn't Dutch if he was a sincere Christian. Does Jack believe in our God at all?"

She began to look very uneasy. "Of course he believes in God. But he thinks it's wrong to scare people into conforming to a bunch of old-fashioned rules and morals with stories of floods and fiery furnaces and whales swallowing people alive. Especially when the people who teach those rules are such hypocrites. We can live good lives without all the false guilt the church tries to scare into us."

I knew those weren't Christina's own words. She must be parroting what Jack had said. It shocked me to realize what a strong influence he'd already had on her, causing her to reject everything we had taught her.

Maarten closed the Bible that still lay open on the table and folded his strong, ink-stained hands on top of it. "If you won't allow us to meet him, then I must forbid you to see him, Christina. You may no longer go out walking alone or sit with your friends in church or lie to us and pretend that you're visiting them. We will take you to and from school from now on—"

"You're making me your prisoner?"

"Only because you've been deceiving us. And because we love you."

Christina rose from the table and stormed off to her room, slamming her door. I agreed with everything Maarten had said and done. I knew he hoped to prevent Christina from ever seeing this young man again—but I knew that he couldn't stop her. She would find a way. We were too late. Our daughter had already slipped away from us like a boat that had become unmoored. Now she was drifting downstream on a powerful current.

CHAPTER 32

Geesje's Story

HOLLAND, MICHIGAN
26 YEARS EARLIER

As I rode to church a few weeks later on that fateful Sunday—October 8, 1871—I couldn't remember the last time it had rained, the last time the clouds had rolled in from the lake bringing relief with life-giving water. The ground was parched and brittle, the air dry and crackling, the creek beds shriveled down to a trickle. At the same time, everyone in our household seemed to be holding his breath over Christina. She barely spoke to us, and when she did, her temper often flared like one of the forest fires that kept erupting outside of Holland. Piles of logs and dry brush lay scattered throughout our area, left over from clearing the land, making the arid countryside a tinderbox. A week ago, Maarten and Jakob had helped the other townsmen extinguish a fire that had threatened the south side of the city and the Hope College campus. But none of our efforts could extinguish Christina's anger. She endured church services with simmering rage, sitting between

Maarten and me like a slowly heating pot, ready to boil over. We waited with hope for her to change, the same way we waited for the weather to change and bring rain. Either Christina would bend her will to ours and to God's, or she would explode.

A dry, brisk wind blew from the south as we rode to church that Sunday afternoon. The air felt gritty with ash from the recent fires. "It's been a month," Christina said as we climbed the front steps between the pillars. "I've done everything you said. When are you going to trust me again and let me sit with my friends?"

"Your mother and I will pray about it," Maarten replied. Christina carefully banked her anger like hoarded coals. She sat statue-still in church. But then everyone seemed to be motionless on that warm afternoon.

Around two o'clock the wind shifted and began to blow harder from the southwest. I could hear it whistling around the church, rattling the tall, multi-paned windows and rustling the dried leaves outside. I had left several windows open at home, and I worried that ash and dust would blow inside. The service was still in progress an hour later when we heard the tower bell at Third Reformed Church tolling the fire alarm. Dominie Van Raalte was out of town that Sunday, and the minister preaching in his place quickly ended his sermon and dismissed us.

"We received word that piles of dry brush are on fire in the swamp near Pine Avenue and Sixteenth Street," someone told us when we stepped outside. The new Third Reformed Church, only recently completed, was on Pine Avenue and Twelfth Street.

"Take your mother and Christina home for me, please," Maarten told Arie. "Jakob and I will go see if we can help with the fire."

"In your Sunday clothes?" I asked.

"There's no time to change." Maarten and Jakob removed their suitcoats and ties and handed them to me. Orders were coming from every direction as the men mobilized. Someone shouted for them to run to the hardware store and get shovels and other tools to fight the fire. Someone else said the president of Hope College needed all the students to return to campus and form bucket brigades to soak the rooftops of the buildings in case the fire spread in that direction again. Farmers were ordered to harness their teams and plow firebreaks to try to stop the flames. As the men mobilized to fight the fire, I sensed Arie's humiliation that he wasn't deemed fit to help. Delivering the women to safety hardly seemed like a heroic job for a seasoned soldier.

"Do you think we should pack up some of our valuables, just in case?" I asked him when we reached home. Smoke already darkened the afternoon sky, blotting out the sun.

"It probably wouldn't hurt." He kept the carriage parked outside and the barn door open. I asked Christina if she wanted to pray with me for the men's safety, but she shook her head. She stood outside on the front porch, staring into the distance, as if hoping Jack Newell would arrive to rescue her.

Maarten and Jakob didn't return home until after nine o'clock that night. By then a layer of smoke hung over the street outside our house like fog, and I was worried sick. In the distance to the southwest, the rim of the sky glowed orange, like a sunset. But the sun had long since set. The men looked battle-weary, their faces smudged with soot, their eyes reddened from the smoke. Both Maarten and Jakob were coughing smoke and ash from their lungs. They had rolled up their shirtsleeves to fight the fire, but I suspected that their Sunday clothes, reeking of smoke, were ruined. I followed Maarten into our bedroom when he went there to change his clothes, and I hugged him tightly.

"What's going on, Maarten? Is the fire out?"

"No one knows. It's spreading faster than we can battle it. We extinguish it in one place, and then the wind carries the sparks and cinders someplace else. The fire skips around as if it's taunting us." He and Jakob had come home to rest for a few minutes and eat something, then they were going back. As they were getting ready to leave again, Christina tore past them through the front door and rushed into the arms of a stranger standing outside. It could only be Jack Newell. The comfortable way they held each other alarmed me.

Maarten couldn't seem to move as he stared at them in shock, but I hurried down the front steps after Christina. I could see why she'd been attracted to him—he had a handsome face and wavy, light brown hair and a sturdy, muscular build. But there was something in his arrogant stance and cocksure grin that made me dislike him on sight. He obviously hadn't been helping the other men battle the fire, or he would have looked as filthy and disheveled as Jakob and Maarten did. "I'm getting out of town before things get worse," I heard him say. "I've come to take you with me, Christina." He and Christina pulled apart as I approached, but he draped his arm around her shoulder as if he owned her.

"She isn't going with you," Maarten said as he also stepped forward. "Christina, could you really respect a man who would run away to save himself without even trying to help save our town?"

Jack shrugged as if it didn't matter to him if Holland burned.

"It's the very least you can do if you love my sister," Arie added. He stood on the porch steps beside Jakob, his crutches propped beneath his arms.

Maarten picked up one of the soot-covered shovels leaning against the porch railing and held it out to Jack. "We're going back out to fight the fire. Why don't you come with us, son?"

Jack sighed in resignation and took the shovel.

"This time I'm going, too," Arie said, hobbling down the front steps. "I want to help."

Maarten stopped him. "I need you to stay here and try to save the print shop and our house, Arie. Some of the other people in town are soaking their rooftops to prevent blowing sparks from igniting the shingles. I think we should do the same."

"Christina and I will help you, Arie," I said. I hugged Maarten again and begged him and Jakob to stay close together and watch out for each other. Then I hurried away to gather up every tub and bucket I could find. I couldn't bear to watch my husband and son go.

The night was pitch black except for the fire's distant glow as Christina and I dragged the buckets and a ladder to the print shop. Arie limped along behind us. He unlocked the door when we got there and stood in the darkened shop, gazing all around. "We can't possibly move the printing press," he said. "I suppose we could try to save some of the equipment, but . . ."

"Our best chance is to soak the roof like your father said." The wind had become so strong by then that it nearly blew the ladder over as we tried to prop it against the shop. I knew Arie couldn't climb it or stand on the sloping roof, so I put him to work filling the buckets with water. Christina carried the buckets to the ladder, and I hauled each one up and doused the roof with it.

The work was exhausting. And it seemed to me that the wind grew stronger by the minute, the distant glow in the sky brighter. When we finished soaking the roof, Arie brought the carriage around and we piled the cash box, record books, and other valuables from the shop into it. Then we dragged the ladder and buckets back across our property to our house and set to work all over again, soaking the shingles and loading our possessions. The carriage couldn't hold very much, so I had to leave all but our most important things behind.

Hours had passed. It had to be nearly midnight. Maarten and Jakob still hadn't returned. We sat inside the house in the dark, waiting. I was too worried about sparks starting another fire to light a candle or a lantern. I closed my eyes and prayed, terrified for the men's safety as the wind howled around our house. *Please don't take Maarten . . . I love him . . . If anything happened to him, I don't know what I would do.*

I heard Christina pacing restlessly in the darkness. "Why don't you sit down?" Arie finally asked her. "Aren't you exhausted?"

"I can't sit down. I'm worried about Jack. Why did Papa make him go?"

"Could you really love a coward, Christina?" Arie asked. "I knew a few men like him during the war. Always looking out for themselves. Selfish to the core."

"Well, Jack went, didn't he?" she said angrily. "He isn't a coward. And now I'm worried that something will happen to him."

"You *should* be worried about him, and about his eternal soul—especially if he isn't a believer."

"Shut up, Arie! You've never been in love! You don't know how it feels!"

But I did. I knew exactly how Christina felt. I had already lost one son. Would I now lose another, along with my husband? And what about our home and our business and our church and our town? Would God really allow everything we had worked for these past twenty-five years to go up in flames? I thought I understood how the biblical character Job felt.

The three of us sat in the darkness, waiting, while the wind shook the house like a hurricane. I had waited in suspense this way after I'd learned that the *Phoenix* had sunk, worrying and praying for Hendrik's safety. The love and concern I felt now for Maarten were just as great—maybe greater. If only God would give me more time with Maarten. I would tell him every day how much he meant to me, how much I loved him. My feelings for him were different from what I had felt for Hendrik—that great rush of passion and attraction that Christina now felt for Jack. But I loved Maarten for his solid, steadfast faith; for being the man who would have sacrificed his dream to take me back to the Netherlands; who would now risk his life to save our home and our town. Maarten never once made me feel abandoned or unloved or insecure all these years. He had grieved with me, laughed with me, raised our children with me. He had never been impatient or angry with me. And in those moments of great doubt and uncertainty over the years, he had always turned to God in prayer, believing in His goodness despite appearances and helping me to do the same. How very blessed I was to have this steady, uncompromising man for my husband.

Please, God . . . I don't want to lose him.

Just after midnight, Maarten and Jakob finally burst through the front door, breathless from running. Their reddened eyes were nearly swollen shut from the smoke. Christina leapt to her feet first. "Where's Jack?"

"He deserted us hours ago," Maarten said. "Come on, hurry! We have to get out of here! We need to run!"

"What's happening?" I asked.

"Third Reformed Church has caught fire. We couldn't save it."

"They just finished building it!" Arie said.

"I know. Now the wind has carried flaming shingles from the church over to Cappon's tannery. The factory buildings and that huge pile of dried hemlock bark—they're all on fire. When we saw flaming chunks of bark from the tannery blowing toward the Eighth Street business district, we knew it was time to run. There's no stopping the fire now."

"The carriage is packed and ready," Arie said. "Where should we go?" I felt so shaky I could hardly stand or walk as Maarten herded us to the door. My heart had never pounded so hard before.

"Some townspeople are heading west to the lake and getting into boats," Maarten said. "I think we should go east, toward Dominie Van Raalte's house. It's on the creek—if it hasn't dried up by now."

Outside, the wind was blowing so hard that Maarten had to support me. A gust snatched the kerchief from my head before I could catch it and blew ash and grit into my eyes. Washtubs and buckets and wooden crates summersaulted down the street as if they weighed nothing at all. We joined hundreds of our neighbors crowding the road that led out of Holland, all desperate to save our lives. As the carriage moved forward, I turned around and gazed in horror at the scene we were fleeing.

It was the middle of the night, but the burning city looked as bright as day. We could feel the heat of it, as hot as an oven, blowing toward us on the wind. I watched the fire jump from one roof to the next, one house to the next, faster than anyone could outrun it. Waves of flames rolled along the ground, consuming everything in their path.

"Hurry, Maarten!" I begged. "We have to hurry!" My eyes watered from tears and from the smoke, which nearly blinded us at times. All the while, the wind battered us, raining sparks down on us like biblical fire and brimstone. I have never known such terror in my life.

At last we made it to Dominie Van Raalte's house on Fairbanks Avenue and collapsed to our knees to thank God. His house was packed with refugees like us, even though he still hadn't returned from preaching in Muskegon. What would he say when he saw his beloved kolonie in flames? We waited there throughout the night, watching the distant fire, ready to flee again if the wind carried the inferno our way.

At dawn, the wind and flames seemed to die away. The rising sun hid behind a haze of smoke and ash. "Jakob and I are going to walk back with some of the other men to see what's left," Maarten said. I was too weary to move, too heartbroken to view the destruction. Christina began to pace again as we waited, but I knew her anxiety wasn't for her father and brother. Hours passed before they returned.

"It's gone, Geesje," Maarten said, his voice hoarse with grief and smoke. "Nearly the entire city is gone. Burned to the ground."

"It looks like a field that's been mowed clean with a scythe," Jakob added. "There's hardly a fence post or a sidewalk board or even a tree stump left."

I drew a shaky breath before asking, "What about the print shop and our house?"

Maarten shook his head. "Gone." He gave me a moment to absorb the news before saying, "But Pillar Church is undamaged. It's a miracle. And the buildings at Hope College were spared, too."

"Did everyone make it out of town? Do they know if everyone is safe?"

He hesitated for a long, dreadful moment. "Only one casualty that we know of for sure—Widow Tolk."

"Maarten, no!" I covered my mouth in grief. I knew Sara Ooms Tolk, an elderly widow who lived alone.

"Someone told us that she stayed too long, that she was trying to save more of her belongings. They couldn't get her to leave. I'm so sorry, Geesje."

As everyone expected, Dominie Van Raalte was heartbroken when he returned to find our twenty-five years of hard work in ashes. Nevertheless, he held his head high and said, "With our Dutch tenacity and our American experience, Holland will be rebuilt."

Later that day, our little family of five rode home in our carriage, packed with our only remaining belongings, to see what we could scavenge from the ruins. I wept when I saw the blackened skeleton of the printing press among the shop's charred beams and debris. That sight hurt me even more than seeing our home's crumbling chimney, the only thing left standing above the foundation of our house. Behind the house were the sad remains of the log cabin that Papa and Maarten had built when we'd first arrived. I looked over at Maarten, wondering if his spirit felt as broken and defeated as mine did. "Can the press be salvaged?" I asked him. He shook his head.

He climbed down from the carriage and rummaged in the back of it for his Bible. I had packed it for him, and he opened it now to read to us from the prophet Habakkuk: "'Although the fig tree shall not blossom, neither shall fruit be on the vines; the labor of the olive shall fail, and the fields shall yield no meat; the flock shall be cut off from the fold, and there shall be no herd in the stalls: Yet I will rejoice in the Lord, I will joy in the God of my salvation.'"

Christina exploded. "How can you say that? The town is in ashes! We lost everything! We don't have food or clothing or even a place to live! You have no way to make a living—"

"And yet we are all alive, Christina. Nothing else matters as long as our family is safe. 'The Lord gave, and the Lord hath taken away; blessed be the name of the Lord.'"

She jumped down from the carriage and stormed off, crossing our property to where our home had once stood. "Let her go, Geesje," Maarten said when I started to follow her. "Maybe when she sees how our brothers and sisters from neighboring churches come to Holland's aid, she'll understand Christ's love." I hated the thought of living on charity, but Maarten was right. The Christians from local churches would gladly help us get back on our feet.

We were among the more than three hundred families left destitute by the fire, the thirteen hundred people now homeless. The final statistics, when we learned them, were incomprehensible: two hundred ten homes destroyed, seventy-five stores, fifteen factories, five churches, three hotels. Then came another shock—unbelievably, the city of Chicago had also caught fire on the same night as Holland and had burned throughout the night and the following day. The destruction and loss of life there had been even greater than here.

I helped Maarten and our two sons sift through the rubble of the print shop. An hour later, my hands blackened, my face smudged, the hem of my skirt soiled with soot, I decided to go help Christina sort through the remains of our home. I found her sitting on one of the foundation stones with the charred, tin tea box on her lap, reading through the letters I had kept inside. Some of them were from Arie, written to us during the war. Most of them were from Hendrik. Why had I kept them all these years?

The angry expression on Christina's face when she looked up and saw me, told me that she had read enough of Hendrik's letters to understand their significance. "These are love letters!" she said. "From another man! Not Papa!"

"They were written before I married your father—"

"You're so against Jack and me, yet according to these, you know exactly how I feel! You were in love with this man—a man who wasn't a Christian!"

"Hendrik became a believer. Your father is the one who taught him about God and—"

"You know perfectly well what it's like to love someone so much you feel like you might die if you can't be together!"

Oh, yes. I knew.

She waved the incriminating letter in the air. "It says here that you would have left your home and family in the Netherlands to run away with him."

"But I didn't run away, Christina. I came to America with my parents. Hendrik decided to come, too. If you've read the letters, then you know he wanted to become a Christian."

"What happened to him? Did he die?"

"No. . . . But when his ship sank, I thought he had. By the time I learned that he was still alive, I couldn't marry him."

"Why not?"

"I was already married to your father."

She jumped to her feet, dumping the tin box and the letters onto the ash-covered ground. "So you gave up the man you really loved to settle for a man from your church, the man your parents wanted you to marry."

"It wasn't like that. You don't know the whole story—"

"You're such a hypocrite! You told me to forget Jack and marry someone from church, someone I could never love as much as him, when all along—"

"That isn't what happened—"

"You couldn't possibly have loved my papa if you kept another man's love letters all these years!"

I grabbed her shoulders, shaking her slightly. "Christina, listen to me. I never should have kept them. I love your father a hundred times more than I ever loved Hendrik. A thousand times more. The attraction Hendrik and I felt for each other never could have survived all the fires and storms I've been through since then. His faith wasn't strong enough, and neither was mine. But the love your father and I share is the real thing. Nothing can ever quench it." I tried to hold her, but she twisted away from me.

"Leave me alone!" She marched off by herself, heading toward the Black River.

"Christina, wait!" Before I could follow her, someone grabbed my arm from behind to stop me. It was Maarten.

"Let her go, Geesje," he said gently. He took me into his arms and held me tightly. I felt his body shake with sobs, and I knew they weren't for his daughter or even because we'd lost everything we'd labored so hard for all these years. Maarten had heard what I'd said to Christina. He'd heard how much I loved him.

"A hundred times more," I whispered as I clung to him, weeping. "A thousand times more . . ."

Geesje

The summer afternoon is warm as Arie drives me up the hill to Pilgrim Home Cemetery in his carriage. We halt, and he climbs down from the seat first, handling his crutches expertly after all these years of practice, then he helps me down as well. Together, we place the containers of flowers from my garden on each of the graves, beginning with Mama and Papa's. I bend to arrange the flowers on their plot and when I straighten up, I look down at the rebuilt city, risen from the ashes and flourishing once again beneath the summer sky, twenty-six years later. "My parents left their families and their home in the Netherlands to build this town," I tell Arie. "I wish they had lived to see what it looks like today. Papa would be so proud of you and your print shop. It was his dream."

I have also brought flowers for Arie's birth parents, the Van Dijks, and we walk the short distance beneath the trees to place a bouquet there. "I don't remember them at all," he says, shaking his head. "I feel so bad about that."

"You were very young, Arie. I'm sorry they died, but I'm forever grateful that God gave you and Gerrit to us to raise."

We turn to Gerrit's grave next. He would still be buried in Virginia if the other members of our church hadn't helped pay to have him shipped home to us. I'm so grateful to them. There is talk of erecting a memorial in this cemetery to honor all of the brave area men who died in the war. I hope I live to see it.

Next to Gerrit's grave is Christina's. Arie's sorrow deepens, as does mine, as we place the flowers on it. Maarten helped me find meaning in Gerrit's death, but there was no explanation for Christina's.

Two days after the fire, we awoke from where we'd been staying at a friend's house to find that Christina was gone. The note she left behind said she had run away with Jack Newell. He had no job now that the tannery had burned to the ground, so he was going to Chicago to look for work. They didn't know then, that much of Chicago had also been destroyed. He'd asked Christina to go with him. *I love him*, she'd written. *I don't want to lose him.*

The way I had lost Hendrik. Christina didn't say those words, but I ached with guilt, wondering if reading Hendrik's letters had given her the courage to do it. She knew what the outcome for Hendrik and me had been.

"We need to go after her," I told Maarten.

"No, Geesje. We can't. Even if we managed to find her in Chicago and bring her back, we couldn't keep her here against her will."

"What are we going to do?"

"We're going to pray and trust God to bring her back. Jesus said that He knows who all of His sheep are, and no one can snatch them out of His hand."

Now, as I stand gazing at Christina's grave, I think about the difference between a mother's viewpoint and a father's. A mother often sees her children's failures as her own. A father sees them as the result of their God-given free choice to defy Him.

"She was coming home to us, Arie," I say, wiping a tear. "She said she had something important to tell us, something she feared we wouldn't be able to forgive. But I'm still waiting after all these years for God to answer one final prayer for me."

"Which prayer is that, Moeder?"

"I asked Him for the assurance that Christina had returned to her faith before she died. I just wish I knew for certain that she had."

Arie wraps his arm around my shoulder. "I wish I did, too, Mama."

When he was alive, Maarten used to quote Jesus' promise to me in my moments of grief and doubt: "'My sheep hear my voice . . . I give unto them eternal life; and they shall never perish, neither shall any man pluck them out of my hand.'" He used to assure me that Jesus still held Christina firmly in His hand, wherever she was, and He would never let the evil one snatch her away for eternity.

We saved Maarten's grave for last. Arie and Jakob had helped me choose his grave marker, which reads, *Safely home with his Savior.* "You know what your father would say if he was here, don't you?" I ask Arie.

He smiles slightly. "'Don't grieve for me. I'm in a much better place.'"

"That's right." I'm smiling, too. "He used to say that our short, troublesome years on earth serve only to prepare us for an eternity that is far, far greater." I kneel down on the grass to arrange the flowers and silently tell Maarten how much I love him, how much I look forward to spending an eternity together. Arie helps me up again.

"Let's go home," I say. "Dinner is waiting."

CHAPTER 33

Anna

I'm a mess of nerves as I prepare for bed. I don't want to go rowing with William tomorrow. I don't want to take the steamship home to Chicago. I feel like I can't breathe when I think about the long voyage across the Atlantic Ocean for our wedding trip. Praying is still very new to me, but I climb into bed and curl into a ball and plead with God to help me. I ask Him to calm the churning waves in my soul the way Jesus calmed the Sea of Galilee for His frightened disciples. I ask Him to show me who I really am and what He wants me to do with my life. I pray and pray until I run out of words—and then something remarkable happens. I feel His blessing of peace on me as if a gentle hand rests on my head in benediction. It's just like the dream I had when Mama knelt in front of the altar in the castle church and the minister rested his hand on her head. I drift off peacefully to sleep.

The sound of running feet and voices in the hallway awakens me.

I sit up in bed, my heart racing. It's still very dark in my room, but a dull orange glow flickers outside my window around the edges of the curtains. I have left the window open and the air that drifts inside smells like a campfire. The agitation in the hallway grows louder. I hear someone say the word *fire*.

I scramble out of bed and yank the curtains open. A short distance away on the opposite shore of Black Lake an enormous fire is raging. Flames leap and dance as they consume one of the big resort hotels across the lake. The reflection of the flames on the water makes it seem as if the lake is burning, too. Thick black smoke billows into the sky, snuffing out the stars above the burning building. Showers of sparks ascend into the air along with the smoke like a flock of flaming birds. Black Lake isn't very wide at this point. Might the sparks fly across the glowing water and set our hotel on fire, too?

I hurry to the connecting door to Mother's room and knock on it to awaken her. "There's a huge fire across the lake from us," I tell her. "I think we should get dressed and gather up our things in case we need to evacuate." All my life I've heard stories about the Great Chicago Fire that destroyed the city in 1871, just three years before I was born. People say it spread out of control faster than the firemen could battle it. For a while, they'd hoped the Chicago River would halt the fire's spread, but flaming debris blew across the water on the wind, incinerating the city. If the wind is just right tonight, might debris cross Black Lake just as easily?

I'm all dressed except for my shoes when someone knocks on my hallway door. I open it to find William standing there. He has pulled on his trousers without a belt or suspenders and he's wearing shoes without any socks. He's wearing a linen blazer over his striped pajama top. "Anna, thank God you're all right!" he says as he lunges to embrace me. "When I first woke up and smelled the smoke, I thought our hotel was on fire."

"I did, too, for a minute."

"They say it's the Jenison Park Hotel that's burning, but I still wanted to find you and make sure you're fine. I was so panicked

317

at the thought of you trapped in the flames that I threw on my clothes and came to see you."

"I'm fine. I got dressed, too, just in case . . ."

He holds me close, stroking my sleep-tousled hair. "I'm so glad I was here to take care of you. If anything happened to you, I don't know what I would do." His words touch me, and I hug him tightly in return. A moment later he releases me, and Mother opens the door we share.

"Oh, William, thank goodness you're here to take charge. I'm so relieved." I suddenly understand why women like my mother and Honoria Stevens choose to look the other way when their husbands have brief affairs. Mother would be lost without the security of a man in her life. My father makes her feel safe and gives her an identity. He makes her who she is—Mrs. Arthur Nicholson. Now that William is here to take care of us, she feels secure. And so do I. It's the same sense of safety I always feel in my nightmare when Father's strong hands hold me above the waves to keep me from drowning.

"I don't believe we're in any danger at the moment," William says. "But I think we'd be wise to stay vigilant until the fire is under control. The wind seems to be blowing very briskly."

"I would like to go outside and watch," I say, putting on my shoes. "Do you want to come with us, Mother?"

"I'll watch from the window. I'm not presentable." She says this even though she is fully dressed. But her hair is still in a long braid for the night.

"I'll come back for you if there is any danger," William promises.

We head downstairs toward the main door holding hands. With so many windows open on this warm, summer night, smoke has drifted into the hallways and stairwells. Outside, we join dozens of other guests from our hotel as we stand near the shore in a mishmash of clothing and watch the inferno across the glowing lake. The opposite shoreline is lined with people who have fled the burning building. I can only imagine their terror. The Jenison Park Hotel resembles a flaming skeleton as fire engulfs the roof and licks through the windows.

"I feel so sorry for all those people over there, watching their hotel burn," I say, "I hope everyone made it out safely."

"Yes . . . It's going to be a total loss from the looks of it."

"How horrifying fire is! I've seen photographs of Chicago after the Great Fire. And to think, it happened only a few years before I was born." *To parents who then abandoned me.* The thought brings tears to my eyes, which already sting from the smoke. William slips his arm around my waist as we stand together, and I wrap mine around him, as well. The uncertainty and fear on this strange night have broken down our reserves with each other. After a while, I notice that William is looking at me, not the fire.

"You're so beautiful, Anna," he says, brushing a blowing strand of hair from my face. "The glow of the firelight has turned your hair to pure gold."

My hair. It's another reminder that I don't know who I am or where I came from. I remember how Derk mistook me for someone else the first day we met—for a Dutch woman—and I feel prompted to say, "William, there's something I'm not sure you know about me. . . . I was adopted. My father and mother aren't really my . . . I mean, they've raised me since I was a baby, but . . . but I'm not really their daughter."

"I didn't know that."

"Does it matter to you that I don't know anything about my background?"

"Not in the least." He pulls me closer. "It's the woman you are now that I care about." We watch as a section of the building's wall crumbles like a child's tower of blocks. We hear the distant rumble a few seconds later. "Anna, when I woke up tonight and thought our hotel was on fire . . . when I imagined losing you . . . I guess we don't realize how important the people in our lives really are until we fear we may lose them. I don't want to lose you, Anna. I'm so sorry we quarreled."

I look up at him and smile. His face is sprinkled with bristles of dark whiskers that need to be shaved. I've never seen him without his beard well trimmed, and I reach up to brush my fingertips across his cheek. "I'm sorry, too."

"I know I'm probably at fault for over-reacting, but I've heard stories about people who've been swindled out of all their money by unscrupulous clergymen and so-called religious groups. I admit I don't know much about that particular church except that they're not really our sort of people."

"You mean not wealthy?"

"I suppose."

"The pastor of that church isn't unscrupulous. And many working-class people do attend there. But I've been reading the Bible this summer, and I've learned a lot of things. It's hard for rich people like us not to rely on our wealth, and Jesus warns us not to put our trust in money instead of in Him. I don't intend to foolishly give away my money to anyone, but I do want to grow in faith and learn to trust God more. I want to keep reading my Bible and learning for myself what Jesus taught. I hope you'll allow me to do that after we're married."

William lets out his breath in a rush. "I admit that your sudden religious fervor isn't something I understand. Other people in our social circle seem content with the role that religion has always played in our lives." He pauses and we both gaze at the shocking scene across the lake as the flames rage out of control, devouring the once-grand building. William's arm tightens around my waist, drawing me closer. "I suppose I'd be willing to listen more closely to what you're saying from now on. I don't want your pursuit of God or faith or religion or whatever you might call it to come between us again."

I feel a prickle of hope. I recall the sense of peace that had overwhelmed me earlier tonight. "One of the reasons I kept going back to that church was because I needed to find answers to all my questions. But during my time alone here, I've learned that God will lead me to the answers if I seek Him. I can honor your wishes, William, and not return to that church again."

He turns away from the fire and looks down at me. "I'm glad. And I want to make you happy, too, Anna."

His words bring tears to my eyes, a smile to my face. He truly means it. I wish our marriage would be like this, like tonight. That we'd always feel this close to each other. That we would be able to talk this freely and really listen to each other. I know that marriages in our social circle aren't usually close, but why couldn't William's and mine be different? Perhaps it's a goal I could aim for.

We watch the fire until there is little more for it to consume. Thankfully, the wind has died down and the risk of the fire spreading from blowing sparks seems to have lessened. By the time we go back inside, I feel closer to William than ever before.

"Let's choose a date for our wedding when we get back to Chicago," he says. "So we can begin our life together."

"I would like that." It's the truth. He gives me a long, lingering kiss that leaves me feeling dizzy before we part.

I lay down on my bed without bothering to change into my nightgown again, unsure if I'll be able to fall asleep, even though it's still dark outside. Things seem different between William and me now. He seems different. I want to share my life with him and be a good wife to him. Demanding that I be allowed to visit the LaSalle Street church seems silly to me now, and very childish. As Derk has assured me, I can talk with God in prayer anyplace, anytime. I fall asleep with the same sense of peace that I had after praying earlier tonight.

It's still very early in the morning when I do wake up. I practically leap off the bed with an overwhelming urge to go outside and find Derk. I want to talk to him one last time before I return home to Chicago and tell him about the changes I saw in William last night. I want to thank him for his friendship and for the Bible he gave me. And I want to find out what he decided to do about his girlfriend, Caroline.

The grass is damp with dew, the air faintly smoky as I make my way down to the bench where we so often talked. I don't see Derk anywhere, so I sit facing Black Lake and the charred, still-smoking ruins of the Jenison Park Hotel.

"You're up early this morning," someone says behind me. I know it's Derk even before I turn around.

"Yes, I—"

"I heard that was quite a fire last night."

"It was. William and I watched it from here. I hope everyone got out all right."

"The morning news reported that everyone is safe, thank heaven."

"I'm glad. . . . Listen, I got up early because I wanted to talk with you. Can you spare a moment?"

"Of course." He sits down on the bench beside me, careful to keep a respectable distance between us.

"I can only imagine what you must think of William now that you've met him."

"It's not my place to judge—"

"I know he has a strong, forceful personality at times, but he needs to be aggressive in order to be good at what he does, and to get ahead in the banking business. But he can be very tender and loving, too. Last night when the fire woke everyone up, he was very concerned for me. We had a chance to talk as we stood here watching the flames, and he told me how much he cares for me. He promised to try to be more understanding as I search for answers to all my questions. I feel very certain about marrying him now. I know he'll be good to me."

"I'm glad. . . . But may I offer just one more word of advice?"

I hesitate, unsure if I want Derk to shatter the sense of peace I finally feel. "I suppose so."

"In your world you're taught to be genteel and submissive. You're a quiet, gentle woman, and you hold all your feelings inside. But I know you can speak up, Anna. You told me exactly what you thought that day we walked up Mt. Pisgah. You weren't afraid to offer your opinion."

"I'm sorry if I—"

"No, listen. You need to do the same thing with William. Don't let him run over you like a team of horses. If you don't want to go out rowing in one of these boats, tell him so. Don't let him bully you."

"You make it sound so easy. It's not."

"I understand. Maybe you could just pretend he's me for a moment and then tell him what you really think." We both laugh, and I know Derk and I are good friends once again.

"Thank you for that advice. Now, if you don't mind me being nosy, I'm very curious to hear what happened when you talked with Caroline—unless it's none of my business."

He exhales in a huge sigh. "Well, it didn't go the way I'd hoped it would. Tante Geesje helped me see that I had to choose between wanting my own way and wanting God's will for my life. So I told Caroline that I couldn't accept her compromise. My calling to be a pastor hasn't changed. I told her if she loved me enough to try to cope with the demands of my job, I would promise not to let my congregation take advantage of me at the expense of my family. I would promise to be sensitive to her and to our children. But I've been called and trained to be the pastor of a church, and I have to obey God."

"What did she say?"

Derk seems to steady himself. "She started crying and told me to leave. I hate knowing that I caused those tears."

"Was it real grief or was she using tears to try to sway you?"

Derk looks surprised, as if he hadn't thought of that. "I don't know. But I think it's over for good between us."

"You advised me to stand firm with William so I'm glad you did the same with Caroline."

"Tante Geesje says that if it's the Lord's will for Caroline and me to be together, everything will fall into place. If not . . . well, I want His will, not my own."

"That's very good advice. I'm sorry I never got to meet your aunt. She sounds like a wise and wonderful woman." I look out at the row of boats, and as I contemplate crossing the lake with William in a steamship later this afternoon, an idea begins to form. "Are you supposed to start work now, Derk?"

"Well . . . actually, I'm not working today. It's Sunday, and I don't do any work on the Sabbath Day." I notice for the first time that he isn't dressed in work clothes. He has on nice trousers and a dress shirt. A jacket with a tie sticking out of the pocket is slung over his shoulder.

"Then why are you here?"

He looks embarrassed as he stares down at the bench, not at me. "I was hoping to talk to you one last time. I heard William say he'd come to take you home."

It takes me a moment to absorb his words. I rose early today in hopes of seeing Derk, and he did the same to see me. I don't know what to make of the coincidence. Perhaps God has prompted both of us for mysterious reasons of His own. I look at the rowboats again and say, "I have a favor to ask you. I want to rent one of your rowboats."

"You mean later today? With William?"

"No. Right now. I want you to take me out on the lake so I can get over my fear of the water. I need to go rowing with William today, take the steamship home to Chicago with him later, and go on a honeymoon to Europe and see those canals in Italy. I can't remain afraid."

"Are you sure you want to go now?"

"I'm positive. I trust you, Derk. Will you take me?"

He rises to his feet. "Let's go."

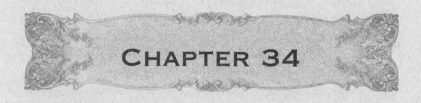

CHAPTER 34

Geesje

I don't know why I'm awake so early this morning. Our Sunday church service doesn't start for hours. The sun isn't even up yet. But rather than lie here tossing in bed, I may as well get up and make some tea and sit down to finish the last chapter of my story. It's been sitting like a heavy weight on my heart, and I doubt if that weight of sorrow will lift until I finish writing it.

I sharpen my pencil, worn almost to a nub after all the words I've written, and begin.

Geesje's Story

HOLLAND, MICHIGAN
20 YEARS EARLIER

I can't begin to describe my excitement when I received Christina's letter telling us she was coming home. We hadn't seen her or heard from her in nearly seven years. I ran out of the house on that warm September day and jogged all the way through town to our new print shop to show the letter to Maarten and Arie. We had rebuilt the shop on west Seventh Street, constructed from bricks this time. We also sold our original plot of land and built the house I still live in today. Since the fire had taught us the folly of accumulating material goods, Maarten and I decided that we needed only a handful of rooms, enough for the two of us. Arie lived in an apartment behind the shop, and Jakob got married and moved to the neighboring village of Noordeloos to pastor a church.

Tears rolled down Maarten's cheeks as he read Christina's letter. "Thank God! Oh, thank God," he repeated over and over. He had trusted God to bring our daughter home to us, and He had been faithful.

"What do you suppose she means," I asked him, "when she says we may not forgive her? Of course we'll forgive her. I can't imagine any reason why we wouldn't, can you? She's our precious daughter."

Arie's eyes also welled with tears when he read the letter. "I want to go with you to Grand Haven to meet her ship. We can close the shop for half a day, can't we? For news as wonderful as this?"

Maarten smiled and wiped his cheeks. "I would kill a fattened calf for her if I had one."

Christina had booked passage from Milwaukee, Wisconsin, to Grand Haven, Michigan, on a ship called the *Ironsides*. On the September morning when she was due to arrive, Maarten, Arie, and I left in our carriage before dawn for the twenty-mile trip north up the coast of Lake Michigan. I worried that her ship would be delayed since a violent storm had blown in during the night, but we decided that after waiting all these years, we would willingly wait in Grand Haven for as long as necessary for Christina to arrive.

The wind blew fiendishly as we left home, and it rained so hard during the journey that we were soaked and shivering by the time we reached Grand Haven. Muddy roads and downed tree limbs made the trip take longer than we'd hoped but when we arrived we learned that Christina's ship hadn't docked yet.

"That's the *Ironsides* out there," one of the clerks told us as we warmed ourselves inside the shipping office. He pointed to a dark shape bobbing offshore, barely visible through the clouds and driving rain. Enormous waves churned Lake Michigan and lashed the pier, creating plumes of spray that looked as though they would sweep away anyone who dared step onto it. "The captain tried once already to bring her into the channel," the clerk continued, "but the waves dragged him off course. He's swinging the ship around now to try again."

More and more people jammed inside the office to await the steamer's arrival. No one spoke above a whisper as we watched and waited. Fear rose up inside me like the towering waves. All I could do was grip Maarten's hand and pray.

"Here she comes," someone said. "Looks like the ship is heading toward the channel again." We all crowded around the foggy window. Arie went outside in the rain with a few other men to watch. The *Ironsides* rose and fell sickeningly on the waves, visible one moment, then disappearing in a watery trough the next until all we could see were her two billowing smokestacks. I remembered the storm we'd endured on the Atlantic and how seasick we'd all been. I held my breath and squeezed Maarten's hand tighter.

The ship was no match for the relentless waves. They shoved her off course once again, causing her to miss the channel entrance as she wallowed like a helpless toy. For a second time, the captain was forced to swing the ship around before attempting to dock again. "He'd better keep his eye out for sandbars," someone said. "They're always shifting around out there."

The third attempt failed almost before it began. "What's happening?" one of the worried onlookers asked the clerk. "What's the ship doing now? Is it backing away?"

"Looks like it. Looks like the captain isn't going to try again after all. He'll probably ride out the storm offshore."

Arie had come back inside and a short time later I heard him say to one of the clerks, "I noticed that the ship's stacks are no longer putting out smoke. Is that normal?"

The clerk grabbed his spyglass and opened the door to get a better look. "You're right . . . her boilers must have quit."

"What would make them do that?" Arie asked.

"She might be taking on water. . . . Looks like she's in trouble." Even without the spyglass I could see Christina's ship rolling helplessly on the breakers. "Uh-oh," the clerk said as he continued to peer at the floundering ship. "She's flying a distress flag. She needs help." He ran outside, shouting into the wind, "Get a rescue team! The *Ironsides* is in trouble!" An alarm bell began to toll, ringing and ringing to summon help.

Maarten released my hand. "Tell us what to do," he said, as he and Arie rushed outside with the other men. "How can we help?"

I stood listening in the doorway as the gathering dock workers and volunteers discussed the rescue. "We don't stand a chance of sending boats out to her. The lake would just swallow them up and spit them back."

"We'll have to wait and see if she lowers her lifeboats. In the meantime we can build a bonfire and get help ready when they do come ashore."

"Do you think their lifeboats can make it in?"

There was a long pause before someone said, "It'll be risky."

"But if the ship is sinking . . ."

"Right. I imagine the captain will wait as long as he dares before lowering the lifeboats, hoping the storm dies down a bit."

I covered my mouth in horror as Maarten and Arie set off with an ever-growing crowd of workers and local residents and volunteers, summoned by the clanging bell. This couldn't be happening. Not when we'd waited and prayed so long for our Christina to come home. Not when she was this close. The only thing I could do was pray.

Another hour passed. The *Ironsides* seemed to be settling deeper in the water, her stern dipping lower than her bow. It looked to me like she was sinking. On shore, the waiting men gave a shout when they finally spotted lifeboats being lowered—they counted five of them. I ran outside to watch with the others, heedless of the wind and drenching rain. The lifeboats looked like tiny specks as they began crossing the distance between the floundering ship and the shore, surrounded by towering waves. The boats were no match for the deadly waves. The screams and cries of the frightened passengers carried on the wind as the lake tossed the tiny lifeboats helplessly.

I closed my eyes. *Please, God . . . please, God . . . please, God . . .*

When the watching crowd gave a collective gasp, I opened them again. "Dear God, no!" Arie cried out. A huge wave had struck one of the lifeboats, flinging it upside down and spilling its flailing passengers into the water. Then an even bigger wave swallowed two more boats, capsizing them, as well. The two remaining lifeboats battled to reach the shore. I covered my ears to blot out the heartbreaking screams and cries for help.

Not Christina . . . Please, God, not my Christina . . .

Even the strongest swimmer didn't dare go out alone in such huge, pounding waves. In desperation, volunteers began forming human chains, hand gripping hand, stretching out into the water from the shore to rescue as many people as possible. I saw Maarten in the middle of one chain, braving the icy water, grasping a man on either side of him in his strong hands. Arie had dug in on his knees at the edge of the water, crutches flung aside, anchoring the end of another chain. The surf hurled the three overturned lifeboats toward land along with the floating bodies of the dead, men in dark suits and women with colorful skirts, their long hair fanned out on the water.

I fell to my knees and was sick. I couldn't watch. My prayers became one long, desperate wail for God to have mercy. . . . *Mercy . . .*

I don't know how much time passed. When I could stand up again, I staggered over to where the first chain had managed to pull a man to shore. A huge bonfire blazed on the beach and rescuers quickly wrapped the man in a blanket and helped him over to the fire. A few of the drenched volunteers warmed themselves briefly before running back to the beach to try to save someone else. I stood near the fire among a crowd of local women waiting with quilts and blankets to warm the survivors. I shivered with fear and cold, unable to stop groaning and weeping until a kind woman wrapped her colorful patchwork quilt and her arms around me.

"My daughter . . . my daughter is on that ship," I told her. She held me tightly, praying with me.

At last the two surviving lifeboats made it to shore. I left the stranger's comforting embrace and staggered toward them with the other women as they rushed to help, the quilt still wrapped around my shoulders. I would give it to Christina. I would envelop her in it and never let her go.

But Christina wasn't among the shivering survivors in either lifeboat.

As another dreadful hour passed, the human chains pulled as many people as they could to safety. I stayed near the fire and searched for Christina among the living—but I couldn't find her among the surviving passengers and crew members. When I saw a young father clutching his terrified child, I gave them the quilt I'd been wearing, draping it around his shoulders.

Someone tugged my skirt, and I looked down to see Arie collapsed on the sand in front of the fire. His face was blue with cold, his eyes rimmed with exhaustion. "Have you seen her? Did they find her?" he asked through chattering teeth.

I shook my head and continued to wander among the dazed survivors calling, "Christina . . . Christina." I studied their faces, searching, searching, as despair overwhelmed me. Then in the distance I saw a group of men hauling bodies out of the water, lining them up on the beach. More men bent over them, checking for signs of life. One of the crouching men was Maarten.

I summoned the last of my strength and ran toward him, calling his name. The wind swallowed most of my cries, but he must have heard one of them because he looked up and saw me coming. He climbed to his feet and staggered toward me, shaking his head, his hands held out in front of him to stop me.

He had found her.

"NO!" I screamed. "Oh, God, no! No!"

Maarten caught me in his arms to keep me from going any farther, and we collapsed to the ground in a tangled heap. "Tell me it isn't her, Maarten . . . please, please, tell me Christina isn't dead!"

His grief-stricken sobs and the strength of his hold on me told me that she was. All of the life drained from me. I should be dead, not my daughter.

I don't know how long we sat huddled together on the sand, but Maarten finally pulled himself to his feet, lifting me in his arms and carrying me to the shipping office where we'd first waited. It seemed as though days and days had passed since we'd left home this morning filled with hope and anticipation. I wasn't looking out the office window when the *Ironsides* finally disappeared beneath the waves, the bow protruding from the water before sinking, but Maarten saw it.

I listened, numb with grief, as the shipping company helped Arie make arrangements to bring Christina home to Holland for burial. Only his courage and strength enabled Maarten and me to get through it. In all, twenty-one people had perished that morning, eleven passengers and ten crew members including the ship's captain.

Our beautiful Christina was gone, and I didn't understand why. Why would God allow this senseless tragedy? Why this, on top of so many other tragedies we had endured?

This time, Maarten had no answers.

**HOLLAND, MICHIGAN
1897**

I close my notebook and lay down my pencil. I walk out to my kitchen and gaze sightlessly through the window. My story is finished. I have written down all of my memories from the past. This final story of how we lost Christina has been the most difficult one of all to tell. I did it for Derk. He already knows all the details of how the *Ironsides* sank, killing his mother as well as our Christina. But I want him to know how hard we all tried—everyone who was on shore that day—to save as many people as possible, many at the risk of their own lives.

I can't write about Christina's funeral because I don't think I have the words to explain how near God was to me on that day, in spite of my sorrow and bewilderment. It was as if He had wrapped me in His quilt and held me close to His heart, His strong, comforting presence a blessing to both Maarten and me. Afterward, God began lovingly wooing us back to His side through the countless small acts of kindness that His family showered on us. We weren't able to understand why He had taken Christina, but slowly, step by step as our grief lifted, He reassured us that one day we would understand. Death wasn't the end but only a new beginning, the way an infant must leave its mother's womb to begin a new, light-filled life.

The sun is rising in the sky as I sit down in my kitchen to eat breakfast. I need to get ready for church soon. I glance over at Derk's house next door and remember my shock when I learned that his mother—Hendrik's daughter, Rosie—had also died when the *Ironsides* sank that day. I'd wondered if she and Christina had met each other and comforted each other in those final harrowing hours. Had they remembered becoming fast friends in front of the cobbler's shop on that long-ago day?

Hendrik found me as I stood alone in the funeral home before Christina's funeral. "Is this our penance, Geesje?" he had asked. "Is God punishing us for loving each other more than we loved our spouses all these years?"

His words shocked me. For a moment I wondered if they could be true. But I quickly shook my head and said, "No, God doesn't do things like that, Hendrik. He doesn't punish the children for the sins of their fathers. Besides, it isn't true. I love my husband, Maarten." I saw that my words had hurt him. "You should go be with Nella now," I told him. "She is surely grieving, too."

When I finish eating, I wash my face and brush my teeth and change into my Sunday clothes, my mind still on those long-ago events. Six months after the *Ironsides* sank, Derk and his father sold their home in Zeeland and moved next door to me. "That house held too many memories," Derk's father told me. "I saw Rosie every time I walked into a room. And yet she wasn't there. This will be a new start for Derk and me."

It was a new start for me, as well. Maarten had caught a terrible chill as he'd battled those icy waves the day the *Ironsides* sank. He developed pneumonia and died three months after Christina did.

From the moment I first saw Derk, I loved that sad little blond-haired boy. I made pancakes for him and held him on my lap and soothed his lonely tears. As he grew older, he came to my house after school each day to wait until his father came home from work, and I helped him with his homework, told him stories, and fed him cookies. We were God's gift to each other to help us heal. And in leading Derk out of his sorrow and grief, I found a way out of my own.

CHAPTER 35

Anna

HOTEL OTTAWA
1897

I watch Derk remove his shoes and socks and leave them on the bench with his suitcoat and tie. He rolls up his sleeves and his trouser legs. I hope he doesn't ruin his good Sunday clothes taking me on this venture. My knees feel like they've come unglued as I follow him to the shore of Black Lake. The water is so calm it looks as though you could walk across it, yet I'm having second thoughts. Derk turns one of the beached rowboats right-side-up and tosses a set of oars into it, then drags it into the shallow water. We haven't signed up with the hotel's concierge to rent the boat, but Derk is probably afraid I'll change my mind in the time it would take him to run up to the hotel and back. He may be right.

And yet I don't want to be shackled by fear for the rest of my life. When he's finished I draw a deep breath and ask, "How do I get in?" The rowboat sits halfway in and halfway out of the water.

"Come here and give me your hand." I do what he says, trusting him. He's standing ankle-deep in the water. "All you have to do is step over the side of the boat and sit down on the wooden seat. I'll keep holding your hand until you're settled. The boat is going to rock a little beneath your weight when you get in, but don't let it scare you. Even if it tipped over, the worst that would happen is that you'd get wet. The water is barely twelve inches deep here."

I laugh nervously and say, "I would prefer to remain dry, if you don't mind."

He laughs and says, "Me too!" When I'm seated, I let go of his hand and grasp the board I'm sitting on in a death grip. "Now, I'm going to push off and then climb in," Derk says. "The boat is going to rock again, but you don't have to be afraid. We'll be fine. You couldn't ask for calmer water."

He gives a hearty push, and I can feel the boat scrape across the ground as it leaves the shore. It begins to float. Derk climbs in, balancing himself expertly as the boat wobbles for a moment. He sits down facing me and picks up the oars. "Good so far?" he asks. I manage a nod, afraid to move a muscle and rock the boat. He pushes us farther from shore using one of the oars, then sets them in the oarlocks and dips them into the water. We glide smoothly out onto Black Lake as he begins to row. "I promise to stay near the shore. And the moment you want to turn back, I will."

"Thank you." At first I'm terrified to move or even breathe, but the rowboat's gentle motion and the sound of the swishing oars and lapping water begin to soothe me. Black Lake is achingly beautiful this morning, the sun warm on my face and hair, the sky cloudless. I realize that going out on the lake with Derk in this tiny boat is a lesson in trust, and a metaphor for a life of faith in God. I'm helpless without Him. My life is in His hands. Yet Jesus promised that not a hair could fall from my head without the Father knowing it. I slowly begin to relax as we row east on Black Lake, away from Lake Michigan and toward the town of Holland. On our left, the shoreline is thick with trees and sprinkled with cottages.

"Thank you for doing this, Derk."

"You're welcome. I'm enjoying it, and I hope you are, too."

"I wouldn't exactly say that I'm enjoying it . . . yet. But I need to conquer my fear."

Derk swishes the oars through the water once, twice, then asks, "Can you remember what caused your fear? Did you have a bad experience on the water in the past?"

I give him a weak smile. "I'm embarrassed to admit it—especially to William—but it's because of a recurring nightmare that I've had ever since I was a small child. William would think I'm being ridiculous, and he's right. It's silly to let a childhood nightmare frighten me now that I'm a grown woman. That's why I need to get over it. That's why I asked you to take me rowing today."

"I was terrified of the water for a long time, too. I didn't have a bad experience myself, but I think I told you that my mother died in a shipwreck on Lake Michigan, just north of here."

A chill shivers through me. "I'm so sorry, Derk. No one could ever blame you for being afraid of the water. How old were you?"

"I was four. As I grew older I wanted to conquer my fear, just like you're doing, so I asked my father to let me learn how to swim and to take sailing lessons. It wouldn't bring my mother back but it would make me feel . . . in control. As it turned out, I discovered that I loved sailing."

I notice dark patches of sweat forming under Derk's arms as he rows. He is all dressed up for church, and I feel bad for making him work in his Sunday clothes. He has kept us near the shore as he promised, but he lifts the oars out of the water for a moment as we gaze at the remains of the Jenison Park Hotel across the water. The boat rocks gently on the lake. A chimney and a section of wall are the only things standing. Smoke drifts into the sky in a few places as people mill around the mound of ruins.

"Life can change so suddenly," I say. "Like it probably did for all those people who were in that hotel last night."

"That's true. I'll never understand how people who don't know God manage to keep going when things like that happen." He lowers the oars and begins rowing again. "Tante Geesje has been letting me read the story of her life. She suffered through so many tragedies, yet her faith was what helped her get through them."

"It sounds like an inspiring story."

"It is. And I learned something I never knew. It turns out that the soldier she was madly in love with was my grandfather."

"Really!"

"He was also in a terrible shipwreck when the *Phoenix* caught fire and sank, and—"

"Oh, Derk! That's horrible."

He stops rowing. "I'm sorry. I shouldn't be talking about shipwrecks when you're trying to . . . you know . . . be brave."

"It doesn't matter. I'm not feeling too scared at the moment. I just thought it was horrible to have two tragedies like that in your family, two shipwrecks. Please go on. You were talking about your grandfather."

Derk pushes his fair hair off his forehead and pulls on the oars again. "Out of some three hundred passengers, only a handful survived. One of them was my grandfather. The Bible says that all the days of our lives are written in God's book before one of them ever comes to be. God knew when my mother's life would end. And He also knew that He had further plans for my grandfather. I'm here because he survived."

"What about all the other people who died?"

"I can't answer that. We may never know why they died that day until we get to heaven. Then we'll say, 'Oh, now I see. It all makes sense.' That's what Tante Geesje used to tell me. Her daughter was on the same ship as my mother, and she also drowned."

I watch a sailboat glide past us, heading west toward the big lake. I sense that Derk needs to talk about what happened to his mother and grandfather, that he draws comfort from remembering them, so I shove my selfish fears aside and say, "Tell me about your mother, Derk. Why was she on that ship?"

"She had gone to Milwaukee to visit my grandmother, who was very sick. I stayed behind with my other grandparents in Zeeland while she was away. She was returning home aboard the *Ironsides* when a terrible storm struck and gale-force winds churned up huge waves. Her steamer was almost to Grand Haven, within sight of the shore. In fact, the captain tried to enter the harbor two or three times, but the waves were too strong and kept pushing them off course. Evidently they struck a sandbar and began taking on water. All the passengers and crew were told to abandon ship and climb into lifeboats."

My entire body begins to tremble. Derk is describing my dream! I can't speak, can't breathe as he continues.

"The lifeboats were making their way to shore when a huge wave smashed into them, capsizing them. My mother and Geesje's daughter, Christina, both drowned. Some of the survivors said that the women's heavy skirts pulled them under—"

"Stop! Derk, stop! I want to go back to the shore right now! Please, please! I need to be on land!"

He freezes, the oars motionless, his eyes wide with surprise. Can't he feel the entire boat trembling along with me? I grip the seat in white-knuckle fear as I shiver uncontrollably. Derk finally recovers from his surprise and rows with all his strength to the closest shore. It's a rugged stretch of coastline with no cottages nearby, and I feel the rowboat scrape the bottom as we come to a halt. Derk leaps out and wades into the water to drag the boat onto land as far as he can. He's out of breath when he's finally done. "Please forgive me. I'm so sorry for scaring you."

"It can't be . . . it just can't be . . ." I say through chattering teeth.

"Anna, what's wrong?

"You were describing my nightmare exactly! How is that possible?"

"Your nightmare? I don't know." He offers me a hand to help me out of the boat, but I shake my head. I'm frozen in place, unable to move. Derk climbs back in and sits facing me again. "Tell me."

"In my nightmare, we're on a ship in a terrible storm. I'm sitting on Mama's lap, and we can barely hang on to our seats because the ship is tossing and rolling so badly. People are getting seasick. We're almost there, we can see land in the distance, but the ship keeps missing the harbor. Then we stop. Someone says we've hit a sandbar. Water starts coming into the boat, and the engines that have been rumbling and pounding all night go quiet. The silence is worse than the rumbling, because we can hear the waves lashing and the wind howling around us. We all sit there. People are crying and praying. Mama rocks me in her arms and sings to me and promises me that everything will be fine, that God is with us."

I don't know how, but as I'm telling Derk my nightmare, I'm remembering more details than I usually recall when I wake up. Derk reaches to pry my arms free and takes my hands in his. "Go on," he urges.

"The crew helps everyone into the lifeboats. But it's a mistake! Now we're being tossed around even worse than aboard the ship. Enormous waves wash right over the sides of the boat and spill into the bottom, drenching us with freezing water. Mama and I cling to each other with all our strength. Then a huge wave picks up our boat and tosses us upside down. We plunge into the water. My skin stings as we go under, and I hear that gurgling sound in my ears that water makes. Everything is pitch dark. I can't see, can't breathe. I feel Mama kicking her legs with all her might, and it seems like hours and hours pass as we're trapped beneath the dark, suffocating waters. At last, we come to the surface again. I drag in a breath of air. Mama and I are both coughing and choking. My father is trying to stay afloat just a few feet away from us, and Mama pushes me into his arms, saying, 'Save my daughter! Save her, please!' I don't want to let go of Mama, but my father grabs me and holds my head above the waves. When I look back, Mama is gone. All I see is her hand, as if she's waving good-bye. Father tries to reach for her, but he's too late. She's gone."

My tears are falling as I finish. Derk moves from his seat to mine and takes me in his arms. "I'm sorry, Anna. I'm so sorry." I let him soothe me, just like Mother used to do when I awoke from the nightmare as a child. When we finally pull apart, Derk takes my hands again and says, "I don't want to upset you even more, but . . . is it possible . . . I mean, do you think it may not have been just a dream? Is it possible that your nightmare really happened to you and that you were aboard the *Ironsides*, too? The details are amazingly similar."

"I don't know. I've had this nightmare for as long as I can remember . . . When did the ship sink?"

"In September of 1877."

"I would have been three years old. . . . Derk, the nightmare has always been exactly the same and so vivid that I can feel the wind blowing my hair in my eyes, how frigid the water is, and how strong my father's hands are when he grabs me." And the terror. Always, I remember the sheer terror. "Do you think it could have really happened to me?"

"There were some survivors. Not everyone drowned. Maybe your parents never talked about it because they hoped you would eventually forget what happened. It must have been horrifying for them, too."

"That makes sense. . . . And yet . . . in my nightmare, I always watch Mama sink beneath the waves. She never comes back. In my dream my mama drowns."

"I think you need to ask your parents about this."

"Yes, I'll ask Mother as soon as we get back. I want to know the truth."

"Did you call her Mama when you were little?"

"What do you mean . . . Why?"

"When you talked about her just now you called her Mother. But when you were describing your dream, you called her Mama. And there was something else that struck me as odd. You said when she handed you to your father she said, 'Save my daughter,' not 'Save our daughter.'"

I start shivering again. "What are you saying?"

"Didn't you tell me you were adopted?"

"Yes, as a newborn."

"Do you know anything about the circumstances? Or about your real parents?"

"Only that my real parents abandoned me and that Father

was traveling on a business trip when . . . No. No. You don't think . . . ?" I can't finish.

"It would explain why you remember a few words in another language. If your real mother was Dutch and she drowned that day . . . and if she gave you to your father to rescue . . ."

"But they told me they adopted me as a newborn." If that was a lie, if they found me when I was three years old, then the parts of the puzzle that Derk is piecing together would all fit into place. Everything would make sense. And so would the dream I had of standing in my familiar bedroom crying for Mama while Mother stood right there. Could that have happened, too? "We need to go back to the hotel. I need to talk to my mother."

Derk glances up at the tangle of woods and brush onshore. "I'll have to row back. I don't think we can walk back from here. I'm sorry—"

"You can row back. I'll be fine."

Derk gives my hands a squeeze before letting go. He stands and climbs out of the boat to push us away from shore, then jumps back in. My mind is reeling, my emotions tossing so wildly I barely notice the boat's rocking motion. Derk lowers the oars and digs into the water with all his strength. In no time at all we're at the hotel. My muscles are stiff with tension and fright as he helps me onshore. I hope my legs can hold me.

"I want you to come with me when I talk to my mother," I tell Derk. He is rolling down his shirtsleeves and pant legs again. He exhales as he drops onto the bench to put on his shoes and socks.

"I would be happy to, but I really don't think that's a good idea. Your mother won't be pleased to see me again or to find out that we've been alone together—and neither will William."

Derk is right. Yet I'm not sure I can face the truth alone. I watch him tie his shoes and say, "But you know all the details about the *Ironsides* and about how much I resemble your Dutch friend and . . . and everything else."

Derk stands and slings his suitcoat over his shoulder. "Just ask her for the truth, Anna. Either you were aboard that ship or you

341

weren't. Either you were a newborn when they adopted you or you were three years old. I'm sure it's been hard for your parents to hold on to so many secrets all these years. Just be sure to let them know that the truth isn't going to change the way you feel about them."

It was good advice. And yet I didn't want Derk to leave. "Where will you be if I need to find you later?"

"Well, for the next few hours I'll be at Pillar Church in Holland," he says with a grin. "Big white building on Ninth Street with six pillars in front. You can't miss it. " He takes my hands in his again and leans forward to kiss my cheek. "You don't need me, Anna. You're a survivor. You can do this."

I watch him walk away.

CHAPTER 36

Anna

**HOTEL OTTAWA
1897**

I take my time walking back to the hotel. Part of the reason is that my knees are still shaky. The other is that I'm afraid to know the truth, afraid to learn that my parents have been lying to me all these years. And I can't bear the thought that I may have lived through a disastrous shipwreck when innocent people like Derk's mother—and perhaps my own—died. I knock on Mother's door before going inside. She is already dressed for breakfast and standing in front of the mirror tidying her hair.

"There you are," she says. "Have you been out walking?"

"Were we in a shipwreck when I was little?" She turns to face me, her mouth open, her eyes wide with alarm. I continue before she has a chance to reply. "I just learned about a steamship called the *Ironsides* that sank in Lake Michigan when I would have been three years old. The details of that shipwreck are exactly like my nightmare."

She sinks down on the edge of her bed. Her hands and her hairbrush fall limply into her lap. "Oh, Anna."

"My nightmare isn't just a dream, is it? It's a memory." I cross the room to stand in front of her. "Tell me the truth, Mother, please. You owe me that much."

"I think we should wait for your father—"

"No! I don't want to wait. I want to know right now! Were we in that shipwreck or not?"

She lowers her head, staring at her lap. I force myself to be patient, to wait, knowing how difficult it will be for Mother to admit she has kept this information from me. It seems as though a lifetime passes before she finally looks up. "Yes," she says. "You were aboard the *Ironsides* before it sank." Her voice is whisper-soft, as if there's a sleeping baby in the room.

"Were you and Father with me, too?"

She shakes her head. "Just your father."

"But you're always in my dream. You hand me to Father and then you sink beneath the waves." Derk had pointed out the odd way I had told him the story: *Save my daughter.* I wait another eternity for Mother to reply.

"It was your real mother who drowned that day."

I can't breathe as I struggle with my emotions. My voice sounds hoarse when I'm finally able to ask, "Did Father know her?"

"No. He'd never met her before. He saw you clinging to her in the lifeboat just before it capsized. She was still holding you when he saw her again in the water. But she could no longer stay afloat so she gave you to him. She wanted you to live. Your father did, too."

This was the place in my dream where I always woke up screaming in terror. I sit down on the bed beside my mother, tears stinging my eyes as I now remember more. "There was a long line of men standing in the water, holding hands. The last one in the chain grabbed the lapels of Father's coat and pulled us in . . . There was a bonfire. . . . Someone wrapped a quilt around Father's shoulders but he gave it to me. He wrapped me up in it because I was so cold and wet. . . . I cried and cried. I wanted my mama, but she had disappeared beneath the waves."

Mother wraps her arms around me, the way she used to do when I awakened from the nightmare. "We believe she drowned, Anna. I'm so sorry. Perhaps your real father did, too, although none of the survivors remembered seeing a man with you and your mother."

"I don't remember being with a man, either. Mama and I were alone."

"We notified the authorities and put notices in all the newspapers—in Grand Haven and Grand Rapids and Milwaukee. They let us take care of you while we waited, but no one came forward to claim you. As the weeks passed, we were relieved when no one did. We loved you from the very beginning."

"But you said I was a newborn when you adopted me. You lied to me."

"That was your father's idea. He wanted you to forget about what happened. He wanted to forget the shipwreck, too. It was a terrifying experience for him, as well, Anna. You weren't the only one who had nightmares about that terrible day."

"I never knew that."

"He hoped that all of your bad memories would fade away if you thought you came to us as a newborn. We wanted you to be happy. And aside from the nightmares, you were. We thought you were too young to remember your mother or to remember losing her."

"And so the handful of Dutch words I remember must be from my mother. She must have been Dutch."

"I don't know. You could barely talk. In fact, you wouldn't talk at all for a very long time. You cried and cried for your mama, and you told us your name was Anna."

"No . . ." I say as I suddenly remember. "It was Anneke. My name was Anneke."

What if all of my other dreams were memories, too? The room with the water stain on the ceiling. The men fighting next door. Mama promising to take me away from that place. The train ride to the dock. And seeing the big ship. Whenever I dreamt of boarding that ship, I would always wake up in terror because I knew what would happen. I suddenly know with certainty that all those things I've dreamt about really happened.

"And the church on LaSalle Street, too," I say aloud. "That's why it seemed so familiar to me the first day I saw it. I went there with Mama." I jump to my feet. "I need to go into Holland. I need to talk with Derk again."

"Right now? Why?"

I want to tell Derk that he was right. I want to share everything with him that Mother just told me and thank him for helping me put all the pieces together. I want to talk about my memories of that day because his mother was there, too. We are connected by the tragedy of the *Ironsides* in a very deep way because we both lost our mothers in that disaster. But I can't give Mother those reasons. I scramble to think. "Well . . . because . . . because there must be a record of all the local Dutch women who drowned that day. People would know and remember. Maybe I can find out who my mother is, what her name is."

"But I told you, Anna. We put notices in all the papers. No one claimed you."

"In the Holland newspapers, too? Were the notices printed in Dutch?"

"Well, no. We didn't think about Holland. We didn't know that your mother spoke Dutch to you."

"Maybe no one came forward because they didn't see the notices. Derk says people around here still speak Dutch to each other and they read Dutch newspapers."

"I don't know what to say, Anna. . . . I can't think . . ." She slowly stands up. She looks as shaken as I am. "Let's go downstairs and find William. We're supposed to meet him, aren't we? We can talk about this over breakfast, and maybe he'll know what to do."

Derk had cautioned me to reassure my parents that nothing would change. I wrap my arms around Mother and hug her tightly. "You're my mother, and you always will be. I love you. Nothing can ever change that. Our lives will go on the same as before, even if I do find out the truth. We'll return to Chicago and I'll marry William, and we'll all be happy. I just need to know who I am."

I see tears in her eyes as we pull apart. "I understand," she says. I don't see how she possibly could understand.

"Why don't you go downstairs and find William," I tell her. "I need to change my clothes and fix my hair. I'll meet you there in a few minutes." She leaves, and I quickly change out of my smoky, wrinkled clothes. I have watched the hotel burn in them, slept in them, rowed out on the lake in them.

I'm so overwrought with excitement that I have trouble pinning up my hair, but at last I'm presentable. I find Mother and William sitting together in the dining room. He rises to greet me, reaching for my hand, and leans close to kiss my cheek. Derk had done the same thing as he said good-bye to me a little while ago. I can barely wait to see Derk again and tell him the news. I had been on the same ship as his mother. And with his aunt Geesje's daughter. Maybe his aunt would remember the names of the other women who died. I need to talk to her, too. I fight to contain my growing excitement as I sit down at the table and place my napkin on my lap.

"Did Mother explain to you what I've learned?" I ask William.

"Yes. It's quite a story." Before we can say more a waiter comes to take our order. I'm too agitated to eat, too impatient to wait while William and Mother do. I order toast and tea, aware that I need to slow down and give them time to absorb all that is happening. If I'm in shock, surely Mother must be as well after carefully guarding this secret for twenty years. I manage to hold my tongue, barely listening as William tells us what he has learned about the Jenison Park Hotel fire. "Thankfully, no one died," he finishes.

By the time our food arrives, I have decided on a plan. "I know we were supposed to go home today," I begin, "but I need to stay for a few more days and try to—"

"Anna," William interrupts. "I now understand completely why you don't want to go home by steamship—"

"No, it isn't that I'm afraid to go back today . . ." I stop; that isn't entirely true. After reliving the memory of the shipwreck, I'm still very much afraid. "It's just that I want to stay a little longer and try to find out more about my mother. This is important to me, William. I need to find out who I am."

"But I can't stay any longer. I have work to do and important meetings to attend in Chicago."

Derk had advised me to speak my mind and stand up to William. I gather my courage. "You should go home without me. You, too, Mother. I'll be fine by myself. I'm going to stay for a few more days and see what I can learn."

If William can't accept that, if he becomes stubborn, then I'll know I need to reconsider marrying him. He gazes at me from across the table as the seconds tick by, and I can sense his struggle. He is used to giving orders and having them followed without question. In the past, he was upset with me for refusing to stop attending the castle church. Our relationship ended. William said last night that he didn't want to lose me again, and I'm guessing that he's trying to decide how far he dares to push me in order to get his own way.

"Does your past really matter that much? You were a child, Anna. The life you have now and our future together—aren't they more important?"

"My mother drowned trying to save me," I say calmly. "She didn't abandon me. I need to know who she was. Then we can move forward with everything we've planned."

He chews his lip, thinking. "You know, the Dutch people in Holland have a reputation for being unfriendly toward outsiders. Their religion is very strict and morally unbending. They can seem intolerant toward people of other religions. I would hate to see you get hurt."

"Even so, they are my family. I need to know who I am."

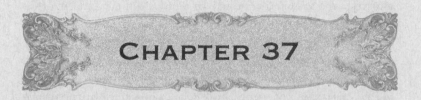

CHAPTER 37

Geesje

I leave my pew after the last hymn is sung, the last prayer is uttered. This morning's worship service has been very uplifting, but there is still an ache in my heart as I make my way down the aisle to the rear of the church, alone. It has been twenty years since Maarten and I sat side by side in this pew.

Of course, I'm not really alone. I'm surrounded by members of my church family, men and women who've lived beside me all these years, children I've prayed for as I've watched them grow to adulthood, marry, and have children of their own. As much as I enjoy Dominie's sermons, one of my favorite things about Sunday morning is the chance to visit for a few minutes after the service with all the people I know and love. I sometimes think this time together is as valuable to all of us as the formal liturgy.

But I miss walking home with Maarten afterward, holding his arm, discussing the sermon and talking about friends and acquaintances who will need our prayers this week. Arie tries to come home for Sunday dinner as often as he can, but I think he finds it difficult to sit down at a table that is surrounded by empty chairs—chairs that were once filled by people we loved. At least once a month I make a point of inviting friends for Sunday dinner, and I'm often invited to their homes, as well. But not this morning. It has worked out this Sunday morning that I'll be returning home alone.

Someone calls my name, and I see a dear friend beckoning to me. I make my way toward her through the dense crowd, enjoying the happy buzz of voices and the giggling children who weave between the adults. I remember how my own children used to be bursting with energy by the time the long service ended and would barrel through the main doors like calves released from their stalls. Especially Christina. She was always the first to leave. I can see her in my mind's eye on a beautiful summer day like this one, kicking off her shoes and socks beneath the pillars and hitching up her skirt so she could run barefooted in the grass in front of the church.

My friend is in the middle of telling me her latest news when I see Derk edging up beside me. He is reluctant to interrupt, but I can tell that he wants to speak with me. He has an odd expression on his face—is it excitement? Worry? I can't tell. I'm concerned that it's more news about his girlfriend, Caroline, and that she is still toying with him like a cat with a mouse. I hold up a finger to let him know we'll be finished talking in just a minute. Derk nods and points to one of the doors leading into the sanctuary. He'll wait for me over there.

A few minutes later my friend finishes, and we embrace as I share her joy. Then she's off to speak to another friend, and I look around for Derk. I don't see him—but I'm very surprised to see my granddaughter Elizabeth standing by herself, gazing all around. I walk up behind her and wrap my arm around her waist.

"Elizabeth! Well, for goodness' sakes! Why didn't you tell me you were going to be here this morning?" She turns and I stare at her in surprise. "Why, you're not Elizabeth!"

350

"No, but I . . . I've been told that I resemble her and . . ." Her voice trails off. We're both embarrassed.

"Are you looking for someone in particular, dear?"

"Yes. I'm trying to find Derk . . . Derk Vander Veen."

"That's funny . . . so am I." We both spot him at the same moment. And then he sees us. He bounds across the crowded lobby so exuberantly that I fear he might knock someone over.

"Anna! What did you find out? Did your mother tell you whether it was true or not?"

"Yes! Everything was true. It was exactly as you'd guessed. I really was on that ship and my mother was probably Dutch and my parents adopted me when I was three years old, not a newborn!" The young woman is breathless and as excited as Derk is. It's all they can do to keep from hugging each other.

"I see you've met my tante Geesje de Jonge," he says, gesturing to me. The young woman seems stunned.

"Oh, I've been wanting so much to meet you. Derk has told me so much about you."

"Tante Geesje, this is my friend Anna Nicholson from Chicago. She's the guest at the Hotel Ottawa I've been telling you about."

It all makes sense to me now, and I'm relieved to know she isn't Caroline. "How do you do, Miss Nicholson. Please forgive my mistake. . . . I thought she was Elizabeth," I tell Derk. I can't stop staring at Anna, astounded by the remarkable resemblance between her and my granddaughter. They're about the same height, have the same slim figure, and the same curly, golden hair.

"I mistook her for Elizabeth, too, the first time we met," Derk says. "The similarity is amazing, isn't it?"

"Please, call me Anna," she says. "I'm beginning to wish I could meet this Elizabeth."

"She's my granddaughter. My son Jakob's daughter."

Anna turns to Derk again, and her words spill out as if she's been holding them back for hours. "Is there someplace we can talk? Maybe outside? Mother and William are waiting for me out in front. We rented a carriage, and we don't have much time because we're supposed to return to Chicago today. But I still have so many questions I need to ask." I start to excuse myself and back away, but Anna stops me. "No, please come, too, Mrs. de Jonge. I would really like to talk to you if you don't mind. If you have time, that is."

Derk tugs my arm. "Yes, please, Tante Geesje. You need to hear this, too." The look of excitement and anticipation on his face intrigues me.

"Of course. Why don't we all go to my house and talk? It's only a short walk from here." I try to remember everything Derk has told me about Anna Nicholson as we head down the front steps. He is very fond of her, I can tell, but she is from a wealthy Chicago family and he is a humble seminary student from a working-class family. Derk had said that Anna wanted to meet me, that she wanted my advice about love and marriage—and the Bible, too. She was engaged to a wealthy Chicago gentleman, as I recall, and I wonder if he's the handsome young bearded man waiting in the street beside a hired carriage from the hotel. An aristocratic woman with her chin in the air is also waiting in the carriage—the girl's mother, I assume. The same mother who wasn't pleased to learn about her daughter's friendship with a hotel worker. I can't imagine what has made them all change their mind about Derk and come into town to find him, but I'm very curious to find out.

Anna introduces us to her mother and William as we all squeeze into the carriage for the short ride to my home. My mind is spinning with hostess details, just like Jesus' friend Martha in the Bible. Do I have enough coffee to serve all these people—or perhaps they drink tea? Do I even have tea? Would they like my cookies, too? And oh! Did I leave my dirty breakfast dishes in the sink? I've never entertained wealthy people before.

I lead the way, and Derk brings up the rear as we walk up the front steps and across the porch to my door. "You don't keep it locked?" William asks in astonishment as I open it.

"I have nothing worth stealing. And I know all of my neighbors. They're honest, God-fearing people. . . . Please, have a seat." I can tell they feel out of place in my sitting room—as out of place as I would feel in their fancy mansions, I'm sure. "Can I get you some coffee or tea?" I ask.

Derk takes my arm and leads me to one of my own chairs. "Maybe in a minute, Tante Geesje. I can't wait a moment longer to hear what Miss Nicholson has to tell us."

I lift my sleeping tabby cat off my favorite chair and sit down, settling him on my lap. I am thoroughly intrigued by these unusual events.

Anna

I sense Mother's impatience as we crowd into Geesje de Jonge's house. It's very neat and spotlessly clean, but so small it would probably fit inside our drawing and dining rooms at home. Despite its small size, the house doesn't feel as claustrophobic as our parlor in Chicago, which is crammed with useless knickknacks and gewgaws and curios. Geesje is a pretty woman in her late sixties with graying blond hair and china-blue eyes. She is tiny and petite, and her eyes seem to twinkle with such joy that she reminds me of the fairy godmother in a storybook I had as a child. I have felt at ease with her from the moment she embraced me by mistake in the church lobby.

Mother and William, on the other hand, seem very uncomfortable in such a plain house with its simple, worn furnishings. We all sit down except for William, who stands behind my chair like a sentry, as if unable to relax. I catch him glancing at his pocket watch, and I know he's concerned about missing our steamship. I was surprised yet pleased that he agreed to hire a carriage to bring Mother and me into town to search for Derk. I promised him I would hurry.

"Here's what we've pieced together so far," Derk says to Geesje. "In an amazing coincidence, Miss Nicholson and her father were passengers aboard the *Ironsides* when it sank—just like my mother and your daughter, Christina."

Geesje gives a little gasp. "That was you? I remember seeing a child in her father's arms that day, standing by the bonfire. I gave him my quilt."

"I told you!" I say, turning to Mother. "I told you I remembered that happening." I shiver to realize how close Geesje and I had been to each other that day, how our lives had briefly touched twenty years ago. "But that man wasn't my father," I say, continuing the story. "At least he wasn't back then. He saved my life that day after my mama drowned. Later, he and Mother adopted me. No one knows who my real mother was. My real family was never found."

"I'm so very sorry," Geesje says. "That was a horrible, tragic day for all of us. Most ships didn't keep a list of their passengers in those days, as I recall. My husband had the terrible task of identifying our daughter. And Derk's father had to identify his wife, too. It was a horrific experience for all of the families."

"Were all the victims identified?" Derk asks.

"I have no idea," Geesje says. "I suppose that information would be in the records somewhere."

"We tried everything we could think of to find Anna's parents," Mother adds. "Even the authorities were unable to locate them."

I see Geesje nodding in understanding as she strokes the cat in her lap. "I vaguely remember some mention of an orphaned child," she says, "and that the authorities were searching for her family. But I was sunk so deep in my grief over Christina that I paid little mind to it."

"I'm hoping you can help me now, Mrs. de Jonge," I say.

"I'll be happy to if I can, but how?"

I move to the edge of my chair in anticipation. I'm trying not to get my hopes up, but I've noticed a little box of peppermints on the end table beside Geesje's chair—the same kind that Mama used to carry in her purse—and I can barely remain seated. "I know my real mother was Dutch because I can remember her speaking to me in another language. And Derk tells me that the phrases I've recalled are Dutch. My real name was Anneke—"

"That's a Dutch name," Derk interrupts.

"I thought so. What I'm hoping, Mrs. de Jonge, is that you might remember the names of the other Dutch women in the area who died when the *Ironsides* sank."

She appears to be thinking as she gazes into the distance. "Here in the Holland area, I know of only two women who died that day—Derk's mother and my daughter, Christina. We're a very close-knit community, and even in the surrounding towns it seems as though everyone is related to someone else. Our church members come together to support each other in times of tragedy and loss, so I'm certain I would have heard about it if another family from a nearby Dutch church was also grieving."

I lean back in my chair as tears of disappointment fill my eyes. William rests his hand on my shoulder in comfort. He and Mother are going to declare my search hopeless and make me return to Chicago with them.

"I'm so sorry I can't be more help, dear," Geesje says. "But . . . hmm . . . I do have one other thought. My daughter left home after the Holland fire to find work as a servant in Chicago. It was the same weekend as the Great Chicago Fire. We didn't hear from her for nearly seven years, and if anything had happened to her during that time, we probably never would have known about it. Perhaps your mother was another young Dutch woman who did the same thing. Maybe she didn't tell her family that she was returning on the *Ironsides*."

"I see . . . that makes sense," I say.

There is so much compassion in Geesje's eyes. She understands my disappointment. "Listen, my son Jakob is the pastor of an area church," she says. "If you'd like, I could ask him to discreetly check with the pastors of other nearby churches to see if any local women are unaccounted for. At least we might learn a name."

"Thank you. That's very kind of you."

William pulls out his pocket watch again and checks the time. "Anna, dear, we've taken up enough of Mrs. de Jonge's time. I'll be happy to pay whatever it costs to keep searching for your mother. I could hire a Pinkerton detective if you'd like. I hear they do good work. But it sounds to me like there's nothing more you can accomplish by staying in Holland any longer. We can always return in the future if it looks as though the professionals are getting close to learning who your mother was."

He's right. And I trust William to keep his word and help me continue to search. I stand up, and I'm about to thank Mrs. de Jonge for her time when Derk leaps to his feet, interrupting me.

"Wait! There's a crazy thought that has been buzzing around in the back of my mind ever since we spoke at the hotel earlier today." He turns to his aunt. "Tante Geesje, would you mind telling me again what Christina's letter said? The last one she sent you?"

"She said she was coming home. That she had something important to tell us but she needed to do it in person. She was afraid we wouldn't forgive her—" She halts and lays both hands on her heart. The color drains from her face so quickly I'm afraid she is ill. She stares at me as if she has just seen me for the first time, her eyes wide and filled with tears. "You don't think . . . Could it be possible that . . . ?"

"It would explain the amazing resemblance," Derk says. "And why no one came forward to claim her."

"Oh, dear heaven . . ." Geesje murmurs. "Yes . . . yes . . ."

"May I tell Anna about Christina?" Derk asks her. Geesje nods. He crosses the room to stand in front of me. "Tante Geesje's daughter ran away to Chicago with her boyfriend. She was gone for seven years, with no contact at all. By the time she returned, you were three years old. Maybe it's possible that—"

I feel dizzy as I put all the clues together. "Do you think Christina could be my mother?"

"It would explain why no one came forward to claim you," Derk says. "Her family didn't know that Christina had a daughter. . . . Tante Geesje, may I show her a picture of Christina?"

She nods and pushes the cat off her lap as she rises from her chair. I hardly dare to breathe as Geesje goes to a little desk in the corner of the room and retrieves a framed photograph. "Christina was seventeen in this photograph," she says. "I saved it from the fire."

"Do you think you might recognize your mother?" Derk asks. "After all this time?"

"I-I don't know . . . but I would like to try."

I'm unable to move, frozen with hope and fear. I catch a glimpse of longing in Geesje's eyes, too, as she hands the picture to me. Everyone in the room is watching me as I take the photograph in my trembling hands. I don't want to get my hopes up. Nor do I want to give Mrs. de Jonge false hopes. I want to be sure—very, very sure—before I say yes or no.

In the center of the photograph is a plain-looking man seated in a chair. He has dark hair and a round face. The woman standing beside him with her hand on his shoulder is Geesje when she was younger. Two tall young men stand in the middle of the photograph behind their father's chair. The young woman standing on her father's left must be Christina. She is very pretty. And she is the only person in the photograph who is smiling, as if she's laughing at the others for being so somber. I can tell even in a black-and-white photograph that her hair is very fair. And curly. Like mine.

I pull the picture closer and stare at her face. Her smile seems to widen as tears blur my vision. I hear her gentle voice saying, *"I love you, lieveling."*

I look up at Geesje. I can barely speak.

"Yes . . ." I whisper. "Christina is my mama."

CHAPTER 38

Geesje

Joy floods through me as I pull this beautiful young woman into my arms. Christina's daughter! Anneke. My granddaughter. I can hardly believe it. We are both weeping as we cling to each other. "My goodness . . . oh, my goodness . . ." It's all I can manage to say.

We finally pull apart because we both need to sit down. I can feel Anneke's body trembling, and my own knees feel as though they've turned to water. We sit side by side on my sofa, gripping each other's hands, the family photograph lying in her lap. There are so many questions I would like to ask her, so many missing parts of Christina's life that I would love to have Anneke fill in for me. But that's probably asking a lot of a child who was only three years old when her mother died. I've noticed her fiancé, William, checking his pocket watch. I know Anneke has a life and a home in Chicago that she must return to, but I don't want her to go.

358

"Can you stay a little longer, Anneke? Please?" I beg. "We've only just found each other. I would love to get to know you, and to have you meet the rest of our family. This is my son Arie," I say, pointing to the photograph. "He's a war hero, and he runs our family's printing business. And this is Jakob. He's a minister, and he and his wife, Joanna, have four children, including your cousin Elizabeth. You must meet them! And this is my husband, Maarten—your grandfather. He's gone now, but I would love to tell you all about him. He never lost faith that God would bring Christina back to us—and here you are! Her daughter!" I hold Anneke's face in my hands as I drink her in. I kiss her forehead. Then I pull her close to my heart again.

"Yes!" she says. "Yes, I want very much to stay!" When we move apart she looks up at her mother and William. Mrs. Nicholson is discreetly wiping a tear with her lace-edged handkerchief. William is moved as well, but he is frowning and chewing his bottom lip in an effort to remain in control. "I know it's time for the two of you to leave," Anneke tells them, "but I'm not going with you."

"She's welcome to stay here with me for as long as she likes. I'll take good care of her," I assure them. In fact, I probably won't let her out of my sight.

"We'll make sure she gets home to you safely," Derk says. "I give you my word." He has tears in his eyes, too, but he's beaming with happiness for both of us. I notice William studying him with a hint of jealousy.

"Are you a family member, as well, Mr. Vander Veen?"

"Please, call me Derk. And no, I'm not really a family member but Tante Geesje has been a second mother to me ever since my own mama died. I live in the house next door."

Anneke rises to her feet and goes to her mother, resting her hands on her shoulders. "Nothing is going to change, Mother. I love you. And please tell Father that I love him, too. He's a hero. He saved my life. But I'm a grown woman now. Tell him I'll be home in another week or so." She goes to William and stands on tiptoes to kiss his cheek. "Thank you for understanding, William. But I think you'd better hurry. You don't want to miss your steamship. Would you please ask the driver to bring my bags inside before you leave?"

I close my eyes in joy. Anneke is going to stay with me. Christina's daughter! My cup is running over with happiness.

I stand on the street with them in front of my house as they say good-bye. I can see that William cares for Anneke—and that he is not happy about her decision to stay. I'm guessing he likes to be in control, to take charge of every situation and quickly fix things. And he probably wants a wife who leaves all the decision-making to him. If Anneke is as strong-willed and independent as her mother was, then I see rough seas ahead for them.

I can also sense the enormous loss that Anneke's mother is feeling. I go to her before William helps her into the carriage and say, "I understand how you must feel. We adopted our two older sons after their parents died. I think every adoptive mother in the world fears that the day will come when she will lose her child to their 'real' family. But please don't worry. I don't think that will happen with Anneke."

"It won't, Mother," Anneke says.

"Mrs. Nicholson, I've learned through the years that all of our children are only on loan to us from God," I continue. "They belong to Him, not to us. Our son Gerrit died in the war when he was nineteen. And then we lost our Christina when she was twenty-four. Arie and Jakob are still with me, but they are adults, with lives of their own to live. I've had to learn to let them go, too. But I thank God every day for all of the years that He loaned them to me."

Anneke holds my hand as we watch the carriage drive away. I'm overjoyed that she will be with me for a few more days and that we can get to know each other. "Let's go inside," I say. "I'll fix us something to eat."

"I guess I'll head home now," Derk says, "and leave you two to catch up."

"No!" Anneke and I both say at the same time. "We have you to thank for this wonderful day," I tell him. "You must stay and have lunch with us." The two of them sit at my kitchen table, watching as I slice my homemade bread and some cheese and fresh tomatoes from my garden. "I'm sorry I don't have more to offer you, but I wasn't expecting company, and I don't usually cook on the Lord's Day."

"This looks wonderful," Anneke says. "I don't need a big lunch, Mrs. de Jonge."

"You can call me Oma, if you'd like. That's what Dutch children call their grandmothers."

Anneke's smile lights up her face. "I would love to call you Oma." I pour coffee and sit down at the table with them, but we're all too excited to eat. "For as long as I can remember," Anneke says, "I've had the same nightmare about the shipwreck. I didn't know it was real until today. I've had other dreams about Mama and me, and now I think they were probably memories, too."

"I would be grateful to hear anything you can remember about your mama—if it isn't too painful for you. You see, we didn't know where Christina was or what she was doing after she left us. We never even had a chance to say good-bye. She had fallen in love with a young man named Jack Newell."

"Do you think he's my father?"

"I don't know. She told us that he was originally from Ohio, and he had left home and a difficult family life with barely a cent to his name. He came through Holland looking for work and met Christina. She ran away with him after the fire destroyed most of the town, including the tannery where Jack worked. Christina said she wanted to find a job in Chicago as a servant for a wealthy family like yours."

"Of course, Chicago was destroyed, too, at the same time as Holland," Derk adds. "They wouldn't have known that when they left, but maybe Jack found work rebuilding the city."

I'm hesitant to admit the truth as I add, "I don't even know if he and your mama ever married. She never wrote to us."

"Maybe William can ask his Pinkerton detectives to check the marriage records in Chicago," Derk says.

"I don't ever recall having a father before the shipwreck,"

Anneke says. "In my dreams, Mama and I are always alone. I dream about living in a tiny room with little more than a bed. It's shabby and it smells terrible, and we can hear men fighting in the room next door. Then Mama says, 'I'm going to get us out of here, Anneke. I'm going to take you home.' If my dream really happened, then we must have been coming here. . . . I had another dream that we're riding on a train that's crowded with poor people like us. The sun is setting behind us as we reach the dock and I see the big steamship. . . ." She pauses for a moment, and I see her steeling herself. "In the nightmare I've had ever since I was a child, I'm in a terrible storm at sea. People aboard the ship are getting seasick because the waves are so rough. It thunders and the lightning lights up the sky outside like daylight, but all we can see is water. Mama holds me tightly, soothing me. She sings to me. She has such a sweet voice."

My eyes fill with tears at the memory of Christina standing beside me in church, singing from the Psalter in her clear, pure soprano. "Yes, you're right . . . she did have a beautiful voice."

"When the ship starts to sink and they make us get into the lifeboats, everyone is terrified! Suddenly a huge wave washes us right out of the boat, and we sink beneath the water. I feel Mama fighting with all her strength to get to the surface, but I think her skirts are making it hard for her to kick, and they pull her down. Father is also trying to stay afloat a few feet away from us. He had been in the lifeboat with us. Mama handed me to him saying, 'Save my daughter! Save her, please!' Then, as soon as I was safe in his arms, she sank beneath the waves."

Anneke pauses again, and I want to weep at the horror of Christina's final moments of life. I hope she is looking down from heaven, and that she knows that the daughter she loved until her very last breath has survived. How proud Christina would be of this lovely, poised young woman. I want to meet her adoptive father and thank him for saving my granddaughter. He could have thought only of saving himself.

"Father had to struggle to keep our heads above the waves,"

362

Anneke continues. "He was growing tired, breathing so hard. Then I saw a man reaching his hand out to us. He was the last man in a long chain of men, all holding hands. He grabbed Father by his lapels saying, 'I've got you . . . I've got you now. . . . Hang on, and you'll both be safe.'"

"Your grandfather was one of those men. And your Uncle Arie. They helped pull you and the other survivors to shore." I wait while Anneke gathers herself. This must be so hard for her, but I long to hear more.

"That's all I remember about my mama," Anneke says with a shrug. "I'm sorry."

"You have no reason to be sorry. Thank you for sharing those memories with me. I know it must be difficult to relive that day."

"Mama loved me with all her heart," she says, wiping her tears. "I know she did. I was always certain of that. I felt safe and happy when I was with her. . . . And lost and alone after she was gone. Even now as an adult, I still feel alone at times, as if I don't really belong with all the other people in our social circle. I guess now I know why." She looks up at me and says, "I'm looking forward to learning more about my mama."

A smile spreads across my face. I always smile when I remember how much joy Christina brought to our family. "She was beautiful and independent and strong-willed from the day she was born—always happy and carefree and full of life. She had three older brothers, and she wanted to be just like them and do everything they did. But as she grew older, she became impatient with our quiet life here in Holland. She wanted to explore the world outside our city limits. She was raised in the church, as all of our children were. We taught her right from wrong and what the Bible says about how to live. Then when she was seventeen she met Jack Newell, and he planted doubts in her mind and heart about her Christian faith. Christina knew it was a sin to run away with him if they weren't married, and so she left without even saying good-bye. She broke our hearts when she did, but our grief was even greater because we knew she was walking away from God. I was overjoyed when she wrote and said she was coming home to us. I wish I knew if she was coming home to God, too."

Anneke looks up, staring at me as if she has suddenly remembered something. "She did come back to Him—she came back to God!"

My heart seems to stop beating. "What? How do you know?"

"Last winter I stumbled upon a church on LaSalle Street in Chicago. They were having some sort of special event there, and the building looked so familiar to me that I got out of the carriage and went inside. I knew as soon as I stepped through the door that I had been there before. The music, the lights, the way the pews were arranged—everything was so familiar. I listened to the preacher for a few minutes, and his sermon fascinated me. He said God loved me and wanted me for His child. After that first day, I kept going back again and again. It was as if I was being drawn there by pulleys and ropes. When William found out, he got very angry with me and forbid me to go back, but I went anyway. I couldn't help it. Then I started having dreams about the church, and now I know why. It's because I went there with Mama. I dreamed that I was sitting beside her in the pew. She gave me peppermints, just like the ones you have on your sitting room table, while she listened to the sermon. The preacher's words must have touched her heart because she wiped her tears on a plain cotton handkerchief with tiny blue flowers on it."

I inhale sharply. "Christina had one like that. I embroidered it for her myself."

"In my dream I asked Mama if she was sad, but she said, no, her tears were tears of joy. When I visited the church last winter, the minister always invited people who wanted to repent of their past mistakes to come to Jesus and find forgiveness. He asked them to come forward so he could pray with them. In one of my dreams Mama takes my hand, and we walk down that long aisle together. She knelt at the front and prayed, I'm sure of it."

I lower my face in my hands as I begin to sob, remembering how Maarten used to remind me of Jesus' promise: "'*My sheep hear my voice . . . I give unto them eternal life; and they shall never perish, neither shall any man pluck them out of my hand.'"* After twenty years of waiting and wondering, God has finally answered my prayer. Now I know for certain that when I join Maarten and Gerrit in heaven someday, Christina will be there with us, too.

CHAPTER 39

Anna

I've been staying here with Oma Geesje for nearly a week, and the longer I stay, the more I dread returning to Chicago. I hate my wasteful life in our mansion, which has more bedrooms than we ever use, closetsful of dresses that I wear only once or twice, and tables overflowing with more food than we can possibly eat. Oma's simpler way of life suits me. I do everything for myself here without servants, even making my own bed. I feel lighter and freer without my petticoats and corsets and gloves and stockings weighing me down. Instead of attending boring teas, I go with Oma to bring meals to people who are sick and deliver warm socks that she has knit herself to needy families. "These are for the cold winter that's surely coming," she tells them as she smiles and pats the children's heads.

I've learned how to dry dishes and to bake cookies, and for the first time in my life I picked a fresh tomato from the vine. I met my wonderful Uncle Arie who lost his leg during the war and who loved

366

my mama dearly. He told me how Mama traveled to the military hospital with Oma and saved his life when he was wounded and in pain and wanting to die. He now runs a print shop like his father and grandfather before him. I also met my Uncle Jakob and Aunt Joanna and their family, including Elizabeth, who could easily be my sister instead of my cousin. And I've spent time with my dear friend Derk, who comes over in the evenings after work to chat with Oma and me and eat the cookies we've baked.

We are in Oma's kitchen, washing the lunch dishes, when a delivery boy comes to the door with a telegram for me. It's from my father. I tear open the envelope and quickly scan it then let out a groan. "I can't believe it! My father has made arrangements for me to return to Chicago by train."

"When?" Oma asks.

"Tomorrow." It's too soon—much too soon. But whether I'm ready or not, the reservations have been made. I'm going home tomorrow.

Oma eases onto a kitchen chair, drying her hands on her apron. I can see from her expression that she is sad and disappointed. But then she smiles and says, "Well, we both knew this day was coming, didn't we?"

"But it's too soon! I feel like there's so much more we need to talk about. I have so many questions I want to ask you about love and marriage and the Bible and our family and—"

"I know," she says. "I know." She studies me for a moment, and I can tell that she's thinking about something. Then she rises to her feet and walks into the sitting room, beckoning for me to follow her. She pulls a notebook from a drawer in her desk and hands it to me.

"Here, I want you to read this. It's the story of my life, Anneke, and a little of your mother's story, too. The city officials asked me to write down my memories to help celebrate Holland's fiftieth anniversary, but I think it might help you answer some of your questions about marriage and life and faith. You can sit out on the front porch and read it, if you'd like. I'll finish tidying up."

I leaf through the lined pages as I carry it out to a chair on the shady porch. The notebook contains page after page of writing, all in pencil. I'm drawn into Oma Geesje's story from the very first page, which begins with the words, *On the night of my fifteenth birthday, a huge brick shattered the window of Papa's print shop and ended my childhood. . . .*

I have no idea how much time has passed, but by the time I finish reading, I'm overwhelmed by how much my grandmother has endured during her lifetime. I now see the town of Holland and the people who moved here and built its homes and churches and schools in a new light. Most of all, I marvel at Oma Geesje's abiding faith in God through it all. I tell her so when she comes outside to sit with me on the porch.

"It has more to do with God's faithfulness to me than the other way around," she replies.

"But you've done so much during your lifetime," I tell her. "I know God probably has a purpose for my life, too, but I don't know what it is."

She smiles and says in her gentle way, "Often, it's not one great, dramatic thing that God asks us to do but hundreds of little everyday things. If we want to be used by Him, if we're ready to be used and aren't all tangled up with our own plans and projects, then He'll show us the work He has for us. He sees your heart, Anneke. You can trust Him to direct your path."

I think about the train tickets that are waiting for me, and I feel a great heaviness in my chest. "I'm not sure I want to go back to Chicago, Oma. Sometimes I feel like I don't belong there. It scares me to think that I'll get all caught up in parties and teas and that superficial life again. I want to stay here. Mama was bringing me back to Holland because she wanted me to live here. With you."

Oma is quiet for a long time, and I can see that she is struggling with what she's about to say. When she's finally ready, she reaches for my hand. "That may be what your mother wanted, Anneke, but I believe God wanted you to live in Chicago. Otherwise, if He had wanted you to grow up here, then things wouldn't have happened the way they did. Maarten and I would have learned that you were Christina's daughter, and we would have brought you home with us. Instead, God placed you in the arms of the father He wanted you to have. As much as I would love for you to stay here with me, I believe your place is in Chicago, in the home where God put you."

"But I—" I start to protest, then stop, remembering that my father's financial problems were the reason I had agreed to reconcile with William. Father saved my life at the risk of his own—maybe now I can repay him. And when William and I talked on the night of the fire, he had seemed willing to change. But there is another reason why I want to stay here, one that I'm reluctant to share with Oma Geesje.

"There's something else, isn't there," she says as if reading my mind. "Is it because you have feelings for Derk? It's plain to see that you two care for each other."

I nod, staring down at my lap. "We've become friends, and I needed a good friend, Oma, someone I could confide in. Derk is the first good friend I've had in a long, long time. I wanted to know more about the Bible, and he answered so many of my questions this summer and now . . ." Now my feelings for him have grown stronger each day as we've spent time together.

"I'm glad that Derk could be a friend to you. I can tell that he is very fond of you, too." Oma sighs before saying, "I'll admit that I've thought about how miraculous it would be if my granddaughter married Hendrik's grandson. But can you picture Derk living in Chicago and working for your father every day? Can you imagine him fitting into your social world and learning proper manners and all the rules of etiquette and so on?"

"He would probably feel even more miserable than I do, at times."

"I have no doubt that Derk is intelligent enough to do the work that your father does—but that's not what God has called him to do."

"I could stay here—"

"You, my dear, sweet girl, would be like a fish on land as Derk's wife. Your Aunt Joanna can tell you that life as a dominie's wife is a very special calling for a woman. Derk won't earn very much money, so his wife will have to cook all his meals and clean his house and raise his children—while taking care of all the extra duties her position as a dominie's wife requires. No, I believe God has prepared you and suited you for a much different future."

"I suppose . . . and I did give William my word that I would marry him."

"But there's no hurry to marry, is there? Can you give yourself more time, first? Get to know him better? I advise you to ask God if this is His will for you before you say your vows."

I nod, remembering how Oma rushed into marriage with Maarten without taking time to pray. "Right now I feel so much closer to Derk than I do to William even though we've only known each other for a short time. I'm able to talk to him like a friend and tell him how I really feel. And he listens to me. Though William and I did have a good talk on the night of the fire, and he promised he would try to be more understanding of my spiritual pursuits. I'm very fond of William, but I don't love him the way you loved Hendrik." I pause before asking, "Do you think I could ever learn to love him the way you loved Maarten?"

"That's up to you. It means making a decision to love him day after day, one loving act at a time. Love is a very powerful emotion, Anneke, but it's also a decision—one you can choose to make. I had an advantage because Maarten was such a wonderful man of faith who loved God—and I'm assuming from everything you've told me that William isn't nearly as committed to his faith as Maarten was. Or as Derk is."

"No. He isn't."

"Then perhaps you should test the waters a bit before you get married. Talk to him about your faith and see how he responds.

In time, you could have the same godly influence on William that Maarten had on me. Imagine all the good that a wealthy man like William could do if his heart was surrendered to God. I can already imagine the good that a woman in your position could do. Think of all the young women like Christina who are trapped in Chicago, poor and alone in a huge city with no family to help them, living in a room like the one you remember, and being taken advantage of by unscrupulous men."

"I see what you mean." And for the first time I feel a glimmer of excitement about returning home.

"God will lead you every step of the way, Anneke. He knows the plans He has for you, plans for you to prosper and have hope and a future. That's why He saved you from the shipwreck twenty years ago and gave you to such wonderful parents to raise." Oma reaches to give me a hug—how I've grown to love her hugs! Then she smiles and says, "I need to start making dinner."

"Is it that late?"

"Derk will be coming home from work soon, and I thought we would invite him to eat with us tonight." Oma returns her notebook to her desk, and we go into the kitchen to make supper together.

I'm putting plates and cutlery on the table an hour later when Derk arrives. My heart can't help speeding up when I see him duck through the door, his face and arms bronzed from the summer sun. "How was work, dear?" Oma Geesje asks him.

"On days like today it hardly seems like work," he says, running his fingers through his fair hair. "I took guests out sailing on Black Lake twice today, once this morning and again this afternoon. The water was beautiful, the breeze just right. It was great!"

"Will you stay and have dinner with us?" Oma asks.

He looks at me and his smile broadens. "I would love to. Let me run home and wash up, then I'll come back."

Derk is his usual, cheerful self as we sit down to eat later, but I feel a lingering sadness from reading Oma's story and from the disappointing news I will have to share with him. "I'm taking the train home to Chicago tomorrow," I say. "Father sent me a telegram today with all the arrangements."

"Oh. I see. I thought you two ladies seemed somber tonight." And now Derk is somber, too, his broad, handsome smile gone. "Your father didn't give you very much notice, did he?"

"No . . . but I suppose I did agree that I would only stay for a week." We all do our best to keep up a cheerful conversation while we eat, but with little success. None of us seems to have much of an appetite.

Oma asks Derk to read today's Bible portion aloud when we finish eating, a ritual she follows every day. Then she says, "Why don't you two go out on the front porch. I'll clear up these dishes and join you in a little bit."

Derk and I sit side by side on the front steps, staring straight ahead. The evening sky stays light here during the summer months, the sun never setting until after nine o'clock at night. I can tell that neither of us knows what to say or where to begin.

"Well!" Derk finally says, heaving an enormous sigh. "I can't believe we have to say good-bye."

"We'll see each other again, I know we will. I'll be back to visit Oma Geesje and . . ." My voice trails off as I run out of words.

"I guess I was hoping that there might be a future for us . . . together . . ." We look at each other, and I have an overwhelming urge to kiss him. I quickly turn my face away, sensing that he longs to kiss me, too. "Anna, I know I could never give you all of the things you're accustomed to . . . and that your way of life is—"

"That isn't it at all!" I say, facing him again. "I would love to have a future with you, Derk. You're the most wonderful, amazing man I've ever met!"

"But . . . ?" he asks with a crooked grin.

I take my time, needing to explain everything to Derk the way that Oma explained it to me. I'm still struggling to understand it all myself. "Oma Geesje thinks I was rescued and adopted by my parents for a reason. That God has a plan for me in Chicago. She says I should return home and trust God to show me what it is, Maybe it means marrying William—maybe not. But for now, I need to go home."

Derk sighs again. "I hate to admit it, but she's probably right. She usually is."

"She let me read her memoir today, and I agree that it would be amazing if you and I ended up together. Imagine Geesje's granddaughter marrying Hendrik's grandson. But that isn't the way God seems to be directing either one of us. You need a partner for the ministry He has given you, and I don't think I would be the right wife for you any more than Caroline was."

He pulls me into his arms and holds me tightly. I feel so comfortable there, and as I return his embrace, I wish with all my heart that it could be different for us—but it can't.

"Derk, I truly believe that God brought you and me and Oma Geesje together this summer for a reason. All three of our lives have been changed. Now . . . now it's just so very, very hard to say good-bye."

"Then we won't," he says, still holding me tightly. "We'll just say . . . until next time." We finally release each other and stand at the same time. "You'll always be in my prayers, Anna. And I hope I will always be in yours."

Tears stick in my throat as I nod. I can't reply. Derk bends to kiss my cheek, and I watch him turn and walk away. I think I understand how hard it was for Oma Geesje to say good-bye to Hendrik on that long ago day, to watch him walk away into the woods and out of her life forever.

Chapter 40

Geesje

Arie comes with his carriage to drive Anneke and me to the train station. He's going to miss her almost as much as I will. She is different from her mother in many, many ways, and yet having Anneke with us has brought back so many wonderful memories of Christina.

When we get to the station we go inside out of the hot sun and sit on a bench while we wait for the train to arrive. I don't want Anneke to leave, but I know that she has to. Tears sting my eyes when I hear the faint sound of the train whistle in the distance. A few minutes later, the engine chugs noisily into the station and halts with a hiss of steam. "We'll see each other again, Oma, won't we?" she asks as we stand on the platform together.

"Of course we will."

"You must come to Chicago for my wedding, if I decide to marry

William. You, too, Uncle Arie. And Uncle Jakob and Aunt Joanna and Elizabeth and everyone else must come, too."

"I would love to celebrate your wedding day with you," I tell her. Although I can already imagine how dreadfully out of place I would feel. I have brought my notebook with my life's story with me, and I pull it out of my bag now and hand it to Anneke. "I want you to have this, dear. Now I know why I felt so compelled to write all of my story, the good parts as well as the bad. It was for you, so you would know who you are and who the people were who lived and loved and trusted God before you."

"Are you sure?"

"Oh yes. I'm very sure." Anneke takes the notebook in both hands and hugs it to her chest as if I've given her something much more valuable than a dime store notebook. Her eyes fill with tears as the train whistle blows a warning. "No tears," I say, acting braver than I feel. "I know for certain that we'll see each other again." I watch my precious granddaughter board the train. Then I remain on the platform, watching until the last car disappears and there is nothing more to see.

Arie puts his arm around my shoulder and gives me a hug. "Let's go home, Mama," he says. I nod, already knowing how empty my little house will feel without her.

My son Jakob comes that evening. He ties his carriage to my hitching post and sits down on my front porch with me for a few minutes. "So, Anneke returned to Chicago this morning?"

"Yes. I hated to see her go."

"I can well imagine." We sit in silence for a long moment before Jakob says, "With so much happening this summer, I wondered if you ever had a chance to finish the memoir you were writing about Holland's history?"

"I did. I'll go inside and get it."

The final version of the story that I show Jakob is only a dozen pages long. He leafs through it and says, "I thought it would be longer than this."

"Well, I explained why Mama and Papa decided to leave the

Netherlands . . . described our journey here and the hardships of getting settled . . . What else is there to say?" I ask with a shrug. "Read it and see for yourself."

In this new version, I don't mention Hendrik or my many struggles to trust God. I don't write about Maarten or how we worked to build a marriage together and found love in the end. When Jakob finishes reading a few minutes later, he looks up at me.

"This is wonderful, Moeder. I think the committee will be pleased with your contribution."

"I'm so glad. And you will take it home and correct my English for me?"

"I'll have Joanna look it over, but it really doesn't need much. Your English is very good."

"It should be after living in America for fifty years." I can see that Jakob is about to leave, but I put my hand on his arm to stop him for just a moment longer. "I know I've told you this before, son, but I'm so very proud of you and what a fine dominie you've become. Your father was very proud of you, too."

"I hope I'm even half the man of faith that Papa was."

"Yes . . . Maarten was a true man of God. There isn't a day that goes by that I don't miss him."

The twilight is fading into night as Jakob's carriage disappears in the distance. I'm alone again—but I'm never really alone. My loving Father, who has been with me through countless joys and sorrows in my lifetime, still holds me tightly in His hand. Indeed, nothing can ever separate me from His love.

Author's Note

I need to thank my dear friends Paul and Jacki Kleinheksel for all their help and encouragement in writing this book. They shared their love of Holland and Hope College with me, as well as their wonderful library of books on Holland's history. I'm grateful for excellent local historians such as Robert Swierenga and Randall Vande Water who made the task of researching this novel so much easier. Thanks also to Ted VanderVeen for loaning me his invaluable book of Dutch immigrant memories, inspiring the idea for Geesje's memoir.

Paul and Jacki Kleinheksel also introduced me to the fascinating work of the Michigan Shipwreck Research Associates. Books by underwater researchers Craig Rich and Valerie VanHeest helped me bring Lake Michigan's sometimes tragic history to life. The account of the *Phoenix* disaster in 1847 is a true story. So is the sinking of the *Ironsides*; however, I took the liberty of moving the date of that shipwreck forward four years to better fit the chronology of my story. The *Ironsides* actually sank off the coast of Grand Haven, Michigan, on September 15, 1873.

All that remains of the grand Hotel Ottawa is a historical marker near the shore of Black Lake—now known as Lake Macatawa.

The splendid hotel burned to the ground in a fire in 1923 and was never rebuilt. The story of the fire that destroyed the Jenison Park Hotel, mentioned in my novel, is true. That hotel burned on the night of July 24, 1897. Tragically, fire also destroyed most of the city of Holland on October 7, 1871, the same weekend as the Great Chicago Fire. Hope College's oldest building, Van Vleck Hall, was spared—and became my dormitory when I attended Hope College nearly one hundred years later.

Bestselling author **Lynn Austin** has sold more than one million copies of her books worldwide. She is an eight-time Christy Award winner for her historical novels, as well as a popular speaker at retreats and conventions. Lynn and her husband have raised three children and live in Michigan. Learn more at www.lynnaustin.org.

More From Lynn Austin

Visit lynnaustin.org for a full list of her books.

After years of exile in Babylon, faithful Jews Iddo and Zechariah are among the first to return to Jerusalem. After the arduous journey, they—and the women they love—struggle to rebuild their lives in obedience to the God who beckons them home.

Return to Me
THE RESTORATION CHRONICLES #1

The lives of the exiles left in Babylon are thrown into despair when a new decree calls for the annihilation of all Jews throughout the empire. In this moment, Ezra, a brilliant Jewish scholar, is called upon to deliver his people to Jerusalem, but the fight to keep God's law is never easy.

Keepers of the Covenant
THE RESTORATION CHRONICLES #2

When news reaches him that Jerusalem's wall is shattered, a distraught Nehemiah seeks God's guidance. As soon as he is granted leave from his duties to the King of Persia, Nehemiah sets out for Jerusalem to rebuild the wall—never anticipating the challenges that lie ahead.

On This Foundation
THE RESTORATION CHRONICLES #3

⬙BETHANYHOUSE

Stay up to date on your favorite books and authors with our free e-newsletters. Sign up today at bethanyhouse.com.

Find us on Facebook. facebook.com/bethanyhousepublishers

Free exclusive resources for your book group! bethanyhouse.com/anopenbook

an open book

If you enjoyed *Waves of Mercy*, you may also like...

Shipwrecked and stranded, Emma Chambers is in need of a home. Could the widowed local lighthouse keeper and his young son be an answer to her prayer?

Love Unexpected by Jody Hedlund
BEACONS OF HOPE #1
jodyhedlund.com

When Brook Eden's friend Justin, a future duke, discovers she may be an English heiress, she travels to meet her alleged father. Once she arrives in Yorkshire, Brook undergoes a trial of the heart—and faces the same danger that led to her mother's mysterious death.

The Lost Heiress by Roseanna M. White
LADIES OF THE MANOR
roseannamwhite.com

Stella West has quit the art world and moved to Boston to solve the mysterious death of her sister, but she is in need of a well-connected ally. Fortunately, magazine owner Romulus White has been trying to hire her for years. Sparks fly when Stella and Romulus join forces, but will their investigation cost them everything?

From This Moment by Elizabeth Camden
elizabethcamden.com

◊ BETHANYHOUSE